"The ultimate vacation read. I didn't want to put it down. The duo deliver a stunning story about the love between sisters and soulmates, and for one's self. Heavy topics such as body positivity and mental health are handled with a light, humorous, and heartwarming touch, and *The Comeback Summer* will leave you grinning from ear to ear."

—Denise Williams, author of *Do You Take This Man*

"Lighthearted and endearing."

—*Parade*

"Another winsome and winning tale that neatly pivots between the two sisters' viewpoints and delivers the maximum measure of sharp humor and smoldering romance, all while insightfully underscoring the importance of the bond between siblings and the rewards found in embracing new challenges in life."

—*Booklist*

UNTIL NEXT SUMMER

Ali Brady

BERKLEY ROMANCE
New York

BERKLEY ROMANCE
Published by Berkley
An imprint of Penguin Random House LLC
penguinrandomhouse.com

Library of Congress Cataloging-in-Publication Data

Names: Brady, Ali, author.
Title: Until next summer / Ali Brady.
Description: First Edition. | New York: Berkley Romance, 2024.
Identifiers: LCCN 2023048277 (print) | LCCN 2023048278 (ebook) |
ISBN 9780593640821 (trade paperback) | ISBN 9780593640838 (ebook)
Subjects: LCGFT: Romance fiction. | Novels.
Classification: LCC PS3602.R342875 U58 2024 (print) |
LCC PS3602.R342875 (ebook) | DDC 813/.6—dc23/eng/20231013
LC record available at https://lccn.loc.gov/2023048277
LC ebook record available at https://lccn.loc.gov/2023048278

First Edition: July 2024

Printed in the United States of America
1st Printing

Title page art: Crossed oars © Anatolir / Shutterstock
Map by Christina Vanko
Book design by Amy Trombat

To the people and places who make us feel like we belong

I want to linger
a little longer
a little longer here with you

—classic camp song

UNTIL
NEXT
SUMMER

Jessie

August

When I was a kid, I had a button on my backpack that read I LIVE TEN MONTHS FOR TWO. When people noticed it, I'd get one of two reactions: total confusion (*Ten months of what? Does this poor girl have a terminal illness?*), or a knowing smile.

The ones who smiled would inevitably ask one question. A question that let me know, without a doubt, that they were my kind of people:

"So where'd you go to camp?"

No matter the age gap or difference in our backgrounds, we'd start swapping stories, sharing memories. The gruff custodian at my elementary school bragged about winning Color Wars when he was fourteen. A bus driver sang his favorite camp song (*The Princess Pat . . . lived in a tree*), complete with hand motions. My pediatrician told me she once caught her marshmallow on fire and then, panicking, waved her roasting stick in the air, causing the marshmallow to fall onto her bare foot. She even showed me the burn scar, taking her shoe off in the middle of her clinic room while I waited for my twelve-year-old vaccinations.

Here's what I took from those conversations: there's something magical about summer camp. Those days stick in your mind like pine sap in your hair, like the scent of campfire smoke on your clothes. Even decades later, the memories remain vivid.

Which is why I decided that I didn't want to spend ten months slogging through what everyone else called Real Life only to spend two months living what felt like *my* real life.

I wanted it all the time.

It's sometimes still hard to believe I achieved that childhood dream. That this is my full-time, year-round, always and forever job. I am the head camp director at Camp Chickawah, and we've just completed another successful summer session.

The big lawn in the middle of the property is abuzz, hundreds of campers milling around, duffels and sleeping bags heaped in messy piles. Counselors try their best to wrangle the kids as they exchange tearful hugs with their cabinmates and friends, promising to see each other next summer. Then we herd them onto buses, double-checking that their gear is safely stowed below, and wave as they take off down the road.

I gather my summer staff—the counselors, lifeguards, kitchen crew, sailing and archery and tennis instructors— and thank them for working so hard. I remind them that camp people never say goodbye; we say "see ya next summer." So that's what they do, exchanging phone numbers and hugs before taking off.

And then everything goes silent.

The only signs of the three hundred people who called

this place home for the past eight weeks are the trampled ground, scraps of trash, and whispers of memory floating through the air: campfires and songs, pranks and crafts, friendships to last a lifetime. I take a deep breath, thinking how grateful I am to be part of it.

At the same time, I'm exhausted. Each day at camp feels like a week, and each week feels like a month. I haven't had a full night of sleep since May—I'm always listening for the knock on my cabin door. This summer, I drove two people with broken bones to the emergency room in the middle of the night (one camper, one counselor), calmed a pack of terrified ten-year-olds when a tree fell on their cabin's porch during a rainstorm, and stayed up all night cleaning vomit after a stomach bug ran through camp.

And most importantly: I kept a calm, reassuring smile on my face the entire time. After all, I set the tone for the summer. The former owners, Nathaniel and Lola Valentine, taught me this.

"Welp, made it through another year," a gruff voice says, and I turn to see my assistant camp director, Dot.

Like me, she's dressed in Camp Chickawah gear—khaki shorts, a polo shirt, and a wide-brimmed hat. Dot is five feet tall and stocky, built like a human bowling pin with short gray hair. I'm nearly a foot taller, with strawberry blonde hair in two braids and skin that freckles or burns within minutes of sun exposure.

I smile. "It was a good summer, right?"

"It was Chicka-wonderful. Nathaniel and Lola would be proud."

Dot's been a staple of Camp Chickawah since my days

3

as a camper, and now she's looking at me for direction—
something I still haven't gotten used to, even after four years
of being her boss.

"Let's do a sweep of the grounds for lost items," I say.
"Then we call it a day. Sound okay?"

"Sounds great!" Dot says, and off we go.

The next morning, after sleeping for ten glorious hours, I head
toward the lake. The air is cool, faintly scented with pine, and
full of birdsong. I pull my favorite canoe from the shed—it's
hand-carved birchwood and nearly a century old—and slide
it halfway into the water, sending ripples across the
shimmering surface. After discarding my hiking boots and
wool socks on the dock, I pop my earbuds in.

It's time for some Broadway magic.

I press play on the original cast recording of *Hadestown*.
The iconic trombone begins wailing, joined by the inimitable
André De Shields, and as I wade into the cool water and
transfer myself into the canoe, I can't help dancing. Luckily,
no one's around to see.

After stowing my phone in a dry bag near my feet, I
shove myself out with my paddle. Our camp hugs the west
side of the lake; the rest is ringed with pine trees. The rising
sun paints a golden streak across the water, and I follow it,
paddling until my shoulders burn.

Canoes can be tricky to navigate solo, especially an old
wooden one, but I love the nostalgia, the knowledge that
countless campers and counselors have sat where I am now.
Soon I relax into the rhythm and pull of paddle on water, and
my exhaustion melts away.

I've spent every summer at Camp Chickawah since I was eight years old. My parents divorced when I was a toddler, splitting custody fifty-fifty because they both "loved me so much." I believe them—but the fact is, packing up and moving to a different house each week does a number on a child's sense of stability. It's not only adjusting to a different home—it's an entirely different culture. Different food in the fridge, different neighbors, different rules and expectations. Every week, just as I'd settled in at one home, I'd have to readjust all over again.

Which is why that first summer at camp felt revolutionary. Eight whole weeks sleeping in the same bed. Associating with the same people, following the same routine. Camp was the stable home I'd never had. Every summer I returned, and when I was sixteen, I applied for the counselor-in-training program, where I was able to teach and mentor the younger campers.

More than anything, I wanted to become a real counselor during my summer breaks in college. My best camp friend and I were going to do it together, but in the end, she bailed on me. It was painful—the kind of hurt that takes years to heal—but I took the job anyway. When I graduated (with a bachelor's in recreation administration—yes, it's a real degree), Nathaniel and Lola offered to keep me on as an assistant director, one of the few year-round positions at Camp Chickawah. When they retired, I became head director.

Nathaniel and Lola were more than my mentors—they were like an extra set of grandparents who instilled in me the values of hard work and integrity, who taught me the importance of giving our campers a place to learn skills, make friends, and grow. Even though they've passed away, it feels like they're still with me. And like Dot said, I think they'd be proud.

An hour later, I'm pulling the canoe onto the shore when I hear footsteps. Turning, I see Dot and two other people: Jack and Mary, Nathaniel and Lola's son and daughter. He's short and stocky, with his dad's square shoulders, and she's short and soft, like her mother. They inherited the camp, but neither of them has any interest in running it, so they've left it in my hands.

"Hi!" I say, putting my earbuds away. "So nice to see you both. What brings you to camp?"

Jack gives his sister a quick glance. "We're wrapping up Mom and Dad's estate. Can we talk?"

"You're selling the camp?" I say, dumbfounded.

The three of us are sitting in the Lodge, a rustic two-story building overlooking the lake.

"The camp hasn't made a profit in years," Jack says, which of course I know. But making money was never Nathaniel and Lola's goal.

"But—but it's been in your family since 1914!" I protest. "Parents depend on this place for their kids each summer."

Mary gives me a sad smile and her eyes crinkle around the edges, just like Lola's. "I've tried to find a buyer who wants to keep operating it, but no one's interested—"

"I could reach out to the camp community," I say, my voice tinged with desperation. I'm part of a huge online group of summer camp directors throughout North America. There has to be someone who understands how important this place is. How irreplaceable.

Jack shakes his head. "Mary's already tried that."

"I'd buy Jack out if I could," Mary says. "But there's no way I can afford it—"

"And your health, Mary," Jack cuts in.

Mary closes her mouth and nods. "Yes. Well, that too."

I don't know what they're referring to, and it doesn't feel appropriate to ask. But Mary looks thinner than I remember, the shadows under her eyes deeper.

Panic is rising in my chest. This can't be happening.

"So . . . what does this mean?" I ask.

Mary and Jack exchange glances again. Mary's eyes fill with tears, like she's silently pleading with him, but Jack gives a shake of his head before turning to me.

"We're listing the property as residential real estate," Jack says, his voice brisk. All business.

I know what this means—I've seen it happen throughout our area. Luxury vacation developments, condos, and town houses crowding the lakefront, rustic cottages torn down to make way for huge, fancy lake houses.

"Of course, you'll get a portion of the sale, Jessie," Mary says brightly.

I startle. "Wait—what?"

Mary turns to her brother. "I thought you sent her a copy of the will, Jack?"

"I'll send it when I get home," Jack says, shooting his sister a peeved glance. Then, to me: "You get one percent. Should be a tidy sum with a sale this large."

He seems offended by this, as if losing a fraction of his own profit is a profound injustice.

For my part? I don't care about the money. I'm not sure I even want it—it would feel tainted somehow, though it was thoughtful of Nathaniel and Lola to think of me.

"But what does this mean for my staff?" I say. "Do you want us to just . . . clear out?"

"No, no, of course not," Mary rushes to say. "The whole process will take a while."

"Probably not as long as you think," Jack mutters under his breath.

Anger flares inside me. I want to grab them by their shoulders and shake them, ask how they can do this. Don't they understand how much this place means? To their parents, to all our campers. To me.

I remember Dot saying Jack *hated* camp as a kid, that he resented how his parents spent all their time and energy here. Mary loved camp, apparently, but she's never been strong enough to stand up to her older brother.

Now she smiles gently. "Don't worry—we haven't even listed it yet. And whenever we get an offer, we'll make sure to delay closing until next fall. We're not going to just toss you out on your keister, you know?"

She gives a little laugh, but I can't join in, even half-heartedly. My camp is closing. After twenty years, this summer will be my last.

two

Jessie

September

It's been two weeks since the news from Jack and Mary Valentine, and I'm still reeling.

I've been going through our standard end-of-season tasks, so every day brings another reminder that this is the last time we'll do any of it. The last time Mr. Billy, our groundskeeper, will repair the shingles on the Arts and Crafts cabin; the last time Dot will inspect the watercraft; the last time I'll count how many bows and arrows survived the summer and how many I'll need to order for next year.

In a few weeks, Dot and I will move into our rented rooms in North Fork, Minnesota, the closest town, a forty-five-minute drive away. Mr. Billy goes to stay with his brother in Florida. Dot and I spend the winter months enrolling campers and hiring counselors and staff. We'll return to the property in April to start prepping for summer.

Our last summer.

Stuffing my hands in my pockets, I head down the path to the girls' area to check the cabins. On the way, I pass Mr. Billy, his angular frame stooped as he pushes a wheelbarrow full of trimmed branches. I wave, and he grunts. He's taken care of the camp for as long as I can remember—a huge responsibility, since we cover three hundred acres of land, with dozens of buildings and a thousand feet of lakefront— but I've never thought of him as old. In the past couple weeks, though, he's aged a decade. His typical vibe is one of mild annoyance, but now he seems almost fragile.

My boots crunch through fallen pine needles; they're dry and brittle, like my mood. When I pop my earbuds in, the revival of *Sweeney Todd* with Josh Groban starts playing. A musical about a man hell-bent on murderous revenge after everything he loves is taken from him . . . maybe not the wisest choice. I turn it off.

The first girls' cabin comes into view. It's over a hundred years old, with a big front porch and a peaked roof. During the summer, the porch railings of all the cabins are covered with a rainbow of drying towels and bathing suits, but today they're barren. I wonder if the future owner will save any of these buildings, or if they'll bulldoze everything, erasing a century of memories.

The thought makes me physically sick.

I climb the steps to the first cabin, open the door, and walk inside. My boots echo on the wood floor. The air smells like decay; the bare bunk beds remind me of skeletons. But I tell myself to stop being melodramatic and inspect the beds, the mattresses, the blinds, checking them off my list. Briskly, I move from cabin to cabin, trying to avoid the onslaught of memories.

Cabin Two, where I stayed as a nervous eight-year-old. Cabin Four, which I pranked as a feisty twelve-year-old, putting sand in the campers' sleeping bags. Cabin Six, where

I was assigned my first summer as an enthusiastic new counselor.

And Cabin Ten: my home for eight summers, from ages nine through sixteen.

When I reach the bunk I always shared with Hillary Goldberg, a shimmering déjà vu comes over me. Standing on tiptoe, I push the top mattress to the side and there it is, carved into the wood: HILLARY AND JESSIE BFFAEAE. Best friends forever and ever and ever.

It's been years since I've let myself think about Hillary—if she ever pops into my mind, I push her right out. But now it rushes back, the exhilaration of arriving on the property and spotting each other. That first big hug. Running to claim our bunk. Knowing we had eight glorious weeks stretching out in front of us.

It's strange to realize Hillary is an adult now. I still think of her as the round-faced girl with messy curls and wide brown eyes who'd always go along with my schemes—including our plan to be counselors together. Of course, that didn't happen. She took an internship with some big company. It was crushing at the time, but it taught me a crucial lesson: camp friends aren't forever friends. Camp life isn't real life. For most people, it's an escape from the real world.

Whereas for me? It's my entire world.

All my camp friends, all the counselors I've worked with over the years, have moved on, and I've stayed right here. I've always felt that this is where I belong, but once camp closes for good, where does that leave me?

Once all this is gone, will anything I've done matter at all?

When I get back to the office, Dot is there, scowling at her ancient PC.

My cabin is one of my favorite places in the world. In addition to the main office, there's a bedroom, a small bathroom, and a kitchen. It's cozy and quaint, filled with handmade wooden furniture that dates back to the original camp. It's also the only place on the property with Internet, and as I enter, my phone starts buzzing in my pocket.

I pull it out to see texts from my parents. Mom sent a picture of her and my stepdad Mitch with my half brothers, Milo and Colin, at the beach near their home in San Diego. Dad sent a picture of him and my stepmom Amanda with my twin half sisters, Amelia and Abigail, after they won their high school basketball game.

I tap out a quick text to each and promise I'll FaceTime later. My parents are good about keeping in touch, but sometimes their messages are a reminder that I don't fully belong to either of their families. The only place I've ever belonged is camp, and it won't be here much longer.

"What're you working on?" I ask Dot, hanging up my coat, hat, and scarf.

"Money's gonna be tight this year," Dot says, her brow furrowed. "We haven't gotten any early registrations yet."

I grimace; this has real financial consequences. Mary Valentine convinced Jack to agree that any profit we make next summer can be used as end-of-season bonuses for my staff. I haven't told Dot and Mr. Billy about this yet, not wanting to get their hopes up, but my plan is to split it between the two of them; I get one percent of the sale of the camp, but they won't have anything but their own savings and retirement.

"Maybe I shouldn't have told the parents that next summer will be our last," I say, worried.

Dot harrumphs. "Not your fault—you're not the one selling this place. Got an email from Jack Valentine that the property was officially listed."

My body stiffens. I knew this was coming, but it still hurts to hear the words.

"Those rat bastards," Dot says gruffly.

I stifle a laugh, thinking of Jack's squinty eyes. They *are* rather ratlike. "I'm not sure Mary should be included in that. It's thanks to her that they're delaying closing until next fall."

"She allows her rat bastard brother to walk all over her, which makes her a rat bastard enabler, which is just as bad." Dot clicks her fingers on the keyboard, punctuating each word. "Nat and Lola must be rolling in their graves. But Jack was never a camp person, not ever."

My eyebrows shoot up. This is the ultimate insult from Dot. In her mind, you're either a camp person . . . or not. And if you're not? You're pond scum.

My eyes drift to the huge bulletin board on the far wall, where we've stuck letters and cards from campers over the years. There's a crayon rendering of Cabin Eleven, signed in blocky letters *RYAN AGE 9*; a pencil sketch of the big tree near the archery area with *to Nathaniel and Lola from Kat S* written in careful cursive. There are countless wedding invitations from couples who met at camp—Lola always said that camp love is the best kind of love, and that was true for her and Nathaniel.

I used to dream of having a marriage like theirs, with

someone who was as passionate about this place as I am. Running the camp together, raising our kids right here on the property.

But after my last failed relationship, I realized that's a silly fantasy. Even more so now that the camp is closing. So I turn my attention to the many handwritten thank-you notes from former campers, now adults.

Camp Chickawah will always be my favorite place in the world.

Thank you for making my childhood so magical.

All my most important life lessons were learned at camp.

Card after card expresses gratitude and appreciation. And something else, too, something I've never noticed before: yearning. An intense longing to return.

I wish I could come back to camp. I know that's ridiculous, but the place meant so much to me.

If only I could capture the magic of camp as an adult.

I'd give anything to experience just one day of camp again.

Goose bumps lift on my arms and legs as an idea sparks.

If we have to say goodbye to Camp Chickawah, I think I know the perfect way.

To: Camp Chickawah Campers Listserv
From: JPederson@CampChickawah.com
Subject: One last summer at camp

Hello, former campers and friends!

Jessie here with some good news, and some sad news. I'll start with the sad news—because like Nurse Penny always said, *You gotta rip off the Band-Aid and get back on the horse!* (In hindsight, I'm pretty sure she was mixing two different metaphors, but we all survived!)

Anyway, the sad news is that Jack and Mary Valentine have made the difficult decision to sell the Camp Chickawah property, which means this summer will be our last.

But now for the good news! As the current camp director, I'm thinking of trying something new this summer—inviting past campers out for one of eight weeklong camp sessions. An adult camp. Think of it as a walk down memory lane, a chance to come and say goodbye to this special place, to unplug and get back to basics for a week.

If this sounds like something you'd be into, either coming as a camper for a week or coming to work for the summer (there will be no counselors, but I'll need people to staff the kitchen, the Arts and Crafts cabin, and the lakefront), please let me know.

Hope to see some of you back at camp! Have a Chick-amazing day!

Jessie Pederson
Director, Camp Chickawah

three

Hillary

November

It's Wednesday evening, which means Aaron is sitting in his usual seat at our usual table in the corner of our usual restaurant, waiting for Roger, our usual waiter, to bring him his usual drink—an old-fashioned, heavy on the bitters.

For the past two years, I've found comfort in the predictability of our relationship. But lately, I've been wondering what would happen if I just . . . stopped.

Of course, I couldn't. I wouldn't. Not when Aaron is the key to the last item I have left on the "Ten Steps to a Successful Life" list I wrote when I was seven years old. I'm pretty sure I was the only kid on the playground who knew what magna cum laude was. Well, I didn't actually know what it meant—I just knew that my dad valued it, so I wanted it.

Before walking into the restaurant, I glance at my reflection in the window. With my black dress pants and turquoise blouse tucked in the front like the sales associate showed me, I look every bit the professional woman my father raised to be an ideal wife for a man like Aaron Feinberg. At least from the neck down. I'm overdue for a keratin treatment, and my brown hair is beginning to revert to its naturally curly state. I give it a quick finger comb, then apply a fresh coat of coral lipstick. Not perfect, but could be worse.

"Sorry I'm late," I say, giving Aaron a kiss, then taking my usual seat.

"I ordered for you," he says, matter-of-factly. There's no chill to his voice or undertone of annoyance. While the man is a lion in the courtroom, he's a lamb outside it. We never argue, which I guess is a good thing. Although it means we never get to make up.

On paper, Aaron is everything I'm looking for in a husband. He's on the partner track at my father's law firm. He's conventionally handsome, his reddish-brown hair neatly trimmed, his clothes tailored to fit. He even gets his back waxed. Honestly, he takes his appearance much more seriously than I do mine, but vanity isn't exactly a flaw. He's a great plus-one at social engagements, making small talk so I don't have to. And my father loves him.

The thing is, lately I've been asking myself: do I?

I like our life together. It's easy, companionable. What we lack in passion, we over-index in other things, like mutual respect. And that's an important foundation for a lasting partnership.

"How was work today?" I ask.

"Interesting, actually," he says, perking up. The man loves work the way I love . . . I'm not sure I love anything as much as he loves work. "You know the Lewin case?"

I nod. Growing up, conversation around the dinner table centered on whatever big case my dad was working on. I became fluent in legalese, a skill that's served me well.

"The deposition is next week, and I haven't had time to

write my opening statement—but I put the facts into that Chat AI thing, and believe it or not, the robot did a decent job."

"Wow."

"It'll make my job much more efficient," he says, then adds, frowning, "but that means fewer hours to bill."

"Quite the conundrum."

Aaron purses his lips, like he's weighing the pros and cons in his head. Almost thirty years as my father's daughter has trained me for the delicate dance of conversation with men who just need a sympathetic ear to talk through their challenges at work.

"How about you?" Aaron asks as our entrées arrive: steak frites for him, cedar-planked salmon for me. "Good day?"

I shrug, taking a bite of salmon. "Good" is debatable. It was a successful day—but heavy. As an independent consultant who helps failing businesses turn the ship around, I'm often the bearer of bad news. Like today, when I informed my client she needs to close thirty percent of her locations. Her reaction was typical: confused and frustrated. Wasn't I there to *save* her business? But I reminded her, as I have so many others, that a strategic loss can leave room for more gains. The key to success in business—and in life—is to make decisions with your head, not your heart.

My ability to separate logic from emotion and find creative solutions to business problems has made me an in-demand leader in the change agent industry. Which is why it's so rare for me to have an opening in my calendar. Much less one that's three months long.

"Did I tell you I won the bid for the Water Tower project?" I say, reciting the opening line I rehearsed last night and again this morning.

The iconic mall in downtown Chicago has never quite recovered from the pandemic, losing stores and foot traffic, and I've been wooing the management team for months.

"That's great, babe, congrats," Aaron says, raising his glass to clink against mine.

"Thanks. They don't want to start until September, and my contract with the bank wraps up in May, so that leaves a few months unspoken for."

"Something will come up," Aaron says. "It always does."

"Actually, something did . . ." I say, letting the word linger.

Aaron cocks an eyebrow.

"I got an email about a job opportunity I might apply for," I say, feeling oddly like I'm about to ask my dad for permission to go to the mall after school. "Running the Arts and Crafts program at my old sleepaway camp."

Aaron laughs, then abruptly stops when he realizes I'm not joking.

"I know it sounds crazy," I say.

"It does."

I frown, trying to summon the surge of excitement that pulsed through me when I read Jessie's email. I haven't been this excited about a potential job since . . . since the summer I was planning to be a counselor at Camp Chickawah. At my father's urging (read: insistence), I turned down that job in favor of a "real" one that would jump-start my career. Which it did. The experience I got interning for a marketing firm that summer was priceless.

Well, not exactly priceless.

It cost me the best friend I've ever had.

"Camp doesn't start until June," I tell Aaron. "So we could take a few weeks to travel. Go somewhere exciting, maybe

Italy and Greece? I've wanted to go since I watched the first *Sisterhood of the Traveling Pants* movie. And you love feta!"

"I do love feta," Aaron agrees. "But you know I can't take time off right now."

"It's not right now; it's in May."

"May's a busy time," Aaron says. But he's forgetting I'm the daughter of a lawyer—the daughter of his boss. I know lawyers don't have "busy times." All their times are busy, but that doesn't mean you never take time off. Is that the life Aaron wants? A chill runs through me as I imagine spending our honeymoon in the halls of the courthouse.

"Babe," Aaron says, putting his hand over mine. "I'm just thinking about our future—you want me to make partner, don't you?"

"Of course," I say.

"And this camp job. What does it even pay? Minimum wage?"

"It's not about the money."

It would help if I could find the words to tell him what it *is* about. But I've never been good at putting big feelings into words. Even if I could, I doubt Aaron would understand the urge I feel to reconnect with this piece of my past. There was a time when Camp Chickawah felt like home. The one place I could truly be myself. A person I haven't been in more than a decade.

"Everything's about money," Aaron says, then adds, "Right, Roger?" to our waiter, who probably wishes he'd picked a different moment to refill our water glasses.

"Nothing's decided yet," I say. "Who knows if I'll even get the job."

But beneath the table, I cross my fingers, hoping with everything I've got that I will.

four

Jessie

January

Mick's Diner in North Fork has the best breakfasts in a five-hundred-mile radius. Pancakes the size of dinner plates, deep-fried bacon, cinnamon rolls dripping with frosting. During the winter, Dot and I come here most mornings and eat, and work, and eat. We always gain back whatever weight we lost during the busy summer months.

"Morning!" I say to Dot. She scoots into our booth and I slide a mug of coffee toward her as she shakes the snow from her short gray hair.

"Hoo boy, it's comin' down out there. But good news: as of last night, we're seventy-five percent booked."

My jaw drops. We opened registration a *week* ago. Usually it takes until the end of April to hit this milestone.

"That's . . . that's fantastic!"

"If things keep going this way, we might even turn a profit this year. Ironic, right? Finally making money and the camp is being sold."

"I have some other good news: Antonio accepted the position as the camp chef. He'll take over the hiring and management of the rest of the kitchen staff."

"That's wonderful," Dot says. "I've been emailing with a young couple about running the lakefront. I'll set up a call with them for an interview."

"Great," I say. They'll need to be certified lifeguards with experience handling canoes, kayaks, and sailboats. We've never had a drowning death at Camp Chickawah, and even though this year's campers will be adults, I'm not about to take chances.

"That just leaves the Arts and Crafts cabin," I say, looking at the to-do list on my laptop. We're planning on hiring a small staff for the summer—we don't need counselors for adult campers, and we do need to save some money.

"We did get one applicant." Dot pauses, then says, "Remember Hillary Goldberg?"

I blink, surprised. "I thought she had some fancy corporate job."

"In finance, I think," Dot says, nodding. "But she has a break this summer."

Hillary, running our Arts and Crafts cabin? Why would she want to spend her summer working at camp? It's exactly what she *didn't* want when we were eighteen.

"Now, I know you two had a falling-out—"

"That was years ago," I say, waving a hand. "Ancient history. I'm not—"

Dot gives me a stern look. "I know how much it hurt you, Pippi."

Dot usually calls me "boss," but sometimes she slips up—usually when she's thinking of my younger self, that long-ago, inexperienced counselor. In this case, she's probably remembering how much I missed my best friend.

Who was supposed to be there with me.

I clear my throat. "That was a long time ago, and it's fine now. Really."

"If you want to tell yourself that, go right ahead," Dot says. "But she'd do a good job."

"If she's been working in finance, how is she qualified?"

"She'll figure it out—that girl spent hours in the Arts and Crafts cabin," Dot says. She's right. Hillary loved it all: pottery, painting, boondoggle, papier-mâché, tie-dye. "Besides, no one else has applied, because, let's be honest, the pay is shit."

"True," I say, sighing. "I guess it's fine, then."

"You got it," she says, and starts working on an email.

I return to my list, but my mind keeps drifting to the image of Hillary Goldberg returning to camp. My chest feels strangely hollow, and I rub it with my palm. Indigestion, maybe. Damn diner coffee.

"Did I tell ya about the reservation we got for the whole summer?" Dot asks, after a while.

I look up, confused. "The whole summer?"

She grins proudly. "Yeah! Someone emailed me about renting an entire cabin for all eight weeks!"

"Are they paying for all twelve spots?"

Dot's smile falters. "Well, no. I figured he'd take the small staff cabin on the boys' side that sleeps four. Sorry, boss."

I give her a reassuring smile; she doesn't know about my plan to maximize profits so I can give her and Mr. Billy a bonus at the end of the summer. "It's okay. I'll reach out and let them know there will be other people assigned to the cabin. Who is it?"

She looks at her laptop. "William Duncan."

"Who?"

"William *Lucas* Duncan," Dot says, and this rings a faint bell in my mind. "He went by Luke at camp. All the girls had crushes on him—tall, blue eyes, looked like a young Paul Newman?"

That *definitely* rings a bell.

"The one Nathaniel used to call Cool Hand Luke?"

She gives a knowing smile. "Yeah. He was The Man."

"Ugh," I say, grimacing, and Dot laughs.

Nearly every summer there's one male counselor who receives this title from Dot. "The Man" is good-looking, charismatic, adored by the campers. Everywhere he goes, he's accompanied by an entourage of kids, doting on his words, laughing at his jokes.

I have mixed feelings about counselors like that. Some can be a director's dream, using their influence to make every activity more fun. But others become arrogant, walking through camp with a vibe that says, "I don't give a shit about any of this."

The first summer I knew Luke, he was the former.

The second? Definitely the latter.

"He's an author now, right?" I say. "Nathaniel and Lola had his books in the library, I think."

"Wouldn't surprise me," Dot says. She doesn't read much; neither do I. But I used to. As a teenager, I read nearly every book in the camp library—a dusty bookcase in the Lodge.

That's how I got to know Luke. I was a CIT, he was a counselor; he'd recommend books to me, and later we'd discuss them. That was the first summer. When he came back the next year, he totally blew me off. And somehow got every single other male counselor to ignore me, too.

"I'll send him an email," I tell Dot, shaking the sting of that memory away as I open my laptop.

Hello Luke,

I'm happy you're coming to our adult camp. We're going to have an incredible time!

I think there was a miscommunication when you registered, though. We hadn't planned on campers coming for more than one week at a time, but I'm happy to be flexible. However, we aren't able to reserve an entire cabin for one person, so other campers will be sharing the staff cabin with you. Dot will be in touch with a new registration form to reflect this.

Thanks for understanding! I'm excited for the summer—it's going to be Chick-amazing!

All my best,
Jessie Pederson, camp director

I send the email as our waitress comes up. "Hi, Lisa!"

Lisa gives us a big smile. She's about fifty, with curly hair and an apron tied around her generous waistline. "Morning, ladies. Ready to order?"

Dot orders pancakes and a side of sausage, and I order two eggs over easy with bacon.

Lisa refills our coffee mugs. Then she glances out the window behind me, and her smile fades. She leans in and says, "Have you seen Nick since you've been back?"

The blood drains from my face. Nick and I dated last year, and our breakup was . . . difficult.

"No," I whisper. "Why?"

"Because he's coming in," Lisa says, straightening as the door chimes. In a louder voice she calls, "Morning! Just the two of you today?"

"Yep." Nick's familiar voice reminds me that the last time we talked, I made him cry. And Nick's a big, tough firefighter.

There's no way he won't see me, so as he's walking by, I say, "Hi, Nick, how's it going?"

He flinches, then turns toward me. Nick is stocky, bearded, and exactly my height—which bothered him. He'd constantly ask me to change my boots to flats when we went out.

He looks good today; his hair is shorter than before, his beard a little longer. A North Fork Fire Department sweatshirt peeks out from under his coat.

Also: he's holding the hand of a very pretty, very *petite* brunette woman.

"Jessie. Hello," he says. "Uh—do you know Gwen? Her family owns the hardware store."

"I'm sure we've seen each other around," I say, holding out my hand to Gwen. "I'm Jessie. Great to meet you."

She shakes my hand, a pained smile on her face. "Nick's told me so much about you."

By her icy tone, it's clear that whatever he's said, it's not good.

"Do you guys want to take this booth?" Lisa asks, motioning to the one next to ours. "Or—"

"No!" Nick and I say at the same time.

He laughs awkwardly, then says, "We'll take a table over there. See you around, Jessie."

As they follow Lisa, Gwen waves goodbye with her left hand, showing off her pink manicured fingernails—and a sparkly engagement ring. I look down at my hands: calloused palms, short nails that only get painted if a camper asks to do it.

"Didn't you break up with him just a few months ago?" Dot whispers.

"Last June." I take a big swallow of coffee, wincing as it burns my mouth.

Dot does some counting in her head. "Seven months and he's engaged to someone else? Wasn't he talking about marrying you?" She shakes her head and mutters, "And people say lesbians move fast."

"I guess when you meet the right one, you know."

Still, I'm stung. And not just by the fact that he's chosen my exact opposite, at least physically. Nick and I dated all last winter; by spring, things were getting serious. I liked having a boyfriend, someone to snuggle with during the long, cold nights. We'd go snowshoeing and cross-country skiing on his days off. Everything seemed to be going well.

But then I moved back to camp in April. We couldn't see each other as often, though I came to town whenever I could and invited him to visit me on his days off. He seemed frustrated, but I assumed he understood this was the nature of my job.

It all came to a head the week before camp started, when he realized we were about to see even less of each other. He wanted a girlfriend who was actually around, he said. A girlfriend who prioritized their relationship.

I told him that I'd take off one evening per week during the summer. I'd never done this—the director is on duty 24/7 for eight weeks straight—but I was willing to compromise. In reply, he started bringing up our future: What if we got married? Would I still spend summers up at camp? Didn't I want to have children?

Of course I did; he knew I've always imagined being like Nathaniel and Lola, running the camp with my husband and raising our kids there. I knew it was unrealistic and unfair to expect Nick to leave his job, but I asked if he could find a way to compromise. Instead, he suggested I think about a more "family friendly" career.

Then he tearfully said he loved me, and I faltered. This was the most serious romantic relationship I've ever had, and I did care about him. He's a good person; he'll probably make a good husband and father. I thought I could even love him someday.

But when I tried to explain how much camp meant to me, he told me that my priorities were wrong. And that pissed me off, so I ended things. It felt like the right decision at the time . . . but now, with this summer being our last at camp?

Maybe I did have my priorities wrong.

My computer chimes with an email. It's from WilliamLucasDuncan@WLDuncan.com.

The terms are clearly stated in the contract I signed. A full cabin for eight weeks. My deposit has been paid. I trust you will work out the details.

—WLD

I press my lips together, annoyed. It's not only the response; it's the tone. Guess his "I don't give a shit" attitude hasn't changed.

"What?" Dot asks.

"Luke—er, William Lucas Duncan—is being a pain about his reservation." She gets a guilty look on her face, and I add, "No, no, it's fine—I'll work it out."

I type a reply:

Good morning! I'm truly sorry, but it won't be possible to have you take the entire cabin. I'll send you an amended contract with the corrected cost.

Also, camp runs from Monday afternoon through Sunday morning, so the standard cost includes dinner on Monday, three meals Tuesday through Saturday, and breakfast on Sunday. Since you'll be here every day of the week, I assume you'll need an additional four meals (lunch and dinner on Sunday, breakfast and lunch on Monday). As an apology for the confusion, I'll cover the cost of those meals for you.

Sincerely and with warm regards,
Jessie

I read the email to Dot. "That's reasonable, right?"

"Very reasonable," she agrees, and I press send.

A reply pings back:

I'll pay for the extra meals. But I cannot share my cabin. I'm writing my next novel this summer and I require privacy.

—WLD

A prickle of irritation runs down my spine. So he's

writing a novel—good for him! That doesn't give him the right to do whatever he wants with no regard to how it affects the rest of the camp.

> Hi again! I understand your concerns, but the cost of those four extra meals doesn't cover the revenue I'll lose from not having three other campers in the cabin with you.
>
> How about this: I can offer you the counselors' quarters in one of the regular cabins. You'll have a separate room, all to yourself. It normally sleeps two, but I'll make an exception. I can also find you a quiet room in the Lodge for writing. Thank you for understanding!
>
> With warm regards,
> Jessie

I press send as Lisa arrives with our food. Dot and I move our laptops to make room. Before I can take my first bite, though, my laptop chimes with another email.

> That won't work. I need an entire cabin to myself, as promised.
>
> —WLD

Fine. If that's what he wants, he'll have to pay for it.

> Unfortunately, that means I'll need to charge you for four campers. I'm sure you can understand we can't afford to lose that revenue.

Let me know if you'd like an amended contract reflecting this, or if you'd prefer to cancel and be refunded your deposit.

Warmly,
Jessie

Two minutes later:

Eight weeks. Full cabin. Original price. I assume you do not wish to face a lawsuit due to breach of contract.

I feel a scream building in the back of my throat. I hack into my eggs, letting the yolk ooze onto my plate, and take a bite.

"Who does he think he is?" I say to Dot after swallowing. "And no, it's not your fault. Any reasonable person would understand. I've been more than fair!"

"You have," she agrees, nodding.

"He can't actually sue us, can he?"

Dot scowls. "I mean, he could . . ."

"*Ugh.* Why? Why is he doing this?" Groaning, I put my head in my hands. I'm going to have to swallow my pride and beg.

Dear Luke,

I understand it must be frustrating to have your plans changed unexpectedly, and I recognize that this was an error on our part. But it would be so appreciated if you could find it in your heart to be flexible on this. This camp means everything to me. I'm just trying to make the last summer special.

I would be eternally grateful if you would consider.

Please.

Within thirty seconds of pressing send, I receive his answer:

No.

What an absolute *ass*. I grab a piece of bacon and take a vicious bite. Not even the smoky, deep-fried goodness can assuage my anger.

"Boss?" Dot says. "You okay?"

I clench my teeth. "Looks like we're stuck with William Lucas Duncan, aka The Man, all summer."

five

Hillary

June

It's been four months since I applied to run Arts and Crafts at Camp Chickawah. Despite being both ridiculously over- *and* underqualified, I got the job. And against the advice of my father and my boyfriend, I accepted it. I'm flying out bright and early tomorrow morning, and the pre-camp jitters are just as rampant as I remember. Only back then, it was all excitement and anticipation.

Now? I'm not sure how to describe this feeling. Nervous, sure. Anxious, definitely.

Also, hungry.

At least tonight's farewell dinner will solve one of the three. The food at camp was never anything to write home about, so Dad always sent me off with a good meal at the restaurant of my choice. Usually somewhere with a Zagat rating. I was a foodie before being a foodie was a thing, taking sushi in my lunch box when my classmates were still getting the crusts cut off their PB&Js. Just one of the many ways I didn't fit in with my peers.

Sometimes I wonder if I would've been such a serious

and anxious kid if we hadn't lost my mom so unexpectedly. I was five when she lay down for a nap and never woke up. Back then, I didn't understand what an aneurysm was. I just knew that life could be scary and uncertain. I became a stage-five clinger, afraid to leave my dad's side. Which meant I tagged along for a lot of fancy dinners, learning to favor coq au vin over chicken fingers and lobster over Lunchables.

My aunt Carol was the only adult I knew who wasn't impressed by how mature I was for my age. To hear her talk, it was a travesty. *I* was a travesty. I knew that word, and it was not something I wanted to be.

So when my dad signed me up for the sleepaway camp my mom and Aunt Carol went to as kids, I didn't protest. Still, it felt like I was being shipped off. At eight years old, I was a problem that needed to be solved.

In hindsight, going to Camp Chickawah was one of the greatest gifts of my life. A gift I ultimately turned my back on.

But now, I'm getting a second chance.

"Sweetheart," my father says, greeting me with a kiss on both cheeks.

"Hi, Dad."

We're on the patio at Quartino, one of my favorite spots in Chicago for Neapolitan pizza and Italian small plates. As soon as we order, Aaron and my dad start talking work. I don't mind; if anything, I'm relieved. I've had a hard time staying present this week. I've got one foot stuck in the past; everything seems to take me back to camp.

The sunset? Even more beautiful on Camp Chickawah's Steamboat Lake, where the sun casts a kaleidoscope of color across the waters. A cheap plastic cup tossed in the trash? We used to turn them upside down and use them as instruments.

A young girl with strawberry blonde braids skipping down Michigan Ave? Jessie.

She's somehow the root of all my excitement and my fear. Because she isn't just my former best friend. She's the person who took away her friendship without a second thought because I made one decision she didn't like.

Jessie was the first, and quite possibly the only, person who managed to unearth the silly, carefree child hiding beneath my mini-adult exterior. She had a way of finding joy in every single moment, and her enthusiasm for camp and for life was contagious. Whether she was dreaming up a moonlit prank or orchestrating my first kiss, Jessie made everything an adventure. And to my delight, I discovered that I *liked* having fun, liked smiling until my cheeks hurt, laughing until I almost peed my pants.

Over the past decade, I haven't just missed Jessie. I've missed the version of myself I was around her. It's like those cheesy BFF necklaces I bought for us the summer we were twelve, the kind where two halves come together to form a complete heart. Jessie completed me. Not in a romantic way. But losing her friendship left a massive hole in my heart that no romantic relationship could ever fill.

"Earth to Hill," Aaron says, knocking on the table by my plate. "Your father's talking to you."

"Sorry," I say, turning to face my dad. It's seventy degrees out, but he's still wearing a suit jacket. I should have him come out to camp for a week, see if *he* can unlock a more carefree version of himself. I can't picture it—although there's apparently a week we'll have campers as old as seventy!

"We were just talking about how well your business is going," my dad says, and I brace myself for the *but* that's surely coming. "How many clients did you have to turn down this summer?"

"Seventeen," I say, watching his brown eyes widen. They narrow again when he realizes I'm kidding.

"I just hate for you to lose momentum," he says, dropping into his courtroom voice.

My father is the one who taught me the value of following a plan, and his plan for me does not include my taking two months "off." But for the first time in my life, I'm not letting his opinion stop me.

"I've got it all figured out," I say. "I'm starting the Water Tower project the week after Labor Day, and I've got two more clients lined up after that."

"Yes, well, it's still a long time to be gone."

His mouth twists, and I'm reminded of his disposition every summer before I left for camp—somber and sentimental, hugging me extra tight and standing in the doorway a little longer before he said good night. It was as if time suddenly became tangible, and he could feel it slipping away. I assume he's feeling the same way now. I reach across the table to cover his hand with mine.

"I'll miss you, too, Dad."

"It's Aaron I'm worried about," my father says with false bravado. "Eight weeks is a long time for a man to be on his own."

This old-fashioned sentiment makes me cringe, but before I can think of a good retort about the patriarchy, Aaron says, "What's eight weeks when you've got forever?"

My dad breaks into an uncharacteristically bright smile and catches Aaron's eye. Are the two of them in cahoots? Having conversations about my life, our future, over the water cooler? Did Aaron ask for my dad's permission to propose?

I flash back to an image of a future without time off, without love, and the table starts to wobble. Or maybe it's my chair.

It's where we've been heading, yet the infinite nature of the word is overwhelming. *Forever.* My chest feels tight; it's hard to breathe. Aaron says something and my dad replies. Their words sound garbled, like Charlie Brown's teacher.

"You okay, babe?" Aaron asks. It's like he's talking to me from the other end of a tunnel. When I don't answer, he lays a heavy hand on my leg. "Babe?"

"I'm good," I say. And somehow, I manage to pretend that I am.

By the time our tiramisu arrives, my pulse has returned to normal. I'm able to enjoy the moment, and the dessert. Then it's time to leave, and I squeeze my father extra tight and promise to send him a postcard every week. Assuming the canteen still sells them. If not, I'll make my own the way we used to, cutting up boxes of cereal and writing messages on the brown cardboard interior.

Maybe we'll do that for one of our weekly craft activities. Simple and sustainable. I mentally add it to the list I've been curating in a Google Doc. While I used to spend all my free time in the Arts and Crafts cabin, I haven't touched a glue gun or colored thread in the decade since. Thank god for Pinterest.

"You were a million miles away tonight," Aaron says, grabbing my hand as we walk down Ontario.

He's not wrong, and I know every self-help book on the planet would tell me that the best way to deepen our relationship is to let him in.

"Sorry," I say, giving his hand a squeeze. "I've got a lot on my mind."

It's a cop-out, but I don't have the energy to unpack how it feels like we're on different pages of different books. He's talking to my father about our future while I can't stop thinking about my past. Even if I tried to explain, I'm not sure he'd understand.

"Did you ever go to camp?" I ask.

Aaron shakes his head, and I'm disappointed, but not surprised. It shouldn't matter that he's not a camp person. I'm not one anymore, but it feels like I'm on the precipice of becoming one again.

Re-coming, not becoming.

Although I don't know if it's possible to reconcile the girl I used to be with the woman I am today. The woman Aaron is planning to spend forever with.

We stop at the corner of Michigan, waiting for the light to change, and I look at Aaron. Really look at him. He's a good man, and he'd make a good husband. Is it the worst thing in the world if we have different priorities? Money does matter, and it affords us the life we live. So what if he doesn't give me butterflies? It's not like anyone else has, either.

Aaron catches me looking at him and leans down for a chaste kiss. I'm usually not a fan of PDA, but I lean into it, opening my mouth, desperate to feel something that will give me an answer to the question that's been hanging in the air all night.

My response surprises Aaron, but he quickly recovers,

pulling me flush against him, deepening the kiss. He doesn't seem to mind the hordes of tourists around us; if anything, it seems to turn him on. He presses his erection against me, and I feel the flutter of something in my belly—but it disappears the moment I lock eyes with a woman staring at us. She blushes, but I'm the one who's mortified. This is ridiculous. I'm too old to be making out in the street, chasing butterflies.

I pull away from Aaron, whose eyes are dark with desire. I may not know what our future holds, but I know I can't leave him hanging like this when I'm about to leave for two months.

Pushing all the things left on my to-do list out of my mind, I slip my hand in his and say, "Let's go back to my place."

Twenty minutes later, after a perfunctory roll in the hay (he came, I didn't), I'm restless. The walls in my apartment feel like they're closing in around me, so I slip out to the balcony for some air while Aaron showers.

This has always been my plan, I remind myself. Engaged by thirty, married by thirty-one, pregnant by thirty-two.

But is it still what I want? And is Aaron the man I want it with? Or is this all one big game of musical chairs and he's the one I'm left with when the music stops?

"Hey, babe," Aaron says, coming out onto the balcony behind me and sliding his arms around my waist. I lean back into him, desperately trying to feel something. What if the problem isn't him or us, but me?

"I know you still have a lot to do tonight, to pack," he

says, and I blink. Does he sound nervous? "But there's something I wanted to ask you."

My heart gallops in my chest. This is it. The big question. Yes or No. Maybe? Is there room for a maybe? If I say no, does that mean we're over? I'll have lost two years of my life—my plan will officially be off the rails. But if I say yes, does that mean this is as good as it gets?

Aaron shifts so he's beside me, but he doesn't look at me. I follow his gaze, staring out at the Chicago skyline, the city lights so bright you can't see the stars.

"Like you said," he begins. "Eight weeks is a long time."

I didn't say that, but I keep my mouth shut, wishing I could manipulate time, fast-forward past this conversation or rewind back two years to when my dad said he wanted to set me up with a promising lawyer at his firm. Or farther, back ten years to when I made the decision to follow my dad's plan instead of my heart.

"Even your dad said a man has needs," Aaron is saying.

My entire body goes stiff—my dad said no such thing, and this is a weird way to start a marriage proposal.

"So I was thinking," Aaron concludes, "maybe we take a break this summer."

I bark out a laugh. Here I am, trying to convince myself I should marry this man, and he wants to take a break? Dazed, I walk away from the railing and sit on the ironically named love seat. Aaron sits beside me and tries to take my hands in his, but I brush them away.

"Listen, I meant what I said earlier. I want forever with you, but . . ."

"But?" I echo.

"But since you'll be gone *all* summer, and I'll be here . . ."

I don't remind him that I invited him to come out for one of the weeklong sessions so he could see this place that means so much to me. Again, I got the excuse of what a "busy time" this is for the firm.

He's still talking, and I force myself to pay attention.

"I thought we could treat this summer like one last hurrah. It wouldn't be anything serious," he says, as if that matters. "Just a little fun, taking care of, you know . . ."

"Your needs?" I don't even try to keep the sarcasm out of my voice. I'm not angry—I'm annoyed. At myself, because I didn't see this coming, and at Aaron for going so far off script.

Aaron doesn't pick up on my tone. "Exactly," he says, relaxing back into the sofa. "I'm so glad you see the logic in this."

"So, let me get this straight," I say, trying to push past the sting of rejection and focus on his so-called logic. "You'll get a free pass to sleep with whoever you want over the next two months?"

"I'll wear a condom every time," Aaron says earnestly.

"And what about me?"

"What about you?" He looks genuinely confused.

"If you're sleeping around, I assume it's okay for me to do the same?"

Aaron laughs, stopping only when he sees I'm not amused. "I mean, if you want, but, well . . . you know." I narrow my eyes, keeping my mouth shut. "It's just, well, you aren't really the type."

"The type to have sex?" I cross my arms over my chest, not sure if I should be amused or offended at this, coming from the man I'm sleeping with.

"No," Aaron says, trying to take my hand again. "I didn't mean that. I meant, well, the type to just have fun."

"You don't think I'm fun?"

Aaron inhales a quick breath. "Being serious isn't a bad thing. It's a great quality for a wife."

Now it's my turn to laugh. "A *wife*? Is this your idea of a proposal?"

"I'm not proposing—not yet, anyway."

"Good," I say, folding my arms. "Because a proposal requires at least a little romance."

And it shouldn't involve sleeping with other people, I add silently.

"Noted," Aaron says, and the sincerity in his voice astounds me. "But, Hill, you should know I'm planning to spend the rest of my life with you. That's why it makes sense to take a break this summer. A lifelong commitment is a big deal, and I think we should both be *really* ready. You know?"

He says all this like it's perfectly reasonable, like I should be flattered. Instead, I'm . . . I don't know what this feeling is. It's like someone dropped a bomb on the path that was so clearly laid out ahead of me, and I'm not sure whether I should find a detour and keep going, or turn back.

"And you think after this summer you'll be *really* ready?" There's an edge to my voice that he either doesn't pick up on or chooses to ignore.

"Absolutely. We're both turning thirty soon. It's the perfect time to have one last summer of freedom before we officially step into adulthood."

I sit silently for a while, trying to process this seismic shift. On the one hand, he's not wrong. If we're going to settle down together, it's smart to be sure. But something about his suggestion doesn't feel right. Maybe because I'm not very fun, like Aaron said. I'm a boring monogamist.

"Listen," I say, standing up. "I've got an early flight. I think you should go."

"So . . . we're good?" Aaron asks.

"I don't know," I admit. "I need to think about it."

He nods, slipping his hands in his back pockets. "Until then . . ."

"Until then, we're on a break. Do whatever you need to do."

A smile lights up Aaron's face until he remembers himself and tamps down his excitement. He gives me a quick kiss goodbye and heads off into the night, eager to get a start on all the adventures waiting for him and his completely average penis.

As soon as the door closes behind him, I sit back on the love seat, wishing I had a girlfriend I could call. Someone to ask advice about what I should do—now, and in two months when camp is over. What I should do *at* camp. Probably nothing? Like Aaron said, I'm not the type to have hot, meaningless sex with strangers.

But that's okay. The relationship I need to focus on this summer is a platonic one.

One more sleep until I'm reunited with my best friend.

six

Jessie

After months of prep work, we're one week away from the start of adult summer camp. Today, my summer staff arrives. Nathaniel and Lola always said that training week was the most important week of the summer, that it sets the tone for the year. *I* set the tone.

Here we go.

I'm wearing khaki shorts, hiking boots, a green polo shirt with the Camp Chickawah logo across the left breast, and my wide-brimmed sun hat. I've braided my hair in two French braids, sprayed myself with bug repellent, and slathered SPF 70 across all exposed areas of my body.

Sunscreen and DEET: the aroma of summer camp.

Years ago, one of my camp flings told me that I'd be a solid six out in the real world, but I'm a nine at camp. I doubt he meant it as a compliment, but I took it as one. All the qualities that make me a good match for camp life—my height, my strength, my Energizer Bunny personality—are "too much" in the real world. No one is impressed that I can heft three duffel bags in each arm, that my loud voice carries over a crowd, that I can stay up until two a.m. comforting a homesick camper, then wake at dawn and work all day with a smile on my face.

But here? I was designed for this.

I head to the dining hall, a big log building with a green shingled roof. It's one of the busiest buildings on the property, the site of three meals a day and other large group activities—plus, it's next to my office and personal cabin.

As I heave open the door, I'm happy to see the lights on for the first time in months. Mr. Billy and his seasonal crew have been busy getting the wooden tables and benches in place. On the far end is the kitchen, its two big serving windows currently closed. I can hear the thump of bass coming from inside.

Time for me to greet our camp chef.

Two weeks ago, the chef I had hired sent an email saying he'd taken a higher-paying job on a cruise ship. Panicking, I sent an SOS email to the camp listserv, asking for leads. Within twenty-four hours, I had a response from Cooper, who was in my year at camp and is now a classically trained chef. As part of his application, he created a week's sample menu. I started salivating just reading the descriptions and hired him immediately.

When I told Dot, she recalled him as "that short, round, asthmatic kid." An accurate description, though I mostly remember him as the boy I paid three Kit Kats and a Twix to kiss my then–best friend.

I push open the swinging door and hear louder music. The counters are covered with crates of food, and the door to the walk-in fridge is open.

"Cooper?" I call.

A man sticks his head out of the fridge. "Jessie!" he shouts, and runs over to give me a hug.

When we pull away, I stare at him, flabbergasted. He used to be shorter than me, and wider, but now he's about my height, stocky but solid, with dark, wavy hair under a Red Sox hat.

"You look so different!" I blurt out.

He grins, which calls to mind the Cooper I remember. "Time and puberty work wonders. You look the same, though. Braids and everything."

I'm not sure if that's a good thing, but I smile anyway.

"Wow, you're already getting started," I say, motioning at the crates of food.

"I shopped for nonperishables and brought as much as I could. I'll need to go to town every week for fresh things, but I've worked it out with the grocery store to supply what I need."

"Great," I say. As Lola always said, *A fed camp is a happy camp.* "Everything is settled with the kitchen crew? You're okay with the people Antonio hired?"

"Yeah, they'll be great," Cooper says, nodding. "They're mostly folks from town, plus some college kids who wanted a summer job. I'll have a breakfast and lunch shift with three people, a dinner crew with four."

"Amazing," I say, impressed with how quickly he stepped in and took charge. "Can I help unpack?"

"If you want. I've got it, though."

He easily hefts a large crate of #10 cans and heads to the pantry. I pick up a similar crate, grunting with the effort, and follow him.

"So how are you?" I ask him as I unpack the cans from my crate. "Excited to be the big kitchen boss this summer?"

When we talked over the phone, Cooper told me that after five years working for a trendy restaurant in Boston, he was taking a sabbatical. That this would be a nice stopgap while he decided if he wanted to go back or move on to something new.

"For sure. I'll do my best to overcome the bland camp food stereotype—though I'm considering wearing a hairnet and support hose. You know, for authenticity's sake."

I snort a laugh. "What else is going on in your life? Do you have a significant other? Kids? Pets? Plants?"

"No pets, plants, or kids," he says, grinning. Then he winces. "No significant other, either."

I raise my eyebrows and Cooper continues, answering my unspoken question. "I was seeing this waitress at my last restaurant. One of us thought it was casual, and one of us thought it was . . . something else. It didn't end well. As in, it ended with a vat of lobster bisque being thrown at my head."

"Yikes. I'm sorry."

"Even more reason to get out of Boston for the summer. Single and ready to mingle, right?"

He winks—playfully, but with a hint of flirtatiousness that could be trouble. I'll have to keep an eye on him. I had my fair share of summer flings as a counselor (throwing a bunch of horny college-aged young adults together for eight weeks leads to *plenty* of clandestine sex). But as director, I hate dealing with romantic entanglements between staff. It causes so much drama.

And this summer, there's an added dimension, in that

our campers are adults. As long as everyone is consenting and safe, I don't care what they do with each other. But I don't want employees hooking up with campers. I need my staff to remain professional and focused.

While we unpack more crates, I catch him up on the staff for the summer—he remembers Dot and Mr. Billy—and the newlywed couple I hired for the lakefront.

"And for the Arts and Crafts cabin . . ." I grin and bounce my eyebrows up and down. "Remember Hillary Goldberg? You two smooched down by the lake when we were fourteen?"

Cooper's eyebrows shoot up. "Of course. So you two have kept in touch?"

"No. I . . . well, we haven't spoken in years."

"Really?" He sounds surprised. "You were so close."

I can feel my smile fading. "You know how it is. Camp ended, and we . . . drifted apart."

"Life does that, right?" he says, then claps his hands. "Thanks for your help—I'm going to start dinner prep. I'll ring the bell when it's ready."

I'm walking across the big lawn toward the campfire with Dot when I hear a voice call, "Jessie! Dot! Is it really you?"

I turn to see a tiny woman, her dark hair flying behind her as she runs. When she reaches us, she throws her arms around me and squeezes.

"It's so good to see you!" I say, a little breathless.

Zoey Takahashi was a CIT during my first couple years as an assistant director. She's bubbly and sweet, and though she can sometimes come across as ditzy, she always took her responsibilities seriously. She and her husband Zac are fresh from their honeymoon, here to run our waterfront—they're both certified lifeguards, and he's a sailing instructor.

"Welcome back to camp," Dot says, then grunts when Zoey gives her a hug, too.

Zoey motions to the man who's come up beside her. "And this is my husband!"

"Zac Takahashi-Zimmerman. Or Zimmerman-Takahashi. We haven't decided," he says, smiling. He grabs my hand in his meaty palm and gives it three big pumps. "Nice to meet ya."

"You too," I say, extricating my hand before he bruises it.

I recognize Zac's Australian accent from our phone conversations, and he looks like I pictured: tall, blond, and broad-shouldered.

"This is Camp Chickawah, baby!" Zoey says, putting an arm around her husband's waist. "What do you think?"

Zac looks around and whistles. "I think you were right—this place is a beaut!"

"I'm so glad we're doing this!" she says, smiling up at him.

"Me too." He leans down and gives her a kiss on the lips, but the quick peck quickly turns into more. And more. And *more*, until they're wrapped in each other's arms, kissing so deeply I'm surprised they can breathe.

I glance over at Dot, who grimaces. We wait awkwardly for them to finish, trying not to watch.

When they break apart, Zoey turns to me, oblivious to any possible discomfort. "Do I have time to show Zac around? He's never been to a summer camp before."

"It's such an American thing," he says. "It's surreal—like being on a film set."

"I've given you two the big room in the Lodge," I tell them. "Your names are on the door. You can get settled whenever."

Zoey squeals and grabs Zac's hand. "Let's go down to the lake."

They run off, hand in hand, their laughter echoing in the evening air.

"They're . . . cute," Dot says.

"Really cute," I agree. "That was a lot of kissing for the middle of the day in front of two people they don't know super well, though. Right?"

Dot's mouth twitches in a silent laugh. "Let's hope Cooper and Hillary are deep sleepers, because you know those walls are thin! Oh, and speaking of Hillary . . ."

"What about her?"

"Are you sure you're going to be . . . okay? Seeing her again?" Dot asks, her voice unexpectedly gentle.

My eyes prickle with sudden tears, and I turn away before she can see. "Of course! It'll be just like old times."

"Well, except that she—"

"Want to help me set up the campfire for tonight?" I cut in.

Dot hesitates. "Sure, boss. Whatever you say." She glances behind her. "Hey, were you expecting anyone else today?"

"Just Hillary," I say, following her gaze. There's a man walking across the lawn toward us. Maybe a delivery guy? "Can I help you?" I ask when he's a few feet away.

"Checking in," the man says. Grumbles, really.

Confused, I take a step closer. There's something familiar about him. He's a couple inches taller than me, dressed in a

gray T-shirt and jeans, with a baseball cap pulled low like
he's hiding from the world.

It's not until he lifts his chin that I catch a flash of
brilliant blue eyes and realize who he is.

William Lucas Duncan. *The Man.*

"What's he doing here?" Dot says in a furious whisper as we
hurry along the path toward Luke's assigned cabin. It isn't
ready for him yet, since he was supposed to arrive next week
with the other campers.

"I have no idea." I glance behind me; Luke is heading
toward the parking lot to grab his stuff. "He didn't ask you if
he could come early?"

"No. And he sure as shit didn't mention anything about a
dog."

That's the other unwelcome surprise. I consider myself a
lover of all living things—but Camp Chickawah has never
been a dog-friendly summer camp. And I am not about to
spend my summer picking up poop.

So I nicely informed Luke that he'd need to make other
arrangements.

"At least the dog will be gone soon," I say.

Dot snorts. "That dog isn't going anywhere."

"What do you mean? I told him to find somewhere else
for the dog before the other campers arrived, and he said
okay."

We reach the cabin and climb the stairs to the porch.
Before going in, Dot turns to face me. "He said 'sure.' That
was sarcasm, honey."

I think back to the blank expression on his face. "Really?"

"Yes. He's one of those deadpan assholes who act like everyone else's concerns are beneath them," she says, then opens the door.

Dot despises rule breakers, so Luke is officially on her shit list. I guess I should have expected this, given his email communications. *I require a private cabin to write my novel.* Pretentious jerk.

Shaking my head in frustration, I join Dot in opening the windows. This smaller cabin, historically used by extra staff members, has four twin-size beds, a table, and a bathroom with a toilet and sink. Luke will have to use the communal shower building, and knowing he'll be forced to interact with the plebians gives me some satisfaction.

Dot checks the mousetraps while I make sure the bathroom is stocked with toilet paper and hand soap. I hope he isn't expecting fluffy white towels and little bottles of toiletries.

When I return to the main room, Luke is walking in the door, a duffel in each hand. He shoves his way past me and dumps everything on the closest bed.

Despite my irritation, I find myself smiling, because that is what my mouth automatically does when I'm playing my camp director role. "So, this is where you'll be—"

He turns and walks back out. I look at Dot, my jaw dropping.

"Dickhead," she mutters. "Don't waste your time worrying about him, boss."

I sigh, but nod. Come Monday afternoon, I'll be busy with the other campers. He can isolate himself as much as he wants.

But I'm going to stand my ground about the dog. I can't have it running around the property, barking at squirrels and bothering everyone. Plus, what if some campers are allergic? No, Luke will have to find somewhere else for it to stay this summer.

I head out of the cabin, ready to confront him, then stop short.

Luke is at the bottom of the porch stairs with his dog, bending over to help it up. The dog is struggling, like each step is painful, and my heart reluctantly squeezes.

My soft heart used to embarrass me—I once cried for days after finding a dead bird at school, and a bunch of my classmates teased me—but my teacher told me compassion was a strength rather than a weakness. I'm not sure about that, since soft hearts are easily bruised. Still, I wait until Luke and his dog reach the top of the stairs, and the dog comes over to sniff my shoes.

"Hello, there," I say, bending down. It's a golden retriever, its face almost totally white, one eye cloudy with a cataract. I let it sniff me, then gently give it a pat on the chest. The dog leans into me, tail wagging. "What's your name, puppers?"

"Scout," Luke says.

I look up, smiling. "Like Scout Finch?"

He nods but doesn't return my smile. There's a palpable sense of gloom surrounding him. So different from the way he acted back in the day, when he was The Man, charming and adored, always laughing and joking. I can't help but wonder what changed.

"She's beautiful," I say. And obviously well cared for; her fur is silky soft. "How old is she?"

"Thirteen."

My heart squeezes again. I can't separate this elderly dog from her owner all summer.

Sighing, I straighten up. "All right, the dog can stay. Just . . . make sure she doesn't bother the other campers. Ticks are a problem here, so check her every day. And pick up her poop, okay?"

"Obviously."

Luke turns to go into the cabin. There's something so sad about watching him head into the dark with his elderly dog. My silly, soft heart gives one final squeeze.

On impulse, I say, "Luke?"

He turns.

"Do you want to come to the lake with us later? The staff is planning to hang out and have a drink as the sun goes down. Scout is welcome, too."

I'm just outside the threshold. He rests one hand on the doorframe and the other on the door, like he's holding himself upright. For the first time since he arrived, he lifts his eyes to meet mine—they're so blue it's startling, and a hot poker seems to hit my spine. His face is lined with exhaustion, or sadness, or both, and when his lips part in a long, heavy sigh, I find myself leaning forward in concern.

He's lonely.

Not a pretentious asshole. Just lonely.

Then he breaks the silence with one word:

"No."

And shuts the door in my face.

seven

Hillary

I forgot how long a drive it is from the Minneapolis airport to camp. When I was a kid, every minute on the bus stretched like an hour. It was torture, knowing my reunion with Jessie was so close, yet so far away. Even now, after ninety minutes in the backseat of a town car heading west on Highway 94 and twenty minutes north on country roads, I'm bouncing in anticipation.

Or maybe that's nerves? Because I'm not sure the excitement is mutual. The few emails I've exchanged with Jessie have been friendly, but they don't hold a candle to the letters we used to send. I pictured us still writing each other when we were little old ladies in the nursing home—but the last letter came much sooner than that.

It was the last month of my freshman year at college. I wrote and rewrote that email four times, trying to find the words to let Jessie understand how sorry I was for breaking my promise of being counselors together.

The response that eventually came was just one short sentence: *It's fine.*

Of course, it wasn't. And I knew nothing I said would

make it better, so I left her email unanswered as the days turned into weeks, then months.

I never imagined it would be more than ten years before we'd see each other again.

Up ahead, I spot the familiar sign with YOU BELONG HERE carved into wood. I hope the words are still true. It's strange to think that Jessie has been here this whole time, that my past is her present. I wonder if she's still stubbornly optimistic with the ability to bring out the best in everyone. If Camp Chickawah is still her whole world. And most importantly, if she'll be happy to see me.

For all I know, I'm one of many best friends she's had over the years. Someone like Jessie wouldn't have the same problem making friends that I did. That I still do. Maybe for her, my return to Camp Chickawah is no big deal.

Either way, I'm about to find out.

The car turns down the narrow road toward camp and my breath hitches as the tunnel of trees takes me back in time. I squeeze my eyes shut, and suddenly, I'm the eight-year-old girl who misses her dad and just wants to go home.

Abruptly, the darkness turns to light. We break through the clearing of trees into camp, and I open my eyes, taking it all in: the Lodge to the left; the girls' cabins to the right; the big open lawn and the boys' cabins up ahead.

"This the right spot?" the driver asks as he rolls to a stop in front of the dining hall. I tell him it is, then step out of the car.

But it doesn't feel right.

Something must be wrong with the space-time continuum, because this place is both everything and nothing like I remember. For one thing, it feels . . . smaller.

Less significant. And the buildings all seem worse for wear. The dining hall, once looming and grand in a rustic way, looks like a worn-down shack. The exterior hasn't been touched up in the last decade, and the wood on the porch is so distressed I'm not sure it's safe to stand on.

If I were here in a professional capacity, my recommendation would likely be to wipe the slate clean and start with something new. The land is still impressive— majestic, even, with its acres of woods and pristine lake. It could be a blank canvas to build a new camp or a year-round vacation community for families.

But Camp Chickawah is not a client, and I'm not here to save it. I'm here to have fun and reconnect with a lost part of myself. Maybe then I'll know what I want for my future.

Behind me, I hear a door open and close. I turn to see Jessie, standing like a vision before me.

Like the camp, she's the same, but different. Older, and somehow even taller. Her strawberry blonde hair is in those familiar twin plaits and she's wearing the uniform the counselors used to wear—a Camp Chickawah shirt and khaki shorts, a walkie-talkie on her hip.

She moves to shake my hand at the same time I move to give her a hug, and we end in an awkward collision of arms and hands. Not exactly the reunion I was hoping for.

"Hillary Goldberg, back at camp," she says, stepping back. "Never thought I'd see the day."

I don't know this adult version of Jessie well enough to know if there's a hidden barb under her words or if she's genuinely happy to see me. I hope it's the latter.

"I missed this place," I say. "And you."

Jessie flinches. It lasts a fraction of a second, but it's long enough for my coffee to curdle in my stomach. She can't still be mad at me, can she? I should have reached out sooner, asked if we could talk and clear the air before I waltzed in, acting as if nothing between us was broken; as if it's been ten months and not more than ten years since we've seen each other.

I'm about to ask if she has time to catch up when static buzzes from her walkie-talkie.

"Go for Jessie," she says.

I can't follow the stream of words, but Jessie seems to understand. "Be right there," she says to the person on the other end of the connection.

Then, to me: "I've got to take care of a situation in one of the boys' cabins. Staff is staying on the second floor of the Lodge—feel free to find your room and unpack."

"Oh," I say, doing a terrible job at hiding my disappointment. I'd hoped to be in one of the girls' cabins, just like the old days: sleeping on the bottom bunk, hearing the slow, measured breaths of my camp friends, knowing Jessie was in the bunk above me.

I should have realized Jessie would be in the small cabin where Nathaniel and Lola used to live, next to the dining hall. I went in there once—halfway through my second summer at camp, when my weekly letter from Dad hadn't arrived. I was inconsolable, certain something had happened to him, that he'd had an aneurysm, like my mom.

Even though it was usually off-limits, Lola brought me into their warm, cozy cabin, which had a phone for emergencies. Hearing my father's voice on the other end of the line was just the elixir I needed.

"Remember where the Lodge is?" Jessie calls. She's already walking off toward the boys' side of camp.

"I remember."

"Dinner's around six—you'll hear the bell when it's ready."

With that, she's gone. And I'm left to ponder if my former best friend is acting distant because this is her job now, or if she's still carrying the hurt I caused by walking away all those years ago.

I sigh and look toward the Lodge, way on the other side of camp, then down at my luggage—two large rolling suitcases and a small bag. A far cry from the army-style duffel that was standard for campers back in the day.

It's clear no one's going to magically appear to transport my stuff, so I start the long haul, dragging one bag a few feet down the gravel path, then going back to drag the other. Drag, drop, repeat. Repeat. Repeat. By the time I arrive at the Lodge, my jeans are sticking to me like glue, and my brand-new hiking boots have left blisters on my heels.

The two-story building sits up the hill from the lake, and like everything else around here, it's not as impressive as in my memory. I used to think the two-toned exterior was beautiful, with flat stones accenting the first floor and wood siding on the second. Now, a few stones have fallen out, leaving gaps of exposed cement, and the wood could use a fresh coat of paint. When I let myself in, I choke on the musty air. Even on the first floor, the Lodge has a distinct attic vibe.

There are three big rooms down here, designed for the rare indoor activities or to offer refuge on bad weather days. Taking the stairs to the second level feels like trespassing.

This was where staff who weren't counselors slept; no campers allowed.

There's a lounge at the top of the stairs with a couch, two chairs, and a tiny kitchenette, which holds a refrigerator, a microwave, and an ancient-looking coffee machine. A wave of homesickness for my Nespresso machine hits me—maybe I can get Aaron to ship it up here. It's the least he can do after the emotional whiplash of yesterday. I'm still unsettled by the conversation—the more I think about it, the less logical his logic seems.

Squaring my shoulders and putting him out of my mind, I walk down the long hallway. There are bedrooms on either side, but we've got such a small staff this summer that only a handful are taken. Each is marked by a simple sign in Jessie's familiar block writing. I study the names of my new coworkers: Dot and then Chef on the right; Zac and Zoey and then me on the left.

In my room, I find simple wooden furniture: two twin beds, two desks, two dressers. Like my reunion with Jessie, it falls short of my expectations.

I've been so focused on the nostalgia of coming back to camp that I didn't think about the reality of "roughing" it. There's no air-conditioning, the corners of the room are dusty, and the mattress is so thin I can feel the wood planks of the frame beneath my butt. Maybe Aaron was right when he said this isn't who I am anymore.

But I've never been a quitter, and I'm not going to start now.

Walking over to the window, I gaze out over the lake. The water glistens in the afternoon sun, and the sight of the dock makes my heart swell with memories—Jessie and I would sit out there and sunbathe for hours, talking about anything and everything. I take a deep breath, smiling. Everything is going to be okay, I just—*ack!*

I jump back, my heart pounding. A spider the size of a quarter is chilling in its cobweb along the windowsill, glaring as if I'm the intruder.

Which I suppose I am.

For an instant, I wish Aaron was here to take care of it, but I'm a strong, capable woman. I put on my metaphorical big girl pants and march out to the kitchenette, finding a cup and a small plate so I can evict my roommate to the safety of the great outdoors.

Next on the agenda: a shower. It's going to take a good twenty minutes to wash off the grime of this day.

The shower is a tiny stall in the communal bathroom at the end of the hall, but everything looks reasonably clean, and the water is piping hot. As much as I'd wanted to stay in a cabin, it's nice not having to put on flip-flops and trek my toiletries to the group bathroom.

When I'm finished, I grab a towel from the linen closet. It's small and a little scratchy, barely covering the important bits. But my room is just down the hall, so I grab my clothes and toiletry bag, then step out of the steamy bathroom—smack into a man's chest.

"Whoa there," a deep voice says.

I stumble back, nearly losing my towel before getting my balance. "Hi! Excuse me! So sorry!"

Looking up, I lock eyes with the deep voice's owner. He's about five foot ten with broad shoulders, wavy brown hair under a backward baseball cap, and a neatly trimmed beard. He's smiling down at me—on second glance, it looks more like a smirk.

"No worries," he says. "You okay?"

I straighten up, trying to act unbothered. "Fine, thanks."

"Your, uh—the towel is a bit . . ." He points, grimacing slightly.

I glance down to see that the top of the towel has drifted downward, revealing approximately one third of my left nipple. My cheeks burst into flames, and I yank it up—then feel the cool breeze below and tug it down. This makes me drop my toiletry bag, and my bottles of shampoo and conditioner go rolling down the hallway toward the guy's feet.

A chuckle rumbles from him, and he stoops to pick them up. "Here, let me help. Wouldn't want you to drop that towel."

"I'm sure you would just hate that," I mutter, my mortification growing.

"Hey, we're gonna be sharing this bathroom all summer, so I'm sure we'll be seeing a lot more of each other," he says, handing me my toiletries. "Here you go."

I snatch the bottles back and stuff them into my bag, squeezing my elbows tightly against my body so the towel doesn't shift.

"Thank you," I say, with as much dignity as I can manage. "Have a great afternoon."

And then I hurry past him and into my room, shutting the door behind me and locking it.

His chuckle echoes through the hallway as he walks away.

Once I'm done shaking off *that* embarrassment, I spend the next hour unpacking and trying to make the room feel homier. It doesn't work, but at least stacking the two twin mattresses on top of each other makes the bed more comfortable.

With just about twenty minutes to spare before dinner, I put on a breezy maxi dress and a minimal amount of makeup. I don't want to look like I'm trying too hard, but first impressions matter. Second impressions, even more so.

As I retrace my steps back toward the dining hall, the camp seems more familiar. There's the crunch of gravel under my feet, the rustling of leaves, the slight chill in the evening air. My shoulders loosen and my stiff exterior chips away, revealing the carefree camper I hope is still in there somewhere.

Inside, the dining room looks the way it always did: shiny wood floors and row after row of long, rectangular tables. The one difference is the rich scent of garlic wafting from the kitchen—our camp fare never smelled this decadent.

The kitchen door swings open, and out walks the guy I ran into earlier, wearing an apron covered in hot pink lips and the words KISS THE COOK. My cheeks heat with the memory of our run-in. He is *definitely* better looking than old Chef Cindy.

Before he can notice me, I make a beeline for the table where Jessie is sitting. She's talking animatedly to Dot, who looks just like I remember: short gray hair and stocky build. Across from them are a young couple—a petite, dark-haired woman sitting on the lap of a big, blond man. Presumably the Zac and Zoey who have the room next to mine. They're all laughing and talking like they're best friends. At the end of the table, I recognize Mr. Billy, the old groundskeeper. He seemed ancient back when I was a camper, and I'm impressed he's still working.

It feels like walking into my junior high cafeteria and realizing everyone has a group to sit with except me.

My muscles tense. Should I leave?

"Get over here, Goldberg," Dot calls. Her voice is gruff, but she's smiling. "Good to see you again."

"Hi." I wave. I literally wave. Like an awkward loser. Quickly, I stuff my offending hand into my pocket before I do something even worse, like give them all a thumbs-up.

"Make room," Dot commands, and Zac slides down the bench, Zoey still in his lap. I take a seat across from Jessie, who barely acknowledges my presence.

I might have been better off sitting by Mr. Billy.

Dot makes introductions, ending with the chef. "And you remember Coop, of course."

My cheeks heat as I look up at him.

"Hi . . . again?" I say awkwardly. Am I supposed to know him?

"Cooper," he says. "It's been a long time, Hill. How've you been?"

He says this so casually I almost wonder if he doesn't recognize me as the nearly naked woman he ran into. And how does he know me?

But then he bites his lower lip, and the gesture brings it all back. The two of us, standing a breath apart down by the lake. I was fourteen that summer, and after Sara Verkest kissed Matt Berger, I was the only girl in our cabin who hadn't gotten to first base yet. I hadn't even made it up to bat.

Jessie, being the best friend she was, set out on a mission to find a guy for me to smooch. She was strategic, narrowing it down to two: Toby from Cabin Eleven, who had kissed a lot of girls, and Cooper from Cabin Twenty-One, who was friends with a lot of girls, but as far as we knew, hadn't kissed anyone. In the end, we decided kissing Cooper would be less intimidating. He wasn't exactly cute by most teenagers' standards, but he was sweet and funny.

I'm still not sure what Jessie did to convince him, but she got Cooper to meet me down by the lake after dinner. The view, with the early evening sun casting a shimmering light across the water, took my breath away.

Unfortunately, I can't say the same thing about the kiss, which was awkward and wet. I tried to look him up once after telling someone the story, but Cooper is his last name, and I never knew his first. I guess I can ask him now that he's here, standing right in front of me, waiting for me to say something.

"Wow," I say. "You look amazing—I never would have recognized you."

I cringe, wishing I could stuff the offending words back in my mouth. He doesn't seem bothered, though. His eyes light up and he flashes me a grin.

"I shot up five inches when I turned seventeen and realized I needed to burn calories instead of just consuming them," he says.

I laugh, and accidentally glance down at his ring finger,

which is bare. Not that it matters. Even though my current relationship status is single, this guy has "player" written all over him. Literally.

"Nice apron," I say.

"Nice dress," he replies.

Is he teasing me for being overdressed? His eyes dip down my body and he gives a smirky little smile like he's remembering exactly how *under*dressed I was just an hour ago.

My cheeks flush. "Uh—thanks."

"Any time." He looks like he's about to say something else, but a timer goes off in the kitchen. "Better go get that."

As Cooper excuses himself, I look over to see Jessie watching me. Her jaw is tight, and I search her face for a glimpse of the girl who orchestrated that first kiss.

I hope she's in there somewhere. Otherwise, it's going to be a very long summer.

eight

Jessie

It's the first morning of Training Week, and the staff is gathered around the firepit. I look around, momentarily unnerved; usually, all the log benches are filled. Having just seven people, including me, is strange.

Especially when one of them is my childhood best friend, who has grown into a polished woman with serious brown eyes and rigid posture. She's wearing jeans and hiking boots, but the jeans look designer and the boots are pristine—plus, her familiar wild, curly hair has been tamed into sleek layers. She feels like a stranger, and it's throwing me off balance.

But I gather my wits and stand, smiling.

"Welcome! Thanks for believing in my crazy adult camp idea—we'll probably hit some bumps along the way, but if we work as a team, we can make this summer Chick-amazing!"

For a split second, I feel silly—this is a group of grown adults—but Cooper raises his coffee mug and says, "Chicka-wonderful!"

Zoey chimes in, "Chicka-wow!"

She nudges Zac, who's staring at the clouds, mouth open. He startles and says, "Chicka-brilliant!"

67

Not quite right, but I give him a smile for trying.

"Let's talk about the structure of camp," I say, instructing the staff to turn to the first page in their informational binders. "We have eight one-week sessions, with a new group arriving each Monday afternoon and leaving the following Sunday morning. We'll have different ages each week. Some in their twenties, some in their forties, and even a group in their seventies!"

I notice Hillary smile when I say this. She's sitting on the edge of the group, keeping to herself. She was like that as a kid, too. I always had to persuade her to get involved, and she'd usually end up enjoying herself.

At least, I thought she did—maybe not. Maybe that's why she didn't want to be a counselor with me. Maybe I was too overbearing. Maybe she didn't like me as much as I liked her.

Focus, I tell myself.

"Each week has a special activity," I continue. "Scavenger hunt, camp musical, canoe parade, talent show, Color Wars. See page two in your binders for the full schedule."

"Question," Zoey says, raising her hand like a schoolgirl.

I smile in her direction. "Yes?"

"Are staff allowed to participate in these activities?"

"Absolutely," I say. "Different staff members will be responsible for various events—you and Zac are in charge of the canoe parade—but I hope everyone will participate in as many other activities as possible."

Zac and Zoey grin at each other, like this is the best news ever.

"The daily schedule is listed on page three," I say, and summarize: flagpole, breakfast, morning activities, lunch, afternoon activities, dinner, then an evening activity. "Since our campers are adults, they get to choose what they participate in. No one's going from cabin to cabin waking them up. But I want to emphasize something."

I pause. Everyone is listening intently.

"Obviously, adults won't need constant supervision, but we still need to be careful. We'll require everyone to pass a swim test—"

"And no swimming alone," Zac chimes in.

"Exactly. No one should go off on their own in the woods, either. It's easy to get lost, especially at night. And remember, we're here to work. Please be courteous and professional. That means no romantic involvement with our campers. Understood?"

I look around, making eye contact with each staff member. Zac and Zoey nod in vigorous agreement. Hillary nods, too, but she's been so aloof it's hard to imagine her hooking up with someone who's only here for a week.

But I hold Cooper's gaze until he nods and looks down. Satisfied, I turn to the next page in my binder. "Please take care of your mental and physical health. Camp is exhausting, so if you're feeling overly tired, let me know, and I'll make sure you get a break. Page four shows the assigned day off for every staff member, but if you need more—"

"When's your day off?" Hillary cuts in.

I look up. "What's that?"

She points to the schedule in her binder. "I have Tuesdays, Cooper has Wednesdays, Zac and Zoey have Thursdays. Dot has a half day off on Wednesdays and Fridays. But you don't have any time off."

I shift my weight in my hiking boots. "I'm the director.

It's a 24/7 job." Before she can say anything else, I shut my binder and smile. "All right, we have time to work individually, but let's regroup for lunch. Any questions?"

The week progresses: Cooper in the kitchen, Zac and Zoey at the lakefront, Hillary in the Arts and Crafts cabin. Dot finalizes registration, and Mr. Billy does last-minute property maintenance. William Lucas Duncan and his geriatric retriever keep to themselves; he doesn't even join us for meals. Apparently, he ducks into the kitchen while Cooper's finishing cooking, grabs some food, and leaves. Which is rude, but for the best. The last thing we need is Luke's black cloud casting a shadow over everything.

Meanwhile, I'm out of sorts. Usually training week is intense—wrangling counselors is often more difficult than wrangling campers—but this has been oddly . . . easy. By Wednesday, I'm out of things to do.

I end up in the office, "helping" Dot. I think I'm annoying the shit out of her, though.

Pretty sure that's why she's sent me on some made-up errand to ask Hillary what supplies she needs.

As I mosey toward the Arts and Crafts cabin, my steps dragging the closer I get, it dawns on me Dot has an ulterior motive: forcing me to talk with Hillary.

I reach the cabin and push open the door. The interior is cozy and colorful, with big wood tables and art from past summers decorating the walls. But last year's Arts and Crafts director—a twenty-two-year-old art student named Clarissa—quit a week early and left everything in chaos. Hillary has her work cut out for her.

"Hillary?" I call. My hands twist together, and I force them to relax by my sides.

She emerges from the storage area, holding a box of tangled yarn.

"Hi, Jessie," she says. "Do you need anything?"

"No, no. Just wanted to check in. See what supplies you need me to order."

She glances behind her. "Right now, I'm trying to get organized so I can see what I need."

"Well, um, when you figure it out, just give me a list."

"Will do."

She smiles politely, and I smile politely. It's hard to believe that I used to feel more comfortable around her than anyone else on the planet. What happened?

No. I know exactly what happened. Beneath the awkwardness is a cavern of loss, and part of me wants to ask her *why. Why did you abandon me? Why did you walk away from our friendship?* But that feels so . . . needy. So dramatic. I don't want to make a big deal out of it. We've both moved on.

"Awesome," I say, slapping my hands on my thighs. "Better get going. See you at dinner?"

"Yep."

I head toward the door, my heart beating oddly fast.

"Jessie?" Hillary says then, and I turn.

"Yeah?"

She twirls a strand of hair around her finger, something she used to do as a kid when she was nervous.

"I . . . I wanted to say that I'm sorry. For how it all happened, back then."

For a moment I'm frozen. The memories of that time—the

feelings—swell inside me, trying to burst free of the tight box where I've kept them locked for twelve years.

Then I pull myself together and smile. "No worries. It's water under the bridge."

Hillary nods, but she looks pensive. "I hope we can be friends this summer."

"Sure," I say stiffly. "See you around."

Outside, I stuff my hands in my pockets and head down the path toward the lake. My chest feels sore, like someone reached inside and rummaged around.

People talk all the time about the heartache and despair of a romantic breakup. What about a friendship breakup? Losing Hillary was a thousand times worse than losing Nick or any other guy I've dated.

More difficult to get over, too.

Maybe that's because when a romantic relationship ends, you usually get some closure—there's a breakup conversation; an evening spent eating ice cream and drinking wine with friends while rehashing the details, followed by the purging of all your ex's belongings (maybe into a campfire . . . if you happen to have one nearby). There's crying and extra chocolate consumption, and eventually, you move on.

But with Hillary? She didn't even call me when she took that internship. She sent an *email*. And then never reached out to me again. Ever. There was no closure whatsoever—I hardly allowed myself to think about it.

Now she's back and she says she wants to be friends, and my heart hurts every time I think about her, and I don't have the emotional capacity to face any of this, because this summer is going to be challenging enough as it is.

Better to keep my distance.

By Thursday, I'm still feeling out of sorts. The staff is eating dinner together—Cooper made chicken fajitas with churros for dessert—and everyone's laughing and talking. Even Mr. Billy is with us, quietly eating at the far end of the table.

"Would you rather . . ." Cooper says, and all the former campers perk up as he starts one of our most beloved dinnertime activities. "Lose one eye, or lose two fingers?"

"Can I choose which fingers?" Hillary asks.

I blink, surprised at how eagerly she jumped in. I've kept my distance from her, as I promised myself, but I'm not sure she's noticed. Which maybe goes to show that she doesn't care nearly as much about me as I care about her.

"Whatever fingers you'd like," Cooper says.

Hillary holds up her two pinky fingers. "I'd give these two up. I could still have good hand function."

"Can't give up the opposable thumb," Zac chimes in.

"How do we lose them?" Dot asks.

Cooper turns to her. "What?"

"Is my eye surgically removed under anesthesia in an operating room, or plucked out with a dirty knife in the woods?"

Zoey shudders. "Do you think it would hurt worse to get your eye cut out or your fingers cut off?"

"Eye," Zac says confidently. "It's one big nerve bundle, you know?"

"It's not the pain, it's the risk of infection," Dot says, dead serious. "You're healing up a few days later and bam! Sepsis."

I glance at Mr. Billy, who's rhythmically shoveling food

into his mouth. I swear I see his lips twitch, like he's holding in a laugh.

"It's not plucked out!" Cooper says, exasperated. "You just become a person with one eye."

Zac points to the middle of his forehead. "Like a cyclops?"

"Or a pirate?" Zoey covers one eye like an eye patch.

"I'm going with losing two fingers," I say. "Depth perception is important."

"Plus you're more likely to survive a postoperative infection in your arm than one so close to your brain," Dot says.

"Smart." Zac looks impressed.

She gives him a little salute. "Got to be prepared for the worst-case scenario."

I hold in a laugh. Dot created a ninety-five-page emergency response booklet that covers everything from tornadoes and forest fires (which are possible) to hurricanes and cholera outbreaks (which are not).

"Would you rather," Zoey says, "have the ability to snap your fingers and create fire or create ice?"

"Ice," Hillary says. "I'd create an ice castle."

I press my lips together, inexplicably annoyed. Hillary threw away her opportunity to be here years ago, and now she's acting like she never left.

"Fire," I say, a little too forcefully. "Would save me so much time on bonfire nights."

Dot narrows her eyes, like she's wondering what's going on with me, and I glance away.

"Ice," Cooper says, and Hillary beams at him, delighted. "I'd never have to worry about losing refrigeration. Once I had a hundred pounds of premium steak spoil because we lost power." He shudders.

"Fire would be good to cook that premium steak, though," Zac says, and I feel a weird burst of triumph. Like this silly game has turned into a display of loyalty.

Dot points her fork at all of us. "Creating ice would be helpful in a future climate apocalypse caused by global warming."

Hillary lights up, and I scowl; why can't Dot be on my side?

"But what if the zombie apocalypse happens instead?" I say. "Fire would be more useful in that case."

There's an edge of defensiveness in my voice. Dot's forehead wrinkles in concern, and my cheeks flush. I'm being immature, I realize that, and I order myself to knock it off. To stop acting like a petty teenager whose feelings were hurt.

"Burn those fuckers alive," Zac says, and I'm momentarily startled.

Zombie apocalypse, I remind myself.

"Zombies aren't alive," a voice says behind me. "They're undead."

Everyone turns; it's Luke. He's holding a dinner tray, glowering at us like we're intruding on *his* meal, rather than the other way around.

"Huh?" Zac says, bewildered.

"Imagine a reanimated corpse," Luke continues in a flat voice, "devoid of vitality or soul."

"Ah, so you have something in common," I say.

Cooper laughs, then covers it with a cough.

Luke's eyes snap to mine. They're icy blue, and I shiver. The rest of the table is silent, everyone staring at him. Luke looks like he's about to fire back a retort, but instead he turns around and stalks out of the dining hall, taking his tray with him.

"What's up with him?" Zoey says when he's gone.

I shrug. "Who knows."

The conversation moves on, but I keep thinking about those cool blue eyes, and the emotion I saw hiding in them. Not anger or contempt, as I expected. More like hurt.

And then I remember something: he was holding a dinner tray. I think Luke wanted to sit with us.

nine

Hillary

Camp is officially on! Or it will be as soon as the first bus arrives.

Our welcoming committee—Dot, Jessie, Zoey, and me—is buzzing with energy as we wait outside the dining hall, which looks festive with an arch of green and white balloons.

"Any minute now," Jessie says, looking at her watch. She's been pacing for the last fifteen minutes. While she's been tense around me since I arrived, this is somehow worse. I wonder if she's like this before every first day of camp, or if my being here has gotten her out of sorts.

Dot seems anxious, too, organizing the already organized welcome folders. Only Zoey seems unaffected.

Suddenly, Jessie stops. She lifts and tilts her head in a catlike motion before turning to us. "You guys ready to welcome our first campers?"

"Eek!" Zoey shouts and gets into place beside Jessie. I stand next to Zoey, and Dot makes one final micro-adjustment of the alphabetized folders.

We hold our collective breath, releasing it when we hear the crunch of the gravel and see the fifty-seat charter bus coming around the corner. I'm practically bouncing out of my shoes by the time it stops in front of us.

The hydraulic doors hiss open, and we all scream, "Chicka-welcome!!" as campers file off the bus, hooting and hollering. It's pure chaos, and I love every second of it, watching these grown men and women step back into a memory. What a gift Jessie is giving us all this summer.

I watch her now, looking genuinely happy as she corrals the campers into a line for check-in. Dot hands them each a folder and their limited-edition Adult Camp Chickawah T-shirts before passing them off to be escorted to their cabins.

Zoey takes the first two, lawyers from St. Louis, to Cabin Six, while Mr. Billy loads their luggage into his four-wheeler—which certainly would have come in handy last week!

I'm up next, showing a couple from Cleveland to their separate cabins. They're giddy on the walk over, telling me how they met here at camp and are now married with two kids. Looks like Lola was right when she said there's no love quite like camp love.

Soon, all fifty campers are settled in. But there's no time for rest—the second bus is already rolling down the path. "Chicka-welcome!" we all scream, somehow with even more enthusiasm.

Four hours and six buses later, my feet are aching and my cheeks are sore from smiling. I just escorted the last two campers, Michelle and Katie from Pittsburgh, to Cabin Ten. Now, instead of heading back to the dining hall, I'm sneaking a quick break at the Lodge. I need a second to catch my breath—all this people-ing has worn me out.

My plan for peace and quiet is short-lived, however. The newlyweds are also back, taking a "break" in their room, which is next to mine. These walls are thin, and Zoey is not shy about vocalizing her pleasure. From the volume—and frequency—of the moans I keep hearing, Zac is extremely skilled between the sheets.

A high-pitched shriek pierces the air, followed by the rhythmic pounding of the headboard against the wall. I blush and put in my AirPods, pulling up one of the podcast episodes I downloaded in preparation for the lack of Internet. It's a show that highlights successful businesses that have reinvented themselves. The host is talking to Lou, a woman at the helm of an empire committed to helping people crush their comfort zones.

It makes me think of Jessie, whose comfort zone is clearly this camp. If she was able to think a little differently about things—like she's started to do with this whole adult camp idea—I wonder if she'd be able to turn a bigger profit. Maybe even keep the camp from closing down.

I close my eyes and smile, relaxing into my own comfort zone: solving other people's problems.

Until Zoey moans again, loud enough that it breaks through my noise-canceling headphones. Have I been having sex wrong my whole life? Because I have never, ever made a noise like that.

The dinner bell rings just after six. My social battery has recharged, but my stomach is running on empty. I can't wait to see what feast Cooper has cooked up. With almost three hundred adults packed into the space, the decibel level inside the dining hall is off the charts. I find myself missing the quiet of last week, when it was just the eight of us for dinner.

I scan the room; every table is full. Back in the day, we used to sit by cabin—but the tables that could easily seat twelve kids only comfortably fit eight adults. And Jessie rightly knew that while couples and friends would be okay sleeping in separate cabins, they'd want to be together for meals. Which is great for them—but for me? I prefer the structure of knowing where I belong. Tomorrow, I'll get here earlier so I can claim an empty table.

Tonight's menu, according to the chalkboard sign by the door, is rustic chicken with oil-cured olives, roasted baby potatoes, and sautéed spinach. There's a roasted cauliflower steak option for vegetarians, and an apple galette with vanilla bean ice cream for dessert. The wine pairing—Jessie's idea—is pinot noir. Each table gets two bottles, and from the looks of it, several people brought more for themselves.

Which gives me an idea.

I wonder if Jessie would be open to suggestions; she could sell additional bottles of wine at a premium to make more of a profit this summer. Three hundred campers six nights a week for seven weeks could be a substantial gain.

"Excuse me?" A timid voice interrupts my thoughts, and I turn to see a first-time camper who's here with her boyfriend. "Do you know if the chicken is gluten free?" she asks, sounding nervous. "I'm also sensitive to xanthan gum."

I don't know the answer, but I do know who to ask.

Cooper's in the kitchen, standing close to an attractive blonde, one of the campers here on a girls' trip. He quickly steps back when he sees me, a guilty smirk on his face.

Flustered, I ask him about the gluten and xanthan gum, then head back to the dining hall, leaving them to whatever clandestine thing they were about to do. It shouldn't surprise me he's already breaking the rules, given how cavalier he was during our run-in after my shower.

Over the next hour, I keep myself busy finding the wine opener for a thirsty bunch, getting more bread for one table, more butter for another, and refilling water pitchers. Then, as the campers are finishing their dessert and I'm about to make a plate for myself, Jessie walks up to the front and uses a triangle dinner bell to call everyone's attention for evening announcements the way Nathaniel and Lola used to do.

"Hello, campers!" she calls out. "For those I haven't had the chance to meet yet, my name is Jessie Pederson, and I'm the camp director here at Camp Chickawah!"

Applause spreads through the room like a wave, and I swell with pride for my old friend.

"This summer is bittersweet for me, since it's the last one we'll have here together," Jessie says. "But it warms my heart to have you all back for one Chicka-wonderful week! We've got a lot of nostalgic events planned, but if you want to participate in any of the water activities, you need to report to the docks tomorrow at nine a.m. sharp for your swimming test."

A collective groan rises from the crowd.

"Don't be a sissy," Zac says. The insult isn't PC, but delivered in his Australian accent, it's almost forgivable. "If you're too weak to tread water for ten minutes, you can spend the week at Arts and Crafts."

"No offense, Hill!" Zoey calls.

"As I was saying," Jessie says, trying to get things back on track. "We're in tick country here, so—"

"CHECK YOUR CREVICES!" several campers shout, a catchphrase from when we were kids.

Jessie nods. "Yep, and—"

"How do we get Wi-Fi?" a man calls out.

"Like we mentioned in the registration email, you won't get any service here," Jessie says. "But you can survive a week off the grid. In case of emergencies, we have Internet in the main office—but it's slow."

"Does needing to watch porn count as an emergency?" another man shouts.

Based on the way the room erupts with laughter, you'd think Jessie was talking to a group of teenagers, not adults in their early thirties.

"All right, people," Jessie says. "Let's focus. Breakfast is self-service from seven to nine a.m. The daily schedule will be posted outside the dining hall each morning. For any type As out there, the schedule for the week—subject to change— is posted at the Lodge and the canteen. Speaking of the canteen, it's open every day from eleven a.m. to four p.m., and you can buy stamps and batteries, chips and candy."

"What about weed?" a woman calls out.

"You're on your own for that," Jessie says, and there's another smattering of laughter. "Last but not least, I'm excited to announce tonight's special activity—in keeping with the Camp Chickawah tradition . . ."

"Campfire!" half the room calls out. So I'm not the only one who's been looking forward to this evening. It doesn't get more iconic than sitting around a roaring fire, singing songs and roasting marshmallows.

"See you all at the firepit at eight o'clock!"

Applause and cheers fill the room, and I wonder how it must feel to get such sincere and audible appreciation for doing your job. The most gratitude I've ever gotten is a firm handshake and a box of Bartlett pears.

Not that I'm looking for any recognition; I just want to earn Jessie's trust. That's the first step in my plan to get her friendship back. Really back, not in the friendly-but-distant way she's been this past week.

I turn to see her walking toward me, and I smile, hoping she'll ask me to save her a seat by the campfire.

"Do you mind grabbing the marshmallows from Coop?" she asks.

I deflate but keep a smile on my face. "You got it, boss!"

And with that, my former best friend is off to take care of the many things I never realized went into making a summer camp run.

Once I get the marshmallows from Cooper—ten bags!—I head to the firepit. It's not dark yet, but I learned my lesson from showing up late to dinner.

Mr. Billy is the only one here, prepping the fire with wood and kindling, so I nab a spot on a log in the second row of the concentric circles surrounding the firepit.

Usually, I use downtime to do something productive, but out here without service, my phone has turned into a very expensive camera. It's made me realize how addicted I am to technology, the urge to always be doing something. Anything but nothing.

I force myself to be still, to breathe and be present. Taking in the golden hour as the sky turns to dusk and the trees surrounding the camp fade into shadows.

The moment is short-lived, as eager campers arrive to claim their spots. Even the sun seems to know we're in a hurry to get the night started. Before long, it's the kind of pitch-black you only get out in the middle of nowhere—so dark I can't see whoever is walking toward the pit, strumming a guitar. The simple melody, combined with the crackling of the flames, gives me goose bumps. All chatter ceases, and we sit together in a moment that feels almost spiritual. It's transcendent.

At last, I make out Jessie walking toward the fire, her face glowing in the flickering light. Next to her is Cooper. And his guitar. I suck in a breath at the sight of him—be still, my teenage heart.

I exhale slowly, watching all the women around the fire watching Cooper, too. The blonde from the kitchen is staring at him like she's marooned on a desert and he's a tall drink of water. I try not to roll my eyes.

Jessie is scanning the circle, looking for a spot to sit. I try to catch her eye, but she passes right over me. I look away, grateful for the dark, which hides my hurt.

Someone to my left passes me a flask. I hesitate, then remember Aaron chiding me about my lack of fun-ness and take a sip. The whiskey tastes like Red Hots and burns going down my throat.

"What does everyone want to hear?" Cooper asks, strumming as he talks.

A cacophony of requests blends together, and Cooper laughs before starting to play "Cat's in the Cradle." Another bottle gets passed my way, and I almost choke on the sweet peanut butter flavor as Cooper starts to sing. His voice is like graveled honey and it does something to me. Or maybe it's the combination of his voice, the whiskey, and the fact that I've been listening to my horny neighbors getting it on at least once a day, every day. Either way, I start to sing along, wishing I hadn't waited so long to come back to camp.

The next morning, my tongue has the texture of sandpaper and it feels like someone's tightened a vise around my head. I'm pretty sure I'm still wearing—*yep*—the uniform I wore all day yesterday. It reeks, a pungent blend of campfire smoke, booze, and sweat.

Sitting up, I take a greedy sip from the cup of water beside my bed. I can't remember coming back to the Lodge, and I hope I didn't say or do anything unprofessional. That's what I get for drinking on an empty stomach. It's not like me to be so careless, to get that drunk and lose control.

But there's no time to dwell on what might have happened. Today is the first full day of camp, and I've got a job to do!

It's just past nine, and the first activity in the Arts and Crafts cabin doesn't start until ten thirty (we're making God's eyes with yarn and popsicle sticks). I tame my increasingly wayward curls into a high ponytail, grab clean khaki shorts and a new Camp Chickawah polo, and head out in search of coffee and food.

There's a chill to the air, and judging by the yelping coming from the lake, the water is freezing. I walk toward the dock, where a group of campers are treading water.

"No touching the dock, mates!" Zac shouts in his delicious accent. "Or each other!"

"My arms are going to fall off!" one camper exclaims.

"My balls are going to fall off!" another calls out.

85

"Your balls and your arms will be fine!" Zoey says. "Three minutes down, seven to go!"

A collective groan sounds, and I laugh, grateful the water test is one experience I don't have to relive.

In the dining hall, I'm disappointed by the picked-over selection of breakfast pastries, granola, and yogurt. Hardly the greasy food I need to quell my stomach. I glance toward the kitchen, wondering if there are any leftovers from dinner.

According to my dad, I got my love of leftovers from my mom. It's strange to be like someone in a way you never knew she was. Nearly everything I know about my mom is secondhand. My dad doesn't talk about her much—it makes him too sad—but growing up, I'd always look forward to marking her *yahrzeit*, when we'd lay a rock on her headstone and he'd tell me stories until his voice got scratchy and his eyes grew misty.

There's a light on in the kitchen, but I still pause at the door. It's not exactly off-limits—I'm staff—but it feels illicit as I slip inside and head toward the two industrial-sized refrigerators.

The first one is filled with fruit and vegetables—too healthy. The second contains rows of eggs, dozens of chicken breasts marinating in glass bowls, and . . . *yes!* Two beautiful containers filled with leftovers. My mouth waters as I reach for the container of roasted baby potatoes I was too busy to taste last night.

No sooner do I lift it than I hear someone clearing their throat behind me.

Shit! I turn to see Cooper, his arms folded across his broad chest. The chest I ran into a few days ago while wearing almost nothing. Today he's wearing a cat-themed apron that reads IT'S MEOW OR NEVER and that same Red Sox cap. I wonder if he's a really big fan or trying to cover a bald spot.

"Can I help you?" he asks, a playful grin on his face. I wonder if he's remembering the one-third of a nipple he saw.

"I'm so sorry," I tell him. "I was just . . ."

"Snooping through my fridge?"

My cheeks flush. "Technically, it's the camp's fridge."

"Touché," Cooper says. "Here, let me."

He takes the container from my hands, and I follow him toward the prep area—a metallic island on wheels, parked in the middle of the room.

"I really am sorry," I say.

"It's all good," he says, popping the lid off. "We might have to rethink this whole continental breakfast thing. It doesn't do the trick for hangovers."

"I . . ." I stammer, not wanting to fess up to my current state. But Cooper quirks an eyebrow, and I know it's silly to pretend otherwise. "I may have been overserved last night."

"It was fun, though, wasn't it?" He turns back to the fridge, grabbing five fresh eggs.

"What I can remember of it," I admit.

He chuckles, and I curse my poor alcohol tolerance.

"I didn't do anything stupid, did I?" I ask. The last time I let myself lose control like that, I ended up passed out on top of a pile of coats at a party with Aaron's friends.

"Not at all," he says. "You were just really, *really* happy. Except for when I suggested it was time to head back to the Lodge. I believe you called me a party pooper."

"Oh, god," I say, burying my head in my hands. "So unprofessional."

"We're allowed to have fun, too," he says, cracking eggs into a metallic bowl.

It's only then that I realize he's cooking. For me.

"You don't have to," I say, motioning to what looks like the makings of an omelet. "I actually love cold leftovers."

Cooper looks at me with mock horror. "Not in my kitchen. But if you don't like what I make after you try it, then you can help yourself to all the cold leftovers you want."

"If you insist," I say with a sigh. "And I assume you won't let me help?"

"You assume right," he says, and I take a seat on the opposite side of the counter, watching as he moves around the kitchen with precision and confidence, biting his lip in concentration as he adds a dash of this, a pinch of that. It's impressive. He's impressive.

Cooper looks up from the bowl where he's whisking eggs, the muscles in his forearms pulsing with each rotation. "Fun being back here, huh?"

"Yeah," I say. "But I'm starting to wonder if I should've come. Jessie and I . . . we had a falling-out, a pretty bad one. And it seems she hasn't forgiven me yet."

"Well, if there's one place to rekindle an old flame, it's camp," Cooper says. His eyebrows dance, and I wonder if he's talking about me and Jessie, or me and him.

But that would be crazy. Cooper would never be interested in someone boring like me when every week will bring a new batch of eligible lady campers, like his blonde friend.

Before I can ask about her, he turns back to the stovetop. My mouth waters as the eggs hit the sizzling pan, letting out a satisfying hiss. Next thing I know, Cooper's sliding an omelet filled with cream cheese, roasted potatoes, and chives onto a plate.

"Bon appétit," he says, handing me a fork.

The explosion of flavors catches me off guard. I let out a moan—not unlike the noises I heard coming from Zac and Zoey's room this morning—and look up, mortified.

"Still want those cold leftovers?" he asks, a smug look on his face.

I'm about to say, "No, thank you," when the door swings open and in walks Jessie, looking fresh as a daisy in her crisp uniform and signature braids.

Her smile falters at the sight of me.

"First activity starts in fifteen minutes," she announces.

"Then you've got enough time for food," Cooper says. "Sit."

Jessie hesitates for a half second before walking over and taking the stool next to mine.

Cooper plates the second omelet, the one meant for him, and sets it in front of Jessie.

Her reaction to the first bite is similar to mine. "If we'd had a chef like you before, maybe we'd have turned a profit," she says. "Then the Valentines wouldn't be closing us down."

Her voice is full of melancholy, and I feel a sudden urge to help her in the best way I know how.

"If you're looking for ways to make the camp more profitable," I say, "that's pretty much what I do. Help failing"—Jessie flinches and I pivot—"er, struggling businesses. I actually had an idea the other day about selling wine at dinner. There are other things you could upcharge for, too. I was thinking . . ."

Jessie stiffens, her soft edges turning hard, and I instantly realize my mistake. She's losing so much with the sale of the camp—not just her job, but her family and her home. Her identity. And here I come, pointing out all the ways she could've done better. No one wants to be friends with that girl. *I* don't want to be friends with that girl. She's worse than un-fun. She's a buzzkill.

I take one last bite of my omelet, but it doesn't mix with the sour feeling in my stomach. One week here, and I already have Jessie questioning why she bothered to give me a second chance.

ten

Jessie

It's just after dawn. The sun peeks over the eastern hills as I push my canoe into the lake. Last night I was up late, keeping watch over a group of tipsy campers enjoying a late-night swim, and I'm in desperate need of solitude before the day begins.

My earbuds are in, playing the original Broadway cast recording of *Waitress*. The music is pure comfort, Jessie Mueller's voice as sweet and rich as the sugar and butter she sings about. I've been obsessed with Broadway musicals since my first camp play, though I've never had the time (or funds) to take a break from my job here and travel to New York. I guess when camp closes, I'll have all the time in the world.

A flash of movement catches my eye, and I glance to the right.

Someone's in the water.

Panic lances through me—a drowning accident is one of my worst nightmares, and we're easily three hundred yards from shore. But this person isn't struggling. I'm not an expert swimmer, but I can recognize the even strokes and perfect form as the morning sunlight glints off the swimmer's wet shoulders and back.

I sigh, frustrated. I made it very clear that no one should swim alone.

Then the swimmer gets closer, and I realize who it is.

William Lucas Duncan.

Irritation prickles through me and I remove my earbuds. I felt guilty after snubbing him at dinner the other day, so I stopped by his cabin earlier this week and invited him to participate in some of the camp activities. It was quite friendly of me, in my opinion. He responded by shutting the door in my face. Again.

"Hey!" I shout when he's about twenty feet from my canoe.

He lifts his head, splashing water droplets through the air. "What?"

"You're not supposed to swim alone. That's rule number one."

"Since when?" Even at this distance, his fiery blue eyes throw sparks my way.

"Since forever!"

"That's a stupid rule," he snaps.

"It's an important rule!" I shout. "There's no lifeguard this early. What if you start to drown? I'm sure as hell not going to save you."

He scoffs. "I'm not going to drown."

"Drowning happens when you least expect it!"

"So where's your life jacket?" Luke yells back.

Alarmed, I glance around my canoe and realize I forgot to grab one; Zac and Zoey moved them to a different storage spot.

"Shit," I whisper.

He smirks. "Better head back, then."

"I'll head back when I'm good and ready," I mutter. I don't know why I'm so irritated—maybe because he's showing such blatant disregard for everything I've done to make camp a safe and enjoyable experience.

But he's treading water so easily. It's clear he's at no risk of drowning, and I feel a twinge of envy. I always struggled to pass the swim test—my body seems biologically designed to sink.

"Relax," he says, brushing dark, wet hair from his forehead. "I'll sign a waiver or something."

And with that, he takes off again with those perfect, even strokes.

Huffing, I paddle back toward shore. Against my will, my mind drifts to my friendship with Luke all those years ago, when he was a counselor. When he was The Man.

He would've been around nineteen at the time and new to Camp Chickawah. I was sixteen, a counselor-in-training, and so awkward and uncomfortable in my body. Being a nearly six-foot-tall, skinny-as-a-rail, flat-chested teenage girl will do that to you. Adolescent boys can be *mean*. Luckily, I had plenty of girlfriends and reasonably strong self-esteem. I tried not to let it bother me.

A couple weeks into the summer, we had a break from our CIT duties. Hillary wanted to do a craft project, so I went to the Lodge to get a book from the camp library.

"Have you read this one?" a voice said behind me.

I whirled around to see the most popular counselor of the summer pointing to *The Hunger Games*. My heart skidded to a stop; he was ridiculously cute, with bright blue eyes and an easy smile.

I shook my head, feeling shy.

"It's awesome." Luke pulled the book off the shelf and placed it in my hands. "When you're finished, come find me. I want to hear what you think."

I read it in one day, staying up late with a flashlight while my cabinmates slept. The next morning, I ran to find Luke, who was hanging out near the canteen with his cabin of boys. One nudged another and said something about how giraffes aren't only at the zoo. The rest laughed.

Then Luke saw the paperback in my hand, and his face lit up, a brilliant smile that made my stomach flip. "You finished?"

I said yes, and he scooted over so I could sit next to him on the bench. He asked me what I thought about the characters, about the themes of the book, if I was #TeamGale or #TeamPeeta. I remember how it felt to have his attention on me, like some of his glow had expanded to include me, too.

Over the next week, I finished the series. Each time I finished a book, I found Luke to talk. He recommended other books—like the Maze Runner and Divergent series—and I devoured them, too. Reading about teenagers like me in a dystopian society was exhilarating. So was chatting with Luke. He seemed to actually care about my opinions, and even though we'd sometimes get into big debates, it was always fun. As a bonus, his cabin of boys stopped teasing me.

Of course I had a crush on Luke, but it was nothing more than hero worship combined with teenage infatuation. I knew he was just being kind. But it made the entire summer better for me.

Which was why the way he treated me the following year was so confusing.

I returned to camp as a seventeen-year-old, excited to see Hillary and be a CIT for the second time. But I was also excited to see Luke. I'd read a new book called *Eleanor & Park,* and I was dying to share it with him.

It was training week, and after we finished for the day, I found Luke hanging out at the lake with a group of male counselors. As I walked up, they all turned to stare at me. They seemed shocked that I, a lowly CIT, would interrupt them—and that I would dare approach Luke Himself.

Luke's face turned white when he saw me. Pale, ghostly white.

"Hey," I said, lifting the book awkwardly. "I wanted to see if you'd read—"

"We're kind of in the middle of something," he said, cutting me off.

I blinked, my face heating with embarrassment. "Oh, sorry, I just—"

"Run along now," he said dismissively, and turned his back to me.

I will never forget the sound of the counselors snickering as I hurried away.

For the rest of the summer, Luke acted the same way. Every time I saw him, he'd ignore me, or cut me off, or walk away—and he got the other male counselors to avoid me, too. It was like a fickle king withdrawing his favor. His minions saw his rejection as permission to be mean to me, and all the comments about my height started up again, compounded now by dumb blonde jokes. Someone started calling me "Camp Barbie," and the nickname stuck. I detested it.

More than anything, I was confused and hurt by the way Luke had changed so drastically. The next year, he didn't come back. And now it's clear that rudeness is his true personality, that the summer he was nice to me was a fluke. Good to know.

No more softhearted Jessie, I tell myself. I'll have him sign a waiver later today, releasing the camp from any responsibility if he injures himself on the water.

When I reach the dock, I climb out of my canoe and look across the lake. Luke is heading back toward shore, still swimming with that perfect form, a lonely speck in the vast blue water.

The rest of the day is full of activities. A camper who's a yoga instructor leads a session on the big lawn; other campers go hiking or swimming, or they nap or read in hammocks. After lunch, a group heads to the Arts and Crafts cabin while Zac and Zoey stage a canoe race across the lake.

But it's like I'm watching from a window, enjoying the scenery while separated from it. I guess I miss having children here—it definitely kept me busier.

Now I'm drifting around aimlessly.

Near sundown, someone suggests playing Capture the Flag in the wooded area north of camp, where the uneven terrain, hills, and old-growth forest make it more challenging—and fun.

"Jessie! Come be on our team!" It's Moira, one of the campers, standing with a group of women.

"Are you sure?" I ask, secretly delighted. "I don't want to ruin the game by having the director involved."

"Yeah," she says. "It's men against women, and Zac and

Cooper are playing for the men. We already have Zoey and Dot—we need you!"

Hillary is sitting not far away, sketching in a notebook, and my old habit of pulling her into activities nearly kicks in. But I squelch it. Ever since she brought up those ideas to "make the camp more profitable," I've been a little defensive. It doesn't feel great to have her show up after years of ignoring this place only to start critiquing it. Critiquing *me*, since I'm the one in charge.

Although I have to admit, she has a point. Nathaniel and Lola weren't great at the financial side of things. That's never been my strength, either. Hillary was probably trying to help.

And since I'm trying to make sure Dot and Mr. Billy are financially taken care of, I ought to stop being defensive and start listening to Hillary's ideas.

Before I can think more about that, Moira invites Hillary, who jumps up like she was just waiting to be asked. A dozen memories flood my mind, past games of Capture the Flag: sneaking with Hillary through the trees, working together to corner our opponents. My chest aches with the specific pain that only memories of Hillary seem to trigger.

Shaking it off, I shift to the side of the group opposite her as our team congregates. The captains—Moira and a guy named Lance, who's built like a linebacker—discuss the rules. We'll each plant our flag in our team's territory; the other team will try to capture it. If someone gets tagged, they go to "jail." They'll be out of play unless someone from their team tags them back in.

Moira then pulls our team into a huddle to talk positions

and strategy; she played professional women's soccer, and it shows.

Across from us, the men's team finishes their huddle. One of them calls, "Don't worry, girls, we'll go easy on you."

Zoey straightens up, eyes flashing. "Don't worry, boys, we *won't* go easy on you!"

"I'm rooting for you, baby," Zac calls to his wife, and his teammates groan and tell him to stop being such a simp.

Zoey and I are tasked with guarding the flag. Three other women, including Hillary, play the midfield, watching for approaching members from the other team and chasing them down. Moira, Dot, and another group of women start sneaking toward the other team's territory.

The sun is setting, casting lengthening shadows through the trees. Soon I spot the first member of the men's team creeping through the bushes on Zoey's side. I catch her eye and point, and she slinks off, sneaky as a cat. When she tags him out, he howls in shock.

"Sorry, buddy," she says, flashing a grin.

He heads to jail—an area behind me that I'll guard.

Zoey and I continue to keep watch. I hold my breath as I peer into the shadows.

"There!" Zoey yells, pointing at a dark blur racing past me. I take off sprinting, coming at him from the side so he's forced to veer northward, where Zoey is hiding.

She pops out and tags him.

"Aw, shit!" he yells, kicking at a rock.

Zoey curtsies, and the guy heads off to jail.

The game progresses, the night getting darker, the moon coming out. An hour in, we have eighteen of the twenty men in our jail—including Zac, who kissed Zoey after she tagged him out and told his teammates to shut their mouths when they razzed him.

Then I see Hillary running toward us, breathing hard. "We're the only ones left," she says, motioning to the three of us.

Zoey trots over. "There are only two men left, so we have the advantage."

My competitive spirit instantly activates. "Cooper's still out there, plus that big guy Lance," I say.

"You two go for the flag," Zoey says to me and Hillary. "I'll keep guarding here."

"Keep watch on the jail, too," I tell Zoey, and she nods.

"Ready?" Hillary asks. In the moonlight, with her face sweaty and her hair frizzing into curls, she looks identical to her teenage self. My chest aches, and I force myself to stay focused.

"Let's do this," I say.

Side by side, we creep through the woods. Every snap of a branch makes me jump as we get deeper into enemy territory.

"The flag's in there," Hillary whispers, pointing toward a thicket of trees about thirty yards away.

"Let's come at it from different sides," I whisper. "The guard can only chase one of us."

We separate and head toward the trees as quietly as possible. My eyes catch movement and I turn; somehow, Cooper has gotten past us. He's going toward Zoey—and our flag.

"Zoey! Cooper's on his way!" I yell.

Hillary and I both start sprinting toward the thicket that conceals the enemy's flag. Instinctively working together, like we always did.

My foot catches on a branch and I stumble to my knees, but get up and keep running. *Almost there.* My heart pounds and my lungs burn, but I can make out the tip of the flag above the thicket. Victory is so close I can taste it.

A hand clamps down on my shoulder. "You're out!" Lance growls.

"Go, Hillary!" I yell, my voice cracking in desperation. "You're our only hope!"

All the years we've been apart vanish and we're kids again, competing against the boys, determined to win.

Lance takes off in her direction, surprisingly fast for his size. I'm screaming and jumping up and down; the other women join in, cheering her on. Hillary is almost there, but Lance is closing in fast.

In the distance, Zoey yelps, and my heart sinks. Has Cooper already gotten our flag?

"Run like the wind!" Dot shouts to Hillary.

"You can do it!" Moira yells.

Hillary barrels into the thicket, Lance right on her heels. Silence.

Then Hillary's voice, triumphant: "I got it!"

A cheer erupts from our team, and everyone rushes toward Hillary, who emerges, holding the flag high. We surround her, jumping in victory. Then she's right in front of me, and I throw my arms around her and pick her up.

"You did it, Hilly Bean!" I squeal. "You did it, you did it, you did it!"

"*We* did it," she says. Her cheeks are flushed, the familiar patches that she always got as a kid. "You distracted him—"

"You were so fast!"

"I was terrified he was going to knock me over."

I gasp. "Oh my god, like the time Wally Higgins—"

"—ran into me playing Frisbee and gave me a concussion?" she finishes.

"You puked on his shoes!"

We're both grinning, but when Hillary's gaze meets mine, I stiffen. There's a question in her eyes, like she wants to know if this moment means anything.

"Jessie," she says tentatively. "What I said the other day—"

"Girls rule and boys drool!" Zoey shouts, and soon everyone is celebrating again. Moira leads us in a cheer; the men come over and congratulate us; Zoey teaches our team a victory dance.

Hillary and I are separated in the crowd. But as I watch her walk off, I'm overwhelmed with how *right* it felt to be on her team. Working together.

"Hey, Hill?" I say, catching up to her.

She turns, surprised.

"What you said about camp. Those ways to make it more profitable?"

"Yeah?"

My heart is pounding, and I take a breath. "I'd be interested in hearing them. I mean, if you want to share."

Hillary's eyes widen with surprise. And then she smiles. "Of course. I'd love to."

eleven

Hillary

Sunday afternoon, Dot, Jessie, Zoey, and I are outside the dining hall, waving as the last bus of campers pulls away. I had no idea it was possible to be this exhilarated and exhausted at the same time. And we get to do it all over again tomorrow with a brand-new group.

But first, family dinner.

It was Cooper's idea to turn our weekly staff meeting into a weekly staff dinner. It's an opportunity to talk about what went well over the last week and what needs improving for the weeks ahead. Selfishly, I'm excited to have one meal where I know I'll have a place to sit and people to eat with.

Dot and Jessie are already at a table when I walk into the dining hall, their heads bent together. Looking at them, I feel a pang of jealousy. I should be grateful that my relationship with Jessie has moved from professional to friendly. I know trust isn't elastic; when it's broken, it doesn't just snap back into place. Especially for someone like Jessie, whose childhood was a constant reminder that letting people in gives them the power to let you down.

But I'm nothing if not relentless. And now that she's opened the door to a conversation, I'm optimistic about saving our friendship. Jessie told me about Mary Valentine's offer for her to use any profits as bonuses for her staff. There's no better way to get back in Jessie's good graces than helping her help them—I have a feeling she's more worried about the pending unemployment of Dot and Mr. Billy than her own.

"Something smells good," I say as I approach the table.

Cooper walks out of the kitchen just in time to hear the compliment. His apron is emblazoned with the words HOT STUFF, surrounded by little bottles of Tabasco sauce, and he has several platters balanced on each of his arms. He describes each dish as he sets them down: kale Caesar salad, bruschetta with roasted Brussels sprouts and ricotta with a balsamic glaze, and the main dish, freshly made pappardelle with homemade pesto and garlic-roasted prawns. His plating looks more gourmet than family style, and I wish I had my phone to take a picture.

Once everyone has helped themselves—Mr. Billy, Zoey, and Zac having joined us—Jessie pulls a tiny notebook and pen out of her fanny pack.

"To borrow one of Lola's traditions, I thought we could each share a rose and a thorn from this past week," she says. "Dot, want to start?"

"Tons of roses," Dot says. "The biggest was having so much love and light back at the camp. And the thorn . . . those campers got pretty cranky once their booze ran out."

Everyone laughs.

"I've already called to double the weekly wine order," Jessie says, looking at me. "Hillary had an idea to have additional bottles on hand to sell."

"We could also stock the canteen with beer and liquor," I say, sitting up a little straighter.

"And condoms," Dot adds, and Jessie scribbles that in her notebook. "Apparently sneaking out of the cabins at night is still en vogue . . . and since we can't stop 'em, we might as well make sure they're protected! I found quite a few wrappers by the lake."

"Litter!" Mr. Billy grunts, and we all know his thorn.

"I have a lot of other ideas, too," I say, before we get sidetracked. "If Zac and Zoey are willing, people could pay extra for private sailing lessons."

"I'm game," Zac says.

"And maybe Cooper could offer a cooking demonstration." I see him nodding out of the corner of my eye, which gives me the confidence to continue. "We could have special event mixers, like speed dating for singles. And you could charge a premium for couples to upgrade to a private room if there are any empty cabins that session. I'd be happy to look at your PNL, because it might be worth it to invest in a queen bed, or at least a better mattress for—"

"Let's get back to the roses and thorns," Jessie says, sucking the wind out of my sails. "Zoey?"

Zoey gives me a sympathetic smile before turning toward Jessie. "Being back here is such a big rose, and so is sharing it with my love." She makes eyes at Zac, and I can practically see the electricity zinging between them. "The thorn was all the grown men being such babies about treading water. Zacky?"

"The food is my biggest rose—it's incredible, mate," Zac says, looking at Cooper, who seems genuinely touched. Zoey playfully elbows her husband, and he quickly adds, "And of course, spending all day on the water with my wife—that's worth a dozen roses."

"Much better," Zoey says, cuddling into his side.

"And the thorn?" Jessie asks.

Zac scratches his chin. "Three of the canoes are leaking. Nothing I can't fix with a little sealant, but it'll take some time."

"Noted," Jessie says. "How about you, Coop?"

My stomach tightens. I'm up next. There's a special place in hell for whoever invented icebreakers. Give me a good pro and con list and I'll go to town. But as soon as you call them roses and thorns and expect me to be charming or clever, my mind goes blank.

"My rose is having the freedom to create a new menu every night," Cooper says. "And my thorn . . . so many dietary restrictions."

Jessie scribbles in her notebook. "Dot started outreach for the next few weeks, so we can plan ahead."

"That'll help," Cooper says. "But it breaks my heart to serve people bland food."

"Their loss," Zac says, going for seconds on the pasta.

"And you, Hill?" Jessie asks.

"Well," I say, stalling. My rose had been coming up with so many ideas to help Jessie increase the camp's profitability, but I'm not going there now. "Everyone's said my roses—the people, the food, the nostalgia . . . but if I had to add something, it's that I—I didn't expect people to be so excited about arts and crafts. Almost every session has been full. And the thorn . . ."

I'm not brave enough to admit the truth—how lonely it is being here without the comfort of Jessie's friendship, the anxiety I feel walking into the bustling dining hall every night and not knowing where to sit.

"I guess the thorn is that I'll have to restock supplies sooner than expected."

Jessie jots that down, then says, "There's a Walmart in town. Cooper, aren't you going tomorrow? Hill, you should go with him and get what you need."

Forty-five minutes to town and back in the car with Cooper? I'm so boring, I'll probably put him to sleep. I'm about to politely decline when he says, "Yeah, you should come. I'm leaving around seven thirty."

"Okay, sure," I say, and that's settled.

"This next group of campers are in their early forties," Jessie says, closing her notebook, "and our special activity for the week is the scavenger hunt."

"Wait, boss," Dot says. "You didn't share yours."

Jessie looks wistful, her mouth turning down at the corners. She fiddles with one of her braids, then clears her throat and says, "My rose is you all being here, helping keep the magic of camp alive for one more year. And my thorn . . ."

Before she can answer, the door to the dining hall opens, and a man walks in. I recognize him as the reclusive writer who booked a cabin for the whole summer—I only saw him briefly one night during training week. He stops abruptly and glares at us, as if we're the ones intruding.

"We're having our staff meeting," Jessie replies, her voice flat.

"We've got plenty of food if you're hungry," Cooper says, extending the invitation that Jessie didn't.

The man looks at Jessie, as if waiting for her permission. She sighs, giving the slightest nod, and he takes a seat across from her.

"Has everyone met Luke?" Cooper asks. "Our resident novelist."

My eyes go wide. I didn't realize the novelist was *Luke*, the hot counselor everyone had a crush on when we were CITs.

Everyone including Jessie.

He's older now, but he's got the same smoldering blue eyes and movie-star looks that made him the topic of many late-night conversations in our cabin.

Cooper gets up to grab another plate, but I'm watching the wordless interaction between Jessie and Luke. She's angled her body away from him, aimlessly flipping through her notebook. Luke's also avoiding eye contact, looking down at his food, but every so often he sneaks a glance at Jessie.

I wonder if something happened between them this week—or if this is a remnant of the way Luke treated Jessie that summer he was a jerk to her for no reason.

Whatever it is, I'm sure she'll tell Dot all about it.

The next morning, I get to the dining hall five minutes early. Cooper's already there, leaning against his red SUV, waiting for me.

"Morning," he says, reaching for the handle of the passenger door at the same time I do. Our fingers brush, and I pull mine back as if the contact stung me.

Way to already make things weird, Hillary.

"Thanks," I say, buckling my seat belt as he closes the door and walks around to the other side.

"Made you a breakfast sandwich for the road," he says, handing me a foil-wrapped package that's warm to the touch.

I salivate in anticipation, unwrapping the egg-and-cheese bagel. I stop just before taking a bite. "Aren't you eating, too?"

Cooper shakes his head, keeping his eyes on the narrow road winding through the trees just beyond the camp. "I had a kale smoothie earlier," he says.

"Yech," I accidentally say.

"Hey." Cooper laughs. "Don't yuck my yum."

"I've got plenty of yums you can yuck," I tell him. "Have you ever tried gefilte fish?"

Cooper pulls a face. "Only once."

"Put some horseradish on it, and mmm! It's my favorite part of Passover."

"I thought it might be hiding the matzah . . ." Cooper lifts his eyebrows and flashes me his winning smile, which has no doubt dropped panties all over Boston and the surrounding tristate area.

Before I can think of a response, my phone bursts to life, vibrating with two weeks' worth of notifications. Apparently, we're far enough from camp to have service.

"Whoa," Cooper says, looking down at the alerts filling my screen. "A lot of people must be missing you."

"It's mostly business," I say dismissively. I have an auto-reply on, but I should probably check in occasionally in case there's anything urgent. "And a guy," I add, when a text from Aaron pops up.

"A guy?" Cooper asks, wiggling his eyebrows.

"It's . . . complicated."

According to the timing on the notification, Aaron sent the text three days after I got to camp. I wonder if the dating waters aren't as warm and welcoming as he thought. Maybe he's had a change of heart and wants to put an end to this silly break.

I tap the message.

Aaron: Hey, what's your Netflix password?

"Actually," I say with a resigned sigh, "It's not that complicated."

"Must have been a good text," Cooper says. "Or a bad one?"

I glance over. He's focused on the road ahead, and something about sitting side by side and the lack of eye contact makes it easier to open up. So I give him the highlights of my relationship with Aaron, from my dad setting us up all the way to what I'm now thinking of as his indecent proposal.

"'We were on a break!'" Cooper exclaims when I've finished. "Sorry, *Friends* reference."

"Oh, I got it," I say, laughing. It feels good to talk about what happened, and even better to laugh about it. "Although I'm not sure if I'm Ross or Rachel in this scenario."

"You're too good-looking to be Ross," Cooper says, and my neck flushes with heat, thinking back to the way he looked at me that first day outside the showers.

"Well, either way, Aaron's back in Chicago, treating this summer like it's one big fling, and I'm here."

"Hey, you can have a summer fling, too," Cooper says.

"I could, but I won't."

"Why not?"

I sigh, struggling to find the words without knocking Cooper's own disregard for the rules or making myself sound too lame. "I guess you could say I'm not fun enough for something like that."

"Says who?"

"A lot of people."

"That guy?" Cooper gestures toward my phone.

"He may have said something about my lacking in the fun department." Cooper scoffs and I hurry to add, "But it's okay. I mean, who would I even have a fling with? The campers are off-limits, Zac is *very* happily married, and Mr. Billy is so ancient . . ."

"How about that cute chef with all the sexy aprons?"

An awkward laugh bursts out of me. It's the worst possible response, but I've never been good at flirting.

That's what this is, right? I mean, the man just implied he'd like to sleep with me. But maybe he was joking. He was probably joking.

I turn to look at him at the exact same moment he turns to look at me. My breath catches. Cooper holds my stare, and it's almost like we're playing chicken—until the car veers and he looks straight ahead, keeping his eyes on the road.

"What exactly are you suggesting?" I ask, trying desperately to hide my shock.

"It was an offer, not a suggestion," he says, his voice casual, like he does this every day. Which he might, based on that blonde in the kitchen. "If you're looking for a summer fling, I could be into that."

"Wouldn't that get in the way of your romancing the campers?" I ask.

Cooper lets out a curt laugh, but there's not much humor behind it. For a moment, I wonder if I've offended him. But he just says, "See? You'd be doing me a favor—curbing the temptation to break the rules."

My cheeks flush and I wonder if this is part of some elaborate prank.

"Are you being serious?" I ask.

"Very," he says. "I mean, we already kissed once, right?"

So he does remember.

"And I already saw your boob."

I cover my face with my hands at the memory. "You only saw *part* of my boob."

He winces apologetically. "Hate to break it to you, but I'm a good six inches taller than you. And that towel had some significant . . . gaping at the top."

My mouth falls open. "So because you saw one boob you think you might as well see *everything*?"

Do I *want* him to see everything?

"No pressure or anything," Cooper says. "Just throwing it out there."

My heart is pounding. I can't believe I'm even considering this. I am not a "fling" person. I've never had a "fling." I approach romantic relationships the same way I approach everything in life—cautiously and with a plan. A casual fling would throw all that out the window.

But it would also prove Aaron wrong.

"I'll think about it," I say, knowing I won't be able to think of anything else for the near future.

Our first stop in "town" is the Walmart Supercenter, which has craft supplies for me and food supplies for Cooper. Not to mention alcohol and sex supplies for the campers.

We exchange numbers in case we can't find each other once we've filled our respective carts. I locate all the craft supplies I need—everything from yarn and embroidery floss to tie-dye materials, pipe cleaners, and construction paper—plus all the comforts of home I need for my room, since camp is so remote, Amazon doesn't even deliver there. I pick out a fan, new sheets, two pillows (one decorative), a soft blanket, two towels, and, most importantly, a robe.

When I'm done, I find Cooper in the cereal aisle, chewing his lip as he studies the nutritional labels on two family-sized boxes of cereal. The sight of him sends a rush of heat through my entire body.

If you're looking for a summer fling, I could be into that.

"Hey!" I say, forcing a friendly smile as I roll my cart up beside his. "Find everything you need?"

"And then some. How about you?" Cooper sounds completely chill, whereas I'm still freaking out about his proposition. Could I actually have a summer fling? Me? With Cooper?

"Same, I think." I look down at my list of supplies and realize there's only one thing left. The last thing I want to shop for with Cooper.

You're an adult, I tell myself. *Stop being so pathetic.*

"What aisle do you think the condoms are in? For the campers?" I add so he doesn't get the wrong idea.

Even if we did have a fling, it's not like I'd jump into bed with him. I've only slept with four people in my entire life, and I was in a committed relationship with each of them. But maybe we could . . . make out or something?

"I'm pretty sure they're in the sexual health aisle," Cooper says, with the knowing look of someone who regularly buys condoms.

I make an "ick" face, imagining any derivative of the word "sex" on an aisle sign at Walmart.

"Kidding," he says. "But let's go look."

We find them in Aisle 17, Family Planning. The selection

is overwhelming—although thanks to my latex allergy, my personal options are limited.

"Which ones should we get?" I ask Cooper, since he's the one with a penis. The thought of that—his penis! Which he just offered to let me get to know!—makes me squirm.

"Hmm," he says, studying the selection. "My gut says the glow-in-the-dark ones. Cuts down on the chance of losing it in the bushes."

A laugh bubbles out of me. The package he's pointing to is right next to the flavored ones. Feeling emboldened, I grab packs of both and throw them in the cart. "Think anyone will need the jumbo size?"

"Maybe just one pack," Cooper says, winking. My stomach flips. "And we should get some that are ribbed for her pleasure."

My cheeks grow hot at the thought of Cooper considering my pleasure. I flash back to the sounds of Zoey and Zac in the room next to mine. I wonder if Cooper has heard them, too.

"None for his pleasure?" I say in an attempt to flirt back.

"Uh . . . the ultra-thin ones are for his pleasure," Cooper says, his eyes twinkling as he slides the packs off the rack. "Think we need anything else?"

I hesitate, eyeing the latex-free packages. "Maybe some of these," I say, not meeting his eye as I toss them in the cart. Just in case.

An hour later, we're finally back on the road to camp.

"That poor checkout lady was so confused by our haul," I say, shaking my head. "And when you said we worked at a camp!"

Cooper laughs. "Hey, the crafts could be for the kids, and the condoms for the counselors."

"If that's what it was like being a counselor, then I really regret my decision not to come back."

"That's what the whole falling-out with Jessie was over, right?"

The tiny hairs on my arms stand at attention. "Did she say something to you?"

"No, no," Cooper says. "I just put the pieces together."

I exhale a sigh of relief. "Yeah, well, that's exactly what happened. It was her dream for us to be counselors together."

"But it wasn't yours?"

I twirl my hair around my finger, feeling a twinge of guilt, even after all these years. "I wanted us to be best friends forever, like we were at camp, but when it came to my future, I was chasing a different dream."

"Did you end up getting it?"

"Some of it," I say, thinking about Aaron and the one item I won't be checking off my list anytime soon. The more distance I get from that last conversation, the more certain I am that I deserve a man who doesn't need a summerlong "break" from me to bang whomever he wants. A man who reaches out to ask how I'm doing, not for my Netflix password.

My attempt at a smile falls flat, and I lean back, looking out the window. The trees pass by in a blur. Time feels like that sometimes, like it's moving so fast that things lose their shape; like you've lost your sense of reality. Then when it all slows down, you look up and don't know where you are or how you even got there.

"How about you?" I ask Cooper, desperate to get out of my head. "What's your dream?"

"For a hot minute, I was living it. Running a kitchen at a top restaurant in Boston."

"What happened?" I ask.

Cooper drums his fingers on the steering wheel, as if he's debating how much to share. After a moment, he says, "A local magazine did a feature on the hottest up-and-coming chefs in Boston, and I was one of them."

"Ooh," I say, intrigued. If I had girlfriends, the kind I'd call to dish about our love lives, I could tell them my summer fling was one of the hottest chefs in Boston.

Except I don't have girlfriends, and Cooper's not a chef in Boston anymore. Plus, I haven't made a decision about this potential fling.

"Don't be too impressed," he says. "It was more about the restaurant than me. But it came with a lot of attention. Too much attention. Things were great for a while, but then they got messy, and . . ."

His voice trails off. A somber expression settles on his face—the first time I've seen him with something other than a smile or a smirk. I get the sense there's more to this story, and I'm about to ask what else happened when he clears his throat and shrugs.

"Anyway—I'm here now. And I'm happy to have a break while I figure out what's next."

A comfortable silence settles between us then, and he continues to drum his hands on the wheel. The tendons pulsing under his skin remind me of piano strings moving during a classical concerto. My mind drifts to all the incredible things his hands can do in the kitchen, and I wonder if I can loosen up enough to see what they can do in the bedroom, too. If I can be brave enough.

Fun enough.

"There's more where that came from, right?" Cooper asks, and I startle.

"Sorry," I tell him. "I was somewhere else."

Cooper turns, his smile stretching so wide I almost wonder if he knows what I was thinking.

"What'd you say?" I ask.

"I was saying how much I liked those ideas of yours. For the camp. And the way you were talking, I assume there's more?"

"A lot more," I admit. "I want to help Jessie, and I think I could, but I don't think she's ready for me to be that honest."

"You should always be honest," Cooper says, his voice sharp. "The truth may hurt, but the not-truth can end up hurting even more."

I nod, sensing the pain beneath Cooper's words. *Whose lies hurt him?* I wonder.

"I especially liked your idea about the new mattresses," he says in a gentler tone. He gives me a flirty wink, and just like that, I'm thinking about the fling again. I appreciate that he's not pushing me to make a decision. But it would be fun. To be the kind of person who had flings.

Just for the summer.

twelve

Jessie

It's week two, and the main event is the Great Chickawah Scavenger Hunt. Each cabin will work together to follow the clues, and the winner gets a prize—usually an ice cream party. This year, it'll be a cocktail party with appetizers and drinks created by Cooper. The campers seem excited, but it's a lot of work for me to set up, since the clues require the use of a compass and a map. We'll see how many of them remember the orienteering skills Nathaniel taught them all those years ago.

As I walk through camp, I say hi to a group playing kickball on the lawn, then head toward the lake, where another group is lounging on the swim dock.

"Hey, Jessie!" one man shouts, waving.

I smile and wave back. "Hi, Mike! How's it going?"

"Awesome!"

I try my best to learn every camper's name on the first day. It's more difficult with a new group each week, but it's important that they feel recognized as individuals.

At the north edge of camp, I place the second clue—the first one will be given to each cabin leader tomorrow morning—and use my compass and map to figure out what direction to head next. I count off my paces, place the third clue in a hollow stump, and continue. My earbuds are playing the *Les Misérables* tenth anniversary concert: Colm Wilkinson and Judy Kuhn from the original cast, plus the legendary Lea Salonga and my personal favorite Javert, Philip Quast (don't even get me started on the travesty of Russell Crowe in the film version).

Then I spot Hillary sitting on the small hill overlooking the camp, scribbling in her notebook. Maybe brainstorming more ideas to make the camp profitable? At first, I was overwhelmed by all the potential changes she suggested. But while she was in town with Cooper, I reminded myself why I'm doing this: for Dot and Mr. Billy. When Hillary returned, I sat her down and said I was ready to listen.

Already this week, we've started offering private sailing lessons, custom picnic packages, and a singles mixer. I can't stop imagining what it'll be like to surprise Dot and Mr. Billy with an unexpected bonus on the last day.

"Hey, Hillary!" I call, taking out my earbuds and walking toward her.

She startles and holds the notebook to her chest. "Oh, hi, Jess. How's it going?"

"Good. Just working on the scavenger hunt," I say, motioning to my compass.

Her eyes light up. "I always loved that!"

"We were good at it," I say, smiling.

"Well, you were. Do you remember the year Tommy Flanagan got lost?"

"Oh yeah. He was bragging about his orienteering skills all week—"

"But then he ended up at the totally wrong end of camp," Hillary cuts in.

"And no one found him until morning—"

"And he kept saying—"

Together, we wail: *"My compass! It's broooooken!"*

We descend into a fit of laughter that reminds me of the teenage hilarity you leave behind when you enter adulthood. Hillary and I were always getting reprimanded for laughing during serious activities like flag ceremony—all I had to do was catch her eye and we'd crack up.

"Now that I think about it," Hillary says, "it would be terrifying to be lost in the woods overnight. Poor kid."

"Yeah, Nathaniel and Lola must have been beside themselves. Safety, safety, safety was drilled into our heads during counselor training."

Hillary's smile falters, and I wince, then clear my throat. "What are you up to?"

"Just sketching," she says, showing me the page—a pencil drawing of the scene below us: rolling hills, pine trees, lake.

"I love that you still do this!" I say, smiling.

She hesitates. "Well, I don't. Not in years, I mean."

"Really? How come?" I'm surprised; when we were kids, she was always drawing something in her sketchbook or creating incredible Sharpie tattoos for the girls in our cabin.

"At some point you have to grow up," she says, with a self-deprecating shrug. "Stop spending time on things that don't move your life forward, as my dad would say."

Her words sting. As if *I* haven't grown up, moved forward. I know that's not what she means—she's talking about herself, not me—but I had my own conversation with my mom yesterday. She kept asking me if I was going to get a "real job" now that the camp is closing. Neither of my parents has ever understood how much this job means to me. That it's not just a job—it's my identity.

But as Dot would say, my parents aren't camp people. They don't get it.

"Uh, yeah," I say stiffly. "I'll let you get back to it."

"You should put the final clue in that big maple tree down by the stream," Hillary says.

"The one we used to climb?"

She nods. "Put it up high. It'll make it more fun."

I continue setting clues until I arrive at the last one, which tells the group that finds it that they're the winners. Holding it in my hand, I stare up at the maple tree, which has grown since the last time Hillary and I climbed it.

Grabbing the lowest branch, I heave myself up. It's been a while since I've climbed a tree, and I scrape my knee and palms on the rough bark. But eventually I get to a good spot and tie the final clue to a branch.

Before climbing down, I sit on a thick limb and look out at the lake's shining blue waters to the east and the green roofs of the cabins peeking through the trees to the south. The wind carries the faint sound of laughter and conversation.

My mom's words come back to me: *Are you going to get a real job now?*

My chest constricts. What's more real than waking up before sunrise to make fifteen dozen pancakes for breakfast because the cook isn't feeling well? Or taking a group of campers out on a clear night to show them the constellations? Fixing a broken tent in the middle of a rainstorm during our annual backpacking trip is real. Wiping the eyes of a frightened new camper after a night of ghost stories around the fire is real. Calling an anxious parent to reassure them that their child is doing just fine is real.

And when it ends, a huge part of me will go with it.

Tears fill my eyes as memories roll through me. I'm still sniffling when I hear a sound below and look down.

It's Luke and his dog, out on a walk.

I freeze, hardly daring to breathe, hoping he'll leave without noticing me. Over the past few days, he's been slightly more sociable—eating his meals in the dining hall, though he doesn't talk to anyone—but he's hardly a paragon of compassion.

He's passing beneath me when a breeze rustles the leaves. His dog looks up—maybe she caught a whiff of my scent?—and gives a soft, surprised bark, which makes Luke look up, too.

"What the . . . ?" he says, his forehead wrinkling in confusion.

"Hi," I say, giving a sheepish wave.

"Are you all right?"

I force a bright smile and wipe my damp cheeks. "I'm great! Just hiding something in the tree."

"As one does."

"It's for the scavenger hunt tomorrow."

"Okay."

I expect him to walk away—in fact, I kind of wish he would, since I'm sure he can tell I've been crying. But he shows no sign of leaving, so I begin my descent. I'm clumsier going down than up, especially with an audience, and my cheeks warm with embarrassment.

When I'm six or seven feet from the ground, my boot slips, and I gasp. But Luke is right there, his shoulder coming under my butt, his hands gripping my thighs. The contact of his palms on my bare skin feels like static electricity.

"Easy there," he says, his voice muffled.

I give an awkward laugh. "Thanks. I got it now."

He backs away, releasing his grip on my thighs, and I lower myself to the ground. Luke's dog comes over to me, so I go down on one knee to pet her, which conveniently lets me delay making eye contact with Luke. My thighs are still tingling from where he touched me; I don't remember the last time I shaved my legs, and I hope he didn't notice the fuzz. Not to mention the fact that he had my entire weight resting on his shoulder and I'm a "solid gal," as Nick once said.

"How long have you had her?" I ask Luke. Scout is so sweet, with her gentle brown eyes.

"Since she was around two years old," he says. "She was my uncle's, but he . . ."

He pauses, and I look up. His blue eyes meet mine for a half second before darting away.

"He died. Someone needed to take the dog, so—yeah. It was hard on her, losing him."

"That was good of you," I say, straightening up. "I'm sorry about your uncle, though."

He scratches at the light stubble on his jaw, like he'd rather not be talking about this. "Yeah, well. It is what it is. You heading back to camp?"

I nod, and we start walking together, Scout trailing after us.

"Is she okay?" I ask Luke after a minute or so, remembering how he had to help her up the stairs to his cabin. "Seems like walking is difficult for her."

"Arthritis in her hips," he says. "The vet said she could do a hip replacement, but with her being so old, it didn't seem fair to put her through it."

"That makes sense," I say.

We fall silent again, but it's a comfortable silence, which surprises me. Luke, aka William Lucas Duncan, aka The Man, is being . . . not awful.

The afternoon sunlight filters through the trees, and the leaves crunch softly beneath our feet. I sneak a glance at Luke, remembering how Lola said he looked like a young Paul Newman, how Nathaniel called him Cool Hand Luke. Yes, there's a resemblance—not just the striking blue eyes, but the straight nose, the full lips, the hint of a dimple in his chin. His forehead is creased, and there's a deep frown line between his eyebrows. But there are also laugh lines around his eyes, which means he must smile sometimes, even if I haven't seen it.

Scout comes up to us with a stick in her mouth, and I look away from Luke, hoping he didn't notice me staring.

"No, Scout, I'm sorry," Luke says quietly to her, then to me: "She loves playing fetch, but running isn't good for her hips. All she can manage are slow walks."

But she keeps pleading with those liquid brown eyes, and Luke eventually sighs and takes the stick.

"Just a little," he says, and tosses it a few feet away. Scout lumbers after it, then trots back to Luke, the stick in her mouth again, her tail wagging proudly.

We continue walking, and every so often, Luke tosses the stick for Scout.

"How's the writing going?" I ask.

I've seen him when I've walked by his cabin—usually out on the porch with his laptop, scowling like he wants to reach through the screen and strangle someone.

He grimaces. "Not great."

"Really? How come?"

"My publisher is going to drop me after this book," he says. He throws the stick again for Scout. "Even if it does well, which I'm sure it won't, because they aren't going to put any money into advertising it. Sometimes it feels like there's no point in finishing. I thought about trying to get out of the contract, but this may be the last book I ever get paid to write, so I don't want to just give up."

I'm taken aback—not only by what he said, which explains his gloomy attitude and desperate need for solitude this summer, but because this is the most I've heard him speak since he arrived.

"That's . . . wow. A lot."

He gives a short, grim laugh. "Yeah."

"Why would your publisher drop you? I had the impression you were, like, this super-successful big-time author. I remember Nathaniel and Lola being so proud when they heard about your book deal."

He shrugs. "I did get a good-sized deal, yeah. Five hundred grand total, for the three books."

"Damn," I say, impressed. It's a sum of money I can hardly imagine.

"Except my first book bombed. Only sold around ten thousand copies."

"Ten thousand seems like a lot to me," I say.

"It would've been okay if they'd given me fifty thousand or something, but those numbers didn't come close to justifying the advance, not to mention what they spent on publicity and marketing. Because of that, they didn't advertise the second book at all. It did even worse—sold less than a thousand copies."

I go silent. Even though I know nothing about publishing, it's clear that isn't good.

Scout returns with the stick, but this time Luke doesn't toss it. Instead, he takes a leash from his pocket and attaches it to her collar—we're getting closer to camp, and I'm guessing this is because I made such a big deal about not letting her bother the other campers.

"Anyway," he says, "now I'm stuck writing the third book in a series no one cares about, knowing my career is ending. I'm struggling to get any words down, and what I do manage to write is just . . . blah. It's due after Labor Day, and every day feels like it brings me one step closer to my execution." He shakes his head. "Sorry, I'm being melodramatic. Most writers never get published, right? I'm glad I got a shot at it, at least."

"We have something in common, then," I say. "For both of us, this is our last summer doing what we love. Your last summer writing. My last here at camp. And it's not melodramatic. It does feel like walking to an execution. I know I'm not going to actually die—"

"But an essential part of you will," he finishes.

He holds my gaze, and something passes between us. A sense of solidarity. Like we see and understand each other.

"At least you got half a million bucks out of it, right?" I say.

His mouth twists in a sour frown. "Well, I lost most of the money."

I try to contain my shock. How do you lose that much? Does he have a gambling problem or something?

Beside me, his entire body has gone rigid, his jaw clamped tight, the line between his eyebrows so deep it looks carved from stone. Better not to ask for details.

"I'm sorry," I say instead, weakly.

He rolls his shoulders, releasing the tension. "Just another reason I need to finish the book. I don't get more of my advance until I turn it in."

We've almost reached his cabin, and I find myself slowing down. I'm not ready for our conversation to end. There's something intriguing about him—maybe because he's so closed off. He's like a locked door to a forbidden room; I'm dying to open it and look inside.

"What will you do after this book is finished?" I ask.

"Probably go back to teaching."

"You were a teacher?" I say, perking up. "What did you teach?"

"Junior high English."

I smile and motion to the dog. "Hence naming your dog after Scout Finch."

"My uncle named her," he says, "but yeah. We both loved that book."

Silence descends between us again as we walk up to the cabin and stop.

"Well," I say, "good luck with the writing."

"Good luck with the scavenger hunt," he says.

I expect him to go inside, but he leans against the stair railing and folds his arms, staring at the ground. His posture—the slump of his shoulders, the slope of his neck—reminds me of something.

He's like a lonely camper, the kind that isolate themselves because they feel out of place. Yes, my soft heart is coming into play again, but I can't help it. It goes against all my years in this job to walk away from someone like that.

So I blurt out, "Do you want to join a team? For the scavenger hunt?"

"I know where the final clue is," he reminds me, his lips twitching like he's holding in a smile.

"Oh yeah," I say, smacking my forehead. "But you're welcome to join any of the activities—oh! We have the camp musical next week. Would you like to help?"

"At what point in our interaction have I given you the impression that I'd like to be on a stage singing and dancing?"

I roll my eyes, but I'm secretly thrilled he's at least engaging in the conversation—it's a huge improvement over slamming the door in my face.

"I don't mean perform—we could use help with the writing."

"I'm behind in my *own* writing," he says, but there's not much weight behind his words. Almost like he wants me to talk him into coming.

"You need to take a break occasionally, right?"

"I suppose."

"Also! We're having a bonfire on Friday night—you should come."

He narrows his eyes. "Are you going to keep bugging me until I say yes to something?"

"Yes. You don't have to talk to anyone at the bonfire—just hang out and watch. Don't writers like observing people?" I'm pleading; I probably look like Scout when she wanted to play fetch. "Come on. I'll save you a seat."

He gives me a long look, his expression unreadable, and something warm unspools inside my chest. The deep groove between his eyebrows relaxes then, just a bit. "I'll think about it."

I grin triumphantly, taking that as a win, and say goodbye.

When I get a few yards down the path, I turn and look back. Scout is slowly making her way up the stairs to the cabin, Luke supporting her hind legs. But I swear there's a hint of a smile on his face.

thirteen

Hillary

We said goodbye to our second group of campers this morning, and I'm no-bones exhausted. But this isn't the time to rest. Not when Jessie's counting on me to make an impact on her bottom line.

I'm sitting at a table near the lake, enjoying the view while brainstorming ideas. It's a shame the Valentines are set on selling the camp—if I was able to implement some bigger structural and systematic changes, I have no doubt I could turn this whole operation around.

I'd need to study the finances, but based on what I've observed, there's a lot of untapped potential. Take the cabins—a little winterization would make them livable for another five months each year, opening additional revenue streams, like corporate retreats or artist residencies. And weddings! From the looks of all the canoodling by the farewell campfire last night, several campers arrived single, but left as couples. It seems you're never too old to fall in love at camp.

I shiver, either from the breeze coming off the lake or from the memory of Cooper's eyes finding mine over the campfire last night, like he was singing just for me.

As expected, Cooper had his fair share of attention from the lady campers this week, but from what I saw—and yes, I was watching—the interest wasn't reciprocated. At least, it wasn't acted on.

He hasn't acted on his offer with me, either.

I'm pretty sure the ball is in my court, but I have no idea how to initiate a conversation, to let him know I'm interested in taking this fling from theoretical to actual. I suddenly sympathize with Aaron having to broach the topic of our so-called break.

No. I push the thought of Aaron away; he doesn't belong here, even in my mind.

It's telling how little I've thought of him since I arrived. How unbothered I am by the idea of him sleeping around. I'm more bothered by the idea of *Cooper* sleeping with other women, which makes no sense. But the thought of him sleeping with me and a rotating roster of campers just feels . . . icky.

Not very "fun" of me, I know. I need to get over my stupid hang-ups and go for it. I had a chance two nights ago back at the Lodge—Cooper's room is across from mine, and we came into the hall at the same time. He raised his eyebrows in a silent question. I was about to say something when Zoey opened her door, went to the bathroom, and spent a million years washing her face. Then Dot came out and the two of them started talking about how tonic and bananas are great natural remedies for leg cramps. Bananas!

My thoughts are interrupted by Jessie screaming, "Get out of here, you witch!"

Quickly, I slip my notebook into my bag and head back up to the main lawn to investigate. The campers should all be gone by now.

"Who are you calling a witch, bitch?" a male voice is yelling.

He doesn't have an accent, so it can't be Zac, and I can't imagine Mr. Billy yelling. I pick up the pace, hoping it's not Cooper. I can't be friends, let alone friends with benefits, with a man who screams at a woman like that.

As I round the corner of the Arts and Crafts cabin, I see Jessie standing on the lawn, her hands on her hips. And she's yelling at Luke. Luke?

"You're such a coward," Luke yells.

"At least I have a heart!" Jessie yells back, furious. "I hope a house falls on you!"

They pause, and Jessie's body language relaxes. "That was great!" she says. "It'll work perfectly for the scene with the Lion, the Scarecrow, and the two witches."

What the . . .

I may have said that out loud, because Jessie turns to look in my direction.

"Hey, Hill!" she says, waving me over. "Want to help us workshop the script for the musical?"

Now this makes sense. Jessie has been working on the camp musical for the last two weeks—a spoof on *The Wizard of Oz*. I wonder how she convinced Luke to help—he hasn't participated in a single camp activity since he got here.

"Thanks for the offer," I say, not wanting to be a third wheel. "I think I'm going to go for a walk. Good luck!"

Jessie gives me a quick wave, then focuses her attention back on Luke. I'm pretty sure she still has the hots for him. Hell, I'd have the hots for him if I didn't already have a camp crush.

Which I think I do.

Not only is Cooper easy on the eyes, but every day last week, he saved a plate of leftovers for me. There is nothing sexier than a man who listens to what you tell him about yourself.

As a thank-you (and an excuse to spend more time with him), I've been drawing the menu board each night. I love playing with the colorful chalk and adding a little flair to whatever Cooper's cooked up.

But now, since I told Jessie I was going for a walk, I guess I'm going for a walk.

Just before six, I'm the first one to the dining hall for our staff dinner. If anyone asks, it's because I'm starving—between the fresh air and the exercise, I really worked up an appetite—and not because I'm eager to talk to Cooper alone.

"Hey," I say, popping my head in the kitchen door. "Need any help?"

He surprises me by saying, "Actually, yeah."

I step into the kitchen and let go of the door, which bounces back and hits me in the butt, propelling me toward Cooper. He glances over his shoulder at the sound of my "oof" and laughs before turning back to finish whatever he's doing on the stove.

He's wearing a lobster-patterned apron today, which I recognize from the photo I haven't been able to stop thinking about.

I was in Jessie's office the other morning, googling the ratio for papier-mâché paste, when I did a quick search for the article Cooper mentioned. Sure enough, there was a whole spread, including a full-page picture of him wearing that apron, tied at the waist. And nothing else.

My cheeks flush with the memory of his broad shoulders, the contours of his chest. The way he stood with his hands on his hips, drawing attention to the apron and the question of what was underneath.

What stood out to me most, though, was his expression. The way he looked at the camera—or the person behind it—with a flirty, seductive stare. I wonder if he was sleeping with the photographer.

"Taste this for me?"

I blink. Cooper's standing in front of me with a spoonful of mashed potatoes. Obediently, I open my mouth, and he holds my gaze as he slides the spoon against my tongue. I close my lips, waiting for him to let go of the spoon, but he doesn't—his gray eyes drift to my mouth as I swallow. Only then does he withdraw the spoon, and I realize I haven't even noticed the potatoes.

As soon as I do, I cringe; too salty. Still, I force a smile and say, "Yum!"

Cooper frowns. "I told you how I feel about the truth."

My smile fades, too; someone really must have hurt him in the past. "Sorry," I say, swallowing again. "In that case, they're a little salty."

His smile returns. "More cream and butter will balance that out." He hesitates before adding casually, "So, do you want to hang out tonight?"

My heart leaps. "Yes. Definitely yes."

"Then it's a date," Cooper says, grinning as he turns back to the stove.

Ten minutes later, we're all sitting around the table, sharing our roses and thorns. My real rose is obviously what just happened in the kitchen, but I say it's how excited the campers were to make friendship bracelets. My thorn is all the pranks the campers pulled—one bit of nostalgia I wouldn't mind leaving in the past.

"Looking ahead at this week," Jessie says, "we've got a lot of thespians coming."

Zac giggles and Zoey elbows him in the side. "*Thes*pians, not lesbians."

"Don't you worry, we've got a fair share of those coming, too," Dot says, giving Zac a wink.

"The script is coming along well, thanks to Luke." Jessie pauses to give him a smile—he joined us for dinner tonight, this time as an invited guest. "And we should be good for the costumes since we're making this a modern retelling."

"But we might need some props," Luke says. "A wicker basket and a stuffed animal to play Toto. Possibly a few tutus."

"Coop and I can pick those up when we go to town tomorrow morning," I offer. "I'm already getting supplies to make the set. We're going to add some extra sessions in the Arts and Crafts cabin Tuesday, Wednesday, and Thursday afternoon for anyone who wants to help."

"I'll put it on the schedule," Dot says, jotting down a reminder.

"We'd better get to work if we want the script to be finished before the campers get here," Jessie says, gathering her things.

Luke nods and takes one last bite before standing up to follow her.

"I think we're going to get going, too," Zoey says. "Testing out a new idea we had for a midnight sail."

"By midnight, she means ten p.m.," Zac says.

"Who cares what time it is as long as it's dark?" Zoey says, her eyes glimmering. The waves won't be the only thing making their boat rock tonight.

Mr. Billy left about fifteen minutes after we all sat down, so it's just me and Cooper now. And Dot. Who is looking at us both, a wide grin on her face.

"Looks like it's just the three of us tonight!" she says, and my stomach sinks. "How about a board game at the Lodge?"

Cooper glances over at me, clearly reading the panic on my face. "Maybe another night," he says to Dot.

"Oh," Dot says, glancing between me and Cooper. "Ohhhh. On second thought." She stands up, grinning. "I'm going to go read my book by the fireplace. You two have fun—you want help cleaning up?"

"We've got it," I say, my eyes still on Cooper.

"Good night, Dot," Cooper says, his lips quirking up in a smile.

Dot chuckles as she walks into the night, leaving me and Cooper alone. *Finally.*

I exhale, nervous. It's been more than two years since I kissed someone new—and I've never, not once, cheated. Although this isn't technically cheating. We're on a break. A break that Aaron suggested. A break that I'm pretty sure I want to make permanent.

"Hi," Cooper says, suddenly standing beside me. He

extends a hand to help me up, and just like the other night in the hallway, we're mere inches apart. Close enough for him to smell the garlic on my breath. Then again, he's the one who put it there.

I must make a face, because Cooper says, "What are you thinking about?"

"The copious amount of garlic I ate tonight," I admit.

A chuckle rumbles through him, and he reaches into his back pocket, pulling out a packet of breath strips. "Here you go—but for the record, I'm sure you always taste amazing."

Heat floods my stomach, and any doubt about his definition of "hanging out" evaporates like the breath strip on my tongue.

"It won't take me long to clean up if you want to wait here," Cooper says.

"It'll go faster if I help," I say. "And I have an idea of where we can go."

He winks. "Then let's get busy!"

Before long, Cooper and I are walking through the empty camp. It's so quiet I can hear my breath hitch when he takes my hand. The calluses on his fingers are rough against my skin—so different from Aaron's soft, regularly manicured hands. I lace my fingers through Cooper's, excited to discover more ways he's nothing like Aaron.

We walk, hand in hand, toward the boys' side of camp, cutting between Cabin Nine and Cabin Eleven. Standing at the threshold between the clearing of the camp and the undisturbed forest, I understand why it's off-limits after dark. It's pitch-black in there.

"Any chance you have your phone?" I ask Cooper.

He drops my hand for an excruciatingly long moment, digs it out of his pocket, and turns on the flashlight.

"Thanks," I say, taking it in my right hand and reaching for his again with my left.

With his phone lighting the way, we retrace the steps I took earlier on my walk. There's a path for the first little while, but when it curves right, circling back toward the girls' side of the camp, we keep going straight. After about fifteen minutes, we emerge into a clearing. Across from us, water cascades down the side of a rocky hill into a small lake.

"Whoa," Cooper says, the same reaction I had earlier.

"It's beautiful, right?"

"Stunning," he says, turning to me, standing kissably close.

As much as I want to go for it, I need to make sure we're on the same page first. My heart pounds, and I force myself to say: "So, your offer is still good? To be my summer fling?"

"So good," Cooper says immediately, and his enthusiasm makes me grin.

"You should know, I've never done anything like this."

"Nervous?" he asks, the corner of his mouth quirking up.

I nod, my heart rate quickening. "A little. Maybe. I don't know. Should we have rules?"

"Sure," he says. "You're in control—nothing happens that you don't want."

I let out a shaky breath, relieved. Establishing rules and boundaries might just be my love language. "First rule: we should probably put a time limit on it."

"Until the end of camp?" he suggests, twirling a strand of my hair around his finger.

"Sounds good. Rule two: no PDA."

Cooper nods. "How do you feel about sleepovers?"

I make a face. That sounds pretty relationship-y. "I don't want anyone to know about this," I tell him, even though it's probably too late with Dot; but for all she knows, we just had plans to platonically hang out. "So rule three: we keep this quiet. And we should probably say no feelings, right? Keep it casual, no strings attached?"

"Deal. Any other rules?"

"Just one more," I say, flashing back to how tense I got every time a beautiful camper put her hands on Cooper last week. "As long as we're doing . . . this, we shouldn't do . . . this with anyone else. None of the campers, I mean. But if there's someone you like, a woman, just tell me and we end it, no hard feelings."

"That won't be a problem," he says, but I'm not sure I believe him. Like Taylor Swift says, a player's gonna play.

And like Aaron said, I'm no fun. Case in point, right now: way to take all the excitement out of a hookup by putting a bunch of rules around it, Hillary.

"Sorry, I told you I'm no good at being fun." I break his stare and look toward the rushing water.

"Hey," Cooper says, drawing my face back toward him. "Your rules are sexy as hell—nothing's more fun than a woman who knows what she wants. And I've got a rule, too."

"Something to do with honesty?" I guess.

Cooper nods. "You want something, you tell me. You like something, you tell me." He pulls me closer, resting his hand on the small of my back. All the blood in my body rushes to the one spot. "And if you don't, you tell me that, too. None of that 'yum' bullshit you gave me when my potatoes were salty as fuck."

I burst out laughing. "Okay! I'll be completely and totally honest, even if it might hurt your feelings."

"Good. So . . . how do you feel about this?" His finger traces the curve of my jaw to my chin, then rests gently against my bottom lip.

"I like this," I say. "I like this a lot."

Even in the dark, I can tell his eyes are sparking with desire.

"That goes both ways, right?" I ask as I reach up and slip the baseball cap off his head. No hair loss. His brown hair is thick and wavy, and I run my hand through it.

Cooper lets out a slow breath, bending his head back with my touch, like a cat. "I like," he says, so I keep exploring, trailing my hand down his jaw, across his neatly trimmed beard.

More confident now, my finger drifts down to his chin, then up to his lips. I've never been this forward with a man—I always let the guy make the first move, initiate the first kiss, the first touch—and it's thrilling. It's fun.

With his eyes locked on mine, Cooper takes my finger between his lips and gently sucks. My breath hitches at the feeling of his tongue against the pad of my finger. He releases it with a soft *pop*, and I wait for him to kiss me. But he doesn't. He just waits, watching me, staying true to his word and letting me be in control.

I remind myself to be brave—and fun—then lean in and kiss *him*. As our lips meet, he cups my face, gently guiding me closer. He tastes like mint and his lips are warm, his beard tickling my chin. Our kisses are soft, tentative, as we taste and tease each other. He's being careful, following my lead, which I appreciate, but soon I find myself leaning in, wanting more. I open my mouth, inviting him to deepen the kiss, and he does, wrapping one arm around my waist, pulling me close. His tongue slides more deeply against mine and heat sizzles down my legs. I let out a soft, involuntary moan. He's kissing me like this is the main attraction, not just the warm-up for something more.

His lips nip my ear, and he trails kisses down the side of my neck. My mind flashes back to our first kiss all those years ago, and I laugh, remembering how awkward and stumbly it was.

"What's so funny?" he asks, pulling away slightly.

I don't want to admit it, but I promised honesty. "I was just thinking about how much you've improved since our last time doing this."

Cooper smiles, tilting my chin so I'm looking into his eyes. "Do you remember the camp dance that summer?"

"I think so," I say, although most of the camp dances have blended together in my mind.

"I asked you to go out and look at the stars with me."

"I brought Jessie out with me," I say, remembering how nervous I was to be alone with him, how I wasn't sure I wanted to kiss him again.

"Yup." Cooper laughs. "This do-over has been a long time coming."

"Well, it was worth the wait," I say, lifting my head so our lips meet again.

He sinks into this kiss, his hands running up my back and pulling me against him. My body feels light and breezy, like it's made of stars, and I let out a sigh of appreciation for this place, for this man.

And, most importantly, for this new version of myself.

fourteen

Jessie

Putting on a musical at camp is always a challenge, but usually we have weeks to get ready. In this case, the cast and crew arrived five days ago, so it's been a flurry of activity. Luckily, the campers are former theater kids, so everyone knows what to do: practicing lines, working on costumes, makeup, and sound. We're staging a gender-flipped, camp-ified version of *The Wizard of Oz*.

"These are perfect," I say, smiling at Hillary. We're on the makeshift stage at one end of the dining hall, seeing everything in place for the first time.

She lights up, pleased. She led the group making the sets, which finished drying last night. "Yeah?"

"They're Chick-amazing. What do you think, Sam?" I ask our stage manager.

Sam gives a thumbs-up. "By far the best sets we've had for a camp musical."

When Sam turned in their registration with a note that they were nonbinary, I was determined to make sure they felt completely welcome. We'd divided the cabins along gender lines—with Sam's application, I realized maybe that wasn't the best idea. Dot and I asked Sam if they'd prefer a men's cabin, a women's cabin, or a private room somewhere else.

Sam asked to be assigned to a women's cabin, and everyone has been incredibly welcoming. Say what you will about theater nerds—they're overly dramatic, they can be petty or cliquish, but god love them, they *will* be inclusive.

"Let's run through the lighting and set changes," I say to Sam, "before the performers show up for dress rehearsal—"

The doors to the dining hall burst open.

"Jessie! You need to see this!" a male voice bellows. It's Paul, who's playing the Wicked Witch, along with two other guys from his cabin. He's holding up his phone.

I walk over to him. "What's going on?"

"Darren has a . . ." Paul hesitates, then sighs. "Just look."

He turns his phone so I can see the screen: a picture of a flaccid penis.

"Ew!" I yelp, shoving it away. "What the fuck, Paul? I don't want to see your dick!"

"It's not my dick, it's Darren's," Paul says. "And the dick isn't the point. What is that *thing*?" He uses his fingers to enlarge the photo, zooming in, and I wrinkle my nose as the thing in question comes into focus: a round, blackish speck against wrinkly pale flesh.

"Looks like a deer tick," I say, grimacing. That won't be fun to remove. For Darren or for Dot, our designated tick extractor.

"I knew it!" Paul says, and his friends agree. "It was those chicks in Cabin Eight. They stole his bedding the other day and hid it in the woods. He had to tromp all through the underbrush to find it!"

Beside me, Hillary sighs in exasperation. I feel the same

way. While innocent pranking is part of the fun of camp, these two cabins have taken things too far. I'm sick and tired of it.

I pull out my walkie-talkie. "Dot? You there?"

A moment later, my walkie crackles. "Go for Dot."

"We've got a situation with Darren in Cabin Five," I say. "He's got a—"

"Dick tick!" Paul shouts into the walkie-talkie, and his friends burst into loud guffaws.

"Yes, a tick on his penis," I say, trying not to roll my eyes. You'd think these guys were thirteen years old by the way they're acting.

"Is it engorged?" Dot asks.

Paul blanches. "Uh . . ."

"The tick, not the dick," Dot says.

An involuntary giggle rises in my throat, and I stifle it. Behind me, Hillary and Sam look like they're struggling not to laugh, too. Maybe we're all still thirteen on the inside.

"I think so," I say.

"He'll need to go to urgent care for antibiotics, then. Can't have him getting penile Lyme disease."

Paul and his friends exchange horrified glances.

"You'll head over to his cabin and check it out?" I ask Dot.

"On my way."

As I replace the walkie-talkie on my hip, something occurs to me: "If Darren has to go to urgent care, we won't have a lead."

It's a ninety-minute drive each way, and the show starts in three hours. Darren's been practicing all week to play the lead role: the wide-eyed farm boy transported via tornado to a fantastical summer camp.

"Exactly!" Paul says. "And no one else knows his lines."

Hillary speaks up, her voice tentative: "Well, *someone* else does."

Hillary and I hurry down the path toward Luke's cabin. I knock on his door, glad Hillary's with me. There's a sense of solidarity in solving this problem together, as a team, like we used to.

The door flings open.

"What?" Luke snaps. His hair is rumpled, like he's been running his hands through it nonstop.

Flustered, I blurt out, "Darren has to go to urgent care for his dick."

Luke's eyebrows shoot up.

"His *tick*," I correct, then mentally kick myself. "I mean, *a* tick."

Luke squints at me.

"There's a tick on his—"

"We need a new lead," Hillary cuts in, bless her. At this point, my foot is embedded in my mouth. "Since you wrote the script and know the lines . . ."

"Not interested," Luke says, and goes to shut the door. I stick my boot over the threshold, stopping it from closing.

"Come on, Luke!" I say, exasperated. "We need you— there's no time for anyone else to learn the part."

His mouth curves in a sneer. "You think I give a shit about this musical?"

Hillary sucks in a shocked breath. But I'm used to Luke's attitude, though he's being extra salty today. I smile patiently and say, "We could use your help. Please?"

"I'm busy." He uses his foot to nudge my boot out of the doorway. "Now if you'll excuse me . . ."

And he shuts the door in my face for the third time this summer.

Hillary's jaw drops open. "That was so rude! Just like our second year as CITs—"

"Exactly!" I say, grateful for our shared history.

"What an asshole," Hillary murmurs, and I nod, although I can't help wondering what's going on. I've spent enough time with Luke to know he's not an asshole by nature, though he plays the part well.

We head down the stairs together.

"What'll we do?" I say.

Hillary gives me a sneaky smile. "I mean, *one* other person knows the script . . ."

It takes me a moment to understand. Then: "Who, me? I can't—it's supposed to be gender-flipped."

She shrugs. "It's gender-flexible." She's right; we have a female Scarecrow and a Tin Woman, but the Cowardly Lion is played by a man. "And it's starting in less than three hours, Jess. Come on. We need you."

It's been years since I've performed in a camp musical, but when we tell the cast and crew, everyone is supportive. Mikayla, the costume designer, gets to work altering Darren's costume (he's smaller than me, which isn't great for my self-esteem). Raul practices my makeup and hair, and Hillary runs lines with me. We break for dinner, after which the crew moves the tables and lines up the benches for our audience.

And then it's time for the show. Nearly every camper this week was involved in preparing for the musical, but only about a third are performing or working the stage crew, so the dining hall is packed.

When the opening music starts, I take my place, butterflies in my stomach. Cooper and Dot are sitting in the front row; he smiles, and she flashes me a thumbs-up. I scan the audience, stupidly wondering if I might see Luke, but there's no sign of him. It feels like a slap in the face after all the time we spent writing this damn play.

Then I glance at the wings, where Hillary is waiting to feed me lines if needed, and she mouths, *You can do it!*

Her words infuse me with confidence. I nod at Sam to turn on the spotlight, and the play begins.

There are mistakes, sure—I forget my lines, the set piece for the house falls over during the tornado, and the sound goes out during the Wicked Witch's final monologue ("Oh, what a world, what a world . . ." as he melts into the floor). But the audience is supportive, laughing and clapping at all the right points. When I click my ruby-bedazzled Chuck Taylors and say, "There's no place like camp," everyone cheers.

After the performers take their bows, I bring out Sam and their stage crew, Mikayla and her costume designers, Raul and his makeup team, Hillary and her set creators. The audience stands, clapping and cheering.

Then I feel Hillary's hand grabbing mine. "You did it!" she whispers.

"We did it," I say, squeezing her hand.

I mean more than just this performance—and more than our efforts to increase profits. We're building our friendship again.

I'm up early the next morning, still basking in the glow of the performance, but tired. The cast and crew were hungry after the show, so Cooper opened the kitchen and made pancakes. We all ended up hanging out long past midnight. I meant to sleep in, but my body is accustomed to waking at dawn, so here I am.

My usual canoe isn't near the lakefront, which means Zac must be putting sealant on the old wood, as promised. The kayaks are lined up and ready to go, though, so I grab one and set off. I'm listening to *The Music Man* revival with Hugh Jackman for the first time. It's good, but I'm still partial to the movie soundtrack. Who can beat Robert Preston, the original Buffalo Bills, and tiny Ron Howard with a lisp?

By the time I've paddled out to the middle of the lake, Marian the librarian is falling in love with Professor Harold Hill, oblivious to the fact that he's a con man. I take a deep breath, relishing the morning breeze and golden sunshine.

But then I realize: my kayak is full of water.

My first thought is that I must have splashed water inside the cockpit; I'm not used to kayaks. But this is more than a *little* water—my legs are submerged, and I forgot to bring a life jacket (again).

A whisper of panic crawls up my spine. Kayaks are very safe, I remind myself. And there doesn't seem to be any obvious structural damage. Maybe I hit a rock and cracked the hull, but didn't notice?

I try to bail water out with my hands but it's totally ineffective. Nathaniel's voice sounds in my head (*Safety first, safety second, and safety third*), and through my panic, I try to recall my kayaking lessons from when I was a camper. I could get out of the kayak, flip it over, and let it drain while I float beside it, but I'm not sure that's a good idea. I'm out pretty far—several thousand yards. I need to make a decision, fast: paddle, or swim back to shore.

Since I don't have a life jacket, the safest thing is to stay with the kayak. Before the water gets any higher, I remove my earbuds, place them in the dry bag with my phone, and stow it back in the hatch.

I set off, paddling as hard as I can. But the waterlogged kayak feels like it weighs a thousand pounds. Every stroke makes my arms and shoulders burn. Plus, there's a breeze pushing against me. When I look down, the water level inside the kayak is even higher.

Fear and confusion rattle through me—I thought kayaks were unsinkable? But it's been years since I've used one.

I'm fine, I tell myself. It's all going to be fine.

But the kayak keeps getting heavier, and the water inside keeps rising.

I have to swim for it.

My heart is beating too fast. I take a calming breath. I can do this. I can see the shore—it's not exactly *close*, but it's close enough. Steeling myself, I lift out of the kayak and drop into the water.

The chill takes my breath away. Out here in the middle of the lake, the temperature never really rises, even in the summer.

It hits me then: I left the dry bag with my phone and my expensive noise-canceling earbuds behind. *Damn it.* I consider going back, but the kayak is already drifting away, so I tell myself to leave it.

I've never been a great swimmer, but I try to remember

what I learned in my swim tests all those years ago, counting off a hundred strokes before lifting my head. My heart sinks—the shore is so far. And I feel strangely naked, floating out here without a life jacket. Hillary never loved being in the lake—she said it was like swimming in soup. *Fish and poop soup*, she'd say.

A hysterical giggle rises in my throat, and I stuff it down. I need to stay focused. My wet canvas shorts are heavy, so I undo the button and wriggle out of them. After that, I feel lighter, which gives me the motivation to set off again. A hundred more strokes, and I take another break.

Still so far from the shore.

I press down the nasty little whisper that says I'm not going to make it and tread water awkwardly, catching my breath. But I suck at treading water, so I roll onto my back. Unfortunately, I also suck at floating on my back. Better to keep moving forward.

Another hundred strokes. The shore is closer, but I'm *exhausted.* My lungs are burning; every muscle in my body aches; I'm so cold my teeth are chattering.

I can't do this.

Panic shoots through me, and I desperately start swimming again, my movements clumsy and jerky. My head goes under; I swallow a gulp of water and cough violently when I resurface.

Then I hear a voice drifting across the lake: "Hey! You okay?"

Straining to keep my head above water, I spot a tiny, blurry figure standing on the dock.

"Luke!" I shout, waving one arm.

"Jessie? Swimming alone is against the rules!"

I'm too tired to respond to that.

"My kayak sank!" I manage to shout, and then my head goes under again. I fight to the surface, coughing and flailing. When I open my eyes, Luke is in the water, swimming straight toward me. I kick myself in his direction, even though my muscles are screaming and I keep inhaling water.

When he's almost reached me, he extends his hand. I lunge toward him, desperate to wrap myself around him and never let go, but he takes my hand firmly and turns me so I'm facing away from him. I momentarily flash with fear, but he's right behind me, his chest pressed to my back, his arm wrapped around my torso.

"I got ya," he murmurs in my ear.

I cough up more water, babbling, "Thank you, thank you, I'm sorry, I'm so stupid—"

"Shhh. You're all right. You're safe. Let's get you back to shore."

Luke clearly knows what he's doing, holding me against his chest as he kicks his legs to propel us toward land. So I relax and let him take over. I'm shivering with cold and fear, but he's warm and calm, his heart beating a steady rhythm. And even though he's only a couple inches taller than me, I realize now that he's bigger. Broader. Stronger. His arm, the one wrapped around me, is corded with muscle. His wrist has got to be twice as thick as mine.

It's strange, feeling small. Being taken care of.

Finally, I feel ground beneath my feet. Luke helps me stagger out of the water, then lowers me to the wooden dock, where I collapse in a wet, shivering heap. He disappears for a moment before returning with his towel, which he drapes over my shoulders.

Relief rushes through my body, and my eyes fill with tears. "Thank you so much."

He wraps his arms around me, rubbing with the towel to warm me up. "What happened?"

"I don't know! My kayak started taking on water. I lost my phone and earbuds, which—ugh. And yeah, I forgot to bring a life jacket, and I know it was stupid, but—"

He's staring at me. His eyes have taken on that fiery blue that could burn someone alive.

"What?" I say.

In a flash, he's on his feet, stalking down the path toward the cabins. I stumble after him, wrapping the towel around my body, trying to cover my wet T-shirt and underwear.

"Hang on," I call out, but he doesn't stop. "I'm sorry, okay? I was distracted this morning—I should have been more careful—"

He makes a sharp right turn. Where the hell is he going?

I try to keep up, but he's faster than I am, somehow unbothered by sticks or rocks in the path, even though his feet are bare and he's wearing nothing but sopping-wet swim shorts. Meanwhile, I keep stepping on sharp things and yelping in pain. I could go back to the lake and get my shoes, but I'm too curious to turn around now.

Luke reaches Cabin Five, takes the stairs two at a time, and throws open the door without knocking. I scramble up to the porch and hear his thunderous yell echoing in the cabin:

"—motherfuckers better wake up!"

I freeze. Better to stay put.

"What the hell, man?" someone murmurs sleepily.

"This stops now, understand?" Luke shouts, punctuating

his words with a fist on the doorframe. "I saw you all down by the kayaks last night."

I have no idea what he's talking about, but by the guilty silence in the cabin, I think the campers do.

"It's their fault I got a dick tick!" a voice says—Darren.

"And they toilet papered our cabin!"

"The girls were talking about going kayaking this morning—"

"We only wanted to slow them down—"

"We just hid the drain plugs so they wouldn't be able to—"

Luke slams his fist on the doorframe again, silencing everyone. "Are you fucking kidding me? Somebody could have died."

A memory fills my mind, something I haven't thought of for years.

The first summer that Luke was a counselor, the thirteen-year-old boys from his cabin played a prank on the eight-year-old girls. It would have been fine for someone their own age (red Kool-Aid in the showerheads), but they did it the morning after telling the little girls about Bloody Barbara, a ghost that supposedly haunted the camp. The girls were terrified and crying, and I overheard Luke giving his boys a strict dressing-down about never pranking anyone younger or more vulnerable. It only added to my blossoming hero worship of him, of course.

"Dude, come on. Zac and Zoey inspect the watercraft every morning," someone says defiantly.

"Jessie took a kayak out at dawn," Luke replies in an icy voice. "She almost drowned."

There's a brief, guilty silence. Then someone pipes up: "We didn't mean—"

"Shut up," Luke snaps. "No more pranks. I expect you to replace the missing drain plugs immediately. Let Zac and Zoey know so they can double-check everything. You'll have to cover the cost of the lost kayak, as well as Jessie's phone and earbuds. And last but not least, you will all apologize to Jessie later today."

With that, he turns and walks out—and nearly crashes into me on the porch.

He stumbles back in surprise, then shoots me an icy glare before walking down the stairs and heading away, down the path.

"Wait!" I shout, running after him.

But he keeps going, his long strides eating up the ground. I struggle along behind, penguin-shuffling, his towel wrapped around me.

"Luke, wait—let me say something."

He spins to face me, his eyes flashing blue fire. "What?"

"Thank you."

In response, he rolls his eyes and stalks off again.

.My temper flares as I run after him.

"What do you want me to say? I'm sorry for forgetting a life jack—"

"It wasn't your fault," he says, without turning around.

"So why are you mad at me?"

"I'm not mad at you."

"Then why are you so goddamn confusing?!" I shout.

He finally stops and turns to face me. His chest is heaving, his wet hair sending little rivulets down his skin.

"Every time I think you're loosening up," I say, "you freeze over and shut me down. I'm trying to thank you for saving my life, and for some reason you're *furious* with me—"

"I'm not—"

"It's like back when you were a counselor, and you were such a shit to me that second year! You wouldn't even talk to me!"

He scoffs. "Oh, I get it. You had a crush on me, and I hurt your feelings."

"I didn't—that's not—" I stop, embarrassed. But I have nothing to be embarrassed about. "Okay, sure. I had a crush on you. Practically everyone did. It was silly teenage stuff— you were a counselor; I was a kid."

"Exactly! I was a counselor having sex dreams about a seventeen-year-old!"

His voice echoes in the morning air.

I stop, shocked speechless. "You—what?"

"Shit," he mutters. He wheels around and starts walking away.

"No, no, no." He doesn't get to leave after dropping that bomb. I catch up to him and grab his wrist. "Explain. Now."

He yanks his arm away and exhales in frustration. "It was inappropriate, and obviously I knew that, but that summer you looked—different, okay? And I wasn't going to *do* anything about it, because you were seventeen and I was twenty and the whole thing disgusted me—"

"*What?*" I cut in, somehow offended.

"—so I didn't talk to you anymore. I would never in a million *years* have gotten involved with a camper or a CIT. But I needed to get you out of my head, so I stayed away from you. Okay? Are you satisfied? Is that what you wanted to know?"

He breaks off, breathing hard, and I stand there, my mouth hanging open.

I don't know what to say—he's obviously still bothered, and I get it: there was a power differential between us, and I was a minor, still in high school. But we weren't *that* far apart in age. It's not like he was having those dreams about an actual child. And he didn't do anything inappropriate—in fact, he did everything in his power to avoid even the appearance of anything inappropriate between us.

"You can't control your dreams," I say finally. "Everyone has weird dreams—"

"I know!" He runs a hand through his wet hair. "Believe me, I know. You were the *last* person on earth I wanted to have that kind of dream about."

Now I'm definitely offended. "So you wanted some distance, fine. But did you have to get the other male counselors to be jerks to me, too?"

He goes still. "I—you don't know what they were saying about you?"

"No . . . ?"

He blows out a breath, shaking his head.

"What were they saying?" I demand, taking a step forward.

"Just . . . comments. Inappropriate comments."

I roll my eyes. "Like Camp Barbie?"

"Worse than that," he says darkly. "Do you remember that tall guy with the red hair? Vince? He would say disgusting things about you, vulgar things, and it started rubbing off on the others. So I told all the boys' counselors to keep their mouths shut and leave you the fuck alone or I'd report them to Nathaniel."

I blink, memories rearranging in my mind. Me, walking up to Luke at the beginning of that second summer. The way the other male counselors stared at me . . .

They were leering. My body had filled out that year, boobs and hips appearing for the first time, but I didn't realize anyone was looking at me that way.

When Luke told me to leave, he wasn't trying to dismiss me. He was trying to protect me.

"Vince ended up being sent home, do you remember?" Luke says.

I shake my head.

"He was getting too close with one of the girl campers. She was, like, fourteen. I told Nathaniel and he fired him immediately."

Nausea twists my stomach. Sexual abuse is every camp director's worst nightmare. It permanently taints (and potentially shuts down) the camp. Even worse, it forever damages innocent young lives.

"Thanks," I say. "For doing that."

He shakes his head. "Don't thank me. I felt sick about the . . ."

"Dreams?" I finish.

He lifts his eyes to meet mine, and something shivers down my spine. Almost of their own accord, my eyes slide down his body: his chest and shoulders, lean muscle and tan skin, still glistening with water droplets. His swim shorts, clinging to his hips and thighs.

My cheeks flare with heat and I shake myself.

"You were a good counselor, Luke," I say, trying to keep

my tone professional. "And like I said, those kinds of dreams don't mean anything."

A muscle in his jaw flexes, and he looks away.

"I'm going to shower and change." I motion to his towel, which is still wrapped around me. "Can I get this to you later?"

He waves a hand. "Yeah, no worries. But I—uh . . . I need to apologize."

I blink.

"For how I acted yesterday. I'm dealing with some stuff and none of it is your fault."

"Stuff like your writing?"

"Among other things. You've borne the brunt of my negativity on more than one occasion, and I'm sorry."

His expression is serious, stiff, like the straight nose and high cheekbones are carved out of marble. Like some talented artist spent days shaping the curve of his lips, the shallow dimple in his chin.

"I forgive you," I say, surprised—in the best way—to receive this apology.

"Would you believe me if I said I'm actually feeling better being here?"

That makes me smile. "Don't tell me the magic of summer camp is warming your frozen heart."

His lips curve up ever so slightly. "Something like that."

"I'm glad you're here." I hold his gaze. All the fear and panic I felt in the water rushes back, and a lump comes to my throat. "Thank you for saving me this morning."

He gives a curt nod. "No problem."

"Come to the campfire tonight," I say. He still hasn't attended one. It's our last night with this group of campers, and with a bunch of theater nerds, the singing is sure to be amazing. "Please. You owe it to me."

He scoffs. "I owe *you*?"

"Yes, I've been traumatized. I nearly drowned, then I learned that my childhood camp counselor was having naked dreams about me. Which he found 'disgusting.' So not only are my lungs damaged from inhaling lake water, my self-esteem has been crushed."

He runs a hand over his face. I swear he's trying to keep from cracking a smile. "Jess . . ."

"Luke . . ."

"I'll consider it," he says. "But I won't sing any camp songs."

"That's okay."

"And do not force me to socialize."

"Of course not."

"And you'd better not tell anyone about those dreams—"

"I would never," I say seriously, then flash him a smile. "Okay, see ya later . . . try not to think too much about me while I'm gone."

He sighs and looks heavenward, as if he's searching for the strength to deal with me.

"Don't think about how it felt to have my body pressed up against you in the water," I add.

He closes his eyes like he's pained. "My god, Jessie Pederson. You're a menace."

I grin. "If you take a nap this afternoon, make sure you don't dream—"

"Shut your mouth."

Chuckling quietly, I turn and walk away. All I hear is his heavy exhale behind me, but I guarantee he's smiling.

fifteen

Hillary

The musical last week was a beautiful disaster. I know *The Wizard of Oz* isn't supposed to be a comedy, but I can't remember the last time I laughed so hard. Seeing Jessie onstage skipping down the yellow brick road with a stuffed dog in her arms was just perfection.

As if my thoughts summoned her, Dorothy herself walks into the Arts and Crafts cabin, where I'm setting up for the first session of the day. It's the Fourth of July, and I have a patriotic craft planned, then I'm helping Zac and Zoey decorate canoes for the parade and fireworks show tonight.

"Hey!" I say, excited for the impromptu visit.

But then I notice her shoulders are slumped, her eyes puffy and red. She looks defeated—which is not a word I'd ever associate with Jessie Pederson.

I drop the red, white, and blue yarn and rush over to her.

"Jess, what's wrong?" I only hesitate for a split second before I wrap my arms around her. Jessie goes soft in my embrace, letting me support her.

"It's okay," I say, rubbing her back. "Whatever it is, it'll be okay," I promise blindly.

We stay like that, with her head resting on my shoulder,

159

until her breathing has returned to normal. I don't know about her, but my eyes are brimming with tears.

"Want to tell me what's going on?" I ask as I continue to rub circles on her back.

Jessie straightens herself up and takes a deep breath. "I got an email from Jack Valentine this morning. It's over."

My stomach sinks, even though I knew this was a strong possibility.

"They have a buyer," she says. "The camp is officially under contract."

"Shit."

This is why I never let my heart get involved in matters of business. Old companies fold and new companies start every single day. It's the cycle of commerce; and it only hurts when you let yourself care.

"I'm so sorry, Jess," I say, reaching for her hand.

"It's fine," she says, even though it's clearly not. "We have until the end of the summer." Her voice cracks on the last word, and my heart breaks for her. She's losing so much—but she won't lose me. Not again.

Jessie takes her hand back and clears the emotion from her throat. "Anyway, I just wanted to let you know."

"Thanks," I say. "I wish there was something more we could do."

"Me too," she says with a sigh.

Neither of us moves. I hope she knows that she's not alone, that I'm here to help shoulder the weight of this immense loss.

The silence is interrupted by the static of her walkie-talkie, pulling us back to the reality at hand.

"Go for Jessie," she says, transforming back into the

happy, shiny camp director she lets the world see. With a small wave, she's off.

The door closes behind her, and I rub my aching chest, trying to make sense of the swirl of emotions. I hate that she's hurting, but I'm grateful she turned to me. For the first time all summer, I feel confident our friendship will survive, even if the camp won't.

Later that afternoon, after the campers have made patriotic flags for the parade and revealed the red, white, and blue (or, in some cases, purple) tie-dyed shirts we made yesterday, I rush out to find Cooper. The kitchen is abuzz with his staff getting ready for tonight's BBQ, and ingredients in various stages of prep cover the counters.

"Has anyone seen Chef?" I ask, trying to sound casual, like I'm seeking Cooper out for a completely legit, work-related purpose. Which I suppose I am.

Somehow, we've managed to keep our fling under wraps, acting professional, yet friendly, when others are near, then sneaking around camp to private places like the walk-in pantry or the empty archery range to make out like teenagers.

Except neither of us was that kind of teenager, which is probably why we're having so much fun with it.

Nothing's gone past heavy "necking and petting," as Nurse Penny used to call it, but that's somehow made it even better. It's like when you become an adult and start having sex, you forget how fun it is to get all hot and bothered, then back away, over and over again until you're both so breathless and horny that a simple touch, a brush of skin against skin, can threaten to undo you. It's been two weeks of nonstop edging—and Cooper seems to be enjoying it as much as I am, dragging out the anticipation until we decide to reach the main event.

"He's out by the grills," one of the guys answers, and I wave in appreciation before heading outside and around the far corner of the dining hall toward the lake.

There's Cooper, standing in front of the grill with his hat on backward, wearing an apron with the words SUCK IT, ENGLAND under a picture of George Washington in shades. His face lights up at the sight of me, and I feel a flutter in my belly that stops me in my tracks. *The elusive butterflies.* So they do exist.

"Hey," he says as I get closer. A quick glance around confirms we're alone, so I slip my arms around his neck and bring my lips to his for what's supposed to be a quick kiss.

But the sweep of his tongue against mine sends the butterflies into a frenzy, and I forget everything that isn't us. Cooper's hand slides down from my waist to cup my butt, pulling me closer. Heat flushes through me, and I can tell he's getting excited, too. The press of his erection against my stomach brings me back to the moment: standing out in the open, in broad daylight where anyone could see us. I quickly step back to a platonic distance.

Cooper clears his throat, then adjusts himself. "To what do I owe this pleasure?"

"Huh?" I say, before remembering myself. "Oh! I have news."

Cooper's smile falters when he sees the look on my face. "It's not good news?"

"Afraid not."

I fill him in on what Jessie told me and explain the way sales of this size work. How being under contract is just the first step in a very long process that could likely take until the summer is over, if not beyond.

"Shit," Cooper says. "Jessie must be a wreck."

"Yeah," I say, twirling a strand of hair around my finger. "It's crushing—and I hate knowing that I could've saved this place for her if things were different."

Cooper quirks an eyebrow. "How so?"

"Finding ways for failing businesses to turn things around is what I do. That's my job." I sit on top of one of the picnic tables, trying to think of the best way to explain the thoughts that have been niggling in the back of my mind for the last few weeks. "But it only works if the owners *want* it to be saved. The Valentines are set on selling—from everything I've heard, Jack has his eyes on the money, and this land is worth millions."

"So you couldn't have saved it?" Cooper asks, confused.

"Not if the Valentines are set on a quick payout," I say. "They'd have to be on board, or at least give Jessie the power to make the decisions. But even then . . ."

"What?" Cooper asks. "You don't think she'd do whatever it took to save Camp Chickawah?"

I shrug. "It would take some drastic changes, and Jessie loves this place so much—maybe even too much. She's still running it the same way Nathaniel and Lola did. And when you do things the same way for so long, you don't evolve. You get stuck. That's why a lot of these old businesses are run into the ground—they refuse to change. But that's what happens when you make one thing your whole life and get *way* too emotionally invested in it."

A creak of a floorboard rings through the air, and Cooper and I both turn to find Jessie standing mere feet away on the porch outside the dining hall.

Her face is frozen into a mask of shock and hurt.

Shit.

I'm about to explain what I meant—that my frustration is with the Valentines, not her—when she turns and speed-walks away. I take off after her, trying to catch up, but her long legs make it difficult, and I end up running.

"Jessie! Wait! Let me explain."

"Not necessary," she calls back, picking up her pace. "Hey, Noah," she says, smiling and waving to a camper walking by. "Looking good, Jenna!"

If I wasn't actively pursuing her, I would stop in my tracks, stupefied at the way she can carry on like her world isn't falling apart at the seams. But I am, so I keep going.

"Jess, slow down!" I shout, my chest burning from the exertion.

She walks even faster, breaking into a run herself as she approaches her cabin. She takes the stairs in two big steps and closes the door behind her, right in my face. I don't think there's a back door, and I can't imagine her climbing out the window to escape, so I take a minute to catch my breath.

Once my pulse has reached non-cardiac-arrest levels, I knock.

Unsurprisingly, she doesn't answer.

Surprisingly, I push past my inner rule-follower and go inside anyway. Jessie is sitting in front of her old desktop computer, staring daggers at the screen while typing furiously.

"Can we talk?" I ask.

"I'm busy," she says, pummeling the keys like she wishes they were my face.

"Listen, about what I said. Out of context I can see how—"

"Don't patronize me, Hillary," she says, her tone cold.

"That's not what I'm trying to do, I just want you to understand."

"Oh, I understand," Jessie says, looking up at me for the first time. Her blue eyes fill with tears, and she blinks them away. "Actually, I don't. Why were you trying to help me at all if you thought I was such a bad businesswoman? Running this camp into the ground?"

"Jessie, that's not—"

"That's exactly what you told Cooper." There's more hurt than anger in her voice, and deep down, I know I deserve it—I was venting to Cooper, processing my own feelings about losing this place, but I should have been more aware of how what I said could have been perceived.

"I *wanted* to help you," I tell her. "If the Valentines—"

"Oh, please," Jessie says, her voice wavering with emotion. "It's over, Hillary. We both know that."

I recoil at her words. Is she talking about the sale of the camp or our friendship? The first, I understand. The latter, I won't accept. I get what happened the last time: I broke a promise and she was rightfully hurt. But this time, I didn't make any promises. I came back to help. I *did* help—she'll be able to give Dot and Mr. Billy hefty bonuses with the increase of cash flow this summer. And my being here—to help *her*—came at the detriment of my own career and personal life. Aaron wouldn't have asked for a break if I wasn't leaving him for two months.

"Everyone in my life said coming back here this summer was a big mistake," I tell her. "I walked away from clients that wanted to pay me a lot of money. But I came back anyway, for you."

Jessie laughs, but there's no amusement in the sound. "Gee, thanks."

My head is a cyclone of emotions, and I stop, trying to find the words that can fix this. But I'm not sure they exist. And the thought of being here four more weeks without Jessie's friendship feels like torture.

"Maybe I should just go home," I say, my voice small and uncertain.

"Maybe you should," she says, her eyes focused on the computer screen.

I blink. Why did I suggest such a stupid thing? I don't want to leave. I want her to turn around and tell me to stay. To say she's sorry she overreacted, that we'll get through this together.

"Jessie, I hope you know I'd never say or do anything to hurt you on purpose. Not in a million years."

"It's fine," Jessie says. Then she stands and, without so much as looking in my direction, walks right past me and out the door.

And just like that, it really is over.

sixteen

Jessie

I hurry away from my office—the *one* place on the property where I can usually find privacy. My heart is breaking. Bad enough to hear from Jack Valentine that they've found a buyer for this place. It's ten times worse to know that Hillary thinks it's my fault.

I have to find Dot—she's the only person who will understand how I feel.

But she's down by the lake, preparing for the canoe parade tonight, which means I have to walk through the heart of camp, which means I keep running into campers, which means I have to pretend to be as happy as a lark, even though I'm falling apart.

Two women dressed in swimsuits pass me. "Hey, Jessie!" they say, waving.

I force a smile and wave back. "Hi, Susan, hi, Ashley! Have fun at the lake!"

I'm sickened by the desperation in my voice. Trying to be a good little camp director, making this summer magical for everyone else before it all burns down.

And it *will* burn down. My favorite place on earth will be wiped away. And there's nothing I can do to stop it.

Two men carrying tennis rackets wave at me, call, "How's it going, Jessie?"

Another forced smile. "Hi, Jeff, hi, Scott—how was the game?"

More campers pass, and it's more of the same. No one seems to notice I'm dying inside.

I'm nearly to the lawn when I see Luke walking toward me with Scout on a leash. I summon my fake smile and chirp, "Hi, Luke, how's the writing going?"

His eyes narrow. "What the hell is wrong with you?"

"Jeez, grumpy much?" I snap.

But as I step past him, he puts a hand on my arm, stopping me. The groove between his eyebrows deepens as he searches my face. "No—something's wrong. What is it?"

I sigh. "I don't need you to rescue me again, Luke."

His eyebrows lift, and he releases my arm. "That's not— sorry."

"It's okay, I just . . ."

I hesitate; *could* I talk to him about this? Dot isn't exactly impartial; she knows my history with Hillary, and she's as upset as I am about the news of the sale.

"Actually, do you have time to talk?" I ask, tentatively.

Luke nods once. "I do."

I haven't been in Luke's cabin since the day he arrived, and as I step inside, I'm surprised at all the ways he's made it his own. He's moved two twin beds together and covered them with a colorful patchwork quilt. The mattress for the third bed is on the floor, with a blanket—Scout is curled up there now, a golden ball of floof, snoozing.

The fourth bed, where I'm sitting now, he's made into a sort of sofa, with pillows propped up against the wall. The picnic table, under the largest window, must be where he works—it's covered with notebooks, pens, and balled-up paper. In one corner he's made himself a kitchenette using the single outlet in the cabin, with a hot plate and electric kettle.

He heats water for tea as I ramble on about the pact Hillary and I made to become counselors together; how she bailed on me; what I just overheard. How she told Cooper that I've run this place into the ground. That I'm too emotionally invested in it.

As I finish my story, I start unraveling my braids so I can avoid looking at Luke. He's been weirdly quiet as I've talked, and I hope he's not silently judging me.

He walks over, a mug of tea in each hand. "Here you go."

"Thanks." I take a sip. The intensity of my initial reaction has faded, and I'm dazed, like I've suffered a blow to the head.

Luke sits next to me on the bed-turned-couch and takes a sip from his mug. He's dressed in a soft gray T-shirt and sweatpants, his hair rumpled, a couple days' worth of stubble on his jaw. It's oddly intimate being here, in this space he's kept closed off to everyone. I wonder if he regrets inviting me, now that he's heard my tale of woe.

"How are you feeling about all this?" he asks.

I take another sip of tea. How to put this into words? The heat of my anger toward Hillary is cooling. Mostly I feel deeply, deeply stupid for allowing myself to get close to her again.

"Well. I guess I should've realized Hillary didn't really care about me or this place. She was barely here a week before she started suggesting all these changes. No respect for tradition. And anyone who loves this camp would never want to change it *that* much."

Luke takes a sip of tea. "Okay."

I frown; does he think I'm overreacting? "I know, I know—she did have some good ideas." I huff, exasperated. "I'm not a total bitch."

Now Luke frowns. "I didn't—"

"No, you're right," I say. "It's not her fault Jack and Mary are selling. It just felt like she's blaming *me* for the camp being a 'failing business'—like if I'd been better at my job, I wouldn't have lost their confidence in the first place."

"Yes, but—"

"I know I'm not great at financial stuff, but I tried my best! There's more to consider than turning a profit. She has no idea how to hire and train counselors, or develop programs for kids, or communicate with parents."

"Right, but—"

"I've given this place everything I have, poured my heart and soul into it, and she's acting like it's pathetic to devote your life to a silly summer camp. And of course she's leaving, just like she did the last time. I'm not going to beg her to stay and let her tell me I'm too 'emotionally invested' in her."

I sink back against the pillows and run my hands through my hair, struggling to contain my emotions.

"Can I say something now?" Luke asks.

My cheeks warm with embarrassment. "Sorry. I was talking too much."

"No, I'm glad you could think through all of that out loud. But I'm still waiting for the answer to my question."

I look at him, confused. His eyes are piercing blue, like he's trying to burrow into my thoughts. "What question?"

"How are you feeling about all this?" he repeats.

"Um . . . I just told you."

"No, you told me what you're *thinking* about all this. How do you feel?"

I give him a sideways glance. "That's a very shrink-y thing to ask."

"It's a very writer-y thing, too, I guess." He takes another sip of tea. "And stop dodging the question."

Scout gets up from her mattress across the room and ambles over; Luke gently helps her onto the bed between us, and she rests her head in his lap.

I pet her absently as I consider. "Honestly? I'm fine. I mean, I'm hurt by what she said, but this whole thing with Hillary doesn't change anything—the camp is still closing."

As I say the words, my throat tightens up. *It's really, truly closing.* For good.

Luke shakes his head like he's disappointed in me. "Still dodging."

I exhale in frustration. "What do you want me to say, Luke?"

"Why does this camp mean so much to you?"

That's easy. "Because it's been part of my life for more than twenty years. It's my career—the only job I've ever had."

"Okay, but *why*, Jessie. Why did you keep coming back here? Why have you made it your career?"

His voice is gentle, prodding me to dig deeper. I lean against the pillows, look up at the rough wood ceiling. As an added benefit, I don't have to look at Luke, at those distracting blue eyes.

Scout nudges my hand with her wet nose, reminding me to keep petting her, so I do.

"This place has always felt like home to me," I say. "My parents divorced when I was tiny, and they split custody, so I was constantly going back and forth between their houses. It was . . . alienating, I guess? I didn't have a place that felt like *mine*. Not until I came here."

"That must have been difficult, bouncing between two homes."

I wave a hand, because "difficult" feels like an exaggeration. "It was challenging, sure. But I have a good relationship with my parents, with my stepparents and my half siblings. Overall it was fine."

"Fine," he repeats.

"Yes. And my summers at camp were good for all of us. My parents got to focus on their own children, take vacations together—"

"Their *own* children?" He sounds mildly appalled.

"No, it's—" I shake my head, flustered. "I mean their kids with their spouse, that's all. I can't blame them for wanting time with their family."

"They'd go on vacations without you?"

"Well, yes!" I say, indignant. Is he not paying attention? "I was at camp. I *wanted* to be at camp."

"Because it was the only place that was yours."

I roll my eyes. "You make it sound like I had a terrible childhood. It was fine."

"You say that a lot."

"What?"

"'Fine.'"

"Because it *was*! I didn't want to go to Disney with my little half siblings when I was fifteen years old!"

But even as I say this, I think of other vacations I missed: the time my dad took his family to Yellowstone, where they saw bison and moose and Old Faithful; the time my mom and Mitch took their kids to New York and saw five different Broadway shows. I remember seeing pictures, hearing them talk about their experiences, and feeling like such an outsider.

But did I tell them that? Of course not. I immediately started talking about all the fun things I did at camp, trying to convince them I'd had an even *better* time.

Or maybe trying to convince myself.

"Okay," Luke says, like he doesn't believe me but isn't going to argue. "But you said everything that happened with Hillary years ago was 'fine,' too. I have a hard time believing that."

Tears prickle my eyes, and I'm grateful for the solid warmth of Scout's back against my leg, her soft fur between my fingers.

"Your best friend," Luke says, "the person you felt closer to than your own biological family, chose to take that internship instead of coming back to camp with you. That must have been crushing."

My chest tightens, and I give a tiny shrug.

"It must have felt like you were losing the only real family you had. Like she was rejecting this world that meant so much to you."

My eyes well with tears, blurring the ceiling above me.

"When you overheard Hillary," Luke says, "I imagine it

brought up all those old feelings. Like she's still rejecting what matters most to you. Like she's rejecting *you*." He shifts his weight, and the bed squeaks. "Am I getting close?"

I can't meet his eyes. It's taking all my strength to contain my emotions, so I nod.

He exhales. "Have you told her any of this?"

"Of course not."

"Why not?"

"Because she's not responsible for my feelings."

"True."

"So what's the point of telling her?"

"So she can understand how you feel. Someone who cares about you would want to know."

I jolt upright. "How is talking about this with her going to make things better? The property is being sold. Facts don't change just because I have feelings."

"Fair enough," he says. He's remarkably unshaken by all this emotional energy I'm pouring into the air. "But you still haven't answered my question."

I exhale and shake my head; it's easier to pretend to be exasperated than to be vulnerable. I haven't allowed myself to examine my feelings in so, so long. I sealed them in that metaphorical box in my mind and shoved it in a corner and tried to forget about it.

But he's right; the emotions are still there. Ignoring them hasn't made them disappear.

Luke sets down his mug. In a quiet voice, he says, "Jess."

Goose bumps rise on my skin. My name in his mouth feels almost intimate, like he's telling me a secret—or asking for one of mine.

"I guess I feel . . ." My throat tightens, and it takes all my effort to whisper the next word. "Betrayed."

He nods, like he's encouraging me to go on.

"Abandoned," I whisper.

He nods again.

"Rejected." My voice gets louder, emotion rushing over me in waves. "Like she never cared as much about me as I did about her. Like she never loved this camp like I do. If she did, she wouldn't be in such a hurry to leave. Which makes sense—she has to get back to her real life. Once this place is history, she'll still have that life. But me?" I swallow. "I won't know who I am anymore."

"And how does that make you feel?" His voice is gentle.

"Sad." My voice breaks. "I'm so sad, Luke."

"Of course you are."

His words feel like permission. I rest my head on his shoulder. Luke sits with me, his cheek resting on my head, as I close my eyes and cry.

Hillary's face appears in my mind, her shocked expression when I agreed that she should leave. I wonder if she regrets coming here, wasting her summer on something that doesn't really matter.

I wonder what she's doing right now, if she's somewhere crying, too.

Tomorrow morning, I promise myself, I'll find her. At the very least, we can talk like adults before she leaves.

I sit up, wiping my eyes. "Sorry for getting your shirt wet," I say, motioning to Luke's damp shoulder.

"I don't mind."

I glance at my watch; it's nearly four, and I spring to my

feet. "I have so much to do for the events tonight. Are you coming to the canoe parade?"

He pushes himself to standing. "No, I need to get packed. I'm leaving early tomorrow morning."

I turn sharply. "What?"

"I need to go to New York and meet with my editor."

"But you're coming back?" I blurt, trying not to betray how sad I would be if he didn't.

"I'm coming back." One corner of his lips twitches upward.

"When?"

"On Sunday. It's a quick trip so I can meet her for lunch. You can handle two days without me."

I nod, surprised at how relieved I am to hear this. "What are you doing with Scout?"

"Boarding her at a place in North Fork."

"Where?"

"Uh, it's called Sweet Suzy's—"

"Dog Motel?" I finish, and he nods. "She can't stay there."

His eyes narrow. "Why?"

"Sweet Suzy is a nutjob. Whenever she takes the dogs on walks, at least a couple get loose and run wild through the streets. Plus, she has a *really* hyperactive husky mix that tries to mate with all the female dogs."

"Scout is fixed."

"She's a senior citizen! You can't put her through that indignity."

Luke purses his lips, peering at me. "Did you just volunteer to watch my dog?"

"No, you should take her *with* you."

"You want me to put a senior citizen in the cargo hold of a plane?" He raises an eyebrow. "Besides, the hotel I'm staying at isn't dog friendly."

"This camp wasn't dog friendly either, and that didn't stop you," I say. Then, remembering the address on his registration form: "Wait—don't you live in New York?"

"Not anymore."

"Where do you live?"

"Right now? Here."

I'm about to fire back a sarcastic retort, but something dark flickers across Luke's face. Then, just as quickly, it's gone. He clears his throat.

"I guess I'll have to take my thirteen-year-old arthritic golden retriever to Sweet Suzy's and hope she isn't too traumatized."

I sigh. "Okay, fine. I'll watch her."

He half smiles, and I can't help the burst of elation I feel.

Luke says he'll bring Scout over to my cabin early tomorrow morning and give me the information about her schedule, feeding, and medications. Then he walks me to the door, and I step out into the sunlight.

I turn back to see Luke leaning against the doorframe, watching me, an unreadable expression on his face. I have a sudden urge to move closer, to put myself into his space and see how he'd react.

Instead, I take a small step away.

"Um—thanks for the tea," I say. "And thanks for listening, Luke."

He nods. "Thanks for watching my dog, Jess."

Just like before, the shortened version of my name feels

intimate. I flash back to the memory of being in the water, his arms around me, his voice in my ear. *I got ya. You're safe.*

That's how it felt, talking with him. Safe. Like he was holding me, gently bringing me to shore, warming me from the inside out.

I want to put my arms around him. I want to lean into the crook of his neck and breathe him in. I want to stay.

But then I shake myself. And give him a small wave before heading down the stairs.

seventeen

Hillary

"I'm going home," I tell Cooper. We're in the kitchen, tucked into the corner by the walk-in cooler. Dinner is starting in fifteen minutes, so everyone is too busy to notice or care what we're doing.

Not that it matters anymore.

I choke back a sob and curse myself for listening to my stupid sentimental heart. Nostalgia is about looking back, not literally *going* back. My dad and Aaron were right. It was crazy for me to come here, to put my entire life on hold and walk away from everything I've worked so hard for. If I'd stayed home or just come for a weeklong session like a normal person, Jessie wouldn't have gotten her hopes up. And I wouldn't have let her down. Again.

"What are you talking about?" Cooper asks, tilting my chin up so I'm looking at him. There's concern in his gray eyes, and I turn away. It hurts too much.

"Jessie wants me to go," I say. "I'll be on one of the buses this Sunday."

"Chef! Where do you want the bacon?"

"Give me a second," Cooper shouts, then turns back to me.

179

"Fire's ready!" another employee yells, and Cooper hisses out a breath.

"It's okay, go," I say, even though I desperately want him to stay. "I'm not leaving today."

"We'll fix this," he says, giving me a kiss on the forehead before getting back to work.

Half an hour later, I'm sitting alone in a shady spot at the edge of the lawn, away from the bustle of activity. It's just me, my feelings, and my plate, loaded with the elevated BBQ fare Cooper and his team made.

If only I hadn't lost my appetite.

Everything looks delicious: a blue-cheese-stuffed turkey burger, champagne-Dijon-mustard potato salad, Chinese coleslaw, and a watermelon-feta salad.

The feta makes me think of Aaron. It's hard to fathom that I was considering—no, planning—a future with him. On paper, he's everything I thought I wanted. Now, I want to crumple up that paper and throw it in the trash. Instead of making my heart grow fonder, this distance has made my head grow clearer. And it's telling me that my heart was never really in it with Aaron at all.

My stomach rumbles, but not from hunger. It feels like an engine revving up, the kick in the butt I need to end things, to make our break permanent. Just because I'm going home doesn't mean I'm going back to him.

I reach for my phone, which is burning a hole in my pocket. I had it on me today so I could take pictures of the flags for the parade. Of course, it's useless out here. I glance longingly in the direction of Jessie's cabin. I haven't seen her since she stormed out of her office. Now I imagine casually walking in as if nothing's happened between us, all, "Hey, boss, mind if I use the Wi-Fi so I can unceremoniously end a second relationship today?"

But even as I laugh at the implausibility, I wonder: does the signal reach outside her cabin walls?

It's worth a shot. I pick up my plate and make my way over, keeping my head down lest anyone try and make small talk. I sneak around the corner to the far side of the cabin. Her bedroom is on the other side of the wall.

Taking out my phone, I suck in a big breath, hoping for a signal. All I need is one bar.

There's nothing.

My heart deflates—until I remember a trick Dot shared the last time I had trouble connecting. I switch airplane mode on, then off, and watch the spinning wheel, holding my breath for good luck. When the tiny single line pops up, I exhale in relief and type out a quick text to Aaron before the signal drops.

> Hey. I know we said this break was temporary, but I think it's time we call things quits. Service out here is awful, but we can talk when I'm back home in a few weeks.

He doesn't need to know I'll actually be back in two days.

I hit send and the message pops up in a blue bubble, the word "Delivered" beneath it.

With that over and done with, I slip my phone back in my pocket and look down at my plate. I'm still not hungry, but if I don't eat now, I'll be starving later. I'm about to take a bite of the burger when my phone vibrates in my pocket.

I jump, the once familiar feeling taking me by surprise. I hesitate, considering what his response might be. We were together for two years; Aaron made it clear he was planning to propose. But he also wanted to take the summer off to sleep his way around Chicago.

I could imagine a world where he responds with a passionate plea for a second chance, unwilling to let the boss's daughter go. But I can also picture a response fueled by logic, agreeing it's best for us to part amicably. I take a deep breath and reach for my phone, hoping for the latter.

It's not that. It's better. Or worse?

I laugh, and rub my eyes, making sure I'm seeing this correctly.

His response: a thumbs-up.

Any glimmer of guilt I felt for ending a two-year relationship over text disappears. I switch my phone back to airplane mode and take a bite of my burger. It tastes like freedom.

After I finish eating, I rush down to the dock to help Zac and Zoey get the canoes and kayaks lined up for the parade. The work is hard; it's physical, and I understand how Zac stays so buff while eating so much. As an added bonus, staying busy helps keep my mind off of everything with Jessie.

Mostly.

Cooper's been busy, too, getting everything cleaned up both outside and in the kitchen. He doesn't get down to the lake until the parade is about to start, so we don't have time to talk before he climbs into the old wooden canoe we're stationed in.

The two of us bob in the water, watching Jessie, who's standing at the end of the dock. She looks so pulled together with her perfectly plaited braids and crisp uniform. No one would guess she's had her heart broken twice today—once by the Valentines, and once by me.

"Good evening, Camp Chickawah!" she says into her megaphone.

It's dusk, and the sky looks like a palette with spilled paint—pink and blue and orange and yellow.

"It is my honor, as your camp director and the grand marshal of this parade, to say . . ." She lowers the megaphone and looks out at the campers lined up in their canoes, their paddles resting on their laps.

I try to imagine what she's seeing; if she sees the adults these campers are today, or the children they used to be. Or if she's thinking about all those years when we were the ones sitting in canoes, full of hope and optimism, believing that this camp and our friendship would last forever.

Jessie clears her throat and continues, "Let freedom ring—and the parade begin!"

The campers hoot and holler, their voices echoing off the water. Jessie climbs into her canoe at the front of the line with Zac and Zoey. Someone hits play on an Americana playlist and Springsteen's voice booms out from the wireless speaker.

One by one, the canoes push off, following the path along the shore before going past the swimming platform, almost to the other side of the lake. Cooper and I are in the last one, bringing up the rear and making sure no one strays off course as the sun goes down.

He's doing most of the work, expertly moving the paddle

from side to side, sluicing it through the water. Lee Greenwood's "God Bless the USA" starts, and I close my eyes. There's a gentle breeze, and I try to memorize this moment so I'll always remember how good it felt to belong to this place, this tradition.

A loud boom shakes me out of my reverie, and I look up at the explosion of light and color filling the dark sky. Zac has been working all week to put together a "bonza" fireworks show, and one of the guys from Cooper's staff is setting them off from the swimming platform.

I've seen plenty of fireworks before, of course, but there's something mesmerizing about watching them on the lake. Everything happening in the sky is reflected in the water, as if the fireworks are moving in reverse, falling up, toward me. It's like living in a mirrored world, more vivid and alive than the everyday one.

The fireworks come faster and faster: white spidery ones that pop like confetti, sparkles falling like rain; then reds and blues, pinks and greens. The dark sky is alive with color, and even though there's a smile on my face, a salty tear slides down my cheek.

After the last firework goes off, gray clouds streak the night sky. They're all that's left, a ghost of the celebration, reluctant to let go. Not unlike me.

Cooper takes his time paddling back to shore. It's just the two of us out on the water now, and I'm grateful he doesn't try to fill the space with words. Between the still of the night and the gentle rocking of the old canoe, any residual tension in my shoulders dissipates. I'm sure the captain of this rusty bucket ship has something to do with it, too.

"Hands and feet inside the vessel," he says, mocking Zac's safety lecture at the start of the canoe parade, Aussie accent and all.

I look up and see we're almost back at the dock. Cooper guides us in for a smooth landing, then hops out and ties a rope around the cleat before helping me up. I keep hold of his hand, even after my feet are safely grounded on the dock.

It's silly, but I love holding his hand, the way it feels to have his fingers laced through mine. Steady and secure. There's so much I like about this man, and I hate that I've held myself back. We haven't even slept together.

"You probably should've picked someone else to have a summer fling with," I tell him.

"No way," he says, pulling me in for a hug. "The point was to have fun—and I definitely had fun. Did you?"

I nod, because I did. But having fun and *being* fun are two different things.

Aaron's face flashes in my mind, but I push it away. He doesn't deserve more of my mental real estate. Not anymore.

"I broke up with Aaron today," I tell Cooper.

"Oh," he says, his brow furrowing.

"Made the break permanent," I explain.

Cooper nods, and I wish I could reach into his head to see what he's thinking. If it matters to him. It probably doesn't, since this is just a fling. But it matters to me, and I realize that, consciously or unconsciously, I was letting Aaron stop me from being all in with Cooper.

But Aaron's a nonissue now, and it's time I stop listening to my head and start following my heart. Without another thought, I lunge for Cooper, kissing him like there's nothing holding me back. The butterflies in my belly flutter to life as our tongues dance. I have never felt more alive. I press my body flush against his and swivel my hips ever so slightly, desperate for friction. He's already hard, and I have a sudden urge not to let his erection go to waste.

"Let's get out of here," I say.

"What do you have in mind?" he asks, his voice low and rumbly.

Cooper has been so respectful with my boundaries, agreeing to take things slow. But it's time to hit the gas. I look up at him, at his beautiful gray eyes full of desire. For me.

I take a deep breath, lower my voice to a whisper, and, as seductively as I can muster, tell him exactly what I want.

"I want you to fuck me."

Cooper barks out a laugh, and I recoil.

"Forget it," I say, pushing past him.

"No, wait," he says, grabbing my hand and pulling me back. "You just caught me off guard—those are the last words I expected from your prim and proper mouth."

He's got a point. My father taught me from a young age that cursing wasn't ladylike. He wanted his daughter to be a lady, and I wanted to make him happy, so I kept my language clean.

But right now, my thoughts are very not clean.

"Okay, so I don't curse a lot," I admit. "But 'sex' sounds so . . . clinical. And 'making love' is too emotional for a summer fling. The f-word felt more appropriate."

"I follow your logic," Cooper says, wrapping one of my curls around his finger.

"Great," I say. "So, do you want to?"

"Do I want to . . ."

He's smiling, and I know I'm the only one who is uncomfortable with this conversation. But I'm also the one who started it. So I let out an exaggerated sigh and put it all out there.

"Do you want to fuck me?"

"Fuck yeah, I do," Cooper says. "Let's go."

He takes my hand, and I don't even care that we're breaking a rule by running on the dock. He starts up the path toward the Lodge, but I pull him back.

"Not there," I say. I know how thin the walls are, and I don't want to hold back tonight.

"Got another idea?" he asks, his voice thick with desire and the tiniest hint of impatience.

We spot the ironically named Yacht Club at the same time and make a run for the wooden shanty, where the life jackets, oars, and other water gear are stored.

Inside, the light is on, a single bulb hanging from a wire. It casts long shadows around the room, which in any other circumstances would give me the heebie-jeebies. But I'm too turned on to be scared.

Fully committed to our plan, I rush over to lock the door—and realize that the lock is on the other side; it's intended to keep people out, not in.

"Shit," I mutter.

"It's fine," Cooper murmurs behind me, taking my earlobe in his mouth, sucking gently. A moan bubbles out of my throat, which is all the encouragement he needs. He turns me so my back is against the door and his lips are on mine. His kiss is urgent, hungry. As he makes my mouth his, I go slack in his arms, my hands splayed on his chest. I can feel the rhythm of his heart, and I want to make it go even faster.

Slowly, I move my hands lower until I find the button of his shorts. It comes undone easily, and as they drop to his ankles, I drop down, too. I reach for his boxers, dragging my fingers lightly over the bulge of him.

Cooper bites his lower lip, and I smile up at him as I hook my thumbs inside his waistband. But before I can free him from the fabric prison of his boxers, he pulls me back up to my feet.

"Hold on," he says.

I take a step back, afraid I did something wrong. But he just smiles and says, "We've been following your rules for this fling, but I've got some of my own. And the number one rule is—"

"Honesty," I say, getting restless. "You already told me."

"That's the number two rule," Cooper says. "The number one rule is: ladies first."

Oh. *Oh.*

Cooper swoops me up and into his arms, cupping my butt with his big, strong hands. I wrap my legs around his waist, heat rushing to my core. He walks us toward the workbench at the far end of the room, moving debris away with one hand while he supports me with the other.

Once a space is clear, he sets me down gently. I glance toward the unlocked door, shocked—and a little impressed— that I'm actually going through with this.

Cooper must read the anxiety on my face, because he says, "You're in control, remember? Nothing happens unless you want it."

"I want it," I say immediately. "I want all of it."

His lips quirk in a tiny, pleased grin. "Well then. I've got you."

For some crazy reason, I believe him. More than that, I trust him.

Cooper steps between my legs and kisses me, more gently than before. This is good; this I know. As his tongue teases mine, his hands slip under the back of my shirt, lifting it up and over my head.

He looks down, admiring me.

"You are so beautiful," he says, moving his lips to my shoulder. He playfully bites down, and I gasp as his fingers unhook the back of my bra. It falls to the table, and he turns his attention to my breasts, taking one nipple in his mouth, swirling his tongue around it while cupping my other breast with his hand. "I've been wanting to do this since that first day. Your towel . . ."

He switches sides, and I close my eyes, savoring the sensation of his wet mouth and persistent tongue as I run my fingers through the soft waves of his hair. When I'm somewhere between satiated and frustrated, desperate for more, Cooper drops lower, trailing kisses down my belly while his fingers undo my shorts. They come off, followed by my underwear.

"Scootch forward," he says, and I obey. I'll do anything this man asks me to do.

Cooper slides me forward a little more and I grimace, hoping the wood under my bare butt doesn't give me splinters. He hooks one of my legs over his shoulder, then kisses the inside of my thigh. I hum with pleasure as he gets closer to the spot where I want him.

Then he's there. I'm there. On the edge. Cooper works magic with his tongue as he slips a finger inside me. *Holy hell.*

"Do you like that?" he asks in a husky whisper.

"I like it," I say through a moan. "I like it a lot." My hands fumble, searching for something to hold on to for fear of falling off the workbench. I grasp on to what turns out to be a life jacket, for all the good that does me. I toss it to the side, aware that I'm drowning in pleasure.

Another moan escapes my lips, and Cooper looks up from between my legs, his eyebrows lifting in appreciation of my appreciation.

"Don't stop," I plead. He listens, sliding another finger inside me, working in tandem with his tongue as the tension builds until—fireworks. I don't just see them; I am them. I cry out, a puddle of nonwords, noises, moans. Sounds I've heard while watching porn with Aaron or listening to Zac and Zoey on the other side of the wall; sounds I've never heard coming from my own mouth.

It's more electrifying than anything I've ever felt, but it's still not enough.

"Do you have a condom?" I ask. I have a few of the latex-free ones up in my room, but that feels miles away. Plus, I'm pretty sure my legs have turned to jelly.

He stands, his hair wild and his expression dazed. "A condom? Here in the boat shack?"

"You didn't stash them everywhere around camp in case we might need one?"

"I should have, obviously," he says, adjusting himself. "I've got plenty up in my room—wait here, and I'll—"

"No!" I shout, startling him. "I'm not staying in here alone. It's creepy."

"Then come with me," he says. "We'll be fast."

I hop off the bench and quickly get dressed, stuffing my underwear in the pocket of my shorts. It'll just slow us down later.

I take Cooper's hand and we stumble out into the darkness, both of us breathless and rushing, desperate to finish what we've started.

When we reach the Lodge, I wait outside while Cooper runs in to get what we need—I told him to grab the ones in the top drawer of my dresser. I bounce anxiously on my toes until he returns, the pockets of his shorts bulging. We duck into the trees a few yards away, and he pulls me into his arms and kisses me. I'm clawing at his shirt, lifting it over his head while he pushes my back against a tree and runs his hand up my shirt, unclasping my bra for the second time tonight.

I'm reaching down to undo his shorts when a sound stops me—a group of campers tromping through the woods toward us, singing "Linger" in a three-part harmony I'd admire under any other circumstance.

Alarmed, I look at Cooper.

"Kitchen," he says, grabbing my hand.

And we're off, running down the dark path toward the dining hall, his shorts undone, my bra unclasped inside my tie-dyed Camp Chickawah T-shirt. We burst through the doors—the kitchen is empty and dark, the only light the glowing numbers on the twin industrial ovens. I'm not sure where we're going to do this, but Cooper leads me to the large, movable island with the stainless-steel top and locks the wheels.

"Condom," I exhale.

He pulls half a dozen packages out of his pockets and tosses them on the surface. "I've got one of every kind we bought," he says, looking proud of himself.

"Latex-free?" I say, hopeful.

He flips through the foil packets. "Bingo."

"Hurry," I beg, slipping my shirt over my head. I let my bra fall to the floor as I slip out of my shorts.

"Hop up here," he says, patting the counter, then tugging off his shirt. The stainless steel cools my burning skin, and I watch hungrily as Cooper (finally!) takes off his shorts, removes his boxers, and slides the condom on. He's not as buff as in the photo spread, but I like this even better, broad shoulders and solid chest but soft in all the right places. And hard in the right ones, too. He steps between my open legs and kisses me like we've got all the time in the world.

And maybe we do, but I want him now. I slide forward, desperate to feel his length inside me. The counter is the perfect height, and it feels like it was made for this, made for us. I rest my hand on Cooper's shoulder for balance and wrap one leg around his waist, then the other.

He reaches a hand down, guiding his shaft to where I'm wet and ready. He teases me with the tip, slipping it in and out, going a little deeper each time. I rock my hips toward him, making a noise that's somewhere between a growl and a moan. Cooper laughs, but I don't care. I'm more comfortable in this moment than I've ever been the first time with someone new. Because it's him. It's . . .

"Wait!"

Cooper startles, pulling back. The movement is so quick, I lose my balance and slip off the counter, thankfully landing on my feet.

"Did I hurt you?" he asks.

"No," I say, embarrassed by my outburst. "It's just . . . I don't know your first name."

"Oh. Well, it's Ben."

"Ben," I say, testing out the feel of his name. "Or Benjamin?"

"Cooper," he says, stepping back toward me. "Now, you good?"

I nod, and he presses me against the counter, lifting my leg and hooking it around his waist. The time for teasing is over, and he pushes inside, stretching and filling me in the best possible way. He rolls his hips, slowly at first, groaning about how good I feel. I arch toward him, urging him on, matching him thrust for thrust.

When he's as deep as he can go in this position, he lifts me up, setting me on the counter where we started. I lean back, my hands splayed on the cool steel for support. With this new angle, his strokes are longer, reaching new depths, and I cry out as he fucks me as promised. The locked wheels of the counter squeak against the floor, moving us inch by inch across the kitchen.

Cooper's gray eyes, intense in the dark, lock onto mine, and warmth pools in my lower belly. I'm dangerously close to unraveling when he leans down and slips my nipple between his teeth, tugging gently on one, then the other. I let out a guttural moan and pray no one shows up hoping for a midnight snack.

Just the mere thought of a snack makes my stomach sound its alarm, a rumbling growl.

"You hungry?" Cooper asks, a laugh in his voice.

"Only for you," I say, wrapping my legs around his waist and pulling him closer. He leans toward me, and I meet him halfway so we're chest to chest, our skin slick with sweat and our breath coming fast. I reach my hand down between us to apply pressure where I need it, and my body clenches around him as the intensity builds and builds until I finally combust.

I attempt to silence myself by biting down on his shoulder, but he doesn't stop thrusting and I can't stop my cries from coming, rolling with waves of pleasure as we fall apart together.

"Is that what you wanted?" he whispers into my neck.

"And then some," I say, allowing myself to relax into him.

Once we catch our breath, I pull on my underwear and T-shirt, he pulls on his boxers, and we retreat to clean up in our separate bathrooms—me to the girls', him to the boys'—then meet back in the kitchen.

I stop in the doorway, admiring the sight of Cooper's backside, illuminated in the light of the open fridge. "What are you doing?" I ask.

"Feeding you," he says, taking out last night's spaghetti and meatballs. "I'll heat this up—"

"No!" I blurt, then flush. "I mean, can we have it cold?"

"That's right, your weird leftover fetish." He shrugs and sighs. "Fine, but only because I'm still not thinking straight after what we just did."

"If you really want the full experience, we'll forgo the plates and eat right out of the Tupperware."

"You're a heathen, Hillary Goldberg," Cooper says. "But I'm in."

We sit on top of what I'll forever consider "our counter," two forks and the open container between us.

"Isn't it good?" I ask, after taking a big bite and swallowing.

"I'm not about to yuck your yum."

I laugh. "Do you remember what my cabin used to call spaghetti and meatballs when we were teenagers?" He shakes his head. "Noods," I say, pointing to a noodle, "and balls."

"Noods and balls?" he repeats, choking on a laugh.

"Yup. And speaking of balls," I say, glancing down at his package. "Can we do that again for dessert?"

"We can do that anytime, anywhere you want," he says, giving me a sweet kiss. I let out a satisfied sigh, happier than I can ever remember being. We could've been doing this for the last three weeks!

I'm going to do my damndest to make up for the time we lost, getting as much of him as I can until camp is over.

Which, for me, is in two days.

"Hey," Cooper says, turning my face toward his. "What's wrong?"

"I'm just so happy," I tell him. "And so incredibly sad."

He slips an arm around my waist, and I lean into the crook of his neck.

"I'm sad you're leaving, too," he says, kissing the top of my head.

"It's not just that. I'm sad that we're losing Camp Chickawah, that I couldn't save it."

"If I had a million dollars," he says, "I'd buy the property from the Valentines and decree that the land only be used for a camp from now until the end of time."

"More like a hundred million dollars," I say, exaggerating slightly.

"If a hundred former campers each had a million bucks, we could buy it."

I laugh and up the ante. "Or if a million former campers each threw in a hundred bucks."

Cooper sits up straighter. "Hang on—the sale's not final yet, is it?"

I shake my head and twirl cold spaghetti around my fork. "No, but it doesn't matter since I don't have millions of dollars lying around. Do you?"

"No," he says. "But how many adult campers are coming through here this summer?"

I do a quick calculation in my head: about three hundred campers a week for eight weeks . . . "More than two thousand."

Cooper's eyes light up. "There's this restaurant in Boston," he says. "It's one of the oldest in the city, and the family couldn't afford to keep it running. The community didn't want to let it go, so a bunch of locals invested."

"A co-op." As I speak, I feel that tingle in my belly, the one that comes along with an idea—*the* idea—that could save a business.

Cooper nods. "Exactly."

"Benjamin Cooper, you are brilliant!" I drop my fork and bring my hands up to either side of his face, kiss his smiling lips, then hop off the counter. "I'm going to find Jessie."

"Can't it wait till morning?"

As much as I'd love to sneak back up to his room at the Lodge and spend the rest of the night wrapped in his arms, rules are rules. No sleepovers. And I can't wait to talk to Jessie.

I have to tell her now.

Cooper must see this written all over my face, because he sighs and stands, putting his feet on the floor. "Hand me my shorts," he says. "We're going to sanitize this counter real quick, and then I'm going with you."

eighteen

Jessie

I wake in the dark to a knock on my door. It's been so long since this happened that it takes a moment to orient myself. Maybe I dreamed the knock? Maybe I'm nostalgic for the old days, when people needed me in the night. When I knew my role.

On my nightstand sits a copy of Luke's first novel—I found it in the camp library. It's a YA dystopian, with all the elements we both loved as teenagers: adventure, political intrigue, a love triangle. I'm six chapters in and would have read more, but I was so exhausted and sad after the canoe parade that I passed out.

I'm drifting off again when the knock repeats, then a voice: "Jessie?"

Shaking myself, I step out of bed and stumble to the door. The night is so dark and I'm so tired, it takes a moment for everything to sink in.

First, I notice something strung across my porch, through the trees, and around my cabin: white streamers, fluttering in the breeze. Toilet paper. Someone pranked me.

My heart sinks—I'm too tired for this shit.

Then I see two people in the darkness, five feet from my door.

"Hillary?" I say, shocked. "Cooper? What are you . . ."

I look at the toilet paper, and it clicks. All the emotions I've been struggling to contain come bubbling up, all at once. "Why would you do this to me? It's not enough to blame me for losing my favorite place in the world? You have to pull a stupid prank on me, too?"

I move to close the door, but Hillary takes a step forward, looking alarmed.

"Jessie, wait—we didn't TP you. This was already here."

I pause. "You didn't?"

"Of course not," Cooper says. He's holding his cap in his hands, like he's beseeching me.

"What do you want, then?" My heart aches; just yesterday, she implied that I've run this place into the ground.

"We have a new idea," she says. "An idea to save the camp."

I squint at her. "You . . . what?"

"Can I come in? I'll explain everything."

I'm not sure I can trust her. But curiosity wins out, and I open the door. "Fine."

In the little sitting room off my bedroom, I turn on a lamp. Cooper leaves, saying he wants to give us a chance to talk, and I wish he'd stayed as a buffer. The hurt from Hillary's words feels like a raw, tangled coil in my stomach. She has on a tie-dyed Camp Chickawah shirt, and the immature, petty side of me wants to tell her to take it off. That she doesn't deserve to wear it anymore.

"I'm so sorry about what I said," Hillary says. Her face is pale and earnest. "That's the first thing I want—"

"It's fine," I cut in, not because it's true, but because I don't want to hear apologies from her. There's no point anymore.

"It's not," she says. "I was overwhelmed and sad, and I was venting to Cooper, but I went overboard and said some things I didn't mean."

I appreciate the apology, but my frustration bubbles over. "You made it sound like it's my fault this camp is failing! I've done my best, Hill. Jack Valentine has held the purse strings ever since Nathaniel and Lola passed away—it's not like I had the freedom to make any big changes."

"I know," she says. "I'm sorry, and I know how much this place means to you—"

"You said I was too *emotionally invested*," I say, my throat tightening.

Her eyes fill with regret. "Only because I've spent the last twelve years trying to *never* get emotionally invested in anything—my dad raised me to believe that's a weakness." She shakes her head. "But honestly? I envy you."

"Me?"

"You've always known exactly what you want to do, who you want to be, and you made it happen. Meanwhile, I've always done what was expected of me." She runs a hand through her hair, then glances up at me. "Like when I bailed on our plan to be counselors together."

The old feelings—resentment, confusion, despair—are pummeling me, and I automatically try to stuff them down. But then I remember my conversation with Luke.

She's leaving anyway. How can it hurt to be honest with her?

"That broke my heart, Hill." My voice sounds tiny, mournful. "It wasn't the same without you."

Her face softens. "I know. I spent the whole summer wishing I was here."

"Then why did you take that internship?"

"My dad said it was time to stop 'playing' and start focusing on my future. I couldn't handle disappointing him." She winces. "Only, I ended up disappointing you. And myself, too."

The tightness in my stomach eases, just a fraction. "It felt like you never cared about me as much as I cared about you."

"I cared about you so much. I've never had a friend like you, Jessie. Not before and not since."

"So why didn't you reach out?" My voice is rough; this part is the hardest to say. Remembering how I kept expecting her to email or call—maybe even show up one day in person to explain. But she never did. As if I didn't matter to her. As if all our memories, our entire friendship since we were eight years old, meant nothing. I'd never felt so abandoned.

"I—" She shrugs helplessly. "I thought about calling you, but the summer started, and you were at camp, so I thought about writing you a letter, but then I got busy with the internship, and time kept passing . . ." She looks down at her lap, shakes her head. "I was ashamed of myself, Jessie. I didn't think you'd forgive me."

"I would have," I say immediately. "Even if we weren't counselors together, we didn't have to stop being *friends*. But you vanished from my life, Hilly! I didn't know how to handle that."

She looks up, her cheeks flushed with those familiar red

patches. "I messed up. I know I did. But all you said in your reply was 'It's fine.' What was I supposed to do with that? I didn't know if you even wanted to hear from me again." Eyes fixed on mine, she says, "You could have reached out, too."

The words hit me in the stomach, hard.

All these years, I've blamed her—and yes, she was the one who backed out on our plans—but she's right. Luke's called me out on my habit of saying "It's fine" instead of communicating.

"I wish I had," I say. "I'm sorry."

She nods, like she appreciates that, and silence descends between us.

Then I remember her earlier words. "Wait—you have an idea to save the camp?"

She nods eagerly. "Yes!"

"That's not possible—Jack's set on selling it."

"So we buy the camp ourselves."

I tilt my head. No way I heard that correctly. "What are you talking about?"

"What if I help you clean up the toilet paper outside while I explain?"

I'm still confused, and definitely not optimistic, but I'm not ready for Hillary to leave yet, either. We have more to talk about—and not just this idea Hillary has. We owe it to ourselves, to our history, to work through our past together.

"Sure. That would be great."

We head out, but Hillary stops before she leaves the room. "You still have this?"

She's pointing at the hooks I've stuck in the wall to hang my necklaces: the one my mom gave me when I graduated high school; the one I inherited from my grandmother when she passed away.

And the half of the friendship heart that Hillary gave me when we were twelve. One of those "Best Friends Forever" necklaces every teenage girl seems to have. I've thought about throwing it out so many times, but something stopped me.

Maybe because deep down, I hoped I'd have another chance.

"Yes, I kept it," I say, feeling awkward. "Isn't that what forever means?"

Hillary smiles, tentatively. "Forever and ever and ever."

We head outside, each with a garbage bag. The sky is cloudy—no moon, no stars—and my cabin is surrounded by tall trees and dense underbrush; the only light is the golden glow from my porch. Streamers of toilet paper, caught in the branches, flutter in the breeze. Little white flags of surrender.

As we start cleaning, I glance over at Hillary. Her hair is up in a messy bun, her eyes lit with a familiar fire. She always looked like this when she was excited to start a new craft project. Like her brain was overflowing with ideas.

"Okay," I say, "tell me about this plan you came up with."

She grins. "Have you ever heard of a co-op?"

nineteen

Hillary

It's Sunday night, and I'm still here.

And if that's not enough of a reason to celebrate, Cooper made one of my favorite camp meals: walking tacos. As thrilled as I am by the taco fixings and snack-sized bags of Fritos, I know it doesn't please him. He takes pride in cooking something special for our family dinners—but his attention was needed elsewhere today.

The moment the last bus drove away—the bus I was supposed to be on—Cooper, Jessie, and I hunkered down in the office. Luke's dog, Scout, was with us; she hasn't strayed from Jessie's side since Luke left.

Together, we went through all the paperwork Jessie could find related to the sale, did research on how much similar pieces of property in the area have sold for, and ran numbers to see how much we'd need to raise to make Jack Valentine a competitive offer he won't be able to refuse.

"Explain this one more time," Dot says now, looking up from her spot on the ground, where she's petting Scout. "I thought the Valentines already accepted an offer."

"They did," Cooper says. "But the sale isn't final yet—it's just under contract."

"Sales this big take time," I explain. "There are all sorts of things that have to happen, like escrow, due diligence, title documents, that sort of thing."

"It helps that Mary got Jack Valentine to agree to stall so the sale won't be final until the end of the summer," Jessie adds.

Dot turns to me, giving Scout one final pat before getting up. "You really think they'll agree to this hullabaloo?"

"I don't see why not," I say, trying to sound more confident than I am. "From everything I've heard, Jack Valentine is all about the money. It shouldn't matter where that money comes from. And if we play on Mary's sentimentality, hopefully she'll help convince her brother."

Dot mutters something about Jack that I can't make out, then scoops a spoonful of taco meat into her bag of Fritos. Once it's clear there are no more questions, Jessie fills everyone in on what else we found in the camp's historical paperwork.

My best friend looks effervescent, like the weight of the world has been lifted off her shoulders. I bet our conversation last night has something to do with it. Finally talking about some of the hurt we've been holding on to for the last decade helped me, too. Now that it's all out in the open, I hope we'll be able to move forward and heal.

"What now?" Zoey asks. "How can we help?"

"We're going to start by seeing if people are willing to put their money where their hearts are," Jessie says, glancing at me.

She wanted to make the Valentines an offer first thing tomorrow morning, but I convinced her we should make sure the interest was there first. We're talking about raising a few million dollars at least.

Not that I'm concerned. From what Jessie's said, the adult sessions this summer filled up almost instantly—I have no doubt those same campers will want to help save Camp Chickawah for future generations, for their children or grandchildren. Especially after revisiting that magic this summer.

"Jack and Mary are going to be here in a few weeks to walk through the property with the buyers," I tell the group. "We're going to invite them to come up the night before so they can be wined and dined by one of the hottest chefs in Boston."

The words are meant as a compliment, but they make Cooper wince. Again, I get the feeling there's more to the story of why he left such a lucrative job. And now that I'm staying put, I've got time to delve into the depths and figure out what wounds he's holding on to.

"While they're here," I continue, "we'll present them with the counteroffer and hope like hell they agree to pull out of the deal."

"I wish Nathaniel had pulled out the night that rat weasel was conceived," Dot mutters. I bark out a laugh, and Jessie rolls her eyes.

"Let's be grown-ups here," Jessie says, and I attempt to straighten my expression.

"So the Valentines can just . . ." Zoey hesitates. ". . . back out?"

"It's possible," I say. "There would be some penalties, but we'd cover those costs. We're counting on Mary, since Jack doesn't seem to have a sentimental bone in his body."

Dot grumbles to herself, something about Mary this time. There is no love lost between her and this generation of Valentines.

"What we're saying is, we've got a chance." Jessie's voice is bright, but I can tell there are nerves hiding under that relentless optimism.

The door opens then, and everyone turns to stare as Luke walks in, back from his trip to New York. It's not that he's here—he's become a fixture at our Sunday night dinners—it's that he looks so dapper, dressed in dark jeans, a button-down shirt, and a blazer, like a real-life author headed to a book reading at some fancy gentleman's club.

"Nice threads," Zac says as Luke approaches the table, going straight for Scout, who's asleep at Jessie's feet.

I've never seen Zac in anything but board shorts and a T-shirt, but his assessment of Luke's outfit is spot on—the jacket looks like something Aaron would wear, expensive and tailored to fit. Maybe we should hit Luke up to be the first donor to our co-op.

"Welcome back." Jessie slides over to make room for him. "Scout missed you."

As if on cue, the old dog lets out a loud fart, and everyone laughs.

"Really seems like it." Luke bends his head toward Jessie and whispers something that makes her smile shine even brighter. It's good to see her so happy. I hope Luke reciprocates her feelings. If anyone deserves some carefree camp fun, it's Jessie.

I blush at the memory of last night in the Arts and Crafts cabin—and earlier this afternoon in the walk-in pantry. As if Cooper knows exactly what I'm thinking, he places a hand on my thigh and gives it a squeeze. A flock of butterflies takes flight in my belly, and for the thousandth time today, I send a silent thank-you to Jessie for letting me stay.

"Dinner looks . . . interesting," Luke says as he surveys the table and all the empty bags of chips.

Cooper tenses beside me, but Jessie swoops in with an explanation. "There's a reason for that," she says, and fills Luke in on everything he missed.

"Wow," he says when she's finished.

"Wow, as in 'that sounds like an impossibly crazy plan'?"

Luke shakes his head. "No, wow, as in 'I think that sounds brilliant.'" Jessie glows at his praise, but then he asks, "Have you started work on the fundraising materials?" and just like that, her face falls.

"We haven't gotten that far yet," she says.

"I can help with any writing," he offers. "And maybe build a rudimentary website."

Jessie narrows her eyes. "You're in a weirdly helpful mood. Are you feeling okay? Did you hit your head in New York?"

"If my assistance is unwanted . . ." Luke says, acting like he's about to get up and leave.

Jessie grabs his arm and tugs him back down. "Of course it's wanted. You know how to make a website?"

It looks like Luke's smothering a smile. "Sure. The only problem would be the Internet access . . ."

"You can come to my cabin," Jessie offers, blushing as soon as the words leave her mouth. Everyone around the table chuckles—I'm not the only one who's picked up on the chemistry between them—but she quickly recovers. "To use the Internet."

"How fast can we start raising money?" Dot asks. "This next group of campers is mostly in their fifties, and I'd bet they have plenty of cash to burn."

Jessie nods and takes a deep breath. I have a feeling she's overwhelmed by all these plans. "We can talk about it, start laying the groundwork—and campers can make pledges if they're interested. But we have to figure out a few things before we can collect the money."

"Take too much time, and time will run out," Dot says, sounding like a fortune cookie.

"We'll start as soon as we can," Jessie says. "In the meantime, we've got to get ready for Color Wars this week."

With that, the conversation turns to what we're all here for: bringing our beloved camp memories to life.

If we're lucky, this won't be our last summer after all.

twenty

Jessie

A new set of campers has arrived, a group in their forties and fifties. We're all gathered in the dining hall and I'm doing my welcome speech—the schedule, the rules, check your crevices for ticks, where to buy booze and condoms.

But this time, there's something more.

"Finally," I say, "I have an interesting proposition. You know that the Camp Chickawah property is under contract to be sold—"

Someone boos loudly, and other people join in. Never takes long for these adult campers to regress and start acting like kids.

"I know, I know," I say, smiling. "But as a staff"—I motion behind me to Hillary, Cooper, Dot, Zac, and Zoey—"we have an idea. A way to save the camp. And we need your help."

"Tell us the plan!" someone shouts.

"Tell us! Tell us!" another table starts chanting, pounding their fists. More and more people join in, until the dining hall is full of thunderous noise.

"I'm getting there!" I shout, gesturing for quiet. "The idea is simple: form a cooperative business of former campers and staff and purchase the property ourselves. Every person who joins will have partial ownership and a stake in the camp."

I explain the details, using the talking points Luke put together for our website.

"Let's do it!" a camper shouts, and a bunch of others cheer.

"I'm in," a deep voice booms.

Others call out: "Me too!"

I glance at Hillary, whose eyes are bright with excitement. She's standing next to Cooper, and when she notices me looking, she takes a discreet step away—but not before I notice that their hands were touching, their fingers intertwined.

Hmm. What did Cooper tell me about the last person he dated? A waitress at his restaurant. She threw lobster bisque at him, something like that? I have no idea if he deserved it or not, and I can't imagine Hillary blowing up and hurling stuff, but any drama could be a huge problem for the rest of the summer.

Plus—and the surge of protectiveness surprises me—I might claw out Cooper's eyeballs if he hurts my friend.

Making a mental note to ask her about it later, I turn back to the campers. "Anyone interested, please come up and we'll talk details. And thank you!"

Within two days, we have over a hundred thousand dollars pledged. I'm having trouble believing it. But like Dot said, these campers seem to be at a stage in their careers and lives where they have extra money to invest. One, an attorney with a practice in Minneapolis, has offered to draft sample articles of incorporation. Two successful entrepreneurs volunteered to help Hillary with the business plan, and several others are interested in being on the steering committee.

I'm out on the lawn, talking with a group of campers about the co-op, when Dot comes up to me. She looks nervous, and my anxiety spikes. I haven't had to bring a single camper to the emergency room yet, which is unusual this far into the summer.

"Is something wrong?" I ask.

"Not with the campers," she says quickly; she knows where my mind is heading. "I . . . need to talk to you about something. Something personal."

My stomach clenches. "Okay, sure. Do you want to go somewhere private?"

She glances around; a group of campers is playing Frisbee on the lawn, but no one's close enough to hear. "This is fine. Listen, what you said during training week. About staff not getting involved . . . romantically."

"Oh!" I get it now. "You mean Hillary and Cooper? I know—I keep meaning to talk to her about that, but—"

"Not them. Me."

I stare at her for a beat. Dot's never been romantically involved with anyone as long as I've known her.

"Okay . . . tell me more."

"There's someone here this week that I . . ." She pauses. "Well, we—"

"A camper?"

She nods. "I know you said nothing should happen with staff and campers, and I didn't anticipate this, but—"

"It's fine," I say firmly. "I know I'm the director, but you have decades more experience than I do. I trust you implicitly." Her shoulders droop in relief, and I nudge her, grinning. "So, who's this lucky camper?"

She brightens, flashing me an unexpectedly sweet smile.

"Yvonne. Yvonne Schafer. We knew each other as teenagers here, but times were different back then, so . . . anyway. We've reconnected."

I call Yvonne to mind: warm brown skin, long gray braids. "She seems wonderful, Dot. I'm happy for you. And you know what Lola always said about camp love . . ."

"Yeah, yeah, don't get all sappy about it," Dot says, but she's smiling. "Yvonne's only here for the week. But I wanted to be honest with you. So you aren't surprised when you see us together."

Her voice softens on the last word, and it's so out of character for Dot that I impulsively pull her into a hug. When we pull away, I wipe a stray tear from my eye.

"Enough of that," she says, her voice mock-stern. "Back to work, boss."

I smile. "Back to work."

As I head to the campfire that evening—after a delicious meal of roasted salmon, freshly made bread, and sugar snap peas—I hear singing on the breeze. There's a new energy this week, a sense that we're all in this together, working to save Camp Chickawah. I've spent hours with Hillary, crafting emails to former campers about the co-op, including some with big connections they might leverage. Already, quite a few have responded that they're interested.

It's a little glimmer of hope, but that's all I need right now.

I reach the campfire and breathe deeply, taking it all in: the scent of roasting marshmallows, the flickering firelight, the laughter and singing. All the benches are packed. Dot is sitting next to Yvonne, their heads bent together, hands clasped. Zac and Zoey are cuddled up, and I can hear Zac's voice—loud and off-key—as he joins in the song.

Hillary is sitting across the circle from Cooper, who is playing his guitar, but she's clearly making eyes at him. I haven't talked to her yet—but what will I say? Hillary's an adult. She doesn't need me to police her romantic decisions any more than Dot does.

My chest feels hollow, looking at all the couples.

Back when I was a counselor, I'd have some kind of romantic attachment each summer—some that even lasted a couple months into the school year. But then I became director, and it wasn't appropriate for me to hook up with my employees, so I invested in a good vibrator instead. That's when I gave up my silly dream of falling in love with a fellow camp person, too. During the off-season, I dated a few guys in town, but nothing serious, not till Nick. We weren't right for each other, but I did enjoy being half of a couple. Knowing there was one person in the world who wanted to sit next to me in the dark and hold my hand.

I take a step back. Maybe I'll head to my cabin and read more of Luke's book. No one has even noticed I'm here; they don't need me.

I'm tiptoeing off into the darkness when I hear a voice: "Jess."

My skin prickles. I whirl in the direction of Luke's voice and see him relaxing in a hammock strung between two trees. His legs are stretched out and crossed at the ankles, his body all lean muscles and long limbs. There's a notebook on his lap, a pen in his hand.

"You're here!" I say, surprised at how happy I am. "I didn't even have to beg you to come."

"Indeed. Not quite socializing, but not hermit-ing, either."

He brings one hand up to rest behind his head, which tugs the edge of his Henley up, exposing a sliver of flat stomach. I flash back to the memory of him in his swimsuit, dripping wet, and shake myself.

"Are you writing?" I ask, motioning toward the notebook.

He nods. "Working on an outline."

"For . . . ?"

"My next book."

I smile. "You're not giving anything away, are you?"

"And you're not skipping the campfire, are you?"

I glance back over my shoulder. "I was late getting here, and there's hardly any space left. I didn't want to force my way in."

He stares at me, that groove between his eyebrows deepening. The distant firelight casts shadows on his face, his lips, his cheekbones. "There's room here."

He indicates the space beside him, and I freeze, imagining lying next to Luke in the hammock, pressed against his side, his arm around me, my head on his chest. My body flushes with warmth.

No way in hell. I already have crush-adjacent memories of him from my teenage years, compounded by his revelation about his sex dreams, in addition to the fact that I'm becoming fond of him.

Plus: he's absurdly handsome. There's also that.

He must notice my hesitation, because he sits up, swinging his legs so they're dangling off the side. "Come on," he says, and scoots over.

I sit next to him. The hammock swings and sags, squishing us both to the middle, and I catch a whiff of the clean laundry scent of his clothes. Carefully, I shift away, leaving two or three inches of space between us.

Now I can breathe again.

"Where's Scout?" I ask.

"Back at my cabin. Sleeping." His voice catches, but he clears his throat and goes on before I can ask if anything's wrong. "Thank you for watching her."

"It wasn't easy. She's pretty high maintenance," I say, smiling. Scout is so mellow it's easy to forget she's there: she slept twenty hours a day and followed me around the other four. I missed her last night, her quiet breathing from the foot of my bed.

"I appreciate it. And I'm guessing you and Hillary made up? You used your big-girl words and had an actual conversation?" His voice is gently teasing.

I roll my eyes, smiling. "Yes, we talked. And yes, we made up."

"I'm proud of you," he says, and I glow inside. Which is silly; I'm acting like a starstruck CIT again, hero-worshiping the coolest counselor of the summer.

"It's a great idea, creating a co-op," he continues. "I'd be interested in supporting something like that."

I glance at him. "You would? How?"

"You mean how can I afford to, since I'm dirt poor?" he says dryly.

My cheeks warm. "You said you lost all the money from your advance . . ."

"I didn't gamble it away or anything, if that's what you were thinking."

"That's not—"

"You were, weren't you?" Amusement plays on his lips.

"You think I'm such a moron that I squandered half a million dollars."

"I'm sorry, okay!" I say, laughing. "It's not like you're forthcoming about your personal life. You could have lost the money in a Ponzi scheme, for all I know."

Around the campfire, everyone is singing "This Land Is Your Land," accompanied by Cooper on the guitar. I lean back in the hammock and look up. The trees overhead obscure most of the sky, but here and there stars peek out, the Milky Way a smudge behind them.

I glance over at Luke. He's gazing up at the sky, too, one hand tucked behind his head. Again, his profile reminds me of something out of an art gallery: straight nose, full lips, perfect chin with that shallow dimple. A sparkler seems to light inside my chest, and I look away. Sitting this close to Luke, in the dark, is dangerous.

"I lost most of it in my divorce," he says, breaking the silence.

"You—you're divorced?" I sputter. "How?"

"Well, ya see, my wife didn't want to be married to me anymore, so she contacted an attorney and filed a—"

"I know how divorces work, Luke. I'm just . . ." *Confused.* It doesn't sound like he initiated things, and maybe I'm biased, given my latent crush—which seems to be resurrecting itself—but I can't imagine any woman who'd willingly let him out of her life. "Why?"

He gives a harsh laugh. "I was a shit husband, that's why."

I swallow, stunned. "I'm sorry, it's none of my business—"

"I didn't cheat," he cuts in. "Nothing like that. But I was

wrapped up in my writing, didn't pay enough attention to her, and when things didn't go well with my first book, I got even more obsessed with making the next one a success. I can't blame her for getting sick of all that. Anyway." He clears his throat. "Officially divorced since March. Separated for about eighteen months before. It was messy, working everything out. She got half my advance in the settlement. And after paying my attorney's fees . . ."

He trails off, and I nod.

His email responses about the mix-up with his cabin registration make more sense now. He was going through a nasty divorce, had no extra money, and needed a place to get away.

He shifts his weight, making the hammock swing. "I'll get another payment when I turn this next book in. I'd love to use some of it to help save Camp Chickawah."

I can tell he's turning the topic of conversation away from himself, but that's okay. I get it.

"Thanks," I say. "That's kind of you."

After a pause, I can't resist. "How's the book coming? Can I see?"

I try to grab the notebook from his hands, but he pulls it away and holds it against his chest. The movement makes me fall against him, which gives me another jolt of sparks.

"Get your grubby hands off that," he says. There's amusement in his voice, like he's close to laughing but won't let it out.

I push myself up, putting space between us again. I'm getting way too comfortable around him.

"I'm reading your first book," I say. "Almost done with it."

His face goes blank. "You are not."

I can't help grinning at his obvious discomfort. "It's really good—"

"Stop. Now."

"Can't. I'm desperate to find out what happens between Zolara and Prin when they reach the forbidden city and find Jax. I'm #TeamPrin, by the way."

He leans back, exhaling. "God. You *are* reading it."

"And you can't stop me." I give his rib cage a poke.

He grabs my finger, holds it tight. "You really are a menace."

"I'll try to behave," I say, locking eyes with him.

"That's too bad." He quirks an eyebrow at me, and my breath catches. Is he flirting with me? Or making fun of me?

Either way, time for a change of subject. I retrieve my finger and fold my hands across my stomach. "How's the writing going?"

"Better, actually. I want to go in a different direction for the third book. So far, so good."

"I'm glad," I say, sincerely. He's seemed less gloomy lately, and this must be why.

"We'll see. I'm basically starting over, but the deadline hasn't changed: the day after Labor Day. I'll be writing nonstop." He shakes his head. "Good thing I'm already divorced."

There's an edge of sadness to his voice, and I shake my head. I'm not buying this whole I-was-a-shit-husband routine.

"Okay, but here's the thing," I say. "Why is it your fault that your ex-wife couldn't keep herself occupied while you wrote? I mean, it's your job. Not just your job—your passion."

He gives me a wry look. "Not sure if you're aware, but

there's an unspoken expectation in relationships that you spend time with the other person."

"Why? I mean, yes, of course. But why can't the other person accept that other things in your life are also important?" I roll onto my side to face him. He's listening intently, his full bottom lip caught between his teeth. "I had this boyfriend last year, right? He lives in town, and things were great during the winter, when I was staying there. But once summer started, he was upset that my priority was the camp."

"He broke up with you?"

"Oh, no, I dumped him," I say, waving a hand. "He cried. It was a whole thing."

Luke raises his eyebrows, but I keep going.

"My parents are divorced, as you know, and the things that drove them crazy about each other are the exact things their new spouses love. Like, my mom enjoys doing home renovations, and my dad hated it, but my stepdad loves doing them with her. My dad? He loves watching sports, and my mom felt like he was ignoring her, but my stepmom is one of those obsessive scrapbookers. So he watches games, and she scrapbooks. It's a win-win."

"Right," Luke says dryly. "I need to find a woman who enjoys being neglected sixteen hours a day."

"My *point* is that just because you weren't compatible, it doesn't mean you were a bad husband. Was I a bad girlfriend because I wanted to spend my summers here, doing my job? Some people may think so, but I don't. Nick didn't even try to understand why this camp was so important to me."

My voice wobbles on the last words. Luke must notice, because he reaches out his hand and places it on mine. I don't think it's a romantic gesture—more like solidarity. Even still, the world seems to narrow to this: me and him, side by side in a hammock, his warm hand covering mine.

"He was a fucking idiot to let you go," he says softly.

My chest warms with a mixture of confused feelings—attraction? Friendship?

I swallow. "I don't want to be with someone who doesn't care about what matters to me, even though that means I'll probably be single forever."

"True."

I give him a side-eye. "Thanks for the vote of confidence."

He sighs, exasperated. "Jess. I'm saying you're right—no one should be with a person who refuses to understand what matters to them."

"I'm wise beyond my years," I say.

"That you are."

"Maybe I'll embroider it on a pillow and sell it on Etsy."

"I'll be the first to order one."

"Just one? Come on, Luke."

"I'll order ten in each color and size."

I grin. "That's better."

He slides his hand under mine, and I hold my breath as he laces our fingers together. Now we're definitely holding hands, and I have no idea what it means, but I don't want to let go.

So I relax into the hammock, staring up at the sky, grateful to have someone next to me.

twenty-one

Hillary

The energy around camp this week is nothing short of electric—
and not just because it's Color Wars. The optimism and
excitement about the co-op has seeped into every aspect of
camp life. From raising the flag in the morning to drinking
"bug juice" at lunch and sitting around the campfire at night,
everything is more joyful.

I didn't realize how big a shadow the impending sale had
cast until it started to lift. In its place is a sense of hope, the
growing belief that there might be more summers at Camp
Chickawah, for all of us. I've been crunching numbers, and if
the pledges continue at this rate, we'll be within spitting
distance of our goal.

I've been working on a few ideas to put us over the edge.
Jessie told me not to hold anything back this time—an
invitation I'm going to put to the test this afternoon. She isn't
going to like what I have to say, but the more I look into the
camp financials, the more I understand why the Valentines
decided to sell.

"Hello!"

Jessie's voice rings through the Arts and Crafts cabin,

bringing me out of my anxious mind and into my anxious reality.

"Out here!" I call. I left the back door open and set a bottle of rosé and a small charcuterie board that Cooper put together out on the picnic table behind the cabin. I'm learning there are more benefits to this summer fling than the sexual variety.

"What's all this?" Jessie asks, walking outside. "Are you trying to seduce me, Goldberg?"

I shrug. "I mean, if there's nothing going on between you and Luke . . ."

Jessie's eyes flash with mischief, and my suspicions about her feelings are as good as confirmed. But I won't push for details. Yet.

"Honestly, I thought you could use a break," I tell her as we settle across from each other at the picnic table. "And I wanted to show you something I've been working on."

Jessie's face lights up. Shoot. I hope she isn't expecting to see one of the craft projects we've been working on for Color Wars—although the medals the campers made by wrapping cardboard circles with tinfoil are pretty awesome.

I should have started this conversation differently: with wine.

"Here," I say, grabbing the bottle and two glasses. "Don't tell the boss I snuck the good plastic cups out of the dining hall."

"Your secret's safe with me," she says, filling hers almost to the top. "Here's to delayed endings and new beginnings."

"I'll drink to that." I clink my cup against hers and take a sip, hoping that one of the new beginnings she's thinking about is our friendship.

The wine is sweet and a little tart—not unlike this

moment. It's just after five, but the summer sun is still high in the sky, casting tree-shaped shadows over the table. Dragonflies zip past us; in the distance, laughter and splashing echo from the lake.

We sit in companionable silence, sipping our wine, while I try to gather my nerves.

"You wanted to show me something?" Jessie asks.

"Yeah," I say, fumbling my notebook out of my canvas tote bag. "I've been working on some ideas to help us raise more capital. A few of the campers mentioned their companies having corporate matching programs—the co-op doesn't qualify, but if we form a 501(c)(3), a nonprofit arm of the camp, then we can accept donations and get their matches."

"Brilliant," Jessie says, taking a big sip of wine.

"And I was thinking about the Willis Tower," I say.

"The what?"

"It used to be called the Sears Tower," I explain, and she nods, the Chicago building's old and more familiar name ringing a bell. "But another company bought the rights, so now it's the Willis Tower."

"As in Bruce Willis?" she says, grinning at me.

"Sadly, no," I say, chuckling. "But I was thinking we could sell naming rights to places around camp—like the Valentine Lodge or the Pederson Swimming Dock. People would pay a pretty penny to have things named after themselves or their loved ones."

"Oooh!" Jessie says, rubbing her hands together. "I like that! And maybe we charge more to name things after people's enemies—like the Jack Valentine latrines!"

I laugh. "Exactly! That's one of the most important parts of fundraising: the value of everything is directly proportional to how valuable we make it. A rock can be worth ten grand if you position it right."

Jessie's nodding enthusiastically, and I hate that I'm about to pop her bubble.

"But there's something else," I say, dropping my voice to hopefully convey the shift to a more serious topic. "When we were in the office the other day, I saw a historical document of the camp's financials. The profit margin has dropped significantly over the last five or six years."

Jessie narrows her eyes, taking a slice each of cheese and prosciutto from the charcuterie board. "I'm aware of that."

"I know you are. I'm just saying, if a co-op buys a failing company, it will still be a failing company."

"Do you think I'm trying to trick people into investing?" Jessie asks, a wounded expression on her face. "That I'll take their money, sit back, and let the camp fall apart?"

"No, no, not at all." I take a sip of my wine, rethinking my approach. "I just have ideas—more drastic changes that could help the camp do more than survive. Jessie, it could thrive."

My heart is pounding so loud I can feel it pulsing in my ears. As much as I want to keep going, to convince Jessie that I know what I'm talking about, my father taught me that sometimes the most persuasive thing you can say is nothing.

"I'm listening," Jessie says eventually, taking an olive off the board, and I exhale a sigh of relief.

"We both know that registration for sleepaway camps is down across the country," I say. "But there are more and more people like Luke who are looking for an escape or a retreat year-round."

"I've actually thought about that," Jessie says. "But the cabins aren't winterized."

"Yes, exactly! That's one of the first things we should do once the sale goes through. Winterize the cabins so we can use them in every season. And maybe give the Lodge a little facelift."

I hope she doesn't balk at my use of the word "we." I'm so invested in this idea; I want to stay a part of it. This could be a new chapter for both of us.

"I was thinking, summer camps only run from mid-June to mid-August because of school schedules. That gives us two weeks on either side where the weather is still great, and we could offer adult sessions. This thing you've created is too good to let go—and with fewer spots available, people will pay even more to relive their favorite camp memories."

I'm talking too much, so I pause and spread some Brie on a cracker, leaving space for Jessie to take in what I'm suggesting—a shift in the way she thinks about the business. Rather than being viable two months of the year, it could work for all twelve.

"I like it," Jessie says, and I exhale in relief. "I've had similar thoughts . . . what I'd do differently if I was really in charge, you know?"

"This could be amazing, Jess," I say, the wheels in my mind spinning with possibilities. "The two of us working together? It's a dream come true."

"I know companies pay a lot for your time and talent," Jessie says, and I start to protest, but she holds her hand up, and I stop. "We obviously don't have much disposable income at the moment, but we could definitely pay you three Kit Kats and a Twix."

There's a sparkle in her eye, and I feel like I'm missing

something, but I'm not about to question her. Not when this is the outcome I wanted.

"Deal," I say, clinking my glass against Jessie's. "And to think I was going to do it for free."

Jessie laughs and takes another sip of her wine. "Thanks for this break. I needed it."

"You should thank Cooper," I say, suddenly feeling an urge to let her in on my little secret.

"Cooper, huh?" The suggestive lilt to her voice says she already knows.

"Let's just say I highly recommend a summer fling with a chef."

She grins, delighted. "Hillary Goldberg finally got a camp boyfriend!"

"Not a boyfriend—it's super casual," I say.

"Casual?" Jessie looks skeptical. "Aren't you the girl who planned your entire camp schedule two weeks in advance? You've changed since we were kids, but not *that* much, Hill."

"True. But honestly, the predictability of my life has been stifling. I think I've been itching to break free, only I didn't know it till I got here. I want to stop obsessing about what I *should* do and start focusing on what I *want* to do. On doing what feels good."

"And doing Cooper feels good?" Jessie says, her eyes alight with mischief. My cheeks heat up, which answers her question. She leans back, laughing out loud. "Go, Hillary!" Then she looks at me. "Wait—so that guy in all your Facebook photos . . ."

"Aaron?" I ask, surprised but secretly pleased that Jessie was paying attention to my rare social media posts. "We were on a break, but I made it permanent on the Fourth."

This piques Jessie's interest, and I fill her in on the rapid demise of my relationship. She gasps and shakes her head in all the right places, and it strikes me that this is exactly the kind of conversation I craved the night Aaron made his indecent proposal. My heart swells, knowing that whatever lies ahead—the good and the not-so-good—I'll finally have a best friend by my side again.

I finish by telling her about Cooper, how kind and patient he's been. In and out of bed—though, come to think of it, we haven't actually been *in* a bed yet.

"Sounds amazing, Hilly," Jessie says, resting her hand on top of mine. "Just be careful with that heart of yours."

Her words remind me of another warning I got earlier this week. I was sitting around the campfire, subtly (or so I thought) admiring Cooper from a distance. Then the woman sitting next to me started talking about him. She was from Boston, and according to her, my fling left a trail of broken hearts in his wake, sleeping with "anything that had a pulse."

I shake the memory away, trying to dislodge the unsettled feeling it gave me.

"Speaking of romantic entanglements, what's happening with you and Luke?"

Her smile fades. "Oh, nothing."

"Nothing?" I prod. "Come on, I told you about Cooper."

Jessie sighs. "If there was anything to tell, I would. But there's nothing. I thought there might be, but it's probably my overactive imagination conjuring up that old teenage crush."

"Everyone had the hots for him when he was a counselor," I say.

"Yeah, well, turns out he had the hots for me back then,

too." Jessie's cheeks flush and she covers her face with her hands.

"Wait, what?"

She peeks out from beneath her fingers, a giant grin on her face. "He may have mentioned having erotic dreams about me when I was a CIT."

My jaw drops. "Jessie May Pederson! I'm going to need more details, stat."

"It's pretty much what it sounds like," she says. "That's why he got so weird with me back then—but it doesn't mean anything's going to happen between us now. He's got a lot going on, and so do I."

"Hot, no-strings-attached sex is something you want to make time for," I tell her. "Trust me."

"Oh, I'm all about summer flings—it's just been a while since I've had one." Jessie hesitates, then tilts her head, studying me. "Actually, maybe I can ask you something. Google has *not* been helpful."

"Go ahead."

"I've been thinking about . . . I mean, wondering . . ." She hesitates, fiddling with her braids. "And if you don't want to tell me, it's okay, I just—"

"Just spit it out!" I say, laughing. "Whatever it is, it can't be *that* big of a deal."

She takes a deep breath, then blurts, "Whatarethepubichairstylesnowadays?"

I stare at her. "Wait . . . what?" My mind slowly catches up. "Jessie, are you planning on letting Luke go to Virginia? When he hasn't even been to Cleveland yet?"

At this reference to the geographical locations we used as

teenage campers to describe sexual activity, she bursts out laughing. Paris was kissing (for obvious reasons); Cleveland was for touching boob, since it sounded kind of like cleavage; the Netherlands was anything in the underwear region; and Virginia was "all the way." Back then, we didn't know anyone who'd let a boy go to Uranus.

"No. I don't know," Jessie says. "I mean, nothing's happened. But if it does . . . I guess I want to be prepared? I've been living in the forest for ten years, and he's from, like, the most citified city in the world. I'm sure things have changed . . . out there . . . with regards to grooming. Down there."

"Grooming down where?"

We both glance up to see that Zoey has somehow snuck up on us. She's fresh from the lake, her dark hair in a wet braid, her dimples winking. "Ooh, wine! What are we talking about?"

"Nothing, nothing!" Jessie says brightly. Her cheeks are pink. "We're talking about nothing."

"Jessie wants to know about pubic hair styles with the youths," I say pointedly, passing Zoey the bottle of wine, since I only brought two cups.

"Girl talk. Yay!" She plops down beside me and takes a swig, wiping her mouth with the back of her hand. "Well, you know, it's really whatever you want to do with it. Some girls put a little gel in it, bring out the natural waves."

Jessie's eyes bulge.

"I hear they're doing middle parts nowadays," I say, barely holding in a laugh.

"You're messing with me," Jessie says.

"You could shave it into fun little shapes—like a heart or

a triangle. Ooh!" Zoey lights up. "A little arrow pointing the way."

"Pointing the way to what? Hey, that meat looks good."

Now it's Dot, walking toward the three of us, her walkie-talkie swinging from her belt.

Jessie shakes her head. "Please, join us. Let's make this a full staff meeting."

"It's good to get opinions from a wide demographic," I say, then turn to Dot and motion her to sit. "We're talking pubic hair. To shave or not to shave."

"Or wax," Zoey adds.

"Nah, you gotta let that grow," Dot says. She swings her leg around to sit sideways on the bench next to Jessie, helping herself to some salami. "I'll tell ya, I shaved it all off *one* time and I looked like a plucked chicken down there for weeks." I wrinkle my nose at that mental image. "And the regrowth!" Dot shudders. "Nope. It's there for a reason. Keeps things hygienic. Plus . . ." She winks. "Wilderness is fun to explore."

"It shouldn't matter what you have down there," Zoey says, getting more passionate with each word. "If a man has a problem with it, he's not worthy. He should be honored to even *be* there. He should bow down and worship the queen of the jungle!"

"Who's this 'he'? Are we talking about someone specifically?" Dot asks.

"No!" Jessie shouts, at the exact same time I say, "Luke."

Jessie shoots me a death glare as Dot chuckles and says, "Ah, The Man's getting acquainted with the ol' Vulvarine?"

Jessie's cheeks flame red. "No. No acquaintance."

"Yet," I add.

Jessie rolls her eyes. "*Nothing* is happening."

"Then why are we talking beav?" Dot helps herself to another big slice of salami, topping it with cheese before popping it in her mouth.

Jessie presses her lips together and squeezes her eyes shut; I can't tell if she's mortified or trying not to laugh. Or both. "I just don't want to look like a forest troll."

"You'd never look like a forest troll," Zoey says. "Trolls are short. You're more like a . . . forest ogre?"

"Thanks," Jessie says dryly.

"Who's a forest ogre?"

We all turn our heads to see Zac walking up, shirtless in his swimming shorts, a towel draped around his shoulders.

"Annnnnnnd we're done!" Jessie says, standing up. "Good talk, gotta go."

I reach across the table and grab her arm, pulling her back down. "Actually, Zac, it's great you're here. We need a guy's opinion."

"Sure," Zac says, sitting next to his wife and giving her a kiss. "Can I have some?" he asks, motioning to the food.

"Please do," I say, pushing the charcuterie board toward him. He dives in, stacking meat, cheese, and dried fruit high on a cracker.

"Do men have pubic hair preferences for women?" Zoey asks him, matter-of-fact.

Zac pops the entire cracker in his mouth, then chews, taking the question seriously. "I mean, I know some guys say they like it bare, but doesn't that seem a little . . . prepubescent?"

He smiles broadly, like he's proud of himself for using such a big word.

"Good job, baby," Zoey says. "So you don't mind a full bush?"

"What kind of Aussie would I be if I didn't like the bush down under?" He grins, loading up another cracker. "Wilderness is meant to be explored, I'd say."

"That's right," Dot says, and she and Zac high-five. Jessie buries her face in her hands.

"What are we exploring?"

It's Cooper, and he's carrying over another bottle of wine. At the sight of him, Jessie groans and slumps onto the table, her entire face hidden. "If Mr. Billy comes out next, I'm going to pass away. RIP me."

"We're talking pubes," Zac tells Cooper cheerfully.

Cooper's eyes widen as he looks at me.

I shrug. "Yeah. Jessie wanted to know what the styles are nowadays."

"And if men have preferences," Zoey adds.

Jessie, head still in her hands, lets out another groan. "Oh my gooooood."

"You want my honest opinion?" Cooper asks, squeezing in beside me.

"No. No, I do not," Jessie mumbles, her voice muffled, but I nod at Cooper to continue.

"You should do what *you* prefer," Cooper says. "Whatever makes you feel most confident. Nothing sexier than confidence."

He glances toward me, and I squeeze my thighs together and look away.

"I'd feel most confident if we never spoke of this again," Jessie says, lifting her head, her cheeks blazing red.

"Honestly?" I say, smiling. "I think you should just put it in two braids, so the carpet matches the drapes."

Dot's holding in a grin as she adds, "Or a mullet—business in the front, party in the back."

"All right, we're done here," Jessie says, swinging her leg around the picnic bench. "Back to work, everyone. That's a direct order."

As she walks away, I call after her, "Good luck with your next visitor from St. Petersburg!"

Without turning, Jessie flips me the bird.

Zac whispers to his wife, "We're getting a camper from Russia?"

The next morning, instead of my normal camp uniform, I put on a pair of running shorts and my Blue Team T-shirt, then head to the flagpole for the official opening ceremony of Color Wars.

"You're just in time," Jessie says, sounding as excited as I feel. Luckily, she didn't rescind her offer to be partners for the games today after the whole pubic council.

"Ready?" Zac says, coming up beside us. He and Zoey are both on the Orange Team.

Jessie nods, and he hits play on his phone, sending an Olympic fanfare blasting from his Bluetooth speaker. I'm not sure what's going on, but audible gasps and whistles rise from the crowd. I stand on my tiptoes, trying to figure out what the fuss is about.

And that's when I see him.

Cooper, dressed in a toga tie-dyed with all four team colors—red, orange, green, and blue—and a crown of leaves around his head. He's holding one of the torches Jessie asked me to make for the opening ceremony. She forgot to mention my fling would be the one carrying it. Or that his toga would show *that* much leg. I've never found calves particularly sexy before, but the way Cooper's flex when he runs is nothing short of hot.

When he reaches the flagpole, leaving several women and a few men looking lustily after him, he hands Jessie the papier-mâché torch. She holds it high above her head and shouts, "May the best Color win!"

The Blue Team wins our first team event (kickball) and crushes it in the individual competitions, adding ten points for winning the egg and canoe races and five points for coming in second for the balloon race and apple bobbing.

My personal best activity is flip cup, a new addition to these adult games. I haven't played since college, but apparently, I've still got it. That win put us in the lead by twenty points with two events left.

"Hill, over here!" Jessie shouts. Our team is huddled by the flagpole, watching tug-of-war. If the Red Team wins and we lose, they'll move into first place.

"Shit!" Jessie mutters as the Orange Team tumbles and the Red Team celebrates. Then she remembers herself and gets back into team captain mode. "It's okay, we've got this. Who has the most upper body strength?"

"Not me," I say, stepping back.

Jessie scans the rest of our group, identifying a woman and two men who look like they work out.

"One of you should go in the front, another in the back,

and the third right in the middle," she says. "Everyone, make sure you stand with your feet a little wider than shoulder-width apart. We are not going down!"

"Hell yeah!" the man who volunteered to be the caboose yells.

"Places, everyone!" Cooper calls out. He's the judge for this station, and I'd be lying if I said I didn't want to impress him. I take a deep breath, rubbing my sweaty palms against my shorts.

"Everyone, pick up your rope!" Cooper shouts.

The twined material feels heavier than I expected, and it's so thick I can barely wrap my hands around it.

"At the sound of my whistle," Cooper says, "tug! First team to pull the other over the halfway mark wins."

He pauses, standing right beside me, close enough to touch. Then he brings the whistle to his beautiful lips, lips that have explored every inch of my body, and my mind drifts to last night around midnight, behind the hay bales at the archery range; the way he pressed me against the . . .

The rope is yanked out of my hands as our entire team stumbles forward.

"Ooh!" I cry as I fall, scraping my knee, the rope burning my hands.

Cooper officially declares the Green Team victorious, then calls the Red Team to take our place for the final round. I walk toward Jessie, who's wiping dirt from her knees.

"It's okay," she says. "If Green takes the Red Team down, we still have a shot."

The match begins, and we turn to watch as the Red Team suffers the same fate, toppling over in less than thirty seconds, thanks to the former NFL player on the Green Team.

"Yes!" Jessie roars, pumping her fist in the air.

It's fun seeing this competitive side of her again. I just hope history doesn't repeat itself in the final event: the dreaded three-legged race.

Jessie and I are in the last of sixteen heats. If we win our race, it'll give our team enough points to win the whole Color Wars. If someone from the Red Team wins and we get second place, we'll go to a tie. Third place, it's over.

"You got this, boss," Dot says, tying a blue bandana around our ankles, binding me and Jessie together.

There are six other pairs in our heat—two from each team—including identical twins Avi and Olive on the Red Team. I wonder if they have an advantage; sharing DNA probably makes sharing a leg easier.

But Jessie and I have an advantage, too: this isn't the first time we've run this race. The last time, though, I tripped, taking Jessie down with me. It knocked us out of the lead, and we ended the Color Wars in second place. "First losers," as Jessie called it.

As if reading my mind, she wraps her arm around my waist, holding me tight.

"Just stay in sync with me," she says. "The only way we win is if we work together."

Dot blows the whistle and we're off. It takes a few steps for us to get our rhythm down, but soon, we're walk-running in tandem, as if we're one.

Inside, outside. Inside, outside. Inside, outside.

Before I know it, we cross the finish line—neck and neck with the twins. I turn to see if we won and upset the balance, almost falling. But Jessie catches me, holding me steady in her arms. I stay there, hugging my best friend, as Dot declares a victory for the Red Team.

Our teams are tied for gold.

"What happens now?" I ask, rubbing my ankle.

"Tiebreaker," Jessie says. "I volunteered us—so I hope you know your eggs."

Ten minutes later, I'm sitting in a chair, Jessie standing behind me, facing two players from the Red Team in the same position. A carton of eggs is on the table between us, and the entire camp community is gathered, watching.

"Before you are a dozen eggs," Cooper says, projecting his voice for all to hear. "Eleven are hard-boiled. One is raw. You won't know which is which until you smash it on your partner's head."

I cringe at the thought of wet, sticky yolk running through my hair.

"Take your first egg," Cooper instructs, and I hold my breath. "On the count of three, crack it on your partner's head."

I wince, closing my eyes as Cooper counts to three and Jessie knocks the egg against my head. To my relief, nothing happens.

Our rivals also get a hard-boiled egg. Two down, ten to go.

The next round, two more hard-boiled ones. The crowd is getting restless.

"Round three!" Cooper yells. "First to get the raw egg loses, giving gold to the other team."

Jessie reaches past me for an egg, changing her mind at the last minute and selecting another.

"One, two, three!" Cooper says, and I hold my breath.

The crowd erupts and I cringe with my whole body, folding myself away from Jessie. It takes a full ten seconds before I realize that I don't feel anything dripping down my scalp.

I look up and see my opponent covered in egg.

"We won!" I shout, leaping from my chair. "We did it!"

Jessie and I hug before getting swept up by our overjoyed Blue Team. They're chanting, "Blue gets gold!" over and over, and my eyes sting with happy tears.

It feels like I finally deserve to have Jessie's friendship back. And I hope this won't be the only victory in our future.

twenty-two

Jessie

During the sixth week of camp, the weather is perfect: blue skies, eighty-degree days, a light breeze drifting off the lake. The campers, in their seventies, have been a delight. The week's big event is an art festival Hillary's been working on, showcasing projects from the whole summer—and selling them to raise money for our plan to buy the camp property.

I start the day with my usual canoe paddle, listening to the original Broadway cast recording of *Moulin Rouge!* with the one and only Aaron Tveit as Christian. When I get back to the dock, Luke is there in his swimsuit, the morning sun bathing his skin in golden light.

A jolt runs through me. Since that moment in the hammock, there's a new energy between us. An awareness. Like we're dancing around each other, but neither of us is willing to make the first move.

He reaches down and steadies the canoe as I climb out. "I see you're taking your personal safety more seriously."

He motions to the life jacket I'm wearing over my one-piece swimsuit and shorts. It's unzipped, but at least I have it on.

"Yeah, because guess what?" I lean in like I'm telling him a secret. "A couple weeks ago, when I wasn't wearing one, I

almost drowned. Luckily, this really grumpy guy
rescued me."

His eyes crinkle at the corners. "A really grumpy guy,
huh?"

"So grumpy. Haven't seen him around lately, though."

He cracks a tiny smile, which feels like a victory, and
helps me lift the canoe and stow it next to the others. It takes
all my strength not to stare at his bare torso, his muscles
flexing under his tanned skin.

"What are you up to today?" he asks.

"We have the art show later on. You should come."

"Sure."

I do a double take. "Really? You feeling okay?"

He narrows his eyes. "Don't make me change my mind."

"Is this a bad time to ask if you'd write poems on demand
to raise money?"

"I don't write poetry."

I hang up my life jacket and face him. His eyes dip down
my body, snagging on my chest. But then he clears his throat
and takes a step back.

"Oh, it can't be that difficult," I say. "Go ahead, make one
up about me."

"There once was a camper named Jessie," he says.

I smile. "Starting off strong."

"With hair in two braids, never messy." He gives one of
my braids a tug, making my heart flip. "She paddles at dawn,
and listens to songs . . ."

"Okay?"

"And wears a life jacket, no stressy."

I grimace. "Yikes. That last line could use some work. But
since we don't have anyone else, you're hired. See you there!"

The art show is a hit: all our campers from this week attend, and some from prior weeks return to show off their projects or purchase others. Everyone's milling about on the big lawn, munching on Cooper's baked goods (also sold to benefit our co-op). Dot invited her sweetie, Yvonne, back up; they're holding hands and beaming like two people who never got the chance when they were teenagers.

Hillary, who has spent the past few days running around like a headless chicken, now looks relaxed and relieved.

"It's going so well!" I say, walking over to her.

She beams. "Thank you!" Inclining her head toward him, she adds, "And it looks like Luke's poems are a hit."

He's sitting under a canopy, surrounded by elderly women. For the first time this summer, he seems at ease. Maybe even cheerful.

"Has anyone told you that you look like a young Paul Newman?" one woman says to him. The other ladies murmur their agreement.

"I've never heard that in my life, but thank you," Luke says, his eyes twinkling.

"When I was young," a third lady says, "everyone said I looked like Elizabeth Taylor."

"I can see that," Luke says, smiling. It's a genuine smile, teeth showing, the corners of his eyes crinkling, so different from the tiny, guarded smiles he's given me. Half the ladies visibly swoon. "Now, what's your name?"

"Nora Burbridge," the woman says, and Luke starts working on her poem.

Later that evening, after a delicious dinner by Chef Cooper, the staff—plus Luke—work together to clean up, putting away tables and chairs. Zac and Zoey peel off to the lake, where some campers are taking a sunset kayak ride. Dot and Yvonne go on a walk; Cooper heads to the kitchen, and Hillary goes with him. Mr. Billy's wandering around with his trash picker-upper, grumbling about how litterbugs never change.

Which means it's just me and Luke. He's sitting at a picnic table, scribbling in his notebook. He must have gone back to his cabin to get Scout, because she's curled up at his feet, asleep.

"What are you working on?" I ask, walking over. His face brightens when he sees me. "Redoing my poem?"

I bend down to pet Scout; she barely lifts her head, but shifts her body toward me.

"No, just some ideas for the next book."

"What? No way!" I gasp and snatch the notebook out of his hand; he lunges to grab it back, but I run off across the lawn, triumphant.

I've been low-key dying to find out what happens next—I finished the second book in his series last night, and it ended on a cliff-hanger. Literally: the main character, Zolara, is hanging on with one hand to the edge of a seventy-story building as Prin, one of her love interests, reaches for her— only for Zolara's hand to slip and send her plummeting into blackness.

"Give that back," Luke grumbles, coming after me.

I dart away, grinning as I read.

I never felt like I belonged anywhere until I came to camp.

I stop and look up, confused. "Wait—what's this for?"

"My next book." He looks defensive, or maybe just uncomfortable, folding his arms and staring at the ground. "It's about a teenage boy coming to summer camp for the first time."

"The third book has kids going to *camp*? That makes zero sense."

"No, I'm not finishing the series—"

"What? Why?"

"Because no one will read it—"

"I will!"

"Well, no one else."

"Then tell me what was going to happen," I say, pleading. "Please! I have to know if Zolara makes it."

He glances at me, his expression pensive. "I have no idea what happens. I wasn't in a good place when I wrote that—throwing my character off a cliff seemed like an apt metaphor."

"I'm sorry. I didn't mean—"

He waves a hand. "No, I know. That ending made writing the third book impossible. But being here gave me an idea for a new story. When I went to New York, I pitched it to my editor."

"And?"

His cheeks flush; a tiny smile. "She loved it."

I jump and scream. "She did? Amazing! Luke! What's it about—other than a kid who goes to camp?"

He runs a hand over his mouth, like he's trying to wipe away the smile, but he's flushing even more, and I'm delighted. I've never seen this bashful version of Luke before.

"The kid who goes to camp has cystic fibrosis. That's a genetic lung disease—it's what my uncle died from. I didn't know him well growing up, but taking Scout made me feel, I don't know, connected to him? I've been thinking about what it would've been like to grow up knowing you wouldn't survive past forty."

The sadness in his eyes makes my heart squeeze. "What happens in the book?"

We head back to the picnic table where Scout is sleeping. "The camp is for teens with chronic diseases. He loves it there, he's making friends. There's a girl . . ."

I grin. "Is it a romance?"

"Not exactly. After a couple weeks he notices that he's getting better. At first he thinks it's just the fresh air, but pretty soon, he doesn't need his treatments at all. Other kids are improving, too—"

"Ooooh," I breathe. "Like a healing lake or something?"

His lips quirk. "No spoilers. But when kids start disappearing, he realizes something more sinister is going on at Camp Shadows."

"It sounds amazing," I say sincerely. "I'm so excited about it that I won't even bug you to write me another poem."

He chuckles softly. "I'll make up a new one. Let me think."

We walk down the path to his cabin, Scout trailing behind us. The sun has set; fireflies are dancing on the lawn. I don't know why I'm going with him, except that I don't want to say good night yet.

"There once was a camper named Jess," he says eventually. "Her freckles were surely the best."

I grin. "Go on."

"She had pretty eyes, and nicely toned thighs—"

"Whoa!" I burst out. "That's rather personal, don't you think?"

"And they called her Camp Barbie, no less," he finishes.

I groan. "I hated being called Camp Barbie."

"It was a compliment, though."

"No. A true compliment is about something you can control, something you achieved, a challenge you faced. Like, 'Wow, Jessie, you've done a great job putting this adult summer camp together.' That's a compliment. Being compared to a ten-inch plastic doll is dehumanizing and objectifying."

He presses his lips together as he studies me. "Point taken. But what about being told that I look like a young Paul Newman? Is that objectifying?"

I scoff. "Paul Newman was one of the most famous actors of the twentieth century, a humanitarian, a devoted husband and father. That's not just a compliment, Luke, that's high praise."

"Or is it a subtle way of saying that I look like him, but the rest of me falls short?"

"Most people fall short of the Paul Newman standard."

"True. How many people have a successful salad dressing enterprise with their face on the bottle?"

"I love those salad dressings," I say. "The ranch especially. He wore a cowboy hat. I'm sorry, it was hot!"

"Compliments should be about what someone can control," Luke says, nudging me with his arm. The contact sends a wave of sunshine through me.

We turn toward his cabin, which takes us up a slope. Scout struggles to navigate a rock in the path, and Luke bends down, guiding her around it.

"There you go," he says. "That's a good girl."

His voice goes husky on that last sentence, and I know he's talking to his elderly dog, but my dirty mind spins it in a new direction. I wonder what he's like in bed, if he's gentle like this. What it would take to make him say *That's a good girl.*

Heat flashes through my body, and I shake it away.

"Her eyesight is going," he says, straightening up. We continue walking, more slowly now, letting Scout pick her way across the uneven path. "She can't hear much, either. She still knows when it's breakfast time, though—she wakes me up at six o'clock every morning."

"You take good care of her."

He shrugs. "She took good care of me when Nicole left. Maybe that's pathetic, having a dog as your primary emotional support—"

"Not at all. Sounds like you're lucky to have each other."

He clears his throat, shoots me a glance. "Yeah. Anyway—I'm sorry about the Camp Barbie thing. I understand why you wouldn't feel it was a compliment. The boys just thought you were hot."

"Why would I care what a bunch of boys thought about me?"

"I thought you were hot, too. Frustratingly, maddeningly, distractingly hot."

Another zing of heat runs through me, but I'm not sure how to take this; there's a sardonic smile on his lips, like he's mocking me.

"Ah, you *thought* I was hot. So glad you've come to your senses."

He shakes his head, mildly exasperated. "Jess . . ."

"Luke . . ."

"I still think you're hot."

I ignore the flush of exhilaration. "And I still don't think that's a compliment because—"

"You have no control over it, I get it." We reach his cabin and stop at the porch stairs. He faces me, that tiny smile playing on his lips. "Let me try again. Jessie, you've done an incredible job with this adult summer camp. Well done."

I scoff. "Nice try."

"Jessie, you're an excellent conversationalist."

"Hmmm."

"Jessie, you're good at making me laugh."

"Except I don't think I've ever made you laugh. You always stifle it!" I say.

His lips twitch. "You're good at *almost* making me laugh," he amends. "And it's sometimes very difficult to stifle."

"Okay, okay. You do know how to give a compliment—"

"I'm not done." He tilts his head, regarding me with a serious expression. "Jessie, you're incredible at bringing people together, creating a community, and helping everyone feel welcome. You even made *me* feel welcome, and I was an asshole to you."

A tiny glow sparks in my chest. *This* feels like a compliment, like a gift.

"You're still kind of an asshole to me," I say, trying to keep from smiling.

He rolls his eyes. "All right, smart-ass. Get out of here."

I turn to go, but he wraps his hand around my arm and stops me. "Can I say one more thing? It's not anything you can control, so it's less of a compliment and more of an observation."

I turn to face him. His hand is around my upper arm, and we're only a foot apart. My breathing goes shallow. "Go ahead. What's this observation?"

"That you're beautiful," he says. "Frustratingly, maddeningly, distractingly so. That I could write an entire paragraph about the freckles that live in the curve of your smile." He lifts his hand, brushes the backs of his fingers against my cheek. His eyes are intensely blue, locked on mine. "That I keep thinking about how it felt to be in the water with my arm around you." His other hand skims to the small of my back, pulling me closer. "That I've been having dreams about you again."

I find my voice. "What kind of dreams?"

"You know damn well what kind."

Liquid pools low in my belly, warm and slick. This is not the kind of interaction I ought to be having with a camper—because that's what he is, a guest at the camp. But I can't seem to step away. Especially not when Luke moves his hand to cradle my face. I lean into his palm, closing my eyes as his thumb strokes across my cheek, down my chin, up to my mouth. He traces the curve of my lips, sending goose bumps across my skin.

I inhale a shaky breath and open my eyes. He's staring at me, focused and curious, like I'm a puzzle he's trying to solve. I'm mesmerized, watching as his lips part. I want nothing more than to feel his mouth on mine, and I lean forward, closing my eyes.

Instead, I feel his forehead press against mine, the whisper of his breath as he sighs.

Then he pulls back, and his warmth is replaced by the cool night air.

I open my eyes, confused. He's shut down, his arms folded across his chest, and I immediately feel silly, like I misread this moment.

"Jess," he says, an apology in his voice. "I'm not at a point in my life where I should get involved with anyone. Even for a few weeks."

"Oh! Of course not. Me neither!" My voice is too loud, too bright. I take a step back, stumble over a root, and catch myself. "I—I should get going. Good night, Luke."

In response, all he does is nod.

By the time I'm a few hundred yards away, my embarrassment has morphed into irritation. How dare he act like *I* was coming on to him? *He* was the one who did the coming on!

I'm about to turn right, onto the path that will loop back toward the big lawn in the center of camp, but I pause.

Turning left will lead me to the Lodge. To Hillary.

And I could *really* use a girlfriend right now.

When I approach the Lodge, I'm relieved to see the window of Hillary's room glowing yellow. Soon I'm hurrying up the stairs and knocking on her door.

She opens it, her eyes wide with surprise. "Jessie. What's going on?"

"Can you talk?" I don't wait for an answer, just push my way past her. Then I see Cooper sitting on one of the twin beds and stop short. "Oh."

He and Hillary exchange a glance. They're fully clothed, but it's still awkward.

"I'll go," he says, and stands. But as he passes Hillary, he murmurs something to her, and she blushes.

"I'm sorry for interrupting, but . . ."

"It's okay. What's up?" she asks, motioning for me to sit next to her on the bed.

"Luke, that's what."

"What happened?"

I yank the elastic off one of my braids and pick at the loose strands. "What *didn't* happen, you mean? And he has the *gall* to act like I was *throwing* myself at him. Ugh!" I flop back on the bed like a dramatic teenager. "*He* was the one giving me compliments. *He* was the one saying I'm distractingly beautiful—"

"The nerve," Hillary says, smiling.

"Right? And then he's all, I could write a paragraph about your freckles, and I can't stop thinking about your body next to mine in the water, and I'm having dreams about you again—"

"Oh. My. God. You're kidding."

"I'm dead serious!" She's listening with rapt attention, like we're fourteen, in our cabin, talking about boy drama. "He's literally touching my *lips*, Hilly, so did I think he was going to kiss me?"

She hesitates and says, "Yes . . . ?"

"Of course I did! Wouldn't you? And when I leaned in— involuntarily, I might add—"

I break off, seething with frustration.

"Yeah?" she prods.

"He stepped away from me!"

She gasps. "He did *not*."

"He did!" I run my hands through my hair, my braids

thoroughly unpicked. "And then!" I stand and mimic Luke's posture, folding my arms and looking at the ground. "He's all, 'I'm not in a place in my life where I should get involved with anyone.' Like I even *want* that." I slump back on the bed, throwing an arm across my face. "I guess now I just avoid him for the rest of the summer."

"That's one way to handle it."

I move my hand, peeking out at her with one eye. "Do you have a better idea?"

Her lips curve up in a mischievous smile. "Oh yeah."

Thirty minutes later, we're sneaking through the woods, trying to be quiet even though we have to keep stopping because we're laughing too hard to walk. We're "camp drunk," as we used to call it—stone-cold sober but acting like sorority girls leaving a party at three a.m., giggling and stumbling. Deep inside, I know that what we're about to do is ridiculous and immature, but no way in hell am I stopping now.

We creep closer to Luke's cabin, and Hillary and I each stand behind a tree, peering out. His lights are on, giving us a full view inside.

"Can you see him?" I whisper.

"Yes. He's at the table, typing on his laptop."

"Guess what?" I whisper, revenge making me gossipy. "His wife divorced him because he's obsessed with his writing, did you know that?"

Hillary leans in, intrigued. "Oh, yeah? How do you—"

"I'll tell you later. Can you see if he's wearing headphones or anything?"

"He sure is," she says, grinning at me.

"Perfect."

We creep forward, climbing the stairs carefully, hoping they don't creak under our weight. Hillary catches her toe on a loose board and almost falls; I grab her arm, both of us shaking with silent laughter. Together, we set up the classic "bucket on the door" prank we must have played a dozen times as campers—though usually with water.

The ante has officially been upped.

Soon, it's ready: one bucket full of syrup we stole from the kitchen, another full of feathers from an old pillow at the lodge, both strategically balanced to tip over when Luke opens the door.

We creep down the stairs, back to our hiding place in the trees.

"Can you see him now?" I whisper to Hillary.

"Still typing."

I grin. "Ready with the pebbles?"

She nods, and we each toss a pebble at his door, then another. And another.

"He's getting up!" Hillary hisses.

"Hide!"

We freeze, standing straight behind our trees, holding our breath. There's a creaking noise as he turns the doorknob, a squeak of rusty hinges, then—

"WHAT THE FUCK?"

Luke's roar echoes through the forest, followed by grunts of disgust as the buckets overturn on his head. I'm dying to know what he looks like, but I'm laughing too hard to see. I glance at Hillary; she's doing the same, tears of laughter running down her face.

"WHO'S OUT THERE?" Luke yells, prompting a fresh

round of stifled giggles from us. "THIS ISN'T FUNNY. AT ALL." More grunts, followed by stomping. "What is this, *syrup*?"

I catch Hillary's eye. "Go," I whisper, pointing ahead.

She nods, and we race off through the woods.

"I can hear you out there!" Luke shouts. "Ugh—this is disgusting!"

His angry grumbles follow us as we run down the path toward the lake. We collapse on the dock, finally letting ourselves laugh until our stomachs hurt.

"That was *amazing*," Hillary says.

"That'll teach him." I sit up, looking at her. "Was that immature of us?"

She tilts her head, thinking. "Nah."

We both burst out laughing again.

"Jess? Hill?"

We whirl toward the lake, see bobbing heads in the water, a few yards off the dock.

"Dot?" I ask, squinting. I recognize her and Yvonne, plus a bunch of the campers, silver and white hair glinting in the moonlight. I'm pretty sure they're skinny-dipping.

"Come on in! Water feels great," Dot calls, and the women around her agree.

I glance at Hillary. "You want to?"

She cringes. "Ew, no. That water is like—"

"Fish and poop soup," we say at the same time, and laugh again.

"Who cares?" I say, then put my hands together like I'm praying. "Come on, *please*, Hilly Bean?"

"Okay, fine." Standing, she strips down to her bra and underwear. "I'm not going totally naked, though."

I shrug. "Suit yourself."

I strip everything off, which makes the women in the water hoot and holler, then grab Hillary's hand. We take off, running down the dock until we reach the edge, then launching ourselves into the air, where we hang suspended for one glorious moment before crashing into the cool water below.

twenty-three

Hillary

At Cooper's request, we're having the Sunday staff meeting over brunch today, because he's busy tonight. He's being cagey about it, avoiding my questions about his plans. I stopped short of reminding him about rule number five—he can end this thing between us at any time, but if he's sleeping with other women, he won't be sleeping with me.

Which is a depressing thought, and the reason I've been in a funk all day.

In the last two weeks, Cooper and I have more than made up for our slow start, giving Zac and Zoey a run for their money. Cooper's a quick study, learning how and where I like to be touched. He's more attentive than anyone I've ever been with. And probably more experienced . . .

I think back to what that woman from Boston said, and to Jessie's gentle warning. It's true; the old Hillary wouldn't have been comfortable with such a casual relationship—but maybe I'm changing, going through a metamorphosis like those butterflies in my belly. A caterpillar about to get her wings.

As always, we start the meeting with roses and thorns. We all agree on one big rose—*no one broke a hip!* The septuagenarian campers seemed to have the time of their lives, as evidenced by their generous pledges toward the co-op. We even sold our first naming rights—from here on out, the bench at the spot separating the boys' side from the girls' side (the one we used to call the French Bench) will be known as the Cohen Canoodling Bench. It's got a nice ring to it!

Jessie's going over the details for the week ahead—we're staging the camp talent show, and a few VIP former campers are coming—when the door opens and Luke stomps in, fury radiating from him like a thundercloud. Not unlike the last time I saw him, only now he isn't covered in syrup and feathers.

"Who did it?" Luke snaps, his terrifying ice-blue eyes sweeping over us all.

Everyone goes silent. Jessie looks up, her face the picture of innocence. "Did what?"

"You know damn well. Where were you last night?"

"In my cabin," Jessie says evenly.

"I was with her," I chime in, but my voice wavers. I'm not convincing anyone.

Luke's eyes widen. "You—"

"We were all together," Zoey cuts in.

Dot nods in solidarity. Jessie told her and Yvonne everything while we were skinny-dipping, and Dot must have told Zoey, which means Zac and Cooper are the only ones in the dark.

And Luke.

"Doing what?" Luke demands.

"Girl stuff. Face masks, mani-pedis, that sort of thing." I slide my hands under the table, hoping Luke didn't notice my nails are polish-free.

"Skincare is important," Jessie says. "Gotta take care of my freckles. Someone once said they could write a *whole paragraph* about them."

Luke's face reddens, and I can't tell if it's from anger or embarrassment. "You'd better watch—"

"Watch yourself," Dot cuts in, her face a stony mask of disapproval. "You may have been The Man years ago, but Jessie's The Boss now."

His jaw clenches. "That took me all night to clean up."

"I have no idea what you're talking about," Jessie says, giving him a crafty smile. "Would you like some eggs? Cooper was planning on making pancakes, but we're all out of syrup."

Luke's eyes flash, and he turns to Cooper.

"Don't look at me," Cooper says, holding his hands up. "I have no idea what's going on."

"Me neither," Zac pipes in. "But I'm on Jessie's side."

Luke turns to me and Jessie. "You'd better watch your backs," he snaps, "because I'm gonna—"

"Now, now," Dot says. "You're not thinking of starting a prank war, are you? Because between the four of us"—she indicates herself, Zoey, Jessie, and me—"I'd say we have about fifty years' worth of pranking experience."

I hear a thud, followed by a deep voice that's almost a growl. "Closer to a hundred, if you count me."

We turn to see Mr. Billy holding a shovel in his hands. The expression on his face makes me certain he wouldn't hesitate to use it in our defense. He may not know what this is about, but his loyalties are clear.

Luke takes a step back. "Fine," he says, an edge to his words. "What do you expect me to do?"

"I don't know," Zoey says in a snarky voice. "Maybe you could apologize?"

Luke scoffs. "For what?"

"For being frustratingly, maddeningly, distractingly rude," Dot says.

Luke goes pale.

"Just say you're sorry," I tell him.

"Tell Jessie she's a perfect queen and you're a dumb little dweeb," Zoey adds.

"Admit you're a pretentious prick," Dot says.

From Mr. Billy: "Grovel."

Next to me, Jessie folds her arms and smiles up at Luke. His hands clench into fists as he stares down the line at each of us. Then, without a word, he turns on his heel and walks out.

Once he's gone, Cooper's forehead wrinkles in confusion. "Wait—do you guys know where all the syrup went?"

I glance over at Jessie, and we dissolve into giggles.

Later that afternoon, I'm in my room, running numbers and working on a business plan for the co-op, trying not to think about what—or who—Cooper is doing, when three quick raps sound on my door. Our secret code.

I bolt out of bed and open the door. Cooper's there, wearing dark jeans, a green Henley, and his blue Red Sox hat. He's holding a bouquet of the tissue paper flowers he made in one of my arts and crafts sessions last week. "For you," he says, giving me a kiss on the cheek.

"I thought you had plans tonight?" I ask, confused but delighted.

"I do," he says. "I'm taking you out on a date."

"I'm not dressed for a date," I say, looking down at my leggings and tie-dyed Camp Chickawah T-shirt.

He reaches down to pick up something that's just out of sight in the hallway. It's a giant wicker basket, packed full of containers of food, two bottles of wine, and a blanket.

"But you're dressed perfectly for a picnic," he says with a playful grin.

Twenty minutes later, Cooper and I are walking through the empty campgrounds, hand in hand—I'm feeling more date-like after taking ten minutes to freshen up, changing into a sundress, and putting on makeup for the second time all summer.

As we stroll, Cooper suggests we make a "no talking about camp" rule—with the exception of me filling him in on what happened between Luke and Jessie, which I eagerly do. I finish the saga—and apologize for stealing the syrup—and he agrees that the punishment fit the crime.

The path through the woods is familiar; he's taking me to the waterfall—aka, the place where we had our second first kiss. My heart flutters. I bet Cooper is the kind of guy who remembers birthdays and anniversaries.

Which will be very lucky for some other girl, I remind myself, *since this is just a fling*.

"Wait here," he says as we reach the clearing.

Cooper takes a blanket from the picnic basket and spreads it out for us to sit on. I settle in, folding my legs beneath me as he sits on the other end.

"What did you make for us?" I ask, looking at the picnic basket, my stomach growling.

Cooper winces. "It's actually a little embarrassing . . ."

I arch an eyebrow. What could possibly embarrass Cooper?

He lifts the first container: the garlic-parmesan green beans we had for dinner last night. I gasp, bringing my hands to my face. "You didn't!"

"I did," Cooper says. His tone is self-deprecating, but there's a look of pride on his face.

I don't know how to respond—it's such a thoughtful gesture, and definitely outside the bounds of a no-strings fling. Instead of analyzing what it might mean, I lean over the picnic basket to kiss him. He shoves the Tupperware out of the way, and I crawl toward him. My lips never leaving his, I settle into his lap and enjoy devouring him as an appetizer.

One more benefit of leftovers: you don't have to worry about them getting cold.

We stay like that until my rumbling stomach interrupts the moment. Cooper laughs and pulls back. "I guess I should feed you," he says, taking the containers out one by one. "I am curious—do they have to actually be left over, or does it count as long as they're made in advance and saved for the occasion?"

"That would count."

Cooper shakes his head, and his confusion is adorable.

"I know it's strange," I say. "I think it might be a genetic abnormality. My mom apparently liked leftovers, too."

"Apparently?"

I nod, the dull ache that usually accompanies thoughts of my mom settling in my chest.

"She died when I was five," I tell Cooper. "But according to my dad, she barely ate a thing when they started dating.

She'd get most of her meal to go. He thought she just had a really small appetite—but one night after they moved in together, my dad found her in the kitchen, eating the leftovers in her pajamas. She said most dishes taste better that way, and I've always agreed."

Cooper hands me the container of penne alla vodka and a fork, and we both dig in. I sigh happily as I take a bite.

"So, have I convinced you of the virtues of leftovers?"

"There is a certain appeal—the chewiness of the pasta, the cold sauce." He takes an enormous forkful, then adds, "If you ever tell anyone I said that, I'll deny it until the day I die."

We pass the containers back and forth, trading stories of our lives back home. Mine are mostly about work and weekly dinners with Aaron and my dad—which makes me realize how small my life back home is. Even smaller now that I've ended things with Aaron.

Cooper, for his part, has me in stitches as he tells story after story. About the neighborhood cat named Chicken and the regulars at the bar near Fenway where he watched the Red Sox win the 2018 World Series. He convinces me that the trendy restaurant he worked for was named BIB after Bibb lettuce, that every dish was served on a bed of greenery. Turns out it's actually an acronym for Better In Boston, and to hear Cooper talk about the city where he was born and raised, things do seem better there.

I wonder if he would've given me a second glance if we'd met in Boston. If I'd even like the person—the womanizer— he was there. The other camper's words drift back to me like smoke from a campfire: *He'd sleep with anything that had a pulse.*

Almost involuntarily, I shift away from him. As if

putting space between us will remind my heart that he doesn't belong to me.

"Where'd you go?" Cooper asks, and I blink, see him watching me, a curious expression on his face.

I shake myself and force a smile. "I'm right here."

He narrows his eyes. "You promised honesty," he says, his voice low. "What's going on? You sort of . . . closed down there."

I sigh. "It's nothing. I was . . . thinking about something a camper said a few weeks ago."

"Which camper?" By the tone of Cooper's voice, I have a feeling he already knows.

"Her name is Olivia. She's from Boston."

Cooper takes his hat off and runs a hand through his hair before putting it back on. "What did she say?" His voice is hard, and I wish I'd just made something up. But it's too late now—I've ruined this lovely date night, and the only way out is through.

"She said . . . yousleptwithanythingwithapulse," I say, the words coming out in a rush.

Cooper flinches, like I've slapped him.

"I didn't believe her," I say, reaching out to take his hand in mine.

"You should have," Cooper says. He clears his throat and is quiet for a moment before he continues. "It's true. Not that I'm proud of it."

"We all have things in our past we're not proud of. Trust me, I have regrets, too," I say, eager to get the light and breezy feeling back.

He stays quiet for an excruciatingly long time, staring at our hands, our fingers intertwined. He doesn't look up as he starts to speak. "Remember that magazine spread I told you about?"

I nod, wondering if I should admit to googling him and gawking at the image of him and those abs. But then he looks at me with so much pain in his gray eyes that I can't risk saying anything that would hurt him more. I want to crawl into his lap and bring his smile back, but I know Cooper isn't going to let this go.

Stupid honesty.

"I should go farther back," he says. "You know I was a bigger kid. Fat."

"You were cute," I say, protective of young Cooper, the boy I shared my first kiss with.

"I didn't say I wasn't," Cooper says, and I zip my lips. "But at the time, I didn't feel cute. I was king of the friend zone, and I thought I might die a virgin. I told you I had a growth spurt when I turned seventeen, but I didn't tell you that earlier that year, I overheard two girls in my class calling me a 'dick-do.'"

I make a face, not sure what that means.

"My stomach stuck out farther than my 'dick-do.' It was stupid kid stuff, but it hurt—after that, I started counting calories and working out obsessively. By the time I graduated high school, I'd lost eighty pounds and gained some muscle. I kept it up over the next couple years and really started enjoying it. When I went to culinary school, I dated a bit, but inside I still felt insecure."

That explains the green smoothies and why he's so regimented about what he eats. I start rubbing circles on the back of his hand with my thumb. A spark of comfort so he knows I appreciate him opening up like this.

"When that magazine spread ran—" He pauses and blows out a breath. "It brought a lot of attention. At the time, I thought it was great. Everything a guy could ever hope for, right?"

He huffs out a sad laugh, and I squeeze his hand. "What happened?"

"Well. All those women wanting me was addictive. I kept chasing the high, hooking up with a different woman every weekend. Eventually, I realized that once that initial rush was over, I'd end up feeling . . . empty, I guess. I stopped liking the person I saw in the mirror. Started feeling ashamed of him."

He stops talking and looks down at me. "So. You still glad you're hanging out with me tonight?"

"Of course I am," I say honestly. My heart aches for him, for the sweet, chubby kid he was and the man he became. "But just because you *were* that guy doesn't mean you have to *stay* that guy."

He shakes his head. "What's that saying? A leopard can't change its spots?"

"You aren't a leopard, Benjamin Cooper. And one of the coolest things about being a human is that we have the power to reinvent ourselves. Seriously, look at this date—you took me on a picnic and packed my favorite foods, even though it totally goes against your professional standards." I gesture to the basket. "That's incredibly sweet. And thoughtful."

"Well, you're easy to please," he says, but he does crack a smile.

I shift my weight, facing him. "Listen, before this summer, I'm not sure I liked myself, either. I mean, I had the life I always wanted. My business was doing great; professionally, I was in demand; and I was dating the 'right' kind of guy, but I felt empty inside, too. I was so focused on achieving the next thing. I can't remember the last time I sat in the woods and had a conversation and just . . . enjoyed myself."

He leans back on his hands, appraising me. "Are you enjoying yourself?"

"Very much so." I slide closer, tucking myself into the crook of his arm. We sit like that for a while, watching the waterfall crash into the creek below. "Cooper, I have to believe people can change, because *I* want to change. I don't want to go back to being the person I was before—and you don't have to, either."

"Yeah," he says. "Maybe so."

"Definitely so."

I swing my leg around so I'm sitting on his lap and bring my face so close to his that he has no choice but to look me in the eye. We hold each other's gaze, and it feels even more intimate than anything we've done physically.

Cooper rolls us forward so I'm lying down and he's lying on top of me, his leg wedged between mine. His erection isn't the only thing pressing against me; there's a rock beneath the blanket, poking itself into my back.

"Ow," I say, and Cooper stops, the sadness in his eyes replaced with concern.

"Let's go back to the Lodge," I tell him.

"But the rules . . ." he starts.

"Are made to be broken," I finish.

The next morning, I wake up to butterfly-soft kisses on my shoulder and something long and hard against my butt.

"Mmm," I murmur, pressing back into him. Permission granted, Cooper continues, kissing my neck as he slides his hand beneath the T-shirt of his I wore to sleep. I had every intention of going back to my room, but when he suggested pushing the two beds in his room together, I couldn't resist falling asleep in his arms.

I didn't even think about how lovely it would be when we woke up.

"Morning," Cooper growls into my ear as he plays with my nipples. "I love having you in my bed."

"You mean I'm not dreaming?" My eyes are still closed, and my voice is thick with sleep. Cooper chuckles, his left hand traveling down my side, caressing my thigh before drifting up to my center. I'm wet and ready, grinding my butt back against his hardness.

He takes the hint and pushes my underwear aside, slipping one, then two fingers inside me. My breath quickens, but he takes his time, his movements languid and practiced until I can't take it anymore. I shift so I'm on my back and pull him on top of me, sliding his boxers down. Cooper reaches for a condom—we picked up two more latex-free packs last time we were in town—and slides inside, filling me completely.

We move together, slowly at first, like we've got all the time in the world, taking and giving until he picks up the pace, rising to a crescendo. Cooper shudders above me and I'm not far behind. We come together, and I've never, not once, been this in sync, this connected with someone.

Afterward, Cooper goes to shower, and I stay in his bed, floating in the afterglow. I could definitely get used to this. Not just the sex—although our chemistry is off the charts.

It's the way I feel around him, even when we're having hard conversations. Last night, he opened himself up so completely. It was raw and vulnerable. That's not something you do with a fling.

Which is all this is supposed to be. Just fun. No feelings. There aren't supposed to be feelings.

That's what complicates everything and makes it so confusing. Cooper barely checks any of the boxes on my list. He's nothing like what I thought I wanted. But he makes me so damn happy. Happier than I've ever been, which is terrifying, since this fling has an expiration date that's just a few weeks away.

Time needs to slow down, because I'm not ready for any of this to end.

At least there's a good chance Camp Chickawah will go on. The campers have been incredibly generous with their pledges, and if this week lives up to our (admittedly high) expectations, we'll meet our first financial goal.

Speaking of which, I need to get moving. We're meeting with one of our VIP alums, who's agreed to get our story in front of her hundreds of thousands of engaged followers. It's almost too good to be true.

I climb out of bed, debating whether it's better to be late and clean or on time and smelling like sex. Cleanliness wins. I take a lightning-fast shower, and by some miracle, I'm only two minutes late and slightly out of breath when I walk into Jessie's office.

She's behind her desk, sitting across from a stylish brunette who looks vaguely familiar.

"Hey, Hill!" Jessie says. "You remember Kat Steiner."

"Hillary Goldberg!" Kat says, leaping up to give me a giant hug. We were in Cabin Ten together the summer we turned twelve—and I remember being so jealous when Kat discovered her best friend Blake was actually her half sister. I would've given anything to have found out Jessie was my official sister, although I understand now how complicated it must have made things for them and their families back home.

"It's so good to see you!" Kat says, releasing me from her embrace. "Let's take a selfie!"

Before I have time to smile, Kat's iPhone is angled high above us, her cheek pressed to mine. The camera clicks and I freeze, picturing my awkward self being broadcast to her ginormous following.

"Kat and I were just talking about the talent show," Jessie says, getting us back on task.

"Yes!" Kat says. She's somehow managed to look both chic and ready for a day of fun at camp: jeans with strategically ripped holes at the knees, a white crop top with a white button-down shirt open over it, and a tan bolero hat. "I shared a teaser in my stories yesterday, and I'll be posting content about my camping experience all week."

"That's incredible," I say.

Kat brushes it off like it's no big deal, even though her connections could single-handedly save the camp. "I already have a link to the fundraising page in my bio—but the talent show is the real draw. I'm picturing one of those old-school telethons, where we'll talk about the camp and encourage donations between acts. And the whole thing will be live streamed!"

I wince. "But the Internet—"

"—won't be a problem," Kat says. "My brother-in-law Noah is into all that tech stuff—he brought equipment to boost the signal. He's not concerned, so neither am I."

I glance at Jessie, who shrugs before turning to Kat. "And you're sure we can't pay you?"

"The goal is to make you money, not for you to spend it. This is important to me—if it weren't for Camp Chickawah, I wouldn't have met my sister." She pauses and clears her throat, then smiles her bright smile before continuing. "The only thing I want is a slot in the talent show—Blake and I have been waiting sixteen years to perform our lip-sync routine."

I nod, remembering that summer when we were twelve. Kat had to leave the day before the talent show because her grandfather had passed away. The news was an unwelcome intrusion into our camp bubble, a reminder that life was going on back home and something bad might happen at any moment.

Come to think of it, that week was the second time Lola allowed me into the office to call my dad. She knew I was rattled and needed to hear his voice.

A familiar sense of panic stirs in my chest, and I make a mental note to come back to Jessie's office later to give my father a call. He won't be happy I ended things with Aaron, but hopefully he'll be proud of what I'm doing for the camp. Using my business acumen to save a place that's not only special to me, but was special to my mom, too. That's got to mean something.

"I'm telling you, everyone's going to know about this talent show!" Kat is saying.

I gulp. *Everyone?* The last thing we want is for the Valentines to get wind of our plan before we're able to tell them about it.

"We might want to block one or two people," I say.

"Sure thing," Kat says, tapping her phone to life. "Do you know their handles?"

Fifteen minutes later, we're rolling on the floor, laughing. We found and blocked Mary, no problem. Her Instagram account isn't active; her last post was from two summers ago.

But Jack? Apparently the one thing he loves more than money is dollhouses.

His feed is full of them. Ginormous ones. Small vintage ones. Empty ones, and ones with rooms full of teeny tiny furniture. I've never laughed so hard in my life, and I'm pretty sure Jessie peed her pants a little.

It felt good to laugh. Almost as good as it feels to have a solid plan to save our camp.

twenty-four

Jessie

The dining hall is abuzz with conversation as everyone gathers for the talent show. This is one of my favorite events of the summer—and tonight it feels extra special. We're so close to saving the camp.

Jack and Mary are doing a site visit and inspection with the new buyer on Monday. It's the perfect opportunity for me to explain our co-op plan. This morning, I sent the Valentines an email, inviting them to join me and our staff for dinner the night before the site visit, and Jack accepted.

Now I step out onstage, my nerves kicking into high gear. I've gotten used to being in front of a crowd of adult campers, but tonight a few thousand more are watching online.

"Welcome, everyone!" I say into the microphone. The audience applauds and whistles. "I'm thrilled to have so many people gathered for our talent show—in person and virtually. It's a joint effort by all the campers this week, but I want to give a special shout-out to Kat Steiner and Noah Rooney for all the help getting this online."

More whistling and cheering. Blake and Kat are in the front row with their husbands, and Blake shoves Kat to her feet so she can take a bow. Beside Blake, Noah lifts a hand and waves.

"Before we start," I go on, "I want to remind everyone what we're raising money for tonight. We're hoping to purchase the camp and keep it going for generations to come. Please check out our website for information on how to pledge money or otherwise support our cause. The response has been incredible, and we're close to reaching our goal!"

I scan the audience and realize with a start that I'm looking for Luke. We haven't talked since our confrontation the other day—I'm not avoiding him, exactly, but I'm kind of . . . embarrassed, I guess. By all of it. His rejection, my overreaction.

When I can't find him in the audience, my heart sinks.

I miss him. I didn't realize how much until this exact moment.

It would be one thing if I could brush him off as an asshole, but he's not—the other day, I watched him play "fetch" with Scout by throwing a stick into the lake, carrying her into the water to help her get the stick in her mouth, then carrying her back to shore, over and over again. His back must have been aching. It was the sweetest, saddest thing I've ever witnessed.

But if he's not an asshole, that means there must be something about me, specifically, that he doesn't like—which is fine, I'm not everyone's cup of tea.

You're a camp nine but a real-world six, a little voice from the past whispers.

Luke could definitely do better than a six.

Shaking off my dark thoughts, I smile and focus on the

audience. "Without further ado, let's start the show! First up we have Cabin Three, performing a skit they're calling 'The Aquamen'!"

And with that, the talent show is on. Cabin Three starts us off with a classic "synchronized swimming" skit: a blue sheet held in front to represent water, and a choreographed routine performed behind it, complete with matching swim caps and nose plugs. We roll through a variety of talents—an interpretive dance to "My Heart Will Go On" performed on rolling chairs from my office; Kat and Blake's lip-sync and dance to "Build Me Up Buttercup"; Cooper on guitar performing "Yellow Submarine." He's then joined by people playing fiddle, mandolin, and banjo for a rousing folk version of "She'll Be Coming 'Round the Mountain."

For our part, Hillary and I do our favorite skit from childhood—she sits behind me, and I pull my arms inside the big T-shirt I'm wearing while she puts her arms through, so it looks like her arms are mine. Then we re-create "A Day in the Life of a Camp Director," with Hillary attempting to braid my hair, put on my sunscreen, and feed me breakfast. I end up absolutely disgusting, but everyone is laughing, so it's okay.

The grand finale is a sing-along of Nathaniel's favorite song, "Take Me Home, Country Roads," with the changes he made to the lyrics to reflect our camp instead of West Virginia. We sing the chorus over and over, repeating the familiar words about returning home, to the place you belong.

Right here, I think. Doing exactly this.

After the song ends, I wipe my eyes and take the

microphone again. I thank the performers and everyone in the audience, both in person and virtual.

"To wrap things up," I say, "I want to give an update on our fundraising. Dot, do you have the total?"

She hands me a piece of paper. My heart pounds; this is the moment of truth.

Hands shaking, I take the paper. In the front row, Hillary's hands are clasped together as she waits.

I clear my throat and address everyone. "As you probably remember, Dot divides all humanity into two big groups: camp people, and those who aren't. And if you aren't, you're . . ."

"POND SCUM!" the audience yells, clapping and laughing.

"That's right," I say, smiling. "You probably also remember that camp people never say goodbye, we say . . ."

"See ya next summer!" the audience finishes, with more cheering.

I nod. "A month ago, I thought the end of this summer would mean goodbye, forever—and I was determined to make it the best goodbye imaginable. But thanks to the ideas of this brilliant woman"—I point to Hillary in the front row—"my incredible staff, and all you beautiful camp people who joined us tonight, in person or virtually, I finally have hope that Camp Chickawah will be here for many summers to come. And so, I am delighted to announce . . ."

I hesitate, my gaze drifting over the audience. And this time I see him, way in the back.

Luke. He's leaning against the wall, arms folded, watching me.

Our eyes meet, and a jolt runs through my body. For an instant, I falter—he unnerves me, the way he seems to see through my skin, even at this distance. But then he gives a small nod, like I'm doing just fine, and maybe it's pathetic, but that's all I need to collect myself.

"Thanks to your generosity," I say, a huge smile spreading across my face, "we've not only hit our goal, we've exceeded it by three thousand dollars!"

The room erupts into cheers. Hillary jumps up from her seat and runs to give me a hug. Dot joins us, then Zac and Zoey and Cooper, hugging and cheering.

By the time I look over at the door again, Luke is gone.

It's Sunday evening, and Cooper outdid himself with family dinner. Everyone's in a good mood as we discuss Zoey's latest "would you rather"—a choice between having chocolate hair or chocolate fingernails.

"Fingernails," Zac says immediately.

"You're going to eat your fingernails?" Zoey says, giving him a disgusted look. "I'd pick chocolate hair. Always have a little snack on the go!"

Zac tugs at his short hair. "That wouldn't work for me, babe. Can I share yours?"

"Ew, no," she says, and for a moment he genuinely looks like he's going to cry.

"Definitely better to have chocolate hair," Dot says. "Chocolate fingernails wouldn't provide any protection at all. Did you know that nail bed injuries can take six to twelve months to heal?"

I stifle a laugh. "I did, thanks to your first aid book."

"Okay, I have one," Hillary says. "It's chocolate adjacent: would you rather swim in a pool of M&M's or a pool of Skittles?"

"Skittles," Zac immediately says. "Body heat would melt the M&M's."

"What kind of Skittles?" Dot asks.

"I love the sour ones," I say.

Dot turns to me. "Ah, but you wouldn't want to swim in those. They're covered in powder. You'd breathe it in and develop a chemical pneumonitis."

Cooper slides in next to Hillary—he's always last to fill his plate—and says, "Would you rather keep talking about fictitious candy-related situations or our plan to approach Jack and Mary Valentine? They're coming tomorrow."

Everyone goes quiet. A heavy feeling of dread settles over the group.

"Sorry," Cooper says, wincing.

"No, you're right," I say. "We have the money raised. We have a business plan. We just need to get Jack's buy-in."

"And they're still planning on the dinner?" Hillary asks.

"Yep," I say. "Cooper, do you have the menu set?"

"Just about. I'll need to make a special trip to town for some ingredients."

"And Zac and Zoey, the sailboat will be ready?" I ask. We're taking the big forty-footer out on a sunset cruise for the dinner, giving Jack and Mary a view of the camp from the lake.

Zac gives a salute. "I found the perfect spot to drop anchor."

"The financials are almost ready," Hillary says. "I pulled comps in the area, so I know our offer is competitive, but we'll need to cover any penalties the Valentines will accrue from backing out of the sale, too. I also gathered stats on the

individuals joining the co-op, so they can see our plan is
viable."

"Excellent," I say. "And I'm working on my most
persuasive, heartfelt speech." Looking around at my staff, my
heart glows with pride and gratitude. My summer family.
"Let's save our camp."

When I head back to my cabin, there's an envelope stuck in the
doorjamb. It's addressed to me, written in unfamiliar
handwriting.

Jessie—

*Congratulations on reaching your goal. I can't say I'm
surprised—you've always been the kind of person who
achieves whatever she sets her mind to. Including
getting me to apologize (insert self-deprecating smile
from me). Even though you were the one who poured
syrup on my head (insert eye roll from you).*

*So here you go: I'm sorry. You're a perfect queen and
I'm a dumb little dweeb. I'm a pathetic, pretentious
prick. Whatever I have to say to get you to talk to me
again. You are quite literally the only friend I have
here. Which is my own fault for being antisocial, I
know. But still. Come say hi.*

—Luke

twenty-five

Hillary

Today is the day we save the camp—and the day I finally make up for turning my back on this place and Jessie a decade ago.

I've spent so many years feeling guilty for breaking my promise, but if I hadn't, I never would've gained the skills and expertise I'm using right now to help save Camp Chickawah. It's funny, I used to see my ability to separate my head from my heart as a strength when it came to business. But this project—and this summer—has shown me how powerful it can be when your head and your heart work together. It makes everything more meaningful, and it'll make our victory tonight even sweeter.

And we are going to be victorious.

I'm alone in Jessie's office—she and Dot are helping Zac and Zoey get the boat ready while I'm going over the final details of our offer. Usually, I'd have a PowerPoint presentation, each point displayed on a beautifully crafted slide. But we're taking a more casual approach, discussing the deal over dinner and drinks, which we hope will warm Jack's cold heart. Plus, there's the added complication of being out in the middle of the lake. I suppose we could project the slides against the night sky . . .

I laugh at the mental image of Jessie and me gesturing to

a pie chart dotted with stars and look over the numbers one last time before heading back to the Lodge. I've got just under an hour to rest and get ready for dinner. Thanks to my new sleeping arrangement with Cooper, I haven't been getting much sleep. Not that I'm complaining.

Since our date with the leftovers, something has shifted between us. We're not staying up all night having sex, we're staying up all night talking *after* having sex, conversations that feel intense and easy at the same time. The sex is different, too—still excellent, but there's more depth, like our goal has shifted from achieving the best possible orgasm to achieving the best possible connection.

It's feeling less like a fling and more like a relationship. I know it can't last, of course—Cooper's roots and connections are in Boston, and mine are in Chicago—but my chest fills with aching sadness whenever I think about having to say goodbye to him.

I'm doing my best to focus instead on what this experience is teaching me—how it's changed the way I think of myself and what I want in a romantic partner. Next time I meet a potential match, I won't be measuring him against a checklist, determining whether he meets enough of the requirements to warrant a second date. Instead, I'll focus on how he makes me feel—hopefully calm and comfortable in my own skin.

Which is exactly how I feel around Cooper.

Just thinking about him makes me feel warm and fuzzy inside, and I walk out of the office with a smile on my face.

It fades as soon as I see the black town car rolling down the gravel road.

A quick glance at my watch confirms it's only four thirty. *Shit*. The Valentines aren't due for another hour.

I grab my walkie-talkie to give the rest of the staff a heads-up. "The eagles are landing early," I say, before returning the walkie to my holster.

The car rolls to a stop in front of the dining hall. I stand with my hands on my hips and a giant smile on my face, the way I've stood every week for the last two months as we've welcomed each new group of campers. The only difference: those other times, my smile was sincere, and I was actually excited to see our arriving guests.

I strain to see the far side of the camp, hoping to catch sight of Jessie and her braids bouncing toward us. I don't . . . and the car door is opening. But it's okay. I'll introduce myself and take them over to the Lodge so they can—

"Hillary!"

I take a step back, startled. Because the man who just stepped out of the black car wearing a tailored blue suit and holding at least two dozen roses is *not* Jack Valentine.

It's Aaron Feinberg. The Aaron Feinberg I broke up with over three weeks ago. The Aaron Feinberg who had zero interest in coming to camp when we were together—so what in the world is he doing here now?

I'm still trying to process everything when someone else gets out of the car, a woman I've never seen before. She's tall and blonde and dressed in all black. One of Aaron's summer conquests?

Shocked, I stare as this woman pulls a large camera out of her bag and starts snapping pictures like it's her job.

Which, I realize with a sinking feeling, it is.

"Aaron!" I choke out. "What are you doing? This isn't—"

"Hillary," Aaron says. "You look . . . beautiful."

I glance down at myself, and my sense of dread grows. I'm in cut-off jean shorts and a Camp Chickawah T-shirt smudged with paint that wouldn't come out in the wash. There's no way he thinks I look beautiful right now.

The photographer is smiling broadly, snapping pictures, probably interpreting the shock on my face as delight. Which it most certainly is not.

Aaron steps closer to me, then begins to speak, his voice raised, as if he wants to make sure everyone hears him.

"My love," he says, "from the moment I met you, my life transformed in the most extraordinary way. With each passing day, my love for you has grown. I can no longer imagine a future without you by my side."

"Aaron," I say, holding out my hand for him to stop.

He doesn't. In fact, he goes down on one knee, and I freeze with horror.

The photographer keeps snapping pictures, circling us like a hawk.

"Today, as we stand beneath the breathtaking canvas of the setting sun—" He stops, realizing the sun is still high in the sky. Then, flinching, he continues, ". . . beneath the breathtaking canvas of the afternoon sun, I want to ask you a question that has been burning in my soul for the last two years. Hillary Elizabeth Goldberg, would you do me the incredible honor of becoming my wife?"

He pulls a Tiffany-blue box out of his pocket and opens it.

The silence that follows is deafening. The air is still. Even the birds have stopped chirping.

I'm frozen in shock—why on earth would he think this

was a good idea? I've never liked surprises. He knows that. He also knows I broke up with him—he replied with a freaking thumbs-up!

Did my father put him up to this? The thought makes me nauseous. My dad and I haven't been able to talk, but I sent him an email to let him know that I'd ended things with Aaron. I didn't go into detail because A) it's none of his business, and B) I didn't want to jeopardize Aaron's job at the firm. My father's response was curt, imploring me not to make a "stupid mistake" and let a "good guy" like Aaron walk away. I didn't reply.

I'm about to tell Aaron to get up when I hear something behind me. An inhalation of breath so loud it echoes in my ears. I turn to see Cooper, standing in the open doorway of the dining hall. He looks shocked, which is understandable. But he also looks betrayed, which is not. He's known about Aaron from the start, and he knows we broke up.

Before I can ask what's wrong, Cooper takes off, striding toward the lake like he can't get away from me fast enough.

"Cooper!" I yell after him, at the same time Aaron says, "Hillary?"

I sigh, feeling stuck between my past and my present. I want to run after Cooper and ask him what's going on, but I can't leave Aaron hanging. As misguided as this ridiculous proposal is, he flew all the way up here to see me. After two years together, I owe him a conversation.

Aaron's standing now, the pant leg of his designer slacks dusty from the gravel.

"What are you doing here?" I ask, noting with annoyance that the photographer is still snapping pictures.

"Isn't it obvious?" he says with a laugh. "You said you

wanted a romantic gesture. Here it is. I never should've suggested a break this summer. It was a mistake—"

"Why was it a mistake?" I ask, folding my arms. "You didn't enjoy your last hurrah?"

He shifts his weight in his shiny leather loafers. "I mean, not really. If I'm being honest, I thought it would go . . . differently."

I can't help but laugh. "So you didn't get the action you were hoping for?"

"Well, no," he says, "but that's not the only reason. I talked to your dad—"

"What?" I screech. "You told my dad about your ridiculous sexcapades?"

"No, I told him you ended things." He levels a sharp gaze at me. "By text. He was really disappointed in you."

I throw my arms out to my sides. "In *me*? You wanted to spend the summer having sex with other women! But of course, you didn't tell him anything that would make *you* look bad."

"He said I needed to get you back, Hillary, that we're good for each other. That it would be good for our future." Aaron's expression makes it clear that he's thinking about *his* future at my dad's law firm. "And he's right—we should be together. You said you wanted more romance? I'll be better, I promise. I can learn."

He looks so earnest, but I have a sneaking suspicion that this isn't about me at all—it's about keeping my dad happy. My dad, his boss.

"Aaron, come on. This isn't romance. The roses, the proposal—it's all so generic your little AI assistant could have scripted it."

His eyes go wide and his face turns beet red. The photographer focuses in on a close-up, and I can't help but laugh at the ridiculousness.

"Stop with the goddamn pictures," he snaps at her, then looks back to me. "Hillary, it's time to grow up. Your father agrees—"

"My father doesn't get to decide what I do," I say. "And neither do you. I think you should leave, Aaron. Go home."

He seems like he's about to relent, but then he shakes his head and squares his shoulders. "I'm only going home if you're coming with me. I'm sure you've had a 'super fun' time doing crafts and hanging out in the woods, but it's time to come back where you belong."

Anger bursts inside me like a flame. "I'm exactly where I belong, Aaron."

And as soon as I say the words, I know they're true.

Static erupts from my walkie-talkie, and I hear Jessie's voice. "On our way back, Hill."

"Please go," I tell Aaron.

He opens his mouth to protest, then closes it again. It's obvious that he's frustrated and annoyed by all the time and effort he put into flying up here, arranging the photographer, picking out a ring—not to mention taking the time off work. All that, and he didn't get what he wanted, which probably hasn't happened many times in his life.

But he is most definitely not heartbroken.

I can't believe I ever thought it would be a good idea to settle for someone like him. Someone who couldn't be bothered to put a single personal thing about me into his proposal.

"I thought this was what you wanted?" he says, his voice low and sullen.

"I thought so, too," I tell him honestly.

With that, he shakes his head and gets back in the car, closing the door on any future we might have had together. The car starts, and the photographer snaps one more picture before running around to the other side and climbing in.

No sooner does the black car pull away than another one comes rumbling down the road. It's not wide enough for them both, and Aaron's driver lays on the horn. The sound, once a familiar part of my city soundtrack, feels like an assault on my ears. I bring my hands up to cover them until the noise stops.

The second car, which I assume is carrying the Valentines—unless someone else has a jilted ex trying to win them back—backs up to let Aaron's car through. Once there's enough room, the driver hits the gas, sending dust and gravel flying.

I flush with embarrassment. And then I realize I have no reason to feel embarrassed. Aaron is no longer my problem *or* my responsibility. And that knowledge brings relief—that Aaron is gone, and that I wasn't stupid enough to fall for his ridiculous grand gesture. I'm proud of myself for standing my ground, even though I know I'll probably hear it from my dad about my "poor decisions" when I'm back in Chicago.

Growing up, my dad always said I seemed to turn into a different person when I went to camp—almost like that girl was an alternate me and my "real" self was who I was back home. His docile and obedient daughter.

But what if the opposite is true? What if I'm the real me here? Here, where I can sing camp songs with abandon and walk around with paint on my shirt, where I can craft to my heart's content and laugh until my sides hurt?

This summer, I've been able to bring my professional side to camp, too. My head and my heart, working together. For the first time in my life, I'm being my authentic self. All of me, at the same time, in this place.

And now, finally, here comes Jessie, just in time. Impulsively, I throw my arms around her and give her a hug, trying to transmit everything I'm feeling, my gratitude for her friendship, for the opportunity to come back to camp this year and set things right. "Thank you," I whisper in her ear.

When we separate, she raises an eyebrow, looking confused. "What's going on? Who was in that car?"

"I'll tell you later," I promise.

"Was it something to do with Cooper? He stormed onto the boat. Now he's belowdecks, rage-chopping vegetables."

Jessie's words make my stomach twist. I need to find and talk to Cooper. His reaction to Aaron showing up here was bizarre.

"I'll explain that later, too," I tell Jessie. I have to process what happened before I can even think about sharing it.

Her eyes fill with concern. "What's wrong? Are you okay?"

I nod, stuffing the shock of Aaron's proposal and my worry about Cooper into a separate compartment. I'll deal with all that later. Now, I have to focus on what might be the most important business meeting of my life.

As if on cue, the car holding Jack and Mary Valentine rolls up in front of us.

We have a camp to save.

287

twenty-six

Jessie

"You sure everything's all right?" I whisper to Hillary as we hustle down the path toward the lakefront. She seems dazed.

Zoey is about thirty yards behind us with Jack and Mary, charming them with stories of her childhood summers here. Zac's on the sailboat, ready to go, and Cooper has hopefully finished the salad (all fingers intact).

"Aaron just proposed to me," Hillary says in a soft voice.

I whip my head around like a cartoon character. "What? Aaron? The guy you were dating in Chicago?"

That part of her life feels like a separate universe now. Like I forgot that she doesn't live *here*, that summer camp isn't her entire world.

"That was him in the car you saw speeding away," she says. "It was . . . unexpected."

"What did you say?" I whisper. We've neared the lake, and Jack, Mary, and Zoey aren't far behind.

Hillary opens her mouth to answer, then sees Cooper coming toward us, wearing a plain white apron (seems boring for him, but he's trying to look professional), balancing several covered bowls and platters in his arms.

"Cooper!" Hillary calls. "I need to—"

"Excuse me," he says, his voice curt. He climbs on board

the sailboat and disappears belowdecks without a backward glance.

I turn to Hillary. "What was that?"

"He saw the proposal and seemed upset."

"He knew you and Aaron broke up, right?"

"Yeah, so I don't—"

"And here we are!" Zoey calls out behind us, and I whirl around.

Jack and Mary are standing there—Jack with his usual peeved expression, Mary slightly behind him with her usual soft smile.

The show is about to begin.

Everyone boards the sailboat, and Zac guides us out to the middle of the lake, where we'll drop anchor. The ride is smooth, with a light breeze. Cooper serves everyone a glass of wine and sets out an elaborate charcuterie board. Hillary sits next to me, Jack and Mary across from us. I introduced Hillary as our Arts and Crafts director, and if they're confused as to why she's eating with us, they haven't let on.

"Well, this is unexpected," Jack Valentine says, glancing around like he's wondering where all this luxury has been hiding.

"I hope you're hungry," I say. "I don't know if I mentioned that we have a classically trained chef on staff? Before this summer, he worked at one of the hottest restaurants in Boston."

"That's nice," Jack says absently.

"Very nice," Mary says, smiling timidly. "Doesn't everything look lovely?"

It's sunset on a cloudless evening, the lake a shimmering mirror reflecting the sky. The big, old sailboat has been strung with twinkle lights, which are beautiful—and help draw attention away from the peeling paint and worn deck. Looking back toward shore gives a perfect view of the camp: log cabins peeking out between pine trees, the green roof of the dining hall in the background.

While Zac drops anchor, Zoey comes out with the first course, fresh spring rolls and broccolini gomaae. Cooper is bustling around belowdecks and Hillary and I are making small talk; she's on point—I'm dazzled by how cool and confident my best friend is. We've got this.

Back on shore, Dot is getting everything ready for the next group of campers to arrive tomorrow—much to my surprise, Luke offered to help her. I'm overwhelmed with gratitude for all the work my team has put in.

A team that is going to come out on top.

Zoey carries out a tray with the main course, beautifully plated: cold poached salmon over a sesame noodle salad. I take a big sip of wine and remind myself about Nurse Penny's advice: rip off the Band-Aid and get back on the horse.

"There's something I'd like to talk to you about," I say to Jack once we start eating.

He looks up from his dinner, eyebrows raised. "Yes?"

"When she's not running our Arts and Crafts cabin, Hillary is a successful business analyst," I say, "and she's had a bunch of ideas about how to make the camp more profitable."

"That's right," she says, giving a professional smile. "We've implemented quite a few changes this summer, and already we've increased the camp's profits by twenty-three percent."

"Well done," Mary says, smiling.

Jack raises an eyebrow. "I'm not sure why that matters—"

"The adult camp has been a huge hit," I continue. "And there are so many other ways to utilize this property during the off-season, like—"

"What do you mean, *utilize* the property?" Jack cuts in.

"We . . ." I take a deep breath and get to the point. "We'd like to buy the property ourselves. We're prepared to make a very competitive offer."

Jack lets out an incredulous laugh. "An offer? The property is already under contract—it's too late."

"Hear us out," Hillary says calmly. "I've pulled comps in the area, and your buyer appears to be underpaying. We're offering you full market value, plus any penalties for backing out of the original contract. I have the details here—"

"I don't need to see any of that," Jack says. "You have no idea what you're doing, that's clear."

"Our plan is solid," Hillary says. "Hundreds of former campers have pledged to join a co-op to purchase the camp and run it together, with a board of directors and a transparent profit-sharing agreement. The capital has been secured; the business plans are ready."

"That's an interesting idea," Mary says, so quietly I barely catch it.

I turn to her. "You could join the co-op. It would mean a lot to everyone if we had a Valentine on the board."

And if Mary doesn't want to sell, we'd only need the co-op

to purchase half the camp, which would reduce the risk for our members.

"There's no way," Jack snaps. "You can forget it."

"But why?" Hillary asks. "Why does it matter to you who purchases the property?"

"First off, if I back out of the contract, I'll have to pay a penalty—"

"Which we already said we're prepared to cover," I cut in, but Jack goes on as if he hasn't heard me.

"Secondly, I'm selling to a developer that's going to put this place on the map," he says, tapping his finger on the table between us. "Make it an important destination."

"It already is an important destination," I protest. "And we're going to preserve it for future generations. It's what your parents always talked about."

I direct the last part at Mary; she's about to respond when Jack shoots her a glare, and she shrinks back in her seat.

Jack then turns his glare on me. "You don't need to tell me what my parents always talked about—I know very well. Everything in their lives revolved around this damn camp! As for the current buyer underpaying me?" He leans forward, his small eyes locked onto mine. "You don't have all the information about this sale."

Hillary and I exchange glances.

"What do you mean?" I ask.

"As part of the contract, Mary and I are each keeping a prime piece of property. The plans for my lake house are already underway—it's being designed by a world-renowned architect whose work is regularly featured in *Architectural Digest*," he says proudly. "I'll finally feel at home in this place!"

My heart sinks.

"Isn't there anything we can do to change your mind?" I say, desperate. "You know how much this place meant to your parents. Do you really think they'd be okay with you selling it?"

I glance between the two siblings, panic rising in my chest. Mary's eyes are shining with tears, but Jack's jaw is set. My heart plummets into my stomach. All the time we've spent on this plan, wasted.

"The decision has been made," Jack says. He wipes his mouth and leans back, waving at Zac. "Take us back to the dock, please. Now."

"Mary," I say to her, "is there any way—"

"I'm sorry," she whispers, looking down. "I can't."

We wait in awkward silence as Zac pulls the anchor up and navigates the sailboat back to the dock. I'm struggling to contain my emotions, refusing to break down in front of Jack Valentine. Under the table, Hillary grabs my hand, and I concentrate on the feeling of her warm palm against mine.

As soon as we reach the dock, Jack heads off, followed by Mary, who trails after him like a sad duckling.

I look at Hillary. Her face is white; she looks as stunned and devastated as I feel. "I'm sorry," she whispers. "I really thought—"

"It's not your fault," I say. My throat is so tight I can barely get out the words. "I—I need a minute. Okay?"

I stumble off the boat, onto the deck, and away.

Tears flood my eyes as I take the path that leads north, past the boys' cabins, before diving into the wooded, undeveloped part of the property. It hits me all over again that this won't be undeveloped for long—a year from now, most of these trees, some of them a hundred years old, will be gone. Wiped away. Along with everything else.

Stepping off the path, I rush through the trees, branches catching on my clothes and hair. A sob collects in my throat and my knees feel like they're going to buckle, so I lean against a tree, wrap my arms around myself, and cry.

It's over.

I will never welcome another group of children to camp. I'll never tell another ghost story to a wide-eyed group of eight-year-olds, never take the fourteen-year-olds on their overnight backpacking trip, never cook tinfoil dinners in the firepit with the new counselors during training week. This place, these experiences, are an essential part of my soul.

I don't know how I can go on without them.

I have nothing else that matters to me. All these years, I've thought of my life as adventurous, as brave and important. But I've let my world shrink to three hundred acres, all my efforts focused on two months out of the year.

This camp is my life. And I have no idea who I'll be without it. I lean against the tree and let myself cry.

Eventually I hear footsteps approaching, and straighten.

It's Luke, ducking under branches and stepping over logs as he picks his way toward me. Quickly, I wipe my eyes.

"I heard the news," he says. His expression is all gentle concern. "Can I—do you want to talk about it?"

I swallow and shake my head. "I don't know if I can."

"You could try. I'll listen."

My eyes immediately fill with tears again. All my emotions bubble over, and my words rush out of me, raw and aching:

"What was the point of any of this? I put all my eggs in

this basket, and now the basket is broken, and the eggs are splattered on the ground." My voice catches. "I was so stupid, investing my *entire life* in something that could end."

"Jess, everything ends."

I look at him, my cheeks flushed. "What?"

"Nothing lasts forever. We like to pretend it will, because it's too painful to confront the truth that we'll eventually lose everything we love."

I gape at him, aghast. "Do you think this nihilistic bullshit is the best thing to say to me right now?"

"Sorry." He grimaces and runs a hand through his hair. "I'm not good at this. What can I do?"

He says it so earnestly, like he feels inadequate but wants to help anyway.

My response surprises me: "You could give me a hug."

His eyebrows shoot up, as if it's a ridiculous request.

"Ugh, never mind," I say, turning to go.

But he grabs my hand, pulls me toward him, and wraps his arms around me. For an instant I'm frozen, stunned at being this close after all these weeks at a distance. Then my body relaxes, the air emptying out of my lungs in one long exhale, and I lean against him.

"I am so, so sorry," he whispers.

I don't know if he's apologizing for being kind of a dick, or if he's sorry that the camp is doomed, but either way, I appreciate it. I'm trying not to sob, but when I take a shuddering breath, Luke rubs my back gently, and that's all it takes for me to start crying again.

I'm not sure how long we stay like this, locked in an embrace in the middle of the woods, but at some point I become aware that this hug is shifting from friendly and supportive to . . . something else. Luke is touching the loose hairs at the base of my neck, his fingers brushing my skin, sending goose bumps down my spine. His other hand slides lower, to the curve at my waist, pressing me closer.

My breathing goes shallow. I'm exquisitely aware that his mouth is an inch from my cheek. He smells so good I want to bury my face in his neck. My hands are itching to dip under his shirt and feel his skin; my pulse is throbbing between my legs.

Somehow, in the midst of my sorrow, I'm getting turned on.

And so is he, I think; his heart is beating way too quickly for a man standing still. His hand moves up into my hair, his fingers rasping against my scalp, and I bite my lip to hold in a moan. I ought to step away. Luke has been doing this kind of thing for weeks, getting close and then pulling back—but instead, I run my hand up the back of his neck into *his* hair.

His breath rushes out in a sigh of pleasure. I let my hands roam over his shoulders, feeling the planes and ridges of his back. He's doing the same, running his palms down my spine, up the sides of my ribs.

Slowly, he presses his mouth to my jaw, a gentle kiss that makes me sag with relief. With one arm he pulls me flush against him; he's hard. I don't move a muscle, silently praying that he doesn't stop. He kisses my jaw again, then down the side of my neck, his lips parting so I feel his tongue on my skin as he gently sucks. This time, I can't hold in my moan.

Luke pulls back slightly and I get a glimpse of his face: his eyes hazy with desire, the groove between his eyebrows deepening in concentration, his mouth full and soft.

"God, I want you," he murmurs.

I can't seem to find any words, so I nod. *Same.*

His lips curve in a smile as he leans in, and—

My walkie-talkie crackles on my belt. "Jessie? Jessie, where are you?"

It's Hillary. She sounds worried.

I hesitate, not wanting to stop, but Luke takes a step back, turning away so I can't see his face. My heart sinks; is he doing this again? This stupid push-and-pull he's been doing all summer?

"Jessie? Are you there?" Hillary says on the walkie.

Luke is still facing away from me, so I sigh and grab the walkie-talkie off my hip.

"Here," I say into it. "I'm in the woods north of camp."

"On my way."

I replace the walkie on my belt. Luke turns to face me. He's shut down again, all the softness erased from his face. It's like looking at a brick wall, and I'm so fucking sick of this response after *he* initiates something with *me*.

"I should go," he says.

"Yes, you should," I say, not bothering to hide my irritation.

His mouth falls open. "That's not—"

"I'm done with this," I say, motioning between us. "Okay? Don't tell me you *want* me and then pull away and act all shocked that I'm annoyed." I shake my head. "Have the day you deserve, Luke."

I head back toward camp, leaving him speechless behind me.

It doesn't take long before I see Hillary on the path, her face red and blotchy. Behind her is the rest of my staff: Dot, her eyes glassy with tears; Zac and Zoey, arms linked, faces etched with sadness; and in the rear, Mr. Billy, his angular face wrinkled with worry.

No Cooper, though, and I'm about to ask where he is when Hillary pulls me into a hug. She's crying, which makes me start crying again, and this is exactly what I need in this moment: friendship. Support. Understanding.

"I'm sorry," she whispers. "We're all so sorry."

I shake my head. "We did the best we could, and I'm proud of us."

Dot puts her arms around Hillary and me and squeezes. Zoey does the same, followed by Zac, and finally Mr. Billy, his long arms wrapping around all of us.

Out of the corner of my eye, I see Luke moving past, through the trees, watching us.

I close my eyes and pretend like this hug will never, ever end.

twenty-seven

Hillary

It's over. Really, truly, officially over.

And it's all my fault. Jessie says she doesn't blame me, but I don't know how she can't. It was my job to convince the Valentines our plan wasn't just the best option; it was the only one. I had all the data I needed to speak to Jack's wallet and Mary's heart, but I failed.

And I can't even blame Aaron for throwing me off with his surprise proposal. I was on top of my game, but I still couldn't close the deal. And now, Jessie is going to lose the one thing that matters most to her. Camp Chickawah isn't just her job. It's her home, her family. Her whole life.

Jessie has every right to be upset with me, but somehow, she's not.

It's Cooper who's treating me like I have the plague. Mr. Billy has said more words to me in the last forty-eight hours than my so-called fling. Cooper can barely look at me, which makes no sense. I've been honest with him from the start; he knew everything about my history with Aaron: how we were on a break, and—most importantly—that I ended things before I slept with Cooper.

Not that it should have mattered. See aforementioned detail about the break.

And it's not like Cooper's past is squeaky-clean. He admitted as much last week on our stupid, wonderful picnic date. Even so, if one of his former conquests showed up at camp and tried to win him back with a ridiculous unromantic gesture, I wouldn't freak out. I mean, I might be uncomfortable, but I wouldn't push him away.

It wouldn't make sense to get upset over it, because this is just a fling. Sure, we broke some of our rules, but none of the major ones. It's still casual. Purely physical. All that emotional stuff, the way I feel around him, about him, that's just in my head.

Right?

So why is he so upset? And why do I miss him so much?

My ridiculous heart is galloping in my chest, so I take a deep breath and remind myself why I came here in the first place. Having the best sex of my life was just a bonus, and if it's over, so be it. The relationship I came here for was—and still is—a platonic one.

I look down at the friendship bracelet in my hand, the one I've been working on for the last three days. Its base is bright yellow (Jessie's favorite color) with blue accents (mine). I know it's a poor substitute for losing the camp, but I needed to do something. To give her something.

Now, I just have to find her.

She's not in her office, but Dot is, organizing some paperwork. She glances up when she sees me come in and sets it down. "How're you holding up, Goldberg?"

I shrug. It feels wrong to complain to someone who is losing their livelihood because of my inability to close a deal.

"I should be asking you that," I say. "How are you?"

"I'm on this side of the earth, and the sun is shining, so I'm not so bad."

"You're not sad? Or angry?"

She gives a wry smile. "I have my moments—and I'd be lying if I said I didn't look into getting a voodoo doll of that rat bastard."

A laugh bursts out of me, despite how sad I am. "We might have the supplies to make one in the Arts and Crafts cabin. Or an effigy to burn."

"Now you're talking," Dot says, laughing. Then her expression softens. "I know you're disappointed, Goldberg, but you can't control how other people respond. And you did good. Your momma would be real proud of you."

She clearly reads the confusion on my face, because she kicks out a chair on the other side of her desk and motions for me to sit. "Did you know I went to camp with your mom and aunt?"

My jaw drops. "What? You knew my mom?"

"Damn straight," Dot says. "Your aunt Carol was in my cabin, and Becky was like her shadow, always hanging around." She pauses, considering my face. "You remind me a lot of her. She was artsy, and fearless, too—I remember one summer her cabin was doing an overnight hike, and the counselor got stung by a bee. Girl was allergic, and your momma ran all the way back to camp to get help. Three miles, in the dark, all alone. Saved that girl's life. Real brave."

I glance down at my hands. My mom saved a girl's life; I couldn't even save the camp.

"I wish I'd inherited her bravery," I say softly.

"You did," Dot insists. "It was damn brave of you to come

back here. You knew Jessie was upset with you. And you didn't know a thing about running an arts and crafts program. But you showed up. That took a lot of guts."

My cheeks flush, embarrassed. I'd hoped my ineptitude wasn't obvious—but I've got the swing of it now, and it turns out I'm not bad at it.

Dot's still talking. "Not to mention this ballsy plan of yours to buy back the camp."

"Which wasn't successful," I say, slumping forward in my chair. Jessie was my motivation for saving the camp, but part of me wanted to save it for my mom, too. Camp Chickawah was a place she loved. A place we shared, decades apart, even if she never knew I came here.

"I guess that depends on how you define success," Dot says thoughtfully. "It brought you and Jessie closer together—and a friendship like yours doesn't come around every day, or even every decade. So take that for the win it is."

Dot's right, and I'm grateful for her perspective. I'm about to ask if she knows where Jessie is when the phone rings. Dot answers it, and I slip out so she can get back to work, marveling at the idea of her and my mom knowing each other. I wonder what other stories Dot can tell me about her, more things I never knew we had in common.

I continue my search for Jessie, trying the dining hall next. The light is off in the kitchen, and I don't know whether I'm sad or relieved that I won't have another awkward run-in with Cooper.

I'm about to leave when I notice the old camp photos lining the back wall. More than one hundred years of history, black-and-white photos that turn to sepia and, eventually, to color. I don't know why I never thought to look for my mom here.

I locate the summer of 1978 and press my finger against the cool glass of that frame, then the next, looking at each and every girl in the annual camp photos. So many of them could be Mom—brown hair, wide eyes, a button nose, and a shy, knowing smile.

And then I find her. In the second row of the 1984 photo—my mom, Rebecca Katz. She must be around thirteen or fourteen. Her hair is parted down the middle. It's not as curly as mine, but it's just as dark, and she's wearing a Camp Chickawah T-shirt knotted on the side. Her smile is wide and unguarded, a hint of mischief in her eyes. Her arms are linked with two girls on either side of her, and a lump forms in my throat as I remember gathering for that same group photo every summer, surrounded by my own camp friends.

What would my mom tell me if she was here? Would she be proud of me, like Dot said, for coming back and trying to set things right? Or would she be disappointed that I've spent most of my life chasing a future I didn't really want? Checking off boxes I thought would lead to happiness, when it turns out the joy I craved was here all along?

In the place where I belong.

I manage to find more photos of my mom, my aunt, and a much younger Dot. Part of me wants to stay here forever, searching these memories in the hopes of finding answers about who I am and where I ought to go from here. But staying alone in the dark isn't going to give me what I'm looking for. I need to find Jessie.

After striking out on the girls' and boys' sides of camp and at the Lodge, I head down to the lake. Jessie isn't by the boats or near the swimming dock—but then I remember a place we used to go when we were kids. We called it our secret cove; it's just north of the Lodge, past a bend in the lake. No one could see us from land, but it was close enough that we could hear the counselors calling.

Sure enough, Jessie's there, sitting on a patch of sand, her arms wrapped around her knees, staring out at the water. She looks so peaceful and serene that I regret hunting her down. The woman is about to lose everything she cares about; she deserves some solitude.

I'm about to turn and go when she looks up.

"Hey," she says. The emotion in her voice, soft and sad, catches me off guard. But I'm grateful she isn't putting on the smiley veneer she's been wearing the last few days for the campers. This simple act of letting me in means so much more than a silly friendship bracelet.

"I don't want to bother you," I tell her.

"You're no bother," she says, patting the sand beside her.

I accept her invitation, mimicking her position and tucking my knees up to my chest. The sound of the water is soothing, and again my mind drifts to my mom. My brave and beautiful mom. I wonder if she had a best friend here, someone who was to her what Jessie is to me.

I glance over at Jessie, grateful that our friendship has survived so much.

"Thank you," I tell her.

"For what?"

"Being my friend. Despite everything."

Jessie rolls her eyes and knocks her shoulder against mine. "You're stuck with me, Hilly Bean—as long as you stop apologizing. You've hit your quota."

"But I am sorry," I say. "So sorry."

"Zip it," Jessie says. "I will accept no more apologies."

"How about gifts?" I ask. "Will you accept gifts?"

"Always," Jessie says, her eyes sparkling.

I pull the bracelet out of my pocket and hand it to her.

"It's beautiful," she says, turning it around in her hands. "I could never get that V pattern right."

"I can show you," I offer. "It's not that hard."

"Maybe," Jessie says. "I'll have plenty of free time." Her shoulders slump, her body deflating at the intrusive reality of just how close we are to the end of summer.

"That rat bastard," I say, borrowing Dot's nickname. Jack Valentine spent all day yesterday with the buyer, traipsing around the property, talking loudly about the plans for the new development. His custom lake house is going to sit right smack where the Lodge is now—and the thought of him sitting on his porch gazing at the lake while the land behind him is parceled out and sold makes me want to punch someone.

Jessie sighs. "It's going to take all of my acting chops not to be rude when they come up on Saturday for the dance."

"They're still coming?" I say, shocked.

"Yup," Jessie says. "It's tradition—the family comes every year, and this is the last."

"Thanks to them," I mutter, digging my toes in the sand.

Neither of us says anything then, and the sound of campers laughing and splashing in the lake drifts down to our hiding spot. The last end-of-summer dance, ever. My heart clenches. There's got to be a way to make it extra special for Jessie.

I look at my best friend, wearing her usual colorless, comfortable, functional clothes.

"Speaking of the dance," I say. "You aren't going to wear khaki, are you?"

Jessie barks out a laugh. "What's wrong with khaki?"

"Nothing—for everyday wear. But you said yourself, this is the last dance. You should wear something special."

"I don't think I have anything special," she says. "Unless I raid the costume closet."

"You are not going to the dance dressed as Dorothy."

"We did *Beauty and the Beast* last summer," she says. "I could be Belle."

"And Luke could be the Beast," I suggest, knocking my shoulder against hers.

Jessie huffs and shakes her head. Looks like I've stepped on another land mine.

"Do we need to pull another prank?" I ask, cracking my knuckles. "Because I will. I'll cover his toilet bowl with Saran Wrap."

Jessie laughs, but her heart's not in it. "No. I don't know. Maybe."

"What happened?"

"Nothing," Jessie says flatly. "Literally *nothing*. And I don't know why I keep expecting anything different. One moment, he's ridiculously sweet; the next, he's a total jackass again. He's just so frustrating."

"Aren't all men?" I say, my cheeks burning with the

thought of my now-former fling. "Tell you what, he and Cooper can have each other."

"He's still being weird?" Jessie asks.

"Very," I admit.

There's a lot of hurt in that single word. But I'm sure I wouldn't feel this awful if I could have just let this summer be fun, so in a way, it's my fault. I blatantly ignored the rules we made—rules *I* made, to try and protect myself from the very things I'm feeling now. Confused. Sad. Missing him so much my heart aches every time I wake up and he's not with me.

"Have you talked?" Jessie says. "Asked him what's going on?"

I shake my head. "I tried, but it didn't go well."

"What did you say?"

My stomach clenches at the memory of Cooper's vacant stare. How he looked at me like he didn't know me. Like he didn't want to know me.

"I went to the kitchen to talk to him," I tell Jessie. "I said, 'Hey.'"

"And he said . . ."

"He said 'hey' back, then turned and started washing dishes."

Jessie exhales a puff of air, which captures how I felt in the moment. Like the wind had been knocked out of me. It should have been fine; it would have been fine if I'd kept things light and fun. Instead, I had to go and fall for the guy.

My stupid, stupid heart.

"And then what?" Jessie asks.

"Then nothing. I walked away."

I think back to what Dot said about my mom. About me. But she was wrong. I'm not brave. I'm a coward, afraid to hear the boy I like—the boy I *really* like—say he's not into me anymore.

"I wonder if something else is going on," Jessie says. "This doesn't seem like Cooper."

"Yeah," I say, although I wonder if the Cooper we've gotten to know is the real Cooper. Or if the real Cooper is the one that woman from Boston talked about. Maybe he just got tired of pretending.

"I'm really proud of you, by the way," Jessie says.

My eyebrow arches.

"It couldn't have been easy saying no to a proposal," she says. "I remember you wanted to be engaged by the time you turned thirty."

I forgot Jessie knew about my plan and my timeline—I was pretty open about it when we were teenagers. I think I even told Cooper about it once. Maybe that's what happened—seeing Aaron propose reminded him of how much I wanted to get married. Maybe he pushed me away out of fear that I'd try and rope him into a commitment.

"At the start of the summer, I probably would have said yes to Aaron," I tell Jessie. "But spending the last two months here has made me realize I want something different from my life."

"Like what?"

"Wouldn't it be nice if I knew," I say. A small part of me hoped that after the deal with the Valentines went through, I'd be able to stay involved with the camp and Jessie in some business-advisor capacity. But that dream went bust on the sailboat.

"You'll figure it out," Jessie says. "Just follow your heart—it won't steer you wrong."

Maybe she's right. Following my head certainly hasn't worked for me.

"Speaking of your heart," Jessie says, "I wouldn't give up on Cooper just yet. I've seen the way he looks at you."

"What way?" I ask, desperate for even the tiniest bit of validation. Because rules be damned, what we had wasn't just physical. If it was, he wouldn't have been so thoughtful, listening to me and paying attention to the stories I told him. If he didn't care about me, why would he ask me about my mom? Go out of his way to save me leftovers or take me on a romantic date? Spend so much time learning my body, focusing on what makes *me* feel good. Make me come and laugh and cry and feel things. For him.

"The same way you look at him," Jessie says, pulling me back to this moment. "The two of you, I don't know, it's like you always know where the other one is in the room, like there's an invisible string connecting you. And he makes you smile. I swear, Hilly, you smile more around him than anyone else."

Her words make me grin, until I remember I'm not that happy anymore.

"You know," Jessie continues, "when you first got here, you seemed so . . . tense. Like you were here, but not *here*. You were on the edge of everything. Observing, one step removed. But with Coop, you're fully present. You are unapologetically yourself. And I like yourself."

"I like this version of me, too," I say.

Jessie reaches over and brushes a tear from my cheek. I didn't realize I was crying, but the gesture makes the tears fall faster. I'm so incredibly grateful to have her friendship back.

"Cooper's not the only reason I've been more myself," I tell her. "You're a big part of it, too. I haven't been this close—or close at all—to anyone since you."

Her blue eyes fill with concern. "Really? Why not?"

I shrug. "It's not easy for me to open up to new people. And losing your friendship hurt so much that I think part of me was scared to let myself feel like that about anyone else. Not that I'm blaming you—"

"I wish I'd handled things differently, too." She puts her arm around my shoulder and squeezes me against her. "And I get what you're saying. When I lost you, it felt like I lost part of myself. Like my heart was that necklace you gave me—all jagged and half-broken."

"People always talk about soulmates as being romantic," I say, leaning my head against her shoulder. "But is it weird that you're the closest thing I've ever experienced to that?"

"Not weird at all," she says, and rests her head on mine.

We used to sit like this all the time as kids, sometimes here in this exact spot. Just like back then, I gaze out over the lake, feeling the warmth of the sun on my bare arms, the tickle of one of Jessie's braids dangling against the back of my neck.

And for the first time since the terrible dinner with Jack Valentine, I feel like maybe things will be okay. The camp is ending, Cooper isn't talking to me, and I have no idea what I want to do with my life. But like Dot said, this summer has been a success—it brought me and Jessie together again.

"Will you be my date to the dance?" I ask after a beat.

"Duh," Jessie says.

I grin and exhale a sigh of relief. The Valentine Dance—named after the camp owners, not the Hallmark holiday—

was never a big romantic event. It's a party, a fun celebration to mark the end of another incredible season.

And in spite of everything that tried to bring us down, this summer has been incredible.

"Tell you what," Jessie says. "You can have the Belle costume, and I'll find something else."

"Hard pass," I say. "But I have a better idea."

Jessie looks at me, her head tilted in anticipation.

"Think Dot can cover for you during dinner?" I ask.

"Maybe?" Jessie says, her voice wavering.

"Because you are driving the two of us into town to shop for party dresses. Make those boys drool and realize what they're missing."

Jessie laughs. "I hate to break it to you, but our shopping options are Walmart and Walmart."

"I'm up for the challenge if you are," I say, standing. I extend a hand to help her up, and after a long moment, she takes it.

"You're crazy," she says. "But I'm in."

twenty-eight

Jessie

I'm sitting on my bed, finishing my every-other-Thursday check-in call with my dad, which interrupted my morning cry-fest. Ever since the horrible dinner with Jack and Mary, I've been crying multiple times a day, tears spilling out of my eyes almost without warning. Luckily, my dad prefers regular calls, not FaceTime like my mom.

"Any luck on the job front?" my dad asks. Typical.

"I have an interview on Monday for a position at a summer camp in West Virginia."

It's a seasonal position, a supervisor for the female counselors, but the director said after the first summer he'd try to keep me on year-round. It's not Camp Chickawah, but at least I'll be doing what I love.

Still, the thought of working anywhere but here is what started me crying earlier.

"That's great!" My dad sounds excited; he must be *very* worried about me. "Have you thought any more about coming to stay with us for a while?"

"Um, I'm not sure—"

"—because we can put a futon in my office," he goes on. "It'll be fine—you won't be in the way."

"That's . . . very kind of you, Dad," I say, treading lightly.

While I appreciate his offer, I'm less than thrilled about squeezing myself into his family's space, like I did throughout my childhood.

The only place that has ever felt like mine is disappearing.

"Keep me posted," he says, and we say goodbye.

I head out into the morning sunlight and start down the path to the lake. But, almost against my will, I find myself veering onto the path that leads to the boys' cabins. To Luke's cabin.

This is what happens when your sexual awakening is Gerard Butler in the 2004 *Phantom of the Opera* film—you end up falling for the moody, artistic recluse who spends all his time in a dark hovel, hiding from the world. But if I'm going to visit Luke, I need to come up with some excuse. Maybe I'll ask him to join the backpacking group—we're leaving on the traditional overnighter today, one of my favorite events of the summer. Anything but the inexplicable fact that I *miss* him. My brain keeps replaying the memory of him holding me as I cried; his lips pressing against my jaw; his low voice saying *I want you.*

Why can't my brain replay the pure aggravation I felt when he pulled away? That would be smarter. *That* would keep me from doing what I am right now: walking up the stairs to his cabin and knocking.

The door swings open. I peer into the dark interior and see him sitting on the mattress on the floor, Scout curled next to him. His head is bowed, his shoulders slumped forward.

"Luke?"

He raises his head; he looks stricken. "She's gone."

My heart drops.

I walk over; my inclination is to put an arm around him, but I'm not sure he'd welcome that. He seems to have retracted into himself, his eyebrows drawn together, his mouth a grim line.

So I settle next to him on the mattress and wait.

"I knew this was coming," he says. His voice is rough, and he clears his throat. "She's been slowing down, sleeping more, not eating much. Yesterday she hardly moved. It's not a surprise."

"But it's still hard," I say quietly.

"Yes." He wipes his eyes. "I have a spot picked out. To bury her, I mean. She liked it by that stream north of here."

"That's a beautiful spot. Would you like some help?"

"I'll borrow a shovel from Mr. Billy and take care of it," he says. My mind fills with an image of Luke in the woods, all alone, digging a hole, and my chest constricts. "But maybe this evening you could come with me and . . ."

"I'll be there," I say immediately. The backpackers will have to go without me. "Would you like the rest of the staff to come, too?"

"I'd rather not."

I nod, honored that he wants me there. And grateful for something to focus on besides my own impending loss. Again, I feel that urge to wrap my arms around him, but I settle for pressing my shoulder against his. He doesn't pull away.

"You gave her a beautiful life, Luke."

A puff of air escapes his lips; when I glance at him, there's a sad smile on his face. "I know."

And he leans his forehead against my shoulder and quietly cries.

I wish I could stay with him, but I have work to do, helping the backpacking group finish getting ready, giving them directions to the camping spot. I spread the word amongst the staff that Scout died in her sleep last night, and a somber mood permeates the day's activities.

After the backpackers leave with Dot, I stop by Luke's cabin to bring him lunch. He's not there, so I leave him a sandwich and go back to my duties.

Later that evening when I return, he's sitting on the porch, staring into the middle distance. When he sees me, he rouses himself and goes into his cabin. He comes back out with Scout wrapped in a blanket and leads the way to the spot he chose. I stand to the side as he carefully lowers the blanket-wrapped bundle into the hole. Scout looks so small, and my eyes fill with tears.

Luke steps back, his forehead a knot of pain. I ask him if he wants to say anything, but he shakes his head, so I stand there, feeling helpless as he picks up the shovel and fills the grave with dirt, pausing occasionally to wipe his eyes.

By the time he's finished, the sun has set, and it's getting dark, the cool air nipping at my bare arms.

"We should get back," Luke says. It's the first time he's spoken since I arrived.

Silently, we head toward his cabin. I keep fighting the urge to hold his hand, to pull him into a hug—that's what I would want, in a moment like this.

I'm not sure why he wanted me here at all.

When we reach his cabin, I hesitate. "What can I do? Please let me do something."

He meets my eyes; he looks like his heart is breaking. "Will you . . . stay here tonight?" he finally says. "I'm so used to having her here."

My throat tightens. "Of course."

I follow him inside, not sure what I agreed to. Does he want me to sleep here? To stay up and talk? But he climbs into his bed, the one he made by pushing two twins together, hardly looking at me. There's the bed-slash-couch against the wall, but it's piled with notebooks and papers, so I go to the other side of his bed and pull back the covers. The light is off and it's pitch-black. I slip out of my shorts and bra before lying down and pulling the blanket over me.

Luke is already asleep.

When I wake, an hour or so before dawn, the darkness is less intense. It's raining outside, drops spattering on the roof and echoing through the cabin.

Luke is awake, too. He's on his side facing me, his arm tucked under his head. In the dim light he's fuzzy, indistinct.

"Hey," I say quietly. "How are you feeling?"

"Better." His voice is raspy with sleep. "I've been dreading this for months, bracing myself for it. So now that it's happened . . . I wouldn't say it's a relief. But at least it's over." He shifts his weight. "Thank you for staying."

I swallow, not sure how to take this. "No problem."

He exhales. "There is a problem, though."

"What?"

"I don't think I can keep pretending I'm not crazy about you."

His words hang in the space between us, the air thickening with tension until I break eye contact and shake my head, exasperated.

"What does that even mean?" I say. "You're the one who said you 'shouldn't get involved with anyone.' You're the one who pulled away—"

"The other day in the woods?" he finishes, and I nod. Maybe my eyes are getting used to the darkness, or it's getting ever so slightly lighter outside, but I can make out his features now. The groove between his eyebrows. His pouty bottom lip. "Your friends needed you. And I assumed you needed them, too. It seemed wrong to kiss you when you were so emotional. But I wanted to."

I wanted to kiss you, too, I think. I want to kiss him now. But I'm wary; he could pull back at any moment.

Silence stretches between us again until he shakes his head and chuckles, almost to himself. It's nice to hear the sound, after yesterday.

"What's funny?" I ask.

"I'm remembering that first email exchange, when you said I couldn't stay in the cabin by myself—"

"You were so rude," I say, a smile tugging at my lips.

"I know. And you were unfailingly kind in return. I'm sorry—after I got your email about the adult camp, I became fixated on the idea of Scout having her last months here. I didn't want anyone else around to bother her."

I raise my eyebrows, surprised. "You said you 'required privacy' for writing. I thought you were a pretentious asshole."

"I am an asshole," he says dryly, "but hopefully not the pretentious kind. I can write anywhere—I mean, I needed a place to stay, so coming here made sense, and I wanted my dog to be somewhere that would make her happy. Scout loved places like this, with trees and squirrels and lakes. I figured she deserved it after years of living where I wanted. So thank you for that. Really."

My chest warms. "You're welcome. I'm glad you came."

"Me too. And not just for Scout." He pauses, licks his lips. "Being here, spending time with you, it's been . . ."

He trails off.

I nudge him with my foot under the covers, grinning. "What? Terrifying?"

His eyes lock onto mine. "Yes."

A shiver runs down my spine. "Why?"

Outside, the rain has increased, wrapping us in a rhythmic cocoon of sound. He shifts toward me, and I feel his hand on my thigh, just above my knee, his fingertips grazing my skin.

"I was a fucking mess when I got here. My writing career, my divorce, my dying dog . . . I've been stuck in a self-pitying spiral—and here's this gorgeous, outgoing woman who is bound and determined to pull me out of it."

"But why was that terrifying?"

His fingers run up my thigh, stopping at the hem of my T-shirt. My eyes drift closed. His touch is featherlight, but somehow my skin is burning. Even though I'm tempted to roll toward him, I hold still, and his hand runs back down to my knee, his fingers curling around to stroke the soft skin behind it.

A sigh escapes my lips. My eyes are still closed—I'm convinced that if I open them, I'll see that sardonic smile on his face and realize he's toying with me. Trying to see how worked up he can get me before pulling away again.

His hand moves to my hip, gently turning me so I'm on my side, facing him.

And now I open my eyes.

"It's terrifying," he says, "because I could fall in love with you so easily."

I freeze. "Don't say that."

"Okay, I won't. But it's true."

Maybe it is—or maybe he's sad because he lost his beloved dog and I'm in his bed and he could use a distraction. But couldn't I use a distraction, too? I'm losing my beloved camp.

Like Luke said, everything ends—this moment will end. This summer will end, and we'll go our separate ways and never see each other again. So why not enjoy it while we can?

His hand strokes my thigh, and his eyes seem to darken as he looks at me, gauging my response. I hold his gaze and part my legs ever so slightly.

His fingertips move higher, until he's toying with the hem of my underwear. Heat pools there, right there, and I nod. *Yes.* His eyebrow quirks as he runs his hand across the fabric, then lower, until his fingers brush a spot that lights me up. I bite my lip, but a tiny moan slips out nonetheless. His lips twitch, like he's pleased with himself, and he continues circling, teasing, taking his time as the fabric goes from damp to wet to soaking. And then he moves my underwear aside.

At the first touch of his hand, my body tightens involuntarily, and he pauses.

"If you stop right now I will murder you," I say.

He grins—half-delighted, half-devious—as he strokes me, slowly dipping his finger inside, then pulling back out, circling, then doing it all over again. I'm slick and swollen, already so turned on from the weeks of tension building between us. I know it's not going to take much. Heat collects where he's touching me, radiating through me, building to a frenzy until my body tightens and spasms and I cry out, my head rolling back and my eyes squeezing shut.

When I open my eyes again, he's inches away, watching me. I'm shaky, a little dazed, but I manage a teasing smile. "What the hell, Luke? You gave me an orgasm, but you've never really kissed me."

Without hesitation, he leans in and presses his lips to mine. I respond instantly, opening my mouth, our tongues meeting, warm and hungry. We've been waiting for this all summer—these aren't soft, tentative kisses; they're desperate and heated, quickly turning rough. When he pulls away to catch his breath, I bite his bottom lip, growling. In response, he grips my throat with his hand, not squeezing, just holding me in place as he kisses my mouth, my jaw, my neck, scraping his teeth against my skin.

His free hand toys with the bottom edge of my T-shirt, and I lift it a few inches, hoping he takes the hint. He does, running his hand up to cup my breast.

"You're so soft," he murmurs. "I want—I need—"

He lifts my shirt up so he can lean down and put his

mouth on my nipple, sucking lightly at first, then harder, making me squirm. Rain drums on the roof, echoing through the cabin. His other hand stays on my throat, gently pinning me down as he sucks and toys with me until I'm writhing. When he pauses, I take the opportunity to tug his shirt up, and he releases me so I can pull it over his head and off.

The sky outside is lighter now, giving me a view that takes my breath away: his body looks like it was crafted by a master artist. Perfect proportions, perfect symmetry, all lean and toned; my hands ache to touch him.

"You're so goddamn gorgeous, you could be on a salad dressing bottle," I tell him.

His eyes spark with mischief. "And you're so goddamn gorgeous, you could be a Barbie doll."

"Fuck you," I say, grinning.

"Yes, please."

I laugh, then put my palms on his pecs, slide them up to his shoulders, down his arms, across his abs. He closes his eyes and lets me touch him as his breathing turns ragged, until he can't handle it anymore and he grabs my wrists.

"Take off your shirt," he orders, his voice rough.

I obey, and his gaze sweeps over me, fiery blue. He pulls me against him, and the warmth of his skin on mine makes me dizzy. We sink into another deep kiss as we move together, nothing but our underwear between us as we thrust against each other. It's rough and dirty and so fucking hot I can feel another orgasm building.

"Why haven't we been doing this all summer?" he says, and bites my neck—not too hard, but enough to make me startle.

As punishment, I sink my teeth into his shoulder, making him yelp.

"Because," I say, "you were a dumb little dweeb."

He laughs out loud—probably the first real laugh I've ever gotten from him. He kisses my neck, then sucks hard enough to bruise.

"Watch it," I say. "You're going to give me a hickey and everyone will know what we've been doing."

"Oh, everyone will know. I am going to fuck you so hard you won't be able to walk straight."

"Promise?"

He yanks down my underwear, driving a finger inside me, making me gasp—then a second finger, and a third. I take it as long as I can before wriggling away from him; I have something else in mind.

I reach into his boxers and wrap my hand around him. His hips jerk and he hisses. "Fuck, Jess."

I tug his boxers down farther, leaning down to lick him with the flat of my tongue, then closing my mouth around him.

He groans but doesn't let me stay there for too long— soon he's pulling me up again, shaking his head. "I won't last. Not now. Not when I've been wanting this for so long."

"More dirty dreams?"

"You have no idea. Grab my wallet, will you?" He angles his head upward, toward the headboard, and I find his wallet there and hand it to him.

While he's looking inside, I pull my underwear off and throw it somewhere behind me. He finds a condom and gives it to me so he can take his boxers off. My hands are shaking so badly I can't open the package, and a mischievous grin sneaks onto his face as I fumble.

"You like watching me struggle?" I say.

"I'm just glad you're as worked up as I am."

In desperation, I use my teeth to rip the foil open. Luke lies back and I roll the condom on. Then I position myself above him and sink down, slowly. We both groan as he fills me, and for a moment I can't think, can't move, can hardly breathe. Almost unconsciously, I rock against him.

He grips my hips. "Give me a second."

I relax, leaning back to look at him. He's flushed beneath me, breathing hard, his hair messy. Totally unraveled.

Smiling, I motion to him. "I like this. You, at my mercy."

"Fuck yes I am." His voice is almost pained, the muscles in his arms and shoulders tense. "All those dreams I had? They don't compare to reality, not even close. My god, Jess. I could live a thousand years and never forget this. How you look. How you feel."

An unexpected emotion hits me, tender and sweet, making my throat tighten. His earlier words echo in my mind: *I could fall in love with you so easily.* My eyes prick with tears, and I blink them away. I do not need complicated feelings like that right now.

"You ready?" I say, a teasing lilt in my voice.

His eyes flash with heat. "Not yet. Come for me again."

I grin. "Yes, sir."

I begin to move, and he holds my hips as I grind in slow circles. It doesn't take long before heat is building inside me. He's watching me intently, making it difficult to breathe, so I close my eyes and disappear inside myself. I put my hands over his and move them from my hips to my waist, up to my breasts, squeezing and stroking as I rock against him, faster,

faster. My body flushes white-hot and I cry out, shaking and gasping for air.

When I open my eyes, he's smirking up at me. "That's a good girl."

Then he rolls us over so he's on top. He parts my legs with his knee and drives into me roughly, making me whimper, but I tell him it's good, I want more, please don't stop. We move together, slowly at first, but quickly gaining speed. The rain, thrumming on the roof, vibrates deep in my body.

"We're doing this again," he says, panting.

My eyes widen. "When?"

"Tonight. In an hour. After lunch—I don't care. I need to prove I can last longer the next time."

"Deal," I say.

His hands find mine, lacing our fingers together as he rolls into me, his jaw tightening and the tendons in his neck straining until he finally tenses and groans and collapses against me. I wrap my arms around him and bury my face in his neck, inhaling deeply, trying to hold on to this moment as long I can.

But eventually, he rolls off me and goes to the bathroom. I go next, splashing water on my face before returning to bed. He pulls me against him, spooning me from behind.

Outside, the rain is slowing, the sky brightening. I close my eyes, sleep tugging me down.

"How many more days do we have?" he asks.

My eyes open as I realize what he's asking. "I guess . . . four? Unless you want to stay another week while the staff and I—"

"I'll stay," he says quietly. "And until then, you're mine, okay?"

Another surge of emotion threatens to overwhelm me, and I swallow it down. *Everything ends*, I remind myself. *Nothing lasts forever.*

"Okay," I whisper, and he holds me as we drift back to sleep.

twenty-nine

Hillary

The day of the dance has arrived, and like every other year, I'm going stag. Solo. Without a date. Jessie apologized when she told me Luke asked her to go with him—but I would've been upset if she *hadn't* said yes. It makes me happy to see her so happy.

Which I'm trying to remember as I put the finishing touches on my outfit. At least I'll look good when I walk into the dining hall on my own.

We had surprisingly good luck on our shopping trip to Walmart. Jessie agreed to let me pick out her dress if I let her choose mine, and it made the whole excursion more fun. Like we were making up for all the years of best friend memories we missed out on.

For Jessie, I picked an emerald green asymmetrical dress that's long and flowy in back, but short in the front to show off her killer legs. She's going to wear her hair down in beach waves, and we found a floral headband to complete the look.

For me, Jessie picked out a maxi swing dress with a bold pattern of blue and bright pink flowers. It's so low-cut I had to buy a set of stickers that supposedly act like a bra. But the dress looks good. I look good.

Eat your heart out, Benjamin Cooper.

One more application of lipstick, and I'm as ready as I'm going to get. I come into the hallway at the same time as Dot—who's wearing a long black dress that looks like it may have walked out of the *Sound of Music* box in the costume closet. She looks uncomfortable, but pretty.

"Dot!"

"Not a word, Goldberg," she says, pulling at the high neck. "Yvonne wanted me to wear a dress."

"The things we do for love." My voice cracks on the word "love," which is ridiculous. I don't *love* Cooper. I mean, I loved spending time with him. I loved talking with him, and seeing how passionate he was about cooking, bringing flavors and textures together in creative ways. I loved falling asleep with my head on his chest and waking up in a tangle of sheets, his arm draped around me.

Most of all, I loved the version of myself I was around him.

"Shall we?" I ask Dot, grateful that I won't have to walk into the dining hall alone after all.

"Wish I could," Dot says, heading down the Lodge stairs. "Gotta pick up my date in Cabin Six. She wanted to get ready with her friends."

I force a smile as Dot walks away, a skip in her step despite the dress.

A group of women from Cabin Eight arrive at the dining hall at the same time I do, and I'm able to walk in behind them. So close you might even think we all belong together.

Inside, the room looks incredible. Twinkly lights have

been strung from the ceiling. Couples and groups of friends pose for pictures under a balloon arch; there's a fully stocked bar and, just beyond, a long table with an impressive buffet. I spot Jack Valentine loading his plate while Mary follows behind, looking but not taking anything. I hate them for being here, for not being their parents, for starting this whole chain of events.

Although, if they hadn't put the camp up for sale, *I* wouldn't be here, either.

Brushing that thought out of my mind, I scan the room and find Jessie, looking gorgeous in green. She's talking to the DJ, a former camper from St. Paul who owns an entertainment company. Jessie requested a playlist that spans every decade of camper we have in attendance—an impressive range from the 1960s to today. We invited any camper who'd attended a previous session and anyone who made a pledge to the co-op to come back for the dance.

Jessie was shocked by how many people bought tickets— but if I've learned one thing this summer, it's *Don't underestimate camp people.*

I'm about to approach Jessie when Luke saunters up beside her, a glass of spiked bug juice in each hand. He leans close and whispers something that makes her laugh. She's beaming. I don't want to interrupt their moment, so I check out the buffet instead, grateful Jack and Mary have already moved through the line.

Cooper really outdid himself. I fill my plate: baked ziti, salad, chicken Française, shrimp scampi, roasted vegetables, and a tofu dish. I spot an empty high-top table in the back where I can eat quickly, just like I did in the early days of camp.

Every bite is more delicious than the one before it, and I hope Cooper made enough that there'll be leftovers tomorrow.

Not that I'll be invited to partake in them.

It's been almost a week since the disastrous dinner with the Valentines, and Cooper and I have barely exchanged a dozen words since. He's kept to himself, hiding away in the kitchen or his room. This, from the man who went on and on about how nothing is more important than honesty. We agreed at the beginning of our fling that it could end at any time, whenever one of us wanted out. So there's no reason for him to leave me in limbo. It's cruel.

As if my thoughts summoned him, the kitchen door swings open and Cooper walks out, wearing an apron that looks like a tuxedo. My breath catches; he's still very deserving of the "hottest chef in Boston" title. For a second, I almost forget how much his sudden and unexplained distance has hurt me.

Cooper's eyes meet mine, and I stop breathing, waiting to see what he does next. If he smiles, I'll smile back. If he looks away, I'll—

I'm not sure what I'll do. I'm mad at him, I miss him, and I hate that he's the one I want to talk to about how frustrated I am with him.

He's still staring at me, his expression blank. I'm about to turn, to be the one to walk away, when his lips curve ever so slightly, growing into a warm smile.

I start breathing again and match his smile with one of my own.

We stand there, smiling at each other from a distance, until Cooper walks toward me and says, "Hi."

"Hey."

"Listen . . ."

"Everybody to the dance floor!" the DJ shouts, so loud I have to stop myself from covering my ears. "It's time for the Electric Slide!"

Campers rush past us, swarming the dance floor and lining up in rows to grapevine to the left, then the right.

"Did you want to dance?" Cooper asks.

I shake my head. Even if I did, I wouldn't want to interrupt this conversation.

"Me neither," Cooper says, although I can't tell from his tone of voice if he means it.

We stand, side by side, close enough to touch, yet a whole world apart. Once the dancing campers have made a full rotation and are starting on the next one, Cooper says, "Do you want to go look at the stars with me?"

Goose bumps run up and down my arms. That's what he asked the summer we were fourteen.

"You can ask Jessie to join us if you want," he says, sheepishly.

"She's busy." I look up to see Jessie attempting to teach Mr. Billy the Electric Slide. Almost everyone is on the dance floor—even the Valentines. "But I could go."

Cooper looks relieved, and I warn my heart not to get its hopes up.

"Are you done with this?" he asks, motioning toward my plate.

I am, so he hands it off to a member of his staff, then returns to my side. My fingers reflexively reach for his until I remember what's happened between us and curl my hand into a fist.

Four or five campers are coming in from the patio as

we're heading out, and I choke on the remnants of their nicotine cloud. So much for getting fresh air.

"You look beautiful tonight," Cooper says, when we're alone. *Mission accomplished.* "I haven't seen your hair like that before."

I bring a hand up to my hair, running my fingers through the smooth strands. I straightened it because I wanted to look good. And because, growing up, I felt like my curls were synonymous with messy. Unkempt. My dad was always telling me to brush my hair, to pull it back. So I learned to tame it, getting keratin treatments and buying expensive flat irons. For so many years, even my hair has been checking items off someone else's list.

If I could go back, I would have worn it in curls tonight.

We're quiet for an uncomfortable moment, until I tilt my head back and look up, letting out a sad laugh.

"Can't really see the stars from here," I say, straining to see beyond the canopy of trees.

"It was just an excuse to get you alone," Cooper says. The butterflies in my stomach flutter, but I can't tell if it's friendly or ominous. "But we should be able to see them over there."

I follow Cooper to the far side of the patio, where we lean against the railing. Sure enough, the stars are shining above, twinkling like they're putting on a show just for us. It's crazy to think this is the same sky I stared up at all those months ago in Chicago. It's so much more vivid out here. More alive. Kind of like me.

"I've been wanting to talk to you," Cooper says.

"I've been right here," I say, my voice sharp with emotion. The sting of his rejection is suddenly as fresh as ever.

"I know," he says. "I'm sorry. It wasn't you, it was—"

"Oh, please. Don't say it was you."

Cooper takes a step back, surprised at the bite in my voice.

Now that we're here, face-to-face, all the sadness and confusion I've been feeling bubbles into anger. Last week was crushing. It felt like I'd failed Jessie, betrayed the memories of my mom and Nathaniel and Lola, and let down all the future campers who won't know the magic of Camp Chickawah. And without Cooper, I had no one to talk to, to help me process everything.

"I really needed you this past week," I tell him. "And you disappeared."

"I know," he says, his voice small. "I'm sorry."

I think back to what Jessie said, about how Cooper's reaction didn't seem like him. Has he been going through something, too? If I was being the kind of friend to him that I needed, I would have pushed through his withdrawal and asked him about it. Instead, I retreated, using my sore feelings like a shield, protecting me from more hurt.

"I'm sorry, too. I should—"

"No," Cooper says, stopping me. "You don't have anything to apologize for. It really was me. Seeing that jerk down on one knee, it just . . ."

His voice fades. The emotion in his beautiful gray eyes is palpable. Maybe he's fallen for me, too.

But then he looks away, and I know there's more to the story. Something tells me I should sit for this, so I take a seat on top of the picnic table.

"What happened?" I ask.

Cooper blows out a long breath and sits next to me. The few inches between us are buzzing with energy, and I hope that whatever he's about to say brings us closer together instead of pushing us further apart.

"I told you about my reputation back home," he says. "At first, I leaned into it. I loved being wanted by all those beautiful women. It was thrilling; no strings, just sex. But eventually, the physical connection wasn't enough. The highs weren't worth the lows that came afterward. And then I met Julia."

"Did you propose to her?" I ask, desperate to get to the point.

"No," Cooper says. "Someone else did."

I'm relieved, even though I have no right to be. Especially because it's clear this Julia woman hurt him. I reach for his hand, lacing his fingers with mine. It's the first time we've touched in days, and it's such a relief to feel the familiar roughness of his palms, his thick fingers. I feel steadier, just touching him, and I think he does, too—his shoulders relax a little.

After a moment, he continues. "I met her out at an industry night, and we instantly hit it off. She had this way of calling me on my shit, and there was something magnetic about her personality. She would draw me in, then push me away, like it was a game. I couldn't get enough. She traveled a lot for work, and I was busy, but we'd hook up whenever we could. Pretty quick I realized that I didn't want to see anyone but her. I was ready to build a life with someone. And I thought she could be the one."

Cooper pauses, and I start rubbing my thumb over the back of his hand. I know this isn't easy for him to talk about.

"One night, I was in the kitchen at work and I spotted her walking toward the bathroom. I wasn't supposed to be at the restaurant that night, and I thought she was in New York for work. As soon as things slowed down a bit, I went out to the dining room to surprise her. Except I was the one who got a surprise." His voice is shaky; the wound is still fresh. "I got out there just in time to see her boyfriend become her fiancé. Apparently, I was her 'fling before the ring.'"

"Ouch," I say. Cooper grimaces.

"It gets worse. Julia saw me standing in the middle of the restaurant, frozen in place. I was waiting for her to tell me it was a joke, that I was misreading the situation. But she looked away. Kissed her fiancé, left me standing there like an idiot. I managed to hold it in until I went back to the kitchen, then I kind of exploded. Two waitresses I'd hooked up with caught wind of the situation and apparently wanted to get in on my downfall. It got ugly. I ended up getting an entire batch of lobster bisque thrown in my face. Luckily, it was still room temperature."

Cooper takes his hand from mine and removes his Red Sox hat. He runs his fingers through his hair before replacing the hat. "Not my finest moment," he says.

That must've been awful. I don't know what to tell him, so I just say his name. Then:

"Did you lose your job over it?" I ask, remembering how he was a last-minute addition to the summer staff.

"Not exactly. Atlas, my boss, is a good guy. He told me this was rock bottom, which meant the only way to go was up. But I had to be ready to make a change. This summer is supposed to be a sabbatical. A break. I have to let him know soon if I'll be coming back in September."

September. A hollow pit opens in my stomach at the thought of this summer ending, of Cooper going back to

Boston, me going back to Chicago, Jessie going . . . I don't
know where she'll go.

"Anyway, seeing Aaron and you, it brought all of that back."

The hurt in his voice makes my own heart ache. His
reaction makes sense now—Julia didn't just break Cooper's
heart, she made him think less of himself, that he wasn't
good enough to be more than a fling. I feel a twinge of envy
toward this woman who made Cooper want to commit—not
that I expect that from him, of course not; my head knows
that. Unfortunately, my heart hasn't gotten the message.

"But why did you doubt me? You knew I broke up with
Aaron," I say, trying to keep my voice even. "I mean, I
understand why seeing that would remind you of how much
you lost with Julia—"

"No," Cooper says, turning toward me. There's an
urgency in his gray eyes I've never seen before. "It made me
think that for the second time in my life, I was about to lose a
woman I care about. A woman I could see a future with."

I stare at him, digesting his words. "Cooper, I . . . I don't
know what to say—"

"You don't have to say anything." He breaks eye contact,
looking down at his hands. "You've been honest with me from
the beginning about what you wanted this summer. I'm the
one who got confused. And I don't want to keep being the
same guy who confuses good sex with love."

Again, I'm speechless. I had no idea he felt this way,
and I want to be brave enough to tell him I'm on the way to
loving him, too. That I could also see a future with him—
except I can't. I can't see my *own* future, let alone one with
someone else. Everything feels too unsteady and unknown.

For the first time in my life, I don't have a plan, and it terrifies me.

Silence settles between us. I want to say something that will make him feel better, but I can't tell him what I want until I know myself.

"Thank you for telling me," I say, then nudge him with my shoulder. "*Finally.* You were the one who added the honesty rule, remember?"

His face softens, like he's relieved at my reaction, relieved to change the subject. "Yeah. Sorry."

I turn to face him, still holding his hand. "So, honestly, what do you want to do right now?"

I'm not sure what I'm hoping for—part of me wouldn't mind if he hauled me back to the Lodge and had his way with me. But even though I've missed that, what I've missed most is just being with him. Talking, laughing, connecting. I want to soak that up as much as possible before it has to end.

"Honestly?" He meets my eyes. "I'd really like to dance with you."

A smile blossoms on my face, and I stand. "You're in luck. There are only two people in the world who can get me onto a dance floor, and you happen to be one of them. Unless they're playing Chumbawamba. Then I'm out."

"Deal."

Cooper slips his arm around my waist as we walk into the dining hall. The song from *Dirty Dancing*, "(I've Had) the Time of My Life," starts to play, and he takes me in his arms. As we sway to the beat, he sings along, so softly that only I can hear. The lyrics reflect our story. I *have* had the time of my life, and I owe it all to him.

And to Jessie, who looks deliriously happy dancing with Luke.

"Come on, babe!"

I turn to see Zoey running toward Zac, attempting the big lift from the end of the movie. They pull it off: Zac catches Zoey in his arms and she slides down his body, planting a kiss on his lips as her feet hit the floor.

When I look back to make sure Jessie is seeing this, I notice her and Luke walking hand in hand toward the DJ booth. It must be time for her speech—she's been working on what to say all week. Luke gives her hand a squeeze and steps to the side while she takes the microphone.

The final notes of the song fade, which Jessie takes as her cue.

"Good evening, Camp Chickawah!" she says into the mic. "As your camp director, it is my honor and privilege to say a few words tonight, at this, the final dance of our final summer." She pauses, clearing the emotion from her throat. "I'm so glad our special guests, Jack and Mary Valentine, could be here with us."

There's a smattering of unenthusiastic applause— everyone knows they're the reason this summer is the last. Still, the little twerp stands taller, raising his hand in a wave. At least his sister has the decency not to call any more attention to herself.

"But I'd also like to thank each and every one of you." Jessie pauses to scan the room. Her sad smile gets brighter when she sees me leaning against Cooper, his arms wrapped around my shoulders. "Camp Chickawah has been in the Valentine family for over a hundred years—but it's also been a part of my family, and a part of yours."

The crowd applauds, and Jessie smiles as she waits for the noise to die down. "Lola used to say that moments end, but memories last a lifetime, and I know that none of us will ever forget this place."

The room is silent now, everyone watching her.

"But Camp Chickawah is more than this property," she continues. "It isn't the lake or the cabins or the campfire. It isn't the activities, the Color Wars and canoe races and hikes. It isn't the food or the pranks or the songs we love to sing."

Her voice catches, and she pauses, looking down, composing herself. I can hear sniffles from people in the audience, and I see two former campers near me wiping their eyes.

Jessie looks back up, and her voice rings out, clear and strong.

"Camp is the children who came here to grow and develop, the counselors and staff who worked here over the years. It's the friendships we've built and the memories we've made." She smiles warily and says, "Camp isn't just a place. It's us."

The words envelop me like a hug. I've been so focused on saving the actual land that I haven't thought about the intangible aspects. So much of who I am is because of my experiences here as a child, and even though I buried those parts of myself for years, I never lost them.

Now I make a promise to myself that I won't lose them again. I'm trembling a little; Cooper tightens his grip on my shoulder and I lean back into him, appreciating his sturdiness.

"But tonight isn't a funeral," Jessie says. "It's a party.

Nathaniel and Lola would want us to make the most of every single second we have left here. So from the bottom of my heart, thank you for coming, for your support and love. We might not be able to say 'See you next summer,' but I hope you'll all remember this: you can take the people out of the camp, but you can't take the camp out of the people!"

The room erupts in applause, and there isn't a dry eye in the house. The DJ has an upbeat song ready, and soon campers are dancing and singing along to P!nk's "Raise Your Glass."

Amidst the swarm of moving bodies, I lose sight of Jessie. When I finally find her in the crowd, Jack Valentine is walking straight toward her.

"Crap," I say and point toward them.

I don't have to say anything else; Cooper swoops into action. We both know the last thing Jessie needs right now is small talk with Jack Valentine.

"Need you in the kitchen, boss," Cooper says.

He takes Jessie's hand and leads her off. In the kitchen, Cooper's staff is cleaning up from the buffet and getting the dessert trays ready, so we head to a prep area in the back corner.

"Bless you," Jessie says, taking a seat on a stool. "I don't think I could have faked being nice to that man for one more second."

"You shouldn't have to!" I say, taking a cream cheese brownie from the tray Cooper sets in front of us. "Want to hide out in here for the rest of the night?"

Jessie laughs. "Wish I could. But I should probably get back out there."

"Give yourself a minute," Cooper says. "Have some dessert, come back in a song or two."

He gives me a kiss on the head before heading off to rejoin the party.

"These are really good," I tell Jessie, holding up a second brownie.

"Mm-hmm," she says, biting into one. "So, want to tell me what's going on with you two?"

"Not really," I say, because I still don't know. It should be simple—Cooper wants a future with me, and I want one with him—but I can't stop thinking that this whole summer has been an escape from reality, that my real life is going to come crashing down on me once I go home.

But I'm not the only one who had a summer fling.

"Want to tell me what's going on with you and Luke?"

"Not really," she parrots, and we both laugh.

"You were great up there, by the way," I tell her. "I don't think I could have done it."

For a moment, I think she's going to brush that off and say *It's fine*, like she always does, but instead her smile falters and tears fill her eyes. "It was really, really hard."

I shake my head, so impressed with how my brave, beautiful friend has managed to smile through what I imagine is one of the hardest nights of her life. I'm glad I can provide respite, a time for her to stop pretending, just like she's done for me.

I don't know how I made it through a decade without her.

"What you said about friendship . . ." I pause, scrambling to find the words. We've cleared the air about our past, but we haven't talked about what our friendship looks like without the trappings of camp. "With the summer ending—"

"Hilly Bean," Jessie says, giving me a look filled with love and history and deep knowing. "Camp may be over, but our friendship won't be. Not again. Not ever."

"Promise?" I say, my voice wavering.

"Promise."

"Good, because I had a crazy idea. I don't know if you have plans for after camp, but I was wondering if you'd want to stay with me for a while in Chicago? I have a guest room, and I'd love to spend time with you. I know you aren't much of a city girl, but we have beautiful parks, and the lake, and—"

"I'd love to," Jessie says, interrupting my blabbering. "Thank you so much."

We hug, holding each other and crying amidst the chaos of the kitchen. Then the door swings open, and Jessie perks up at the familiar notes of that damn Chumbawamba song. I will never understand how any best friend of mine can like that earworm.

"Come on," she says, grabbing my hand.

I sigh, say, "Only for you," and follow her back out to the dance floor, where we join hundreds of campers from their thirties to their seventies, all having the time of their lives.

For the last time.

thirty

Jessie

Every day of this last week at camp has been bittersweet, in the truest sense of the word.

Bitter: Jack Valentine's smug expression as he watched me pour my heart out in my speech at the dance. The impending goodbyes with my staff, who have become like family. The knowledge that the place I love will soon be wiped away.

Sweet: the smile on Hillary's face when she was snuggling with Cooper. The cream cheese brownies Cooper made. And, of course, waking up with Luke each morning.

I wasn't sure what he meant by, "You're mine until camp ends," but apparently it means sleeping together every night, holding hands wherever we go, and staying up late talking. In short, acting like we're in a real relationship.

A relationship I have for one more week.

Which is the cause of this morning's sob session. Luke is asleep, his body curled behind mine. I'm crying quietly, letting the tears slip down my face onto my pillow.

I care about him. More than I ever did for Nick even after eight months together. Though lately I've been wondering

342

if the appeal of Nick was that having a boyfriend made the off-season feel less like a waiting period between camp sessions. With Luke, it seems impossible that we'll survive out of the beautiful bubble we're in—our lives are too up in the air, taking us in totally different directions. There's no use imagining anything long-term.

Still, every once in a while, the intensity of my feelings for him washes up and nearly drowns me. It's ridiculous. It's way too soon. But that's how time works at camp: a day feels like a week, a week feels like a month.

And I can't stop wishing we had more time together.

The morning light filtering through the windows is soft. I should get up; it's the last day of camp, the day the final campers leave. We have less than a week before the staff and I clear out, too. And shortly after that, the sales documents will be finalized and demolition will begin.

Yesterday, I started to pack up my cabin. I was shocked at how quickly it went. Two duffel bags and a few boxes hold everything I own.

I start to roll away, but Luke holds me tighter.

"Don't leave," he murmurs.

My heart aches. Because I am leaving. We all are.

But it's warm and comfortable here, so I stay where I am. No sense rushing past the sweetness of this morning to the bitterness of the day ahead.

By lunchtime, the campers have checked out, the property is silent, and I'm overwhelmed with the wistfulness I always feel at the end of summer. Only this time, that wistfulness is layered with a piercing grief.

The staff disperses to work on their individual tasks—Zac and Zoey down at the lakefront, Hillary in the Arts and Crafts cabin, Cooper in the kitchen. Mr. Billy is wandering around with his trash picker-upper, grumbling. It feels futile, all of it, because what's the point of putting the watercraft in order, or organizing the craft supplies, or picking up trash, when it's going to be bulldozed anyway?

"Hey, boss."

I turn to see Dot walking across the lawn toward me.

"Hey," I say, and try to summon a smile. But I've been trying to keep it together all morning and I can't anymore, so I burst into tears.

Dot sits on a bench and pats the spot next to her. "Ah, Pippi, come here."

My old nickname makes the tears come even harder. I sit, and I cry, and she pats my back.

"Why aren't you as much of a mess as I am?" I say after a while.

She snorts out a laugh. "Oh, so how hard you cry is a measure of how much you care?"

"That's not—"

"No, I get it. Here's the thing—I've lived more life than you. I have a different perspective. For me, this is a chapter in my life that's closing, and yes, I'm sad, but I'm looking forward to whatever's next."

"You're going to Austin, right?" I say, wiping my eyes. "To stay with Yvonne?"

"Yep."

"I wish I had something to look forward to," I say.

"You do!"

"I really don't."

Dot sighs and shakes her head. "This is why I wasn't so sure about Nathaniel and Lola hiring you full-time right after college."

I look up sharply. "What?"

"Don't give me that look. I knew you'd do an amazing job. I was worried you'd get stuck here."

I bristle. "Stuck? What about you? You've worked here for decades!"

"Yes, in the summers. But I was forty when I started on full-time. Did you know that?" I shake my head, and she says, "Yeah, before that, I did all sorts of things in the off-season. I was a ski instructor. Taught English in Thailand. Spent winters in New Zealand, Greece, Costa Rica—all over the place. Working odd jobs, exploring, meeting new people."

She smiles at the memories, and I think back to my childhood decision to make summer camp my career so I wouldn't have to "live ten months for two."

Seems like I ended up doing that anyway.

"I've never wanted to do anything else," I say, not able to help being defensive.

She pats my thigh. "I know. Camp is your world—that was obvious even when you were a kiddo. But the longer you've stayed here, the more you've closed yourself off to the rest of life. It's like you and that old canoe—"

"I love that canoe—"

"Yeah, and it weighs a ton and is a beast to navigate. But you never considered switching to one of the newer ones, right?"

"I don't—"

"Hear me out," Dot says. "I'm not one of those Pollyanna types who believes there's always a silver lining—this camp being sold is a flat-out crime. But I hope you'll take it as an opportunity to explore, to spread your wings and see what the world has to offer outside of camp."

"I want to work in a camp, though," I say, stubbornly.

"And you can. But don't rush. Figure out what else you love. Travel. Have fun in Chicago with Hillary. Go to New York and see some of those musicals you're always listening to. You're getting a little money from this sale, and that gives you some breathing room."

I look down at my hands, feeling a twinge of guilt for profiting off the loss of my camp.

"You know about that?"

"Of course. Lola told me they wanted to make sure you were taken care of."

I look at her, confused. "Me, specifically? I assumed they meant the current camp director."

"You, specifically," Dot says, nodding. "It's your name in that will, Jessie May Pederson. Whether you worked here or not. Though I bet they suspected their rat bastard kids would sell it while you were still the director."

My heart warms like a glowing campfire. It's not the money that's meaningful—although I've seen the sales numbers; even one percent will be sizable. It's the fact that Nathaniel and Lola thought of me almost as family. Which is how I always thought of them, too.

"Listen, it sucks that this is all ending," Dot says, nudging me with her shoulder. "But don't forget about the possibilities that are just beginning. Okay?"

I hesitate, then nod. "Thanks, Dot."

"Thank you, boss. It's been one hell of a ride."

An hour or so later, I'm organizing the first aid supplies (another pointless task, but I need to stay busy or I'll start crying again) when Hillary comes over the walkie-talkie and says I'm needed in the dining hall.

When I get there, I'm surprised to see Hillary, Cooper, Dot, Zac and Zoey, Mr. Billy, and Luke sitting at a table.

On the floor in front of them are two full backpacks.

"What's this?" I ask. "Who's going hiking?"

Hillary grins. "You are! You missed the overnight campout last week, and we know you were looking forward to it."

I shake my head, confused. "I can't. There's too much to do today."

"We'll take care of it," Cooper says, and Mr. Billy nods solemnly.

"You don't have a choice," Zac says with a smile, and Zoey adds, "We got your backpack loaded up and everything."

Dot chimes in: "We knew you'd never agree to go unless we practically forced you."

I cough out a disbelieving laugh. "But if both Dot and I leave—"

"Oh, I'm not going," Dot says. "I'll stay here and keep everyone on track."

I'm confused; she's the only other person who cares about this activity. "Who's the other backpack for, then?"

"Uh, me," Luke says, speaking for the first time. "If you're okay with that."

My heart fills with gratitude as I look at this dear group

of friends. Family. They're not just giving me an opportunity to do the overnighter one last time. This is a chance to step away from the sadness of closing down the camp.

"Thank you," I manage to say. "This is exactly what I need."

Hillary beams. "We know."

"Now get going," Dot says. "You have six miles to cover before nightfall."

Before I can pick up my backpack, Mr. Billy comes over. "You did good, Pippi," he says to me, his voice gruff. "Real good. You should be proud—I know I am."

A lump comes to my throat; I'm not sure I've ever heard him say so many words all at once. "Thank you for all your hard work over the years, Mr. Billy."

He peers down at me from his full height, his expression grave. "It was an honor."

It usually takes a full day to reach the spot where we camp during the overnighter—young teenagers plus heavy packs equals a slow pace, countless snack breaks, and lots of whining. But Luke keeps up just fine, so even though we set out around three p.m., we're on track to reach our destination with daylight left.

As we hike, he asks me what I'm always listening to on my canoe rides, and I tell him about my favorite musicals; turns out he's seen a lot of them—most recently *Dear Evan Hansen*. This leads to a spirited discussion about poor Evan. Luke insists he's a "lying schmuck who deceived everyone he claims to care about" and I argue that he's a confused teenager searching for meaning in a big, scary world.

Then we talk about what we were like as teenagers. Luke

claims he was a "consummate geek," and when I say that's hard for me to believe, he says he started a Settlers of Catan club in high school (which isn't too geeky, I tell him) and later wrote his college admissions essay about how Catan is a metaphor for life (okay, I agree: total geek move).

We talk about our families; Luke's parents have been happily married for nearly forty years, and he has two younger sisters. In more recent years, he tells me, he was sharing an apartment with a friend, but then the friend's boyfriend moved in, and Luke was in the way. At the start of the summer, he put all his belongings in a storage unit and came to camp.

I remember the time I asked him where he lived, and he said he lived here. I assumed he was joking—but no, he's as untethered now as I am.

I ask where he's going after this, and he says he's heading to a cabin his family owns in Michigan. It's booked all summer, but it'll be empty in the fall. He's planning to finish the draft of his book there. After it's revised and turned in, he'll look for a teaching job in New York state, where he's licensed—a small town, hopefully.

"I realized this summer that the city was too crowded and hectic for me," he says. "From there? I guess I'll figure it out as I go along."

His words bruise my already sore heart. I didn't expect him to say anything about us, obviously. But I'm going to miss him. More than I should.

When we reach the camping spot—a clearing next to a slow-moving river—I spot a ring of rocks still filled with the charred remains of last week's campfire. The flat areas surrounding it seem to hold the ghosts of tents pitched there in years past.

The sun is dropping toward the western horizon, so we get to work: starting a fire, cooking dinner, setting up the tent. We eat as the sun sets, and after we finish and clean up, it's fully dark outside.

"There's only one thing left to do," I tell him.

He grins. "Skinny-dipping?"

"You got it."

When we came here with the campers, the girls would head upstream and the boys down, far enough apart (especially in the dark) for privacy. But tonight, we both know damn well we're doing this together.

We undress on the riverbank, then head into the cool water. He's staring at me with such intensity, it sucks the oxygen from my lungs.

"You've seen all this before," I say, motioning to myself, laughing.

His voice is low and gravelly: "Not sure I'll ever get used to a view like that."

"Well, you don't have to just *look*."

Luke lunges toward me, and I let out a scream of delight as he tackles me, plunging us into the cool water in a tangled heap of limbs. We resurface, sputtering and laughing as we float apart. I'm struck by how relaxed he looks—playful, almost boyish—so different from the gloomy, unapproachable man who arrived two months ago.

"What happened to you this summer?" I blurt out.

"What do you mean?"

I motion between us. "When you first showed up at camp, I never in a million years would've expected this."

"Probably reasonable to not expect to end up naked in a river with someone."

"Oh, I end up naked in rivers with lots of people," I say. "That's not what I mean."

"Lots of people, eh?" He drifts closer, his eyes sparkling with mischief. "And do those other people do this?"

He grabs me by the hips, pulling me flush against him. I suck in a breath at the warmth of his skin against mine. We're inches apart, eyes locked together. Droplets are caught on his lashes, his lips, pooling in the shallow dimple in his chin.

"Usually, yeah," I say, holding his gaze.

He slides a hand up my neck, wraps my hair in his fist and tugs, tilting my chin up to expose my neck. "What about this?" he says, kissing my throat, teeth grazing my skin.

"Occasionally," I say, breathless. Needing to be closer, I wrap my legs around his waist and pull us together. He kisses my jaw, then cups my breasts in both hands, his mouth following in a wordless prayer.

"This?" he whispers.

I'm losing the ability to speak, but I manage to say, "Sometimes."

He sighs, like he's disappointed in me, and puts his mouth next to my ear. "Liar."

Laughing, I lean back into the water, letting my arms drift out to my sides as I gaze up at the night sky, the endless glittering stars. My legs are still around his waist, and he traces my skin with his fingers as we float. The moon slips behind a cloud, lining it with silver. I want to stay like this forever, weightless, breathless, pretending tomorrow will never come.

"You want to know what happened to me this summer?" he says, and I lift my head to look at him. "You did, Jess."

He's gazing at me with an expression I've never seen before—a fierce tenderness that makes my lungs constrict.

"Because I wouldn't stop banging on your door when you wanted to be alone?" I ask, aware that I'm being cowardly, teasing him instead of leaning into the conversation.

His expression softens, like he understands exactly what I'm doing but doesn't blame me. "That's part of it." He pauses, swallows. "I'll never be the same after this summer. I want you to know that."

He's saying goodbye, and my throat tightens. Unsure how to respond, I choose the cowardly route again: reaching for him, pressing my mouth to his. We drift into deeper water, touching, tasting, biting, until I'm so turned on I can hardly breathe.

"I can't get enough of you," he murmurs into my mouth. "This isn't enough. I need more."

Soon we're rushing back to our campsite, drying ourselves with the T-shirts we plan to wear tomorrow. He pulls me into the tent, pressing me down as he comes over me, whispering words that are filthy and tender at the same time, and I close my eyes and pretend this will last forever.

Hours later, I'm still awake. I don't want this night to end. Come morning, we'll pack up and go back to camp, and it'll be over.

Luke's arms tighten around me. "Stay with me," he murmurs.

"I'm not going anywhere tonight."

"I'm not talking about tonight."

I twist around to look at him; he's rumpled and soft, his eyes half-lidded, like he's mostly asleep.

"I want you to stay with me for a while," he says. "At my family's cabin in Michigan."

His voice is warm and gentle, and I want to wrap myself up in it. But something holds me back, something I can't put into words, so instead I say, "I told Hillary I'd stay with her."

He lifts one shoulder in a lazy shrug. "Stay with her while I finish my draft. Then come visit me. It'll take my editor a month or so to get back to me. I'll have nothing to do."

"Ah, so you want something to do," I say, teasing.

"I want *someone* to do." His eyes dance, then turn serious. "You'd love it there, Jess. It's right on a lake, we have kayaks and paddleboards, there's a bike path and hiking trails."

"It sounds amazing. It's just . . ."

I trail off, once again not sure how to say what I'm thinking.

"What's holding you back?" His voice is probing, inviting me to dig deeper, like the time he helped me unpack my feelings about Hillary.

If I was totally honest, I would tell him that I'm already losing so much this summer. I'm not sure I can handle losing him, too, because inevitably I would have to leave, and the more I allow myself to care about him, the more it'll hurt.

But thinking about this makes my chest feel like it's caving in, so all I can manage is, "Aren't you the one who said everything has to end?"

"Ah," he says, nodding. "So why prolong the inevitable?"

"Exactly."

He tucks his arm under his head, looking up at the tent above us. His expression is pensive, the groove between his eyebrows deepening. "Let me ask you something. Back when you were offered the job as director of the camp, if you'd known it would end like this, would you have taken it?"

"Honestly? I don't know. Yes, I have some great memories, but are they worth how painful it's going to be to walk away?"

"I've thought the same thing about my marriage. And those first two books. If I'd known ahead of time how nasty the divorce would be, that the books would bomb—would I have done any of it?"

"Would you?"

"Probably not."

I huff and shake my head. "Great. More nihilistic thoughts from Luke."

He chuckles. "But if we knew the ending before we started, we'd cherry-pick our way through life, only doing things that are guaranteed to work out."

"That sounds kind of ideal."

"Yeah, but if I'd known how fucking awful it'd be to bury Scout, I never would've taken her when my uncle died. And I would've missed out on some great years with her."

"Okay, fine," I say grudgingly, "but are you ready to get another puppy and do it all over again?"

He immediately grimaces. "No."

"See? I put my heart and soul into this camp, especially this summer. So forgive me if I'm wary of letting myself care that much about anything—or anyone—ever again. I'm sorry to be so negative; that isn't usually my style. But what's the fucking point?"

Like in some of our previous conversations, Luke is unshaken by my emotional outburst. He runs his fingers gently through my still-damp hair before speaking again.

"You love *Hadestown*, right?"

I nod, surprised. The musical is a jazz-infused retelling of the Greek myth of Orpheus and Eurydice; after they fall in love, Eurydice ends up in the underworld, and when Orpheus tries to save her, he fails.

"In the opening number," Luke says, "Hermes tells the audience that it's a sad song. A tragedy. He repeats that at the end, too, after you've watched the entire tragic story unfold, right? But then he says—"

"We're gonna sing it anyway," I say, sighing. "Okay, I hear you. I always loved that message, going on a journey, even when you *know* it won't end well, simply because it's worth taking. But facing it in real life?" Tears flood my eyes, and my throat constricts. "I fucking hate it, Luke."

"I know. Same." He pauses. "But in real life, we can't know ahead of time how something will turn out. We don't know if the book will sell, if the plan to save the camp will work . . ." His eyes dart toward me, then away. "Or if the relationship will last."

"So what do we do?"

I'm not just asking about us—I'm asking about life.

About starting over after losing everything I thought mattered.

"I think we ask ourselves if the journey is worth taking. And if the answer is yes . . . then we go for it."

"Why?" My voice catches on a sob.

Beside me, Luke goes silent, like he's wrestling with this as much as I am.

"This sounds trite," he says finally, "but maybe it comes down to deciding what kind of people we *want* to be. The kind who believe nothing is worth attempting if the outcome isn't guaranteed?" He pauses. "Or the kind of people who *try*?"

He's right. I could have let Camp Chickawah close without a fight. But that's not the kind of person I want to be. I hate what's happening, and I'm not sure I'll ever be fully myself again after losing this place, but I don't regret trying.

Luke shifts so we're inches apart, his gaze intense, searching my face. "You have every reason to be wary. So do I. But finding someone who makes me feel like this? It's rare, Jess. So even if we have no idea how it'll end—if we fall apart after a month, or if we spend the rest of our lives together—I think we should *try*."

I force myself to maintain eye contact, to let this penetrate all the way to my core. Dot's words come back to me, how she hopes I'll spread my wings, take some risks, find out what else I love besides camp.

"All right," I say. "After I spend a few weeks with Hillary, I'll come and stay with you."

His face breaks into a smile like the sun, the kind of smile I tried to coax from him for weeks. Now he gives it to me effortlessly, wrapping his arms around me.

All the time I spent this summer trying to get him to smile, to laugh, to engage—none of it was wasted. If nothing else, it led us to this moment, to us holding each other as we open ourselves to the possibilities contained in all these endings.

Bitter, yes.

But also: oh, how sweet.

thirty-one

Hillary

It's been three days since the last bus drove away. It was, by far, the hardest goodbye of the summer. Because this time, we don't have another group of campers to look forward to. Tomorrow, or ever.

The sorrow is palpable; it feels like we're sitting shiva. We might as well be wearing black. Cooper's constantly trying to feed us, and we're all walking around like shadows of our camp selves, going through the motions of closing up camp, but our hearts aren't in it.

All of us except for Jessie. My best friend has been putting on a happy face along with her Camp Chickawah polo each morning, but I know it's a coping mechanism. She even smiled through the goodbyes this morning: Zac and Zoey went back to California; Dot left to go visit Yvonne in Austin; Mr. Billy grumbled something about picking up trash on the beaches in Florida.

It might take a few weeks for the gravity of this loss to hit her, but when it does, I'll be there. That's part of the reason I invited her to come to Chicago. That, and it's pretty much a dream come true. When I was a kid, I considered sneaking her into my duffel bag at the end of the summer. She was tall, but the bag was long. I daydreamed about her walking into my algebra class—school would have been so much more bearable with her by my side. I hope having me by hers now has helped make these final days less painful.

My next contract doesn't start until after Labor Day, so I am more than happy to delay my return to Chicago. And not just because I'm also delaying the mother of all lectures from my dad. He sent me another email last week, expressing his disappointment in my decision to turn down Aaron's proposal.

But that's a problem for another day.

My problem today is the battery of hulking yellow machines the construction crew started to move in. They aren't even waiting for the body to get cold.

In a move that lives up to his rat bastard nickname, Jack Valentine is turning the whole ordeal into a dog and pony show. Tomorrow, he's bringing in a photographer and a reporter to capture the passing of the torch. More like the destruction of his parents' pride and joy.

After they sign the contract in the Lodge at eleven o'clock tomorrow morning, they'll ceremoniously break ground. After that—this is the real kicker—they requested that Cooper make a celebratory lunch. He said no, which I was happy about. But I was a little disappointed he didn't take me up on my offer: the best blow job of his life if he'd serve them undercooked chicken. Unfortunately, his ethics slightly outweighed his rage. And his horniness.

My rage? It's currently at the boiling point, seeing those bulldozers lined up like they're standing sentry at the edge of the camp. The thought of their metal claws digging into this precious soil makes my stomach churn. I can't imagine how devastated Jessie feels.

Speaking of my best friend, I'm on my way to deliver another round of snacks from Cooper: elevated ants on a log, chocolate-dipped celery topped with crunchy peanut butter and raisins.

"Knock, knock," I say, opening the door to her cabin. "Whoa—what happened in here?"

Jessie is sitting on the floor, surrounded by document boxes. Her office, which was meticulous yesterday, looks like a paper war zone.

"I can't find it." Her voice quivers as she continues flipping through the loose-leaf pages.

"Let me help," I say, taking a seat in front of another box. I open it to find stacks of manila folders, all filled to the brim with original and carbon copies of forms. So much history that will soon be shipped off and shredded. "What are we looking for?"

"Lola's will," Jessie says. "Something Dot said . . . I just need to see it."

"We'll find it," I promise, even though I'm not sure what good can come from our search. The Valentines aren't contesting Jessie's right to a percentage of the sale—they're the ones who told her about it.

But if she wants to find the will, we'll find the will. Maybe it'll give her the closure she needs.

Seven boxes and three paper cuts later, Jessie lets out a sigh of relief. "Here it is."

I shove the box wedged between us out of the way and shift over next to her. Jessie feverishly flips the pages, skimming the legalese.

"Dot was right," she whispers. "It says my name, not just the current camp director."

She closes her eyes and holds the papers to her chest. I know she's thinking of Lola and Nathaniel, wishing she could hug them instead of their will. The Valentines were a big part of my childhood, but they were part of Jessie's family.

"Can I see?" I ask.

She hands it over, and I flip through the last will and testament of Charlotte "Lola" Valentine, which was amended a few weeks after her husband passed away. I skim past the Inventory of Legally Owned Assets, the lists of cherished possessions and charitable donations. I slow down when I get to the beneficiary designations.

Jack and Mary Valentine each own 49.5 percent of Camp Chickawah, with Jessica May Pederson getting the final one percent.

"Wait," I say, staring at the document. "Did you know that you own one percent of the camp?"

Jessie shakes her head. "No, I just get one percent of the sale."

I show her the paragraph. "Nope. You're part owner. A teeny, tiny part, but still."

"I had no idea," Jessie says, nodding thoughtfully. "Jack's been cagey about the will since they told me they were selling the camp. I guess this is why? Not that it matters at this point."

We're both quiet—Jessie wrapping her head around the news; me trying to figure out what Lola must have been thinking. Was she hoping Jessie and Mary would team up against Jack as majority owners? She had to know her daughter would never stand up to her son.

I'm searching the paragraph for something, anything, to make this make sense when a provision catches my eye.

It states that if any named beneficiary wants to keep using the land as a summer camp, the other two cannot sell.

The interested party has the right to keep the camp running, splitting the annual profits along the same split of percentages as the ownership.

The hair on my arms stands at attention as I read the line again, focusing on three little words: "any named beneficiary."

Thirty minutes later, Jessie is taking a long, hot shower at my suggestion, and I'm sitting in front of her computer, about to confirm my suspicions.

But first, I have to face the very confrontation I was hoping to avoid. I finger comb my hair and take a deep breath before pressing the button to start the Zoom call.

My father joins moments later, and my heart squeezes at the sight of him sitting in his office, his silver hair perfectly coiffed. I always had the urge to tousle it, but I only made that mistake once. Stephen J. Goldberg doesn't like being ruffled.

"Hi, Dad," I say, my voice cracking with emotion. I've missed him.

"Hillary," he says. His voice is stern, but his expression softens as he takes me in. "Is everything okay? Your email said it was urgent."

"I'm okay," I tell him.

"Clearly you're not," he says. "Aaron is devastated, by the way." My shoulders shoot up, anxiety coursing through my veins. "I told him this camp place turns you into a different person." He's not wrong. "When you were a kid, it would take you weeks to get back to your old self." Again, not wrong.

"That was fine when you were a child, but you're an adult, Hillary. Though recently you seem to have forgotten that."

My voice is gone, and I find myself nodding, even though I don't agree with him, not one bit. Not anymore.

"I told Aaron not to worry," he continues. "When you get back home, you'll come to your senses and see what's good for you. That he's good for you."

Something happens with his words, like a melding of my mind and my body. And they're both screaming: *No!*

In the tiny Zoom box, I see myself shake my head in protest. This is my life. My decision. Apparently, it took me walking away to realize how little I was in control of my own destiny. I've been a puppet, doing whatever it took to make my dad and boyfriend happy.

Well, no more. I'm taking the strings back. I'm going to do what makes *me* happy.

"Stop," I say.

The sharpness of my voice must catch my dad off guard, because he does in fact stop. He looks at me through the screen, one eyebrow raised. I never interrupt him, and I certainly never tell him what to do.

"I'm not marrying Aaron," I tell him. "And nothing you say will change my mind. He'd make a great partner for the law firm, but not for my life."

My father is speechless.

I'm not.

"Besides, my personal life isn't the reason I wanted to talk. I need your advice. Your *legal* advice."

This gets his attention. He clears his throat, then motions for me to continue. I share my screen and show him the pages of the will, which I scanned for his review. He's not an estate lawyer by trade, but he knows his way around a contract. As he looks them over, I tell him the whole story— starting with how Jack Valentine has been purposefully vague about Jessie's role in the will, how he and Mary turned down our offer for the co-op to purchase the land, and finally, the clause we just discovered.

When I finish, my father looks impressed. He's in problem-solving lawyer mode now, not disappointed-dad mode.

"You're telling me you raised more than two million dollars?"

"We did," I tell him. "This place means a lot to a lot of people. Including Mom. And me."

His expression softens again, but only briefly. "Show me the page with that clause again."

I bring up the page in question and zoom in so he can read it, word for word.

"Does this mean what I think it means?" I ask, crossing my fingers beneath the desk.

"It does. As a named beneficiary, Jessica has the right to keep running Camp Chickawah as a camp."

"Thank god!" I say, but my relief is short-lived. I haven't told my father just how imminent the sale is.

He must read the shift in my expression, because he asks, "The contract hasn't been signed yet, has it?"

"Tomorrow morning," I tell him.

He blows out a breath and shakes his head. "It won't be easy—but it's not impossible. Here's what you need to do."

Over the next ten minutes, my father lays out a step-by-step plan involving a judge, an emergency injunction, and a prayer. When he's finished, I'm filled with hope—no, with confidence—that we're going to bring that greedy rat bastard down.

And I think my dad and I might be okay, too.

"Good luck," he says before we end the call. "I may not understand the decisions you're making, but I'm still proud of you, Hillary. You remind me a lot of your mom. And that's a good thing."

I smile at the screen, and he smiles back. "Thanks, Dad. Maybe when I'm back we can get dinner? I'd like to catch up. And maybe we can talk about Mom a little, too?"

He clears his throat. "I'd like that."

We say goodbye and I sit back in the chair, trying to wrap my head around the roller coaster of emotions I've experienced in the last hour. We're on one hell of a ride.

"Hey," Jessie says. She's standing in the doorway, wearing a worn terry cloth robe, her hair up in a towel.

"How much of that did you hear?" I ask.

"Enough," she says, walking over and enveloping me in a hug. She smells like rose water with a little leftover DEET. The official scent of summer camp. The combination makes me smile, and it gives me the nudge I need to keep going.

"Get dressed," I tell her. "We need to fill in the guys."

Minutes later, we're sitting at a table in the dining hall, eating a meal Cooper whipped up from the last of his dwindling supplies. The main course is a breakfast pasta with eggs, parmesan cheese, and extra-crispy turkey bacon. It's surprisingly delicious.

"How far is the nearest courthouse?" I ask.

"It's in the county seat, which is about two hours from here," Jessie says.

I scribble in my notebook, doing a quick calculation: what time Jessie needs to leave to get the judge to sign the paperwork and get back before the official signing of the contract.

"Assuming the courthouse opens at eight, you probably want to leave here by five a.m. Just to give you a little wiggle room."

"I can do that," she says.

"I'm going with you," Luke says, slipping an arm around her waist.

She turns and looks at him. "But your flight?"

"Canceled."

"Really?" Jessie leans back as if she's trying to get a better look at Luke. Studying him. "I'm not used to you being so nice to me."

Luke laughs. "Don't you worry, it's all part of my plan. Get you comfortable, then *bam*!" He hits the table, making us all flinch. "Payback for that syrup stunt when you least expect it."

"You wouldn't dare," Jessie says, giving him her best mean glare—which honestly isn't that mean. Luke kisses her forehead and Jessie concedes, resuming her spot in the crook of his arm.

"Back to the plan," I say. "My dad is emailing the paperwork we need for the judge. It's an emergency injunction that will stop the contract from being signed and the construction from starting. It's just a first step, but it'll buy us time until the judge can fully review the case and make an official ruling."

"Which'll be in our favor?" Jessie asks.

I nod. "From what my dad said, you have a contractual right to keep the camp running as a camp. And the Valentines can either continue getting 99 percent of any profits, or they can agree to let the co-op buy it. Either way, Camp Chickawah isn't going anywhere."

"Which means *I'm* not going anywhere," Jessie says, her eyes filling with happy tears. "I won't have to leave. I can stay right here."

Luke stiffens, but Jessie doesn't seem to notice, even when he shifts slightly away from her, focusing on his plate.

Meanwhile, Jessie's beaming at me like I've single-handedly saved her life. "Thank you, Hill. For everything."

I reach across the table and grab her hand. "Don't thank me yet. You still need to convince that judge to sign the injunction and get back before any demolition starts."

"But if all goes well?" she says, squeezing my hand so tightly it hurts.

"Then this place will be ours," I tell her, hoping I'm speaking the truth. "Forever."

thirty-two

Jessie

I wake in the dark to my alarm, and it takes a moment to orient myself. I'm in my cabin, and Luke and I are leaving soon to drive to the county seat to meet the judge.

Anxiety crackles in my stomach. The camp's future—my future—is riding on the next few hours.

Luke's already up, so I dress in the dark, then head out to find him. He's sitting on the porch steps, writing in a notebook. When he hears me behind him, he flips it shut.

Something in his posture seems odd.

"Hey," I say, touching his shoulder. "You okay?"

He meets my eyes for a split second before looking away, into the darkness of the woods surrounding the cabin. "Yes." He swallows. "No. I don't know."

I sit next to him on the steps, confused. "What is it?"

In response, he shakes his head. His profile, illuminated by the single porch light behind us, is rigid with tension.

"Luke?" I say, my worry growing. "Please talk to me."

"I don't—" He exhales, shaking his head. "There are a bunch of summer camps in New York, did you know that? A couple nights ago, I couldn't sleep, so I was looking them up online, which is bizarre, I'm aware of that, but I couldn't stop myself."

"Hopefully I won't have to look for another job, though," I say slowly. "If everything goes well today."

"I know, and that's so great, Jessie," he says, looking at his hands. "I'm thrilled for you, and for everyone who loves this place—me included. You get to stay here and keep doing what you've always wanted, what you were *born* to do, and I couldn't be happier for you."

"So . . . why don't you sound happy?"

"I am. Honestly—I just . . ." He tosses the notebook down next to him. "I told you this would happen—that it could happen *so easily*, and it has, and it's not like I went looking for this, I didn't—but now . . ."

He trails off, running both hands through his hair in a gesture of pure frustration.

I'm still confused—and worried. "What are you talking about?"

Luke looks over at me, his eyes stormy, anguished. "You told me not to say it, Jess."

It hits me then: we were in his bed, waking up together the morning after Scout died. He said spending time with me was terrifying, and I asked him why. *Because I could fall in love with you so easily.*

And I said, *Don't say that.*

Startled, I sit up straight. "Luke . . ."

"Yeah." He sighs. "I'm sorry."

I turn to him, eyes widening. "Why are you sorry?"

"Because the last thing you need is another complication. If everything goes well today, you'll spend the next few months completely focused on starting this co-op, which is what you *should* be doing. But I can't help thinking about what would happen if I stayed here, too, which is ridiculous because it's not like you've asked me to. But that doesn't change the fact that I'm falling head over heels . . ." He squeezes his eyes shut. "Sorry."

I blink, dazed. Does he think the only reason I agreed to stay with him in Michigan was because I had nothing else to do? That if the camp doesn't close, I won't want him to stay?

"I'm sorry for bringing this up," he says. "I hope you know that I'm rooting for you, and for this camp, no matter what that means for us. Okay?"

My heart fills with something so big and bright and wonderful I can hardly hold it. He's falling in love with me. The knowledge settles over me like sunshine, warming me from the inside, gently coaxing my own confession out of me—feelings I've been scared to express or even acknowledge.

I'm falling in love with him, too. Of course I am—it's been blossoming all summer. When he pulled me to shore after my kayak capsized; when he listened to me cry about Hillary; when he held my hand in the hammock; when he cried on *my* shoulder after his dog died.

But the most miraculous part? Luke understands exactly how much I love this place, my career. He's not asking me to choose him over camp—he's even thinking of staying here. He's rooting for me, for this camp, no matter what that means for us.

And what does this mean for us? I have no idea. But one thing I know for sure is that I have never, not once in my life, felt like this. About anyone.

"Luke," I say. "I'm falling in love with you, too."

His eyes meet mine, startling and blue. "You—what?"

"I'm falling in love—frustratingly, maddeningly, distractingly in love—with you."

His entire body seems to relax, his chin dropping to his chest. "Really?"

The one word contains a myriad of emotions: disbelief, elation, hope.

"Really," I say, my words bubbling out of me in a rush. "And—and no matter what happens today, I would love to go to your family's cabin in Michigan with you this fall, and if we *do* save the camp, then I would love it if you came back here with me afterward. That is, if you want—"

He pulls me into his lap and wraps his arms around me, burying his face in my shoulder. I lean against him, overwhelmed by the tidal wave of emotion rising inside me.

"I never planned on falling in love again," he says quietly. "I tried *really* hard not to. But you wouldn't leave me alone, Jess."

"Sorry about that." My mouth twitches in a smile.

He pulls back to kiss me, laughing. "Yeah, you're not one bit sorry."

I laugh, kissing him again. "No, I'm not."

His watch beeps, and he glances at it. "I hate to say this, but we need to go. You ready?"

I nod. "As I'll ever be."

"Let's go save your camp."

Hillary and Cooper meet us in the parking lot to send us off—Cooper with foil-wrapped breakfast sandwiches, Hillary with travel mugs of coffee.

"We should be back well before eleven o'clock," I say to them.

"Hopefully the buyer and Jack won't show up before then," Hillary says, "but if they do, we'll stall them."

"I'll throw myself in front of the bulldozer if I have to," Cooper says with a smile.

"Same," Hillary says. "I'll throw Cooper in front of the bulldozer if I have to."

I laugh and throw my arms around her. I'm overflowing with gratitude for her, for coming back here and not giving up when I was so resistant to rebuilding our friendship. For standing by my side through it all.

"See you in a few hours," I say when we separate.

She smiles. "I'll be right here waiting."

thirty-three

Hillary

Cooper and I are sitting in the kitchen, trying to eat the cream cheese eggs he made us for breakfast, when we hear the rumble of an approaching vehicle coming up the gravel road toward camp.

I glance at him, alarmed. "It's only nine thirty—that can't be Jessie yet."

Just an hour ago, I went to the office to send Jessie a text to see if there were any updates. She replied that she and Luke had arrived at the courthouse, but there was no sign of the judge. I was planning on going back to the office to check in again soon.

Cooper reaches over and squeezes my hand. "It's okay—we'll stall them. It'll be fine."

I squeeze back, appreciating his certainty. Still, a thousand worries flood my mind: what if the judge refuses to sign the injunction? What if Jessie and Luke run into traffic or road construction or get in a car accident? What if we can't hold the construction vehicles off any longer? The bulldozer is poised a few feet from the director's cabin, Jessie's literal home, a structure that has been there for over a hundred years. It's irreplaceable.

Cooper takes our plates and puts them in the sink, and together we head outside into the morning sunshine. From the patio outside the dining hall, we have a clear view of the parking lot below. Three unfamiliar vehicles have just pulled in.

My heart leaps to my throat.

A stocky man in work pants and a plaid shirt climbs out of a big white Ford F-150—maybe the contractor? He's followed by a tall man in dark jeans and a blazer, exiting a silver Tesla. He's the buyer; I recognize him from the site visit a few weeks ago. Then, finally, Jack Valentine gets out of his shiny black BMW, followed by Mary Valentine from the passenger seat.

"They're not supposed to be here until eleven," I say, panic settling over me.

"It'll be okay," Cooper says, but I catch a hint of concern in his voice, too.

The three men head up the hill toward us, Mary following behind them. The men are talking and laughing, looking so pleased with themselves, it makes me sick.

When the group gets closer, Jack notices Cooper and me, and his smile drops. "Not you again," he says, clearly annoyed. "Don't bother trying to stop us. The sale is as good as done."

"No, it's not," I say, stupidly.

Jack huffs out a dismissive laugh and keeps walking. I feel myself falling in line the way I have around controlling men all of my life—but then I remember how good it felt to find my voice when I was talking to my dad yesterday. I take a deep breath and gather the courage to use it again.

"The sale is off," I say, the words ringing out loud and clear. "The demolition's not happening."

Jack frowns. "We already had this conversation, and I believe I made myself clear. Now—"

"We found your mother's will," I snap, and Jack's eyes widen. "There's a clause that will nullify all of this." I pull the will out of the folder I'm holding and flip through it. "Right here. Page seven, paragraph two. 'If any named beneficiary of the estate plans to continue to use the property as a summer camp, the other beneficiaries may not sell.'"

The buyer of the property speaks up, directing a question to Jack. "What is she talking about?"

Jack brushes this off. "Nothing to worry about—the girl's getting money from the sale, but she doesn't own a big enough percentage to stop us."

"She doesn't care about the money," I say, defiantly. "She cares about the camp. And she's on her way back from the courthouse as we speak with a signed injunction from a judge ordering a stop to the sale—and the construction— until the will can be reviewed."

Jack's eyes narrow, like he's weighing his options and seeing what he can get away with. "She isn't here? Then I'm not sure what you're hoping to accomplish."

"She's on her way—an hour out, tops," I say, hoping it's true. I don't know if Jessie and Luke have even *seen* the judge yet.

The buyer sighs, frustrated. "We have a tight schedule to stick to—"

"You don't want to start demolition on a property you may not legally own, do you?" I say, my voice sharp. I'm channeling my professional persona now, though it feels like a too-tight pair of jeans, ones I've outgrown. They may not be comfortable, but I can still zip them up and get the job done.

Cooper gives me an impressed look.

The buyer glances at the expensive Rolex on his wrist. "Fine. We'll wait until eleven o'clock. If this alleged beneficiary arrives before then, we'll take a look at the injunction. If not?" He shrugs. "We move forward."

"I'm going to go ahead and get things set up," the contractor says, speaking with all the confidence of a mediocre white man. The buyer looks pleased, and the two of them take off across the property. Jack shoots me a peeved look, then scuttles after them.

Before Mary can follow, I put a hand on her arm. "Mary, Cooper just made a batch of Arnold Palmers with fresh basil. Do you want to come sit and have a glass?"

She gives a grateful nod. "Thank you, dear. That would be lovely."

Over the next hour, Cooper, Mary, and I sit on the porch and wait, sipping our lemonade, keeping an eagle eye on everything going on. I reiterate our plan to Mary, explaining that the will is crystal clear and that our co-op is prepared to buy her and Jack out like we discussed a few weeks ago. Jack can have his money, and Jessie can keep the camp.

Then, just in case Jessie doesn't make it back in time, I make sure Mary knows how much power she has. With Jessie's one percent ownership, she and Mary could team up to be majority owners. Mary could be a hero, stopping her evil brother from destroying their parents' legacy.

She doesn't say anything, but judging by the focused way she listens, I get the distinct feeling she's rooting for us.

Several more construction workers show up, as well as a

reporter and photographer from a newspaper in the largest nearby town. If all goes as planned, they'll be here to witness the downfall of the man whose ego they were summoned to boost. Irony at its finest.

Only there's still no sign of Jessie and Luke, and now I have no way of reaching them. The first thing the contractor did in preparation for demolition was to turn off the electricity to Jessie's cabin and the dining hall, which means we have no Internet service. He has a satellite phone on his belt, but I doubt he—or Jack Valentine—will let me use it.

At ten thirty, I start pacing on the porch.

"Where are they?" I whisper to Cooper. Our eyes are fixed on the road that leads to camp, desperate for the sight of the Camp Chickawah pickup barreling down the road.

He's sitting on top of a picnic table, his knees bouncing with nerves. "I'm sure they'll be here soon."

"They better be," I say.

Then something catches my eye and my heart freezes to ice. "Oh my god. They're heading for the bulldozer!"

Behind me, Mary sits up straight. "Oh dear," she whispers.

"Fuck," Cooper says. "We need to stop them. Hold them off long enough for Jessie and Luke to get here."

"How do we even know they're on their way?" I say, trying to keep my voice quiet enough that Mary doesn't hear. "What if something went wrong?"

"They'll be here," he says, though he sounds less certain now. "Come on, let's go."

We take off together, marching hand in hand toward the bulldozer. Everyone has gathered nearby—they're all wearing yellow hard hats, mugging for the camera, posing with their arms around each other. Jack and the buyer each pull out a folder of papers and make a show of signing them with a flourish.

"Hang on!" I say, walking up. "What happened to waiting until eleven o'clock?"

Jack glances at his phone. "It's ten forty-five and there's no sign of her. Even if there was, what's she going to do about it?"

Behind him, a man in a hard hat climbs into the cab of the bulldozer.

"You're going to tell him to wait, right?" Cooper asks the contractor, his eyes flashing with anger.

The contractor shrugs and looks at the buyer. "Up to you, boss," he says.

The buyer gives him a nod. "Go ahead."

The bulldozer lurches toward the cabin, and I take off running after it, not sure what I'm going to do when I get there, but certain I can't just sit by and let this happen.

"Stop!" I yell, darting in front of the bulldozer.

"Get out of the way," Jack snaps.

"Ma'am, you can't be here," the contractor warns. "This is an active construction zone."

"This is an *illegal* construction zone," Cooper says, coming up next to me. Now we're standing shoulder to shoulder in front of the wide yellow teeth of the bulldozer, both breathing hard. My legs are shaking with fear, but we stand firm.

And I think about my mom as a scared camper, running miles back to camp in the darkness all by herself. I'm channeling her. I'm channeling Jessie, and Dot, and

Nathaniel and Lola, too—every counselor and camper from all the years past.

"You don't want to do this," I plead with the buyer. "Just a few more minutes."

He glances nervously at Jack. "You're sure this is all on the up and up?"

"Absolutely," Jack says, his voice full of venom.

"I don't have time for this," the contractor says, and my heart plummets. He gives a nod to the driver of the bulldozer. "Get moving. They'll get out of the way."

The driver gives a nod in return and slowly eases the bulldozer in our direction.

My whole body tenses, but before I can speak or move, Cooper steps between me and the bulldozer, like he's going to face it down on my behalf.

"Wait," I plead, "you can't just—"

"STOP!"

I glance up to see Jessie running toward us, her braids flying behind her, waving a piece of paper wildly in the air.

thirty-four

Jessie

My heart is in my throat as I race across the lawn, taking in the sight: Cooper and Hillary, shoulder to shoulder, facing down the hulking yellow bulldozer heading their way. A group of men, including Jack Valentine, turn to look in my direction. Mary Valentine, standing from her seat on the porch of the dining hall as I run past.

"STOP!" I yell, waving the injunction. "You don't have the right to do any construction or demolition!"

By the time I reach the group, I'm out of breath. I hand the paper directly to Jack Valentine.

The whole process took longer than expected—we waited an agonizing forty minutes before the judge arrived. I'd expected an old white man in a suit, but instead it was a thirtysomething Black woman in leggings and a T-shirt, apologizing profusely because her newborn son had had a terrible night and she'd overslept. She read through the will, instructed her secretary to type up an injunction, and signed it with a flourish. She sent us on our way with a firm "Good luck."

We'd driven back as quickly as possible—Luke driving because I was too nervous. I kept imagining the buildings I love being crushed to the ground, erased because I was a few minutes late.

But everything seems to be intact, and Luke catches up to me as Jack finishes reading the injunction.

When he looks up, his face is so red I think his head might explode. "You can't just—just steal this out from under me!"

"I'm not stealing anything," I say. "As I told you before, we created a business plan to purchase the camp as a co-op—"

"This is ridiculous!" he shouts, getting in my face. He grips my arm, squeezing it. "You and your little—"

"Hey!" Luke shouts, coming up behind me. "Back the fuck off."

Jack releases my arm and stumbles back a step.

"You touch her again and I'll break your hand," Luke says, his voice ice-cold. He's vibrating with fury, reminding me of the time he chewed out that cabin of guys for screwing with the kayaks.

Jack looks terrified, and I'm grateful that Luke's on my side. I may be a tall, strong, capable woman, but it feels *wonderful* to have someone rush in to protect me like that.

"You were saying?" Luke says to me.

"Thanks," I say, and face Jack again. "We have the money raised to buy you both out, unless you want to still be involved. Either way, Camp Chickawah isn't going anywhere."

"I could take you to court for this," Jack says, and the man next to him—the buyer and property developer—nods.

"Go ahead," I say, silently praying that Hillary's dad is right, that there's nothing Jack can do to sell Camp

Chickawah without my blessing. "But you're not starting the demolition today, I can tell you that much."

"And I'm not sure you'll have much of a leg to stand on in court," a timid voice says behind me.

Everyone turns; Mary Valentine is a few feet away from the group, teetering slightly on her feet.

Her brother shoots her a glare. "What are you talking about?"

"I'm willing to testify that our parents intended for Jessie to be considered as a beneficiary," she says, and meets her brother's eyes dead on.

Jack's eyes bulge. "You wouldn't."

"It's what Mom and Dad wanted, Jack," she says, her voice even softer now.

Jack glares at her, then turns to the buyer. "Everything is in order, I promise—"

"I'm not so sure I trust that anymore," the buyer says, peering down at him.

Jack's face turns even redder as he sputters. "I—you—" He whirls on me. "You'll be hearing from my attorney."

"I look forward to it," I say, though I'm terrified that the injunction won't hold, that his attorneys will find a loophole to force the sale through.

For an agonizing moment I'm certain that Jack Valentine is going to laugh in my face. But then he turns and walks away, the buyer following him, the two of them muttering to each other. The contractor rolls his eyes and motions to his guys to clear out, too. The newspaper reporter slips me her card and says to call if I'm interested in telling her the whole story. The photographer snaps a couple extra pictures as they both head to the parking lot.

Before following her brother, Mary Valentine comes up to me. "I'd like to hear more about the co-op," she says. "Will you send me some information?"

A smile stretches across my face, and I give her a hug; she feels like Lola, small and soft. "Of course. Thank you, Mary."

She pats my cheek as she pulls away. "Thank you, Jessie. You know, my parents loved all the kids and staffers they worked with at this camp, but the way they talked about you was special. Like you were a granddaughter to them. Like family."

I smile, her words warming me. "They felt like family to me, too."

She gives me one last smile before heading toward the parking lot, where I expect she'll have an uncomfortable ride home with her brother.

Soon they're all gone, leaving behind a cloud of dust on the gravel road. I turn to face Luke, Cooper, and Hillary.

"It worked?" I say, almost to myself.

Luke nods, a proud smile on his face. "You did it."

Cooper is smiling, too, his arm around Hillary, who has tears in her eyes.

"It really worked?" I repeat, louder, and then it all hits me in a rush: "We did it! We did it!"

Hillary runs toward me, throwing her arms around me, and we're like teenagers again, screaming with joy as we jump in circles and cheer.

We did it.

thirty-five

Hillary

Once the Valentines and their entourage vacate the camp property and move all the construction gear out (see ya, suckers!), the four us collapse in Jessie's cabin. Her home, the century-old building that isn't going anywhere. Thanks to us.

Jessie looks dazed, her eyes shimmering with happy tears. "I should call Dot," she says, her voice cracking with emotion.

"Of course," I say. "Do you want us to leave?"

"No," she says, slipping her phone out of her pocket. "Stay."

I smile and take a seat on the arm of her chair, thinking back to how jealous I was of Dot and Jessie's relationship at the beginning of summer. Now I have my own special connection with Dot, and I know Jessie has more than enough room for both of us in her life.

"Yello," Dot says, answering the phone. Jessie has the call on speaker, and we can hear music in the background. I smile at the thought of Dot living it up with her camp girlfriend.

Jessie tells her the whole story, with me filling in details of the literal standoff. When we finish, the other side of the line is quiet, save for Brandi Carlile playing in the background.

Eventually, Dot speaks. "So camp is back on for next summer?"

"Next summer, and the next, and every summer after that," Jessie says.

"Proud of you, Pippi," Dot says, and the tears Jessie's been holding back break free, sliding down her cheeks. "Nathaniel and Lola would be, too."

We say our goodbyes and end the call with promises to talk more soon. The silence that follows is filled with such relief, it almost feels restorative.

"What now?" Luke asks.

"Usually," Jessie says, wiping her tears away with the back of her hand, "I'd take a few weeks off before starting to prepare for the next summer—planning out the registration calendar, hiring staff, and making a list of repairs. This year . . . Hillary and I had some ideas I think we should talk more about."

My jaw drops. I've been so focused on what saving the camp means for Jessie that I haven't even thought about what it could mean for me. That I could stay and help her, do what I do best: help turn our beloved camp into a thriving business.

"That all sounds great—but I was talking about *now* now," Luke says. "We should celebrate."

"How about one last campfire?" I say, standing up.

Jessie's face lights up. It only seems right. One last campfire that's celebratory and hopeful, that says goodbye until next summer, not goodbye forever.

"I'm sure you have more calls to make," I say to Jessie.

"So why don't you do that, and Cooper and I will go start the fire? You can meet us over there when you're ready."

Jessie agrees, giving me one more hug, squeezing me tight. "Thank you, Hilly. For everything."

Now I'm the one with tears in my eyes, but I blink them away and take Cooper's hand. After two quick stops to grab supplies—his guitar (a campfire isn't complete without music), a bottle of champagne he'd been saving, plus hot dogs and ingredients to make s'mores—we head to the firepit. We're both quiet on the walk over, taking in the beauty and the reverence of this moment. The old pine trees seem to stand taller, the wood cabins more relaxed, and even the gentle breeze feels like a sigh of relief knowing everything is safe. Nothing is going anywhere.

"I can't believe you stepped between me and that bulldozer," I say.

"I couldn't help myself," he says, shrugging. "I know you don't need me to protect you, but—"

"It was hot," I tell him.

He turns and gives me a half grin. "Yeah?"

"Fuck yeah," I say, and he chuckles.

We fall quiet again as we reach the campfire, working to get it started before the night sky goes completely dark. The air is cool, bringing a hint of the autumn that will soon arrive.

"What Jessie said about you having ideas . . ." Cooper says as he sets the wood in the center of the firepit. "Think she'll ask you to stick around?"

I hand him some kindling and matches. "I hope so," I tell him. "None of this was in my plans, but being out here has changed things. It's changed me."

I think back to what my dad said, how I always came home from camp like another person, how it took me weeks to get back to myself. But I wasn't getting back to my real self. I was going away from it. Turning back into the person he wanted me to be. Not the real me, the person I am here.

"For the first time in my life, I don't know what comes next," I say. "I think I've known for a while that I don't want to go back to the life I had before this, but I didn't know what a new life would look like. Especially since I thought the camp was closing."

Cooper strikes a long match and the kindling catches fire, the oxygen and fresh air breathing it to life. I've never felt more solidarity with an open flame.

"Now that the camp isn't closing, do you know what it looks like?" he asks, sitting on a log bench next to the firepit. "Your future?"

I shrug and take a seat beside him, wrapping my arms around myself to warm up. "This still feels like a dream—but in a perfect world, I'd stay here. Help Jessie turn things around and make this business sustainable throughout the year, not just during the summer months."

"That does sound like a dream," Cooper says, his voice wistful.

"How about you?" I ask. "Think you'll go back to Boston once this sabbatical is over?"

"Honestly?"

"It's the only way," I say, giving him a smile.

"I already told my boss I wasn't coming back," Cooper says.

I blink at him, surprised. "What? Where are you going to go?"

The fire is in full force now, the flames dancing, lighting up the night sky, casting a warm glow on Cooper's face. On the hint of a hopeful smile I see there.

"I've never been one of those people who has to know what's coming," he says. "I'm okay with a little uncertainty. But this girl I really like, there's nothing she loves more than a good plan. So I was thinking, if it was okay with her, we'd follow her plan for a while. Whether that was in Chicago—where they have a lot of great restaurants—or in the Minnesota woods, where I'd be the—"

I don't let him finish, launching myself into his arms, kissing the words right out of his mouth, pushing past the discomfort of the unknown and into the comfort of his embrace. And just like that, the hazy vision of my future turns clear: me and Cooper, figuring things out. Together.

"Are we interrupting something?" Jessie calls, a teasing lilt to her voice. I peel myself away from Cooper, resuming my seat beside him, my arm looped through his.

Luke and Jessie take a seat on the bench next to ours, and we pass the bottle of champagne back and forth. The bubbles tickle my throat, and everything about this moment, this night, feels right.

"I've got an idea," Jessie says after a minute. "Roses and thorns for the whole summer."

Cooper blows out an irritated breath. I smile; I love that he shares my opinion on icebreakers.

"Come on," Jessie insists. "I'll start. One of my biggest roses was the talent show. Raising the money was great, but the thing I loved most was feeling like we were one big team, with everyone working toward a common goal. It was like in

Come from Away when the town of Gander pulls together to take care of people stranded after 9/11 . . ."

She trails off, realizing that Cooper and I are staring at her, totally confused. Luke is nodding along, though, as if whatever Jessie's referencing makes perfect sense.

"Never mind," Jessie says. "I'll just say that it was incredible knowing so many people wanted to save the camp as much as I did. And our skit! When Hill put lipstick on my nose—I laughed so hard I almost peed my pants."

"Thank god you didn't—you would have peed on me!" I laugh. "That's my rose: Jessie didn't pee on me."

"That doesn't count," she says. "Give us a real one."

"Hmmm."

I close my eyes and think about the last two months, images flashing before me like a slide show: the first day, when Jessie barely acknowledged me; that first trip to town, when Cooper offered to be my fling; finally feeling butterflies; the nights sitting by the campfire, singing songs under the stars; every single Sunday night dinner; waking up in Cooper's arms. But the biggest rose of all was the way Jessie's friendship came back to me. Slowly at first, then all at once.

And I know what moment I'm going to share.

My eyes well with tears as I say, "My biggest rose for the summer was playing Capture the Flag." The moment I truly believed our friendship was savable. "Not only did we win, but it felt good, being on the same team as you again."

I look at Jessie. Her eyes shimmer in the light of the fire, and I know she knows what I mean. I don't want to leave things on a sad, sentimental note, though, so I add two more roses, quickly, almost under my breath. "Also redeeming ourselves by winning Color Wars—and Cooper wearing that toga . . ."

Cooper suggestively waggles his eyebrows, and we all laugh.

"Boys?" Jessie says.

To my surprise, Luke starts to talk—no additional cajoling required.

"My rose for the summer was finding my muse again," he says, and I wonder if he's talking about the camp . . . or my best friend. "I was so focused on trying to tell an old story that I almost fell out of love with writing. But something about this place—" His eyes land on Jessie. "I found my story, and I think I've found my way forward, too."

"Coop?" Jessie says.

"Well, my first rose is that I finally got to have a camp girlfriend—who's my old camp crush!" There's a flutter in my belly, and I can't believe I spent thirty years thinking butterflies didn't exist. I hate to think I came so close to accepting a life without this feeling. "And my second rose is the pace of life around here. Back in Boston, everything moved so fast I didn't have time to think. I was just going through the motions, trying to win, to be the best. Having time to take a breath and get back to basics helped me think about what I really want in my life. What's important."

Cooper's eyes are locked on mine, and I'm smiling so wide it feels like my cheeks might crack.

This kind of happiness doesn't come from a checklist. It comes from living, from taking risks and following your heart.

"Now for the thorns," Jessie says, lowering her voice. "Let's go reverse order. Coop?"

He sits up straighter and slips his arm around my waist. I lean into him because I know his thorn—and I also know that we're stronger for having been through it.

"I only had two thorns the whole summer," he says. "When I acted like a dick and let my past get in the way of my future." I rest my hand on his thigh and give him a squeeze to let him know all is forgiven. "And all the allergies and food sensitivities. I get it, I do, but it was a challenge to find meals that tasted good and could also be modified for the no-lactose-gluten-free-allergic-to-tree-nuts-keto-paleo crowd."

Luke doesn't have to be prompted to share his thorn: "Losing Scout," he says, his face twisting in pain. "And the fact that I spent far too long pushing people away and acting like an asshole. I appreciate you all being patient with me."

My turn again. "My thorn was those horrible hours when I thought I might have to leave camp early, and when Aaron showed up with that stupid AI proposal."

I shiver at the memory, and Cooper pulls me even closer against him.

It's Jessie's turn. She doesn't say anything at first, just stares into the fire. The rest of us exchange looks, but no one is about to hurry her.

"My first thorn is obviously the dick tick," she eventually says.

I swallow a laugh, and when Cooper lets out a snort, I elbow him in the side. No doubt it was stressful for Jessie, but it was hilarious.

"But the real thorn," she goes on, "was that gut punch that came in the moment after something wonderful happened, when I realized this could be our last summer here."

"But it's not," I say, my voice wobbling with emotion.

"It's not," Jessie agrees.

We're all quiet, and I lay my head on Cooper's shoulder. I close my eyes and try to memorize this moment: the slow and steady rhythm of his breath; the crackling of the fire; the scent of pine, smoke, and Cooper's woodsy cologne.

"Trade spots with me?"

I open my eyes to see Jessie standing in front of us.

Cooper gives my waist a squeeze before getting up and giving Jessie his seat. "You're pretty, man," he says to Luke. "But I'm not going to spoon you."

He sits down on Luke's bench with a good foot of space between them.

"You okay?" I ask Jessie.

"Never better," she says. "Thanks to you."

"What you said earlier, about my ideas . . . if you'll have me, I'd love to stay and help you."

Jessie grins at me, her eyes wide and bright in the firelight. "Really? You want to stay?"

"I do," I tell her.

"I do, too," Cooper says. "You'll need a cook, right?"

"And I can write from anywhere," Luke says.

"We didn't come this far to stop now." Cooper glances at Jessie, then back to me, and we share a secret smile.

"I love you guys," Jessie says, smiling. "I know it will take a while to get things going, but Hill, I loved the idea of having an adult session or two after the regular kids' camp wraps up for the season."

"Yes!" I say, excitement coursing through me. Before, we were discussing theoretical ideas. Now that the camp is ours, it feels like we're making real plans. "And maybe retreats in the fall for artists."

"You could offer a writing residency," Luke says.

"A cooking camp," Cooper suggests.

"We could have a session before the regular season starts with just older kids, where they choose tracks to focus on—sailing, theater, or cooking," I suggest.

"How about a family camp during spring break?" Luke offers.

"It's still snowy here then," Jessie says. "But we could do a snow-themed camp, once we get the cabins winterized."

By the time the fire is reduced to embers, the champagne bottle is empty, and our hands are sticky with the remnants of the sweetest s'mores, we're buzzing with possibilities. With plans for the future of our beloved camp. Plans we're making together.

I think back to that day two months ago when my car pulled up. I had no idea what was in store, but I hoped that familiar sign with YOU BELONG HERE carved into the wood was still true.

Turns out, those words have never been truer. This summer, I didn't just find love. I found myself again. And like Dorothy said in the script Jessie and Luke wrote for the play: there's no place like camp.

Jessie

One Year Later

As always, the last day of summer camp is chaos, but it's the best kind: loading kids and duffels onto buses, calls of "See ya next summer" echoing as they head down the dusty road.

Once they're cleared out, it's time for the counselors and staff to do the same. And then it's over, and I'm standing alone in the middle of the big lawn, that familiar wistfulness crawling over me as I realize I won't see these kids for ten months.

But I'm not *too* sad.

Because adult camp starts next week.

The past year has been a wild ride. There were times I thought we'd made a mistake in believing we could turn the co-op into a successful business venture. Luckily, I have a wonderful team. The Camp Chickawah Cooperative includes hundreds of former campers, with a twelve-person board of directors elected by the members. The board hired me as chief camp director and Hillary as chief operations officer. Her clear financial vision and business acumen have been guiding lights through our most challenging decisions. Running this camp with her is the fulfillment of my childhood dream—though I never imagined doing it with my best friend, my platonic soulmate, whose strengths complement mine perfectly.

"Welp, we made it through another summer," Dot says from behind me.

I turn to smile at her; I was thrilled when she agreed to come back as assistant director. Dot isn't a year-round employee anymore—she's spending the off-season in Austin with Yvonne—and I couldn't be happier for her.

"It was Chick-amazing, wasn't it?" I say.

"Damn right, boss."

I throw my arm over her shoulder as we head back toward the office. Hillary is heading toward us, and I'm struck by how different she looks compared to last summer when she arrived for training week. Her hair is wild and curly, her hiking boots are scuffed, and she has a huge smile on her face.

"Hey, Jessie, hey, Dot," she calls. "Congrats on finishing an incredible summer!"

"Thanks!" I throw my arms around her, squeezing extra tight. "How was Chicago?"

She spent most of the summer here, working with me on plans for the camp (and hanging out with Chef Cooper, because they're obsessed with each other), but she spent the past week in Chicago, meeting with a consortium of women small business owners and visiting her dad.

She'll be running the Arts and Crafts cabin during adult camp this fall, for old times' sake.

"The trip was great—I'll tell you more later," she says. "I've got to find Cooper, but we're still planning on dinner at the lake, right? Seven o'clock?"

I nod. "That should give me and Dot time to wrap things up this afternoon."

"I'll meet you in the office in thirty minutes, boss," Dot says.

"Sure thing," I say.

Dot heads to the office, and Hillary to the dining hall. Cooper bursts out the doors and races toward her, nearly tackling her in a full-body hug, as if they've been apart for months rather than a week. Their laughter floats on the breeze as I head down the path toward the lake, where Zac and Zoey are wrapping up at the waterfront.

His blond hair has grown out to his shoulders, and Zoey has a cute baby bump. They'll stay here through the fall to help with adult camp, then head to Australia for a second summer, scoping out locations near Zac's hometown for a future kids' camp. Zoey is due in February, and they plan to return to Camp Chickawah next summer, baby in tow. I figure if we can make it feasible to raise a child here, someday in the future, if I'm lucky, I can, too.

I walk past the Lodge, which was our second construction project, after winterizing the cabins. Thanks to a big grant from a former camper, it's been renovated and refurbished with big picture windows and a wide porch facing the lake. The garden around it is in full bloom—the campers helped tend the flowers and herbs. Next summer, Cooper wants to add a raised vegetable garden.

Down the shore from the Lodge is a new construction site—Mary Valentine's lake house. She's the largest shareholder in the co-op and retained a half-acre lot for herself, where she'll build a small vacation home that'll be deeded to the co-op when she passes away.

I take the path toward the boys' cabins, climb the stairs of the smallest one, and knock before letting myself in. The air is cooler in here, slightly musty. The beds are gone, but the table remains where it was last year, pushed against the largest window, covered with papers and notebooks. Luke sits there with his laptop. His hair is messy and he's glaring at the screen with that blue-fire stare that lets me know it's been a rough writing day.

He needs a moment to transition back into the real world, so I sit in a chair and wait. *Camp Shadows* came out in July, and it's done well—no bestseller lists, but steady sales, and readers are loving it—so he's working on another novel as part of a new three-book deal. It's not a half-million-dollar deal like last time, but he's happy to be a mid-list author as long as he can keep doing what he loves. He's taken the lead on planning writing and artist retreats here, too, during the off-season.

Last September, I spent a couple weeks in Chicago with Hillary, then headed to Luke's family cabin in Michigan. We spent our days paddleboarding on the lake, playing Settlers of Catan (I finally beat him after two weeks of trying), belting show tunes in the kitchen while cooking dinner (he can do an impressive Phantom), and talking under the stars. Every day I fell more in love with him, but I couldn't shake the nagging question in the back of my mind: did he really feel the same? Or did he get caught up in the emotions when we were back at camp?

Then, one day during our last week there, I accidentally overheard him talking to his mom on FaceTime.

She asked him if things were serious between us, and Luke said, "Let me put it this way, Mom: this relationship can only go one of two ways. Either we'll spend the rest of our lives together, or this will be the most painful breakup I can imagine." "Worse than the divorce?" she asked. And he replied, "So much worse."

That night, I told him that I wanted to figure out how to stay together, and he closed his eyes and said, "Thank god."

Over the winter, we made time for traveling. He took me to New York in January, and we spent an entire week seeing Broadway shows—*Hadestown* and *Moulin Rouge!* and *Chicago* and *Sweeney Todd.* We met up with Hillary and Cooper in New Zealand for two weeks in February, after which they took a monthlong culinary tour through Europe and Asia, and we visited my mom and stepdad in San Diego.

But as much as I enjoyed all this traveling, I was itching to get back to camp.

Returning to the property this past spring felt like having a missing piece of my soul restored. Nothing I experienced during my time away—the musicals, the delicious food, the scenic vistas—could compare to the feeling of being here, where I belong. My world has expanded this past year, but this place is still my home.

Once camp started, I worried that Luke and I would struggle to balance our relationship. But we navigated it like we've navigated everything else this year: together. When I'm busy, Luke feels free to disappear into his fictional worlds, which he appreciates. He made a point to come to most of the meals and bonfires (a gesture of love, since the noise and chaos give him a headache) and he led a weekly writing workshop for the campers. For my part, I realized that being "on the job" 24/7 all summer isn't healthy, so I started putting Dot in charge for one full day each week. She encouraged me to carve out a few hours here and there on other days, too, so Luke and I can get some alone time.

"Hey, you," he says, and I look up. He leans back in his chair and stretches, running his hands through his messy hair. "How did the big send-off go?"

"Good." I walk over and lean against his desk. "How's the draft coming?"

He grimaces. "I spent three hours rewriting three paragraphs."

"Sounds like you deserve a break," I say, grinning as he stands and pulls me against him. With me in my hiking boots and him in socks, we're exactly the same height—something he loves, saying it makes for easier access.

"*You* deserve a break," he says, and kisses me on the mouth. "Have to admit, I'm looking forward to a night with the guarantee of no interruptions. Or even a couple hours without that damn walkie-talkie going off."

I laugh. "I'm looking forward to that, too, but I need to meet Dot in . . ." I look at my watch. "Twenty minutes. Do you think you can be that quick? And remember, we're doing dinner with Cooper and Hillary at the lake later."

"I can be quick," he says immediately. "But then I'll be slow later tonight."

I grin. "Deal."

That evening, Luke and I meet Hillary and Cooper down at the lakefront, where Cooper has prepared an incredible dinner for the four of us still on the property. Dot cleared out to catch a plane to Austin, and the Zimmerman-Takahashis drove to town because Zoey was craving Funyuns and rocky road ice cream, both of which are out of stock at the canteen.

We eat picnic-style on the dock, talking and laughing as the sun sets and the fireflies come out. Cooper says he's looking forward to cooking for adults next week—the kids adore him, but he's grown tired of their limited palates.

"I think it's time for some champagne!" Cooper says, once we're all stuffed. "It'll be our new end-of-summer tradition."

"Sounds lovely," Hillary says to him, "but you forgot to bring it."

He grins, his eyes twinkling with mischief. "We better run to the kitchen, then. Back soon!"

They take off, giggling as they disappear down the path.

"Did that seem a little scripted to you?" I ask Luke.

Luke shrugs. "Maybe they wanted to get it on in the kitchen again."

I snort a laugh. "Probably."

"But since I have you alone for a minute, have I told you about the dreams I've been having?"

I look at him, expecting to see a teasing glint in his eyes. Instead, he looks pensive. Almost somber.

"What kind of dreams?" I ask. "Not like the ones back then, I take it."

He shakes his head. "Not like that. But still . . . well. Unsettling. They always start the same way: I wake up and you're not in bed with me, so I go look for you. I realize I'm in an unfamiliar house—at least, it's a place I don't recognize, though it feels familiar in the dream, if that makes sense?"

I nod, and he continues.

"I step out of the bedroom and into a hall where there are two doors. I open the first one, and it's an office. My laptop is on the desk. My notebooks and scrap paper are cluttering everything."

"Your writing space," I say, smiling.

"Yeah, it's nice. But I still don't know where you are, so I step out of the room and open the next door in the hall. And there's . . ." He pauses, sneaks a glance at me. "A child's bed and a crib. A few toys on the floor. A changing table."

I hold my breath. The only sound is the gentle lapping of the water against the dock, the crickets singing around us.

"No one's in that room, either," he continues, "so I head downstairs to the kitchen and there you are. You're sitting at the table with a little boy and a baby girl with strawberry blonde hair. There's a dog lying next to your feet. And you smile and say good morning."

My eyes fill with tears.

"We eat breakfast together," he says, smiling, "and then you kiss the kids goodbye, and we walk you to the door. And when you go outside, I see the lake and the trees and the cabins in the distance, and I realize that we live here. Right here." He pauses. "That's when I wake up. And every time, I lie there in bed and wish I could go back to that dream." He glances over at me, a few stray tears caught on his lashes. "I want that life, Jess. I want it so badly it hurts."

I want it, too—my heart is overflowing with longing. "But are you sure you'd be happy here? Living in the woods away from society?"

"I don't like society that much."

I let out an incredulous laugh. "But kids, Luke? I mean, I want kids. But how would we make it work? I don't want them to end up like Jack Valentine, resentful of their parents for being so focused on camp."

"I know, but *we* don't run this camp, you and Hillary do. So during the summer, I'd take the primary role in parenting. And I'll do my best to make sure that my deadlines are during the off-season, when you can take more of the primary role. I'm sure there will be challenges, but I think we can figure it out together."

Then he pulls something out of his pocket, and my breath catches.

He's holding a ring. And he looks more nervous than I've ever seen him.

"Those three paragraphs I was working on today?" he says. "They were for this, and I've completely forgotten them now. But I want to marry you more than anything I've ever wanted in my entire life. I want to make those dreams a reality. Please say yes."

My entire body seems to soften. "Luke . . ."

He looks down at the ring, a slim gold band with a channel of diamonds. "I figured you'd want something simple, something you can wear while setting up tents and putting sunscreen on kids and all that, but if you want something else—"

"It's perfect," I say.

And I don't just mean the ring—I mean the life he's imagined for us. It's almost too beautiful to believe, my wildest dreams come true. He pulls me toward him and kisses me, a deep, aching kiss that feels full of promise for the future.

A branch cracks behind us, and I whirl around to see

Hillary and Cooper watching, huge, ridiculous grins on both their faces.

"You guys knew about this?" I say, shocked.

"Of course," Hillary says, "but don't leave him hanging, answer him—he's been nervous about this for weeks!"

I whirl back to Luke. "YES!" I shout. "A thousand times yes!"

Luke's face lights up in a smile, and Hillary and Cooper cheer as he kisses me again.

After that, Cooper pops the champagne and pours a glass for each of us. Hillary's sitting on his lap, snuggled against him, and I'm sitting between Luke's legs, leaning against his chest.

"So . . ." Hillary says, "are we thinking a wedding here next year? I can imagine it on the big lawn, twinkle lights strung through the trees, Cooper in charge of the food."

"I love that," I say, and send her a sneaky grin. "But what if we make it a *double* wedding?"

She blushes and looks away, but Cooper catches my eye and gives me a grin that makes it clear he has his own plan in the works.

We shift to other topics—Cooper tells us about some new menu offerings during adult camp, and Hillary tells us about her trip to Chicago. She says one of the business owners she's working with is an architect who's going to draw up plans for a house for me, not far from Mary Valentine's lot.

"Me?" I say. "Why?"

"Because if you're going to be here on the property with Luke and a family, you can't live in a musty hundred-year-old cabin," she says, smiling. "The entire board is in agreement."

"What about you and Cooper?" I ask. "I want you guys to have a place, too."

"We'd love to be your neighbors," Hillary says, "but for now, we're going to split our time between Chicago and here—maybe stay in your cabin once you move into the house."

After a while, Cooper and Luke gather up the dishes and leave me and Hillary to finish off the champagne. We sit on the edge of the dock, our bare feet in the water, and chat. Each time my eyes catch on the new ring on my left hand, I feel a bubble of excitement. It won't be easy, building a life here with Luke, raising children and balancing our careers, but it's a journey worth taking.

"Remember that button you had on your backpack when you were a kid?" Hillary asks after a while. "What did it say—something about living all year for the summer?"

"'I live ten months for two,'" I say, nodding. "I spent the entire year waiting for camp because it felt like the only real thing in my life."

"And now?"

I lean back on my hands, gazing up at the starry sky. "This past year has pushed me to create a life that's bigger than this camp. I mean, don't get me wrong, I hope we can run this place until we die—"

"You're gonna croak out there in the middle of the lake one morning in your canoe when you're ninety-eight years old," Hillary says, pointing across the water.

"You'll probably die in that Arts and Crafts cabin making friendship bracelets," I say, laughing. "However. Even with our co-op going strong now, there's no guarantee it'll last forever."

"True."

"But if this camp has to close someday, it won't feel like I'm losing *everything* I love." I shrug. "I know that I can still have a full, rich, beautiful life."

"I feel the same way," Hillary says, smiling. "But I have faith in us. I think we're going to be doing this for a long, long time."

She leans her head on my shoulder, and I rest my cheek on the top of her head, the same position we've sat in since we were children. Our feet dangle in the cool water as we stare across the shimmering moonlit surface, our summers to come stretching out in front of us. And I'm filled with an overwhelming assurance that this is just the beginning, that we'll be sitting exactly like this, right here, next summer— and the next, and the next.

Together.

acknowledgments

This book was a joy to write—even if we did have to write it twice! We're grateful to our incredible agents, Amy Berkower and Joanna MacKenzie, for their constant support, guidance, and wisdom. Thank you to our editor, Kerry Donovan, for helping us bring this story to life. We're also indebted to Genevieve Gagne-Hawes at Writers House for giving invaluable feedback (on a very short timeline) to help shape this book and make the kayak scene accurate.

We have an incredible writing community and are so thankful for everyone in it. Thank you to the Berkletes, the Women's Fiction Writers Association, the Ink Tank, the Every Damn Day Writers, the 2022 Debuts, the Eggplant Beach Writers, our Featuring Banana! and Noods and Balls crews (you know who you are).

We are so grateful for the friendship and support of so many authors we admire, including but not limited to: Suzanne Park, Kathleen West, Kimmery Martin, Lainey Cameron, Lyn Liao Butler, Leah DeCesare, Lisa Barr, Renée Rosen, Emily Henry, Christina Hobbs, Lauren Billings, Colleen Oakley, Nancy Johnson, Julie Carrick Dalton, Megan Collins, Kathleen Barber, Kristin Harmel (Alison's literary godmother), Mary Kay Andrews, Kristy Woodson Harvey, Patti Callahan Henry, Amy Mason Doan, Jamie Beck, Kerry Lonsdale, Tiffany Yates Martin, Orly Konig, Rochelle

Weinstein, Kristan Higgins, Barbara Claypole White,
Heather Webb, Liz Fenton, Lisa Steinke, Camille Pagán, Ali
Hazelwood, Zibby Owens, Shelby Van Pelt, Chloe Liese, Lynn
Painter, Katie Gutierrez, Jill Santopolo, Allison Winn Scotch,
Anabel Monaghan, Emily Wibberley, and Austin Siegmund-
Broka.

We'd like to thank the entire Berkley team: Claire Zion,
Cindy Hwang, Jeanne-Marie Hudson, Craig Burke, Ashley
Tucker, Martha Cipolla, Jessica Plummer, Elise Tecco, Kaila
Mundell-Hill, Chelsea Pascoe, Mary Baker, Genni Eccles,
Lindsey Tulloch, and, of course, Sarah Oberrender and David
Doran for the beautiful cover! Thank you to Christina Vanko for
the beautiful map. Thank you to Celeste Montano and the team
at Writers House, and the team at Nelson Literary Agency.

So much of the camp-ness in this book came from our
own summer camp experiences. So we have to give a shout-
out to Camp Birchwood, Camp KeeTov, Brighton Camp, and
Kids Together. Thanks for making us "camp people."

FROM ALISON:

Bradeigh, if I was looking at my life the way we look at our
characters, one of the key scenes that would eventually
(hopefully) lead me to my essence would be the day you said,
"What if we wrote a book together?" Four books later, I still
pinch myself over the fact that I get to be on this journey with
you. I'm so grateful for your partnership, your plotting
prowess, and your ability to steam up any scene. But most of
all, I'm grateful for your friendship.

Thank you to everyone I'm lucky enough to call family:
my mom, Kathy Hammer; my dad, Dr. Randy Hammer; my

little/big sister, Elizabeth Murray; plus Carlene, Nick, Dylan, Alex, and Louie. And I can't forget the Lewins, Bergers, Blocks, Hammers, and Kirbys and Nancy Multin. And then there are my friends who are like family, My Girls, Meg McKeen, D.J. Johnson, Kristie Raymer, Julie Johnson, Krissie Callahan, #LibbyLove, Michelle Dash, Katie Ross, Mia Phifer, Jenna Leopold, Shana Freedman, Robbie Manning, Christina Williams, Pierrette Hazkial, Beth Gosnell, Mary Chase, Peggy Finck, Leah Conner, and Stephen Kellogg. Thank you to the Rock Boat Family, the Rock By the Sea Family, and the Boatcast Podcast crew. And thank you to Brian Glickman for sending camp pictures I could use to reference the location for a certain scene I won't mention . . .

I'm grateful to the Badass Jewish Authors for creating a safe space this past year, and the Artists Against Antisemitism, who helped turn an idea into a movement, and to Therese Walsh and the Writer Unboxed community—especially the covenoonian. Last, but not least, thank you to the Godfrey family for sharing Bradeigh with me, and making me feel like part of the family. Even when we're at a Utah/Florida game. #GoGators

FROM BRADEIGH:

Alison, this book pushed us and I'm so proud of how it turned out. Thank you for being by my side on this journey, for celebrating and commiserating with me, for lifting me up when I'm down and always being a text or FaceTime call away. I'm so lucky to get to write books with you—even when it's challenging and we both feel like our lives are falling apart and we don't know how to fix the book (remember how we completely revised our story outline in two hours via text message?). Thank you to the Women Physician Writers and Physician Mom Book Club, the Bookish Ladies Club founders, and the For the Love of Reading book club. Thank you to my parents, Merrie and Jim, and my siblings, Ellie and McLean, for their support and love. I'm beyond grateful for my wonderful friends, including but not limited to: Amanda, Amy, Suzanne, Erin, Stephanie, Kellie, Susan, and Ashley. I'm lucky to have four wonderful kids (Isaac, Eliza, Everett, and Nora), who are so understanding when their mom is on a deadline. I'm grateful to my two furry sidekicks, Ginger and Beans, for some much-needed dopamine during the hard days. And of course, Nate: thank you for everything. I couldn't do this without you.

We've been lucky to travel to many amazing locations to meet readers and booksellers and librarians. Thank you to the stores who hosted us last year on tour: the King's English in Salt Lake City, the Novel Neighbor in St. Louis, Volumes Bookstore in Chicago, Zibby's Bookshop in LA, FoxTale Book Shoppe in Atlanta, M. Judson Books in Greenville, and the Cuyahoga Library in Cleveland. Thank you to the Savannah Book Festival and Kristin Prentiss Ott for hosting us—we had the best time. Thank you to the Book Bonanza team: Colleen Hoover, Susan Rossman, Stephanie Spillane, and all the unicorns who make the magic happen.

We would also like to thank the bookstagrammers, BookTokkers, bloggers, and everyone on social media who put our book in front of potential readers. We're grateful for this entire community, especially the Bookish Ladies Club; Annissa and Bubba and everyone else in the Beyond the

Pages Book Club; Andrea Katz of Great Thoughts Great Readers; Kristy Barrett of A Novel Bee; Sue Peterson; Robin Kall of Reading with Robin; Lauren Margolin, "The Good Book Fairy"; Ashley Hasty; Ashley Spivey; Cindy Burnett of Thoughts from a Page; Courtney Marzilli with Books Are Chic; and of course, Meg Walker, Ron Block, and the Fab Four of Friends and Fiction.

An extra thank-you for any reader who picks up a copy of any of our books from an independent bookstore. Booksellers are the unsung heroes of the publishing industry, and we are grateful for all they do to bring authors and readers together. A special shout-out to Kimberly and Rebecca George of Volumes Bookstore; Mary Mollman of Madison Street Books; Ann Holman, Calvin Crosby, and Rob Eckman of the King's English; Maxwell Gregory; Pamela Klinger-Horn; and Mary Webber O'Malley.

And last but certainly not least: our readers. Thank you for picking up a copy of our book. None of this would be possible without you. We love hearing from you—so find us online at www.alibradybooks.net and on Instagram @AliBradyBooks.

See you next summer!

—Alison & Bradeigh

UNTIL NEXT SUMMER

Ali Brady

READERS GUIDE

DISCUSSION QUESTIONS

1. What is it about summer camp that makes us feel so nostalgic?

2. Do you think Hillary made the right decision years ago when she chose the internship over being a counselor with Jessie?

3. Did you go to summer camp as a child? Would you enjoy an adults-only summer camp as an adult?

4. Which of the Camp Chickawah weekly activities would you most like to participate in?

5. If you could choose one character to share a bunk or a cabin with, who would it be?

6. Do you think Jessie was justified when she pranked Luke's cabin?

7. Which of Cooper's meals would you most like him to serve you (wearing nothing but his underwear in the camp kitchen!)?

8. What did Hillary learn this summer about herself and what she wants out of life?

9. What did this summer teach Jessie about herself, her career goals, and her love of Camp Chickawah?

10. How do you think Nathaniel and Lola would feel about their children's choices regarding the property and what Jessie did to save it?

11. Last, but certainly not least, what is your opinion on the latest pubic hair trends? (IYKYK)

Continue reading for a preview of the
new romance from Ali Brady,

BATTLE OF THE BOOKSTORES

Josie

When I tell people I run a bookstore, I'm certain they imagine me reading all day, talking books with customers, hobnobbing with authors at literary events, breathing air infused with the tang of fresh ink and cut paper. And yes, those are some of my favorite things about this job. I also love flicking on the lights each morning and gazing at the shelves and stacks, all neat lines and sharp corners. I love unpacking shipments of books and recommending my favorite reads to customers.

But the best part—the absolute, hands-down best part of running a bookstore—is getting to read books before they come out.

A few months before publication, publishers send out galleys to booksellers—uncorrected advanced-reader copies that arrive in brown paper packages, their covers adorned with glowing blurbs from the literary elite—in the hopes that we will read and recommend (and stock multiple copies of) this new title the publisher promises will change the world forever.

Several months ago, a publicist at one of my favorite literary fiction imprints emailed me to ask if I'd consider reading an upcoming release and provide a quote, if I liked it. And did I like it? Well, I stayed up until three o'clock in the morning reading it, leaving damp spots from my tears on the final pages. I spent the entire next week writing and rewriting the perfect paragraph to encapsulate the essence of this epic, heart-wrenching story that I promise will change the world forever.

Last week, I got an email from said publicist saying that galleys were being sent out and oh, by the way, they are using my quote on the back cover (cue internal squeeing!).

And this morning, that package has finally arrived.

My hands are shaking as I rip open the brown paper, a quick glance confirming that yes, indeed, this is the book I adored so much, and I hold my breath as I flip it over to the back cover, scanning through glowing blurbs from many of my favorite authors, and then, there it is:

> "A *stunning meditation on grief and betrayal.* . . .
> *Worth reading and cherishing for years to come.*"
>
> —*Josie Klein, bookseller, Tabula Inscripta*

My breath rushes out and I stifle the teeniest, tiniest burst of disappointment. They only used a fraction of the paragraph I sent. But: it's still my quote. It's still my name. I've spent the past five years learning how to be the best bookseller I can be, determined to prove that a college dropout can still make something of her life, even if my professors didn't believe that. My dream is that someday, readers throughout the city—and maybe even the country—will turn to me for book recommendations. Someday, my voice will matter.

Right now, that seems light-years away. But seeing my name on this galley feels like I've just taken a giant step toward that goal.

My phone chimes with a reminder: MEETING WITH XANDER. I sigh; my monthly check-in with the store owner feels like an interruption to my real work. But we always meet at the coffee shop next door, so at least I can assuage that irritation with copious amounts of espresso.

Xander Liang owns not only the store where I work but the entire block, including the coffee shop, though he doesn't care about books or coffee or really anything except his bottom line. Luckily, he gives me free rein in my shop as long as I pull a profit each month—which I do.

I lock the door and head out into a beautiful May morning, around the corner, and in the door of Beans. The air smells like coffee beans and vanilla, and I take a deep breath, spotting Xander sitting at a table in the corner next to a man I don't recognize.

"Josie!" Eddie, the manager, calls. "Good morning, darling. The usual?"

"Yes, please," I say, smiling as I walk up to the counter and hand over my credit card. "How's business this morning?"

"Well, the morning rush is mostly over, thank god," Eddie says, then lowers his voice and motions over his shoulder at a blonde barista struggling with the levers of the espresso machine—a new employee.

I give him a sympathetic smile.

"We'll have your order right out for you," Eddie says.

I thank him and head over to the table where Xander is

sitting. He's short and balding and wears a perpetual irritated frown, and he gives me a curt nod as I pull up a chair.

"Good morning," I say to Xander, smiling at him while wondering who this other man is, sitting at the table with us.

He grunts and motions between me and the other guy. "I assume you two know each other?"

"No," I say.

"Yes," the guy says.

Confused, I look at him. Nothing about him is familiar. He's around my age, with messy brown hair and tortoiseshell glasses. He's wearing a thick brown cardigan, which strikes me as odd since it's a warm day, and a lanyard stuck all over with colorful pins. I assume the lanyard holds a work badge, but it's unfortunately flipped around, so that's no help in figuring out who he is.

Xander is introducing us, but I only half hear the first part, and snap to attention as he says, "—and this is Josie Klein, who manages Tabula Inscripta."

"I'm sorry," I say. "I don't remember meeting you before."

The guy blinks at me from behind his glasses, a confused smile tugging at his lips. "Well—we have. I mean, I manage . . . Happy Endings?"

I stare at him, not understanding.

"Happy Endings," he repeats, pointing to his right—the opposite side of the coffee shop from my store.

"The massage place around the corner?"

The guy's smile drops abruptly. "No. It's a bookstore."

"Ohhhhh," I say as it all clicks. "You just sell romance."

He blinks, his cheeks flushing faintly, then nods.

I never walk toward that side of the block—I live the

opposite direction—and I don't read romance novels, so I honestly haven't paid much attention. Plus, I'm not great at remembering information that I don't use frequently.

Like, for example, I cannot for the life of me remember this guy's name, and I think back to what Xander just said. Brian, I think?

"Nice to meet you, Brian," I say, sticking my hand out.

He gives me a tentative shake. His hand is huge, like a well-worn baseball glove. "Again, we have met, and it's—"

"I'm going to cut right to the point," Xander says, interrupting. "I've called you both here at the same time for a reason."

I turn to face him, pull out my notebook, and write the date in the top right corner. I consider writing "BRIAN" so I can commit the name to memory, but he might see it, so instead I'll need to work his name into the conversation a few more times.

"I've been considering this for a while," Xander says, "but the time has never been right. The lease on Beans is up, which means it's the perfect time for this project."

"What project?" I ask, pen poised over my notebook.

"Here you go!" a cheery voice says, and I look up to see the new blonde barista. Her name tag says MABEL and she sets a drink down in front of me. "An iced white chocolate chunk macchiato with two extra pumps of vanilla for you, miss."

"Oh, this isn't mine, I get a cappuccino," I say, handing it back to her. It's one of those whipped cream and sprinkles concoctions that make my teeth hurt just looking at it.

Mabel looks horrified. "Oh! I'm so sorry! Eddie said to

bring it to this table, so I figured since you were the only woman here, it must be—"

"It's mine," Brian mumbles.

He takes the cup, his cheeks slightly pink, like he's embarrassed to be caught drinking the "girly" drink. Which: who cares? I certainly don't. Mabel needs to learn not to assume someone's gender based on their coffee order.

"That looks like a delicious drink, Brian," I say, smiling in a way that I hope is supportive.

He grimaces, like my voice hurts his ears. "Actually, it's not—"

"I'll be right back with your order," Mabel says to me.

Brian shakes his head and sighs; I get the distinct sense that he's annoyed with me, which makes me feel all twitchy inside. What did I do? I'm trying to be nice!

But because I'm now feeling uncomfortable, I do what I always do when I feel uncomfortable: start rambling.

"Did you know that drink has about forty grams of sugar in it?" I say, then mentally slap myself as his eyes narrow. "But if it's something that gives you joy, that's great! Although, technically speaking, processed sugar isn't necessary for our body—but it tastes good, and sometimes that's what we all need, don't you think?"

Brian's eyes meet mine. Oh yes, he's annoyed. Maybe even angry. His eyebrows are pulled tightly together and his jaw is tight. Slowly, staring pointedly at me the whole time, he picks up his drink and takes a long, long, *long* sip.

Xander clears his throat. "Are we ready to continue?"

"Sorry." I pick up my pen again and turn toward him, grateful to break the weirdly confrontational eye contact with Brian. "You were saying something about a project?"

"Yes," Xander says. "I'm combining the stores."

Brian coughs on his drink.

I stare at Xander. "You said . . . combining? The stores?"

Xander nods. "That's right. Everything in the building will be combined into one large store. There's no reason this neighborhood needs two bookstores so close together. It's bad for business, having built-in competition."

I'm about to tell him that my clientele is entirely different than that of the romance bookstore, but Xander goes on.

"And you know what people like to do when they shop for books? Drink coffee. Eddie tells me that customers are always coming over here with their books and reading for a while. So I figured, hey, you know what? Let's combine it all. One big bookstore with a coffee shop right in the middle. People can get their Harry Potters and their parenting books and their spy thrillers and sit right down and read them. You know?"

I'm speechless. Appalled. A little nauseated.

Tabula Inscripta has been my domain for five years. I spend hours each season curating a selection of literary fiction and notable nonfiction. I don't sell kid lit. I don't sell parenting books or cookbooks or any other type of how-to book.

And I certainly don't sell genre fiction.

"But our bookstores are totally different," Brian says.

"Totally different customer bases," I add. "We're not in competition with each other."

"Well, you'll figure it out," Xander says. "I mean, one of you will."

I blanch. "One of us?"

"That's another reason for combining the stores: no need for me to pay two managers when it's just one store."

"So—so one of us is out of a job?" Brian says, sounding horrified.

"Who?" I ask, instantly sick. Xander is a man's man. He's going to choose Brian, just by virtue of him being male.

"I'm not deciding right now," Xander says. "Here's the plan."

He launches into a long, detailed explanation, and I do my best to take notes even though my head is spinning. Construction will start within a couple weeks, and the stores will stay open during the process. He anticipates that construction will take approximately three months—he wants it finished in plenty of time to work out any kinks before the holiday shopping season begins. He'll keep the stores financially separated during construction, and then he'll choose the manager who has earned the most profit during that period to be the manager of the new store.

"So you'll hire either Brian or me based solely on financials?" I ask. This is at least an objective measure.

Brian frowns and says, "It's actually—"

"Exactly," Xander says to me. "This is your chance to prove your worth. I anticipate that by Labor Day, my decision will be made."

I swallow, still sick to my stomach, and sneak a glance at Brian. I can't get a read on him. The cardigan, lanyard, and tortoiseshell glasses are giving "aging small-town librarian," which isn't a terrible vibe for a bookseller. But then there's the messy hair, which rubs me the wrong way. He's starting his day at work but he hasn't even taken the time to comb his hair? Maybe that's a good thing for me; maybe he's a mess in other aspects of his life, including his managerial skills.

He shifts his weight, which makes his lanyard slip

forward, revealing some of the colorful pins. They say things like MORALLY GRAY>>>, BOOK WHORE, IN MY SMUT ERA, SPREAD THOSE PAGES.

And one that I cannot for the life of me understand: STFUATTDLAGG.

I force myself to stop staring. He's the competition. This dude who drinks Frappucinos and has poor personal hygiene and wears unintelligible pins could end up with my job, and I can't allow that. I have too much riding on it—not just the paycheck, but all my goals for the future. Everything I've worked for over the past five years, the reputation I've built, the clientele I've cultivated. I have pulled myself out of the humiliating hole of my past to create a beautiful life and the potential for an even more beautiful future. I cannot let that fall apart.

At least I have a decent chance at winning, as long as the playing field is kept even.

I mean, how many books could a romance bookstore sell, anyway?

Ryan

She's called me Brian three times. Make that four.

I always figured Josie—see, I know *her* name—didn't like me. Every time I see her at Beans, she gives me the cold shoulder. Acts like she doesn't know who I am.

Maybe it's not an act?

Which would be crazy. She's run the Tab almost as long as I've been running Happy Endings. And we see each other a few times every week. I know she orders a triple cappuccino with oat milk in the morning, and caffeine-free Earl Grey tea in the afternoon. And one of the extra-gooey Rice Krispie Treats if she's having a bad day. Although, TBH, it almost always looks like she's having a bad day. Maybe her bun is too tight.

I have a feeling Josie never lets her hair down—literally or metaphorically. She's always so serious. I've never seen her without a big, thick book in her hand. She probably carts them around like an accessory, to make sure everyone knows she's Smart with a capital S.

Which she obviously is. At least, she seems to be. And she's also really pretty, in an ice queen kind of way. Which is why I haven't had the balls to talk to her.

"I'm glad you two are being good sports about this," Xander says.

I look across the table, where Josie has her arms crossed over her chest, a scowl on her face.

"Doesn't seem like we have much of a choice," I say.

Xander laughs as if I made a joke. This whole meeting feels like a joke, and I have a feeling we're the punch line. I can picture Xander lying naked in a California king bed (even though he's barely five seven), counting his money and trying to think of ways to make his monkeys dance.

I don't want to dance for him or for anyone, and I don't want to compete against Josie. I hate competition—it brings out the worst in people. I wish there was a way we could both win and neither of us would have to lose our stores.

But the world is not all happy endings, dickwad.

I shake my head to clear my older brothers' words from my mind. They'd probably be thrilled to see me lose so I could get a more "masculine" job, one that wouldn't make them question my sexuality or the fact that I'm single.

The store must be crawling with single hotties, the hopeless romantic type. If I were you, I'd be banging a different babe every day.

Sometimes it blows my mind how the four of us grew up in the same house with the same parents and ended up with such different ideas about love and sex.

It's not that I'm not attracted to some of the women who shop at Happy Endings, it's just—

"All right, then," Xander says, scooting his chair back so abruptly it screeches against the floor. Josie cringes, revealing a dimple I've never noticed before. She really is pretty, even when she's pissed.

"May the best bookseller win." And with that, Xander is off.

I turn back to Josie, hoping for a moment of shared commiseration over this situation we've found ourselves in, but she's scowling at me like *I'm* the enemy.

I open my mouth to say something, forgetting I don't have a witty or charming bone in my body. Another reason I haven't tried to broach a conversation with her before today.

Sally Thorne's *The Hating Game* comes to mind, and I wonder what Josh Templeman might say to Lucy Hutton in this situation.

Josie huffs, then stands and scurries back to her store without a word, leaving me alone with a table full of dirty dishes and an existential dilemma.

Growing up as the youngest of four brothers, everything was a competition. *Everything.* Who could eat the most or the fastest, who could hit the hardest, who had the best aim and could pee the farthest from the toilet bowl. Who was the oldest. (That one didn't make any sense.) And I came in last for every single one of them.

Back then, the only thing at stake was a little ribbing. Nothing I couldn't handle. But now? I couldn't handle losing Happy Endings. And not just because this is the only place I've ever worked. Elaine, the store's original owner and my first and only boss, created this little corner of the world to be a safe haven for the tenderhearted. For those who loved love and didn't always feel deserving of it in the world at large.

She'd be proud of how we've become a welcoming respite for all readers. We have the books to back up our motto that everyone deserves a love story, and it's been an honor and a privilege to serve this community.

If Happy Endings ends . . . there's not another bookstore in town that carries as many diverse and inclusive romance novels as we do. I don't know where our customers will go to browse with no judgement, to sit and read in cozy nooks, to connect with themselves and each other. We've even had a few IRL meet-cutes happen here in the store.

There's too much at stake. I can't let Josie win—even if that means getting my hands a little dirty . . .

Photo by Robin Facer

ALI BRADY is the pen name of writing BFFs Alison Hammer and Bradeigh Godfrey. Their debut novel, *The Beach Trap*, was featured on multiple "best of summer" lists, including those from the *Washington Post*, the *Wall Street Journal*, *Parade*, and Katie Couric Media. Alison lives in Chicago, where she works as an SVP creative director for an advertising agency. She has no kids, pets, or plants, but she does have two solo books, *You and Me and Us* and *Little Pieces of Me*. Bradeigh lives in Utah with her husband, four children, and two dogs. She works as a doctor and is the author of the psychological thrillers *Imposter* and *The Followers*.

VISIT ALI BRADY ONLINE

AliBradyBooks
AliBradyBooks
AliBradyBooks

Ready to find
your next great read?

Let us help.

Visit prh.com/nextread

Penguin
Random
House